When Bombs Fell

On Bath

by

Maggie Rayner

PART ONE

CHAPTER 1

Bath, 1939

The train entered Bath Spa railway station in a billow of steam and smoke, its brakes squealing as it slowed to a stop. In a burst of activity passengers dismounted, new travellers climbed aboard, carriage doors were slammed shut then the guard blew his whistle and the train steamed off towards Bristol. As the air cleared a group of arrivals became visible, huddled together on the platform, exhausted, disorientated, wrapped in heavy coats and hats against the January cold. The leader of a second group of people stepped forward to greet them.

'On behalf of Bath City Council I would like to welcome you all to England. We are so pleased you have arrived safely. I'm going to read out your names so we can identify who your sponsors are, then they will take you to your new homes.'

He paused while an interpreter translated his words into German and people were matched up until a man, his wife and their little girl remained.

'You must be the Blumfeldt family,' said the Council representative, 'and you're staying with Dr and Mrs Roberts.'

A stocky man in his forties wearing a grey mackintosh and a homburg hat introduced himself. 'I'm David Roberts. I'm so very pleased to meet you. If you'd like to follow me, I've got the car outside. Let's get you home.'

The three arrivals followed David out of the railway station and squeezed into the passenger seats of his Austin 7, their suitcases on their knees.

'It's not far,' he said, 'we're about a mile from the city centre.'

They drove in silence until they reached Eagle House, the Roberts' family home. The Victorian villa was set among similar properties on a hill in a part of Bath called Lower Weston. Built from Bath stone, it had a basement, ground and first floors with wide bay windows overlooking the road and a small attic room in the gable. A path bordered by lavender bushes led to the front door.

Wendy Roberts heard the car pull up outside. An official from the Council had rung to tell her the refugees were arriving that afternoon – things were so uncertain, and he apologised for the short notice. Wendy had hurriedly made up the beds for her visitors, bought some basics from the grocers and arranged a bunch of early narcissi in a vase on the table to brighten up their accommodation. Dressed simply in a hand-knitted jumper and a tweed skirt to meet her guests, wanting to set the right tone – relaxed, not formal - she glanced in the hall-stand mirror, quickly put a comb through her fine, fair hair and applied some fresh lipstick. Satisfied with how she looked, she took a deep breath and opened the front door.

The new arrivals got out the car and walked up the path, one behind the other.

'I'm Wendy Roberts,' she said, smiling, shaking hands with each of them and guiding them into the hallway.

'Karl Blumfeldt, and this is my wife Sonia and our daughter Gilda.'

Wendy realised instantly how wrong she had been to worry about her own appearance. She could see plainly how these people had suffered; she could sense their air of loss. And they were so thin! All her own problems paled into insignificance. She caught her husband's eye and saw that he was having the same thoughts. Wendy gathered herself and said, 'welcome to our home. We've prepared rooms for you in the basement, I hope you'll be comfortable there.'

The Blumfeldts followed her downstairs to an unexpectedly light living room with French doors leading to the garden at the back of the house. Wendy had lit the fire, the room was warm and welcoming, and the narcissi filled the room with their strong, rich scent. The visitors put down their suitcases and looked around curiously. They followed David as he showed them the bedroom and the bathroom, 'and the kitchen, through here, all for your own use. There's plenty of food in the cupboard, just help yourselves.'

'Thank you so much,' said Karl, 'this is very good. You are very kind.'

'We'll leave you alone now to get settled,' said Wendy. 'If you'd like to come upstairs at four o'clock, we'll have tea and you can meet the boys.'

Returning to the drawing room Wendy said to her husband, 'it's so different actually seeing them, isn't it? Poor things, they seem so…lost. I do hope we've done the right thing – it's not easy accepting a foreign family into one's home.'

'And it won't be easy for them to accept our charity, either,' he replied.

'But they're better off here than if they'd stayed in Germany…'

When David Roberts first suggested to his wife that they sponsor a Jewish refugee family she wasn't too keen. 'Fifty pounds, Wendy,' he'd said, 'fifty pounds, to rescue a family, give them shelter, help them start a new life - that's what this sponsorship scheme is all about.'

'But won't they eat strange food? And where will they worship? There isn't a synagogue in Bath.'

'I'm sure they'll be able to make their own arrangements. Come on, Wendy, we've got the money, let's give these people a chance!'

'But what about the boys? They won't want to share their home with foreigners…'

'Maybe not – but they'll get used to it. We'll talk to them.'

'So who's coming?' asked Henry, the Roberts' elder son, aged seventeen.

'About twenty Jewish people from a town called Ausberg,' answered his father. 'We've offered to host a married couple with a young daughter.'

'But where will they sleep?' asked Anthony, aged fourteen.

'In the old housekeeper's quarters. It'll need sprucing up a bit, but it should be comfortable enough.'

'How long will they be staying?' asked Henry.

'That depends,' said David, filling his pipe and lighting it. 'It's too dangerous for them to go back to Germany, and if there is a war, well, who knows? But we can give them a home for as long as they need one.'

'Can they speak English?' asked Anthony.

'Mr Blumfeldt can – he's a teacher of languages. We're trying to fix him up with a job. I don't know about the wife and daughter, but they'll soon pick it up.'

'Well, provided they keep away from my room and my model planes, I'm not really bothered,' concluded Henry.

'Nor me,' said Anthony, following his brother's line.

'Good,' said David, drawing purposefully on his pipe. 'Now, boys, I want you to make the family welcome in our home. You might find other people say bad things about them because they're German, and a different religion from us. But the most important thing,' he said, with emphasis, 'is to know that they are in grave danger where they are, and we are helping to save their lives.'

At four o'clock the Blumfeldts duly appeared: he, in his mid-thirties, with a round, kind face, wire-rimmed spectacles and thinning hair, wearing faded grey trousers and a navy woollen jumper; she, of similar age, thin and gaunt, with short dark hair, in a shabby flowered dress and cardigan; and their daughter, a skinny, frightened, eight year old, hiding behind her mother.

'I do hope your rooms are all right,' said Wendy. 'I cannot begin to imagine what you have been through. I hope you will be happy here and feel safe.'

'Thank you for offering us shelter,' said Karl, 'the rooms are perfect.'

'These are our sons, Henry and Anthony,' said David as the boys, just home from school and still in their uniforms, came forward and shook hands.

'And this is our daughter, Gilda,' said Sonia, in heavily accented English. 'Now, Gilda,' she said, looking down at her little girl and speaking in German, 'remember what I told you. Dr and Mrs Roberts are our friends and they have very kindly invited us to stay in their house. So, you must be very good and always polite to them. Now, step forward and say hello.'

The little girl slowly emerged and stood in front of the Roberts family. Her thin, pale face was framed by a shock of frizzy black hair and she stared at the smiling strangers with dark, untrusting eyes.

Anthony squatted down and looked at her on an equal level. 'I'm called Anthony,' he said. 'Welcome to our home. You will be safe here.'

She stared at the gentle, fair-haired boy, her eyes growing wider. She had never met anyone like him before. She couldn't speak.

'Don't worry, Gilda,' he said, 'you'll get used to us. You'll soon be chatting away!' He stood up and went back to join his brother.

They drank their tea and had some cake, then Sonia said, 'we will go to our rooms now, we have things to organise. We are very grateful.'

After they had gone Wendy said to Anthony, 'that was kind of you, to talk so nicely to Gilda.'

'Well…she just looked so scared,' he said. 'I don't think anyone should ever be so scared. I'll always try and help anyone who looks at me like that.'

CHAPTER 2

Bath, 1939

Having two families living under the same roof was never going to be easy. Wendy didn't want to come across as patronising or snobbish but feared that sometimes her reaction was exactly that (especially when it came to the smell of boiled cabbage that wafted upstairs from the basement). Similarly Sonia didn't want to appear diffident and insecure: she was incredibly grateful to the Roberts for letting them share their home but she was perfectly capable of running a household and didn't need superfluous advice. A breakthrough came a month or so after the Blumfeldt's arrival when David contracted a nasty dose of flu.

'I have the cure for him,' said Sonia.

She went to the market, returned with a full shopping bag, stayed in her kitchen for the rest of the morning then produced a pot of the most delicious, life-affirming Jewish staple - chicken soup. Sonia seemed to have the magic touch: David quickly recovered and from then on, when comfort food was needed, Sonia would provide.

Karl was found a teaching job in a local school, the first step in enabling his family to lead independent lives.

Most of the staff were sympathetic to his situation but he knew that, with war on the horizon, he would have problems with certain pupils and their parents who had concerns about their children being taught by a German and a Jew.

The Roberts were proud of their home city and delighted in showing the Blumfeldts around Bath, explaining its history and visiting the Roman baths. Gilda took a drink from the hot waters and spat it out in disgust, exclaiming '*schrecklich!*' and they all laughed, agreeing that it tasted dreadful. The boys pointed out famous landmarks of Georgian architecture including the Royal Crescent and the Circus, finishing in the Parade Gardens where they sat down by the River Avon among the neatly-planted beds of Spring flowers and David bought ice creams for everybody. The Blumfeldts were charmed by the beautiful, genteel city, thankful to have escaped into a different world.

The Jewish community in Bath was small and in the absence of a synagogue, religious services were held every Saturday at a hotel in the city centre run by a Mr Greenstein which soon became the refugees' focus for religious and social activities.

On Fridays the Blumfeldts maintained the tradition of Shabbat when Sonia would serve her husband and daughter a special meal accompanied by prayers, incantations and the lighting of the menorah.

As the family gradually settled in, Karl asked David about Eagle House.

'The eagle is the symbol of Germany. I wonder why your house has this name?'

14

'I'm not sure,' said David. 'The stone eagles on the pillars by the front gate have always been there. I don't know anything about a German connection. My parents bought the house from new in the 1880s, and I and my two older brothers were born here.'

'What happened to your brothers?'

'Both dead, killed at Passchendaele. It was a terrible time…my mother never got over it. My father was a Doctor and he encouraged me to join the Army Medical Corps – I served in Northern France.'

'You must have been very courageous.'

'It was my duty.'

David sighed and looked into the distance. Then he said, 'I met Wendy just after the war at the hospital here, in Bath, where I work now. She was a nurse and very pretty. It was love at first sight! When my parents died I inherited the house, we had our two sons and have been very happy here.'

'And now you have opened your home to your old enemy!'

'I can assure you, Karl – as a Medical Officer one treats every patient alike. I have no personal animosity towards the German people – it's the Nazis that we have to stop.'

On Gilda's first day at school Sonia was in a nervous state all day. When she collected her daughter at three o'clock Gilda ran towards her and burst into tears. In German, between sobs, she cried, 'I hate it! I'm not going back! I can't understand what they say and they all laugh at me! Mama, I want to go home!'

Sonia tried to comfort her distraught daughter. 'You are home, *liebchen*, this is your new home, in England.'

'NO! NO!'

'Gilda, you must try and forget about Ausberg, it's all different there now. Your life is here, in England, with Papa and me.'

Sonia led the crying child back to Eagle House and tried to console her. When Karl returned he spoke to his daughter. 'Now, Gilda, it is very difficult for all of us. You will have to go back to school tomorrow – and the day after that, and the day after that. It will be all right, in time. You will make friends and things will become easier. But first, we must help you improve your English!'

Over the next few weeks with lessons from her father, chats with Wendy and the Home Service on the wireless, Gilda began to understand the words and rhythms of the language and her confidence grew. Anthony helped her with her reading, lending her his favourite childhood book - *The Wind in the Willows*. One day she opened it, traced her finger over the inscription on the inside cover and read aloud: *'To Anthony, from Mummy and Daddy, Christmas 1932'.*

'That's right!' said Anthony, 'I was eight – the same age as you.'

Gilda stared at him, entranced. 'I like this book,' she said.

Anthony gave Gilda some back numbers of a popular new comic, hoping it might make her laugh – something he'd never heard her do.

They knew they were making progress when one evening, in order to encourage her daughter to eat her vegetables, Sonia said, 'they will make you strong.'

Gilda replied, 'like Pansy Potter!'

'Who is that, *liebchen*? Someone at school?'

'No,' replied Gilda scornfully, 'Pansy Potter The Strongman's Daughter.'

Her parents looked at her, curiously.

'She's in the *Beano*!'

Henry tolerated the German Jewish family that was sharing his home but spent most of his time playing sports with his friends or studying. He was expected to go up to Oxford to read Maths but in his heart he had other ideas.

For as long as he could remember he had been fascinated by the idea of flying and his ambition was to join the Royal Air Force. The walls of his room were plastered with pictures of aircraft he'd cut out from magazines and on a shelf were displayed the model planes he'd made, including his favourite, a Sopwith Camel. He had read all the books about flying he could lay his hands on and had recently sent away for RAF recruitment literature. His parents were aware of his passion and hoped he'd grow out of it, but Henry was determined.

And while everyone was worrying about the likelihood of war, and how awful it would be, he had other ideas – he was desperate for the war to begin so he could gain his pilot's wings and go out there and fight.

Over the next few months Gilda's English rapidly improved. She even began to pick up the local Bath accent, although David thought it had gone far enough when she started calling a 'vase' a 'valse'. In August, at Wendy's suggestion, Gilda invited some friends for tea in the garden to celebrate her ninth birthday. Afterwards the two families sat outside in the evening sunshine, relaxing and listening to music by the bandleader Glenn Miller on the gramophone. Henry was absorbed in reading 'Flight' magazine while Anthony and Gilda sat on the ground playing 'Snap!'

David was at ease, smoking his pipe, thankful that the Blumfeldts had settled in so well and become their friends.

Wendy said to Sonia, 'Gilda looks the happiest I have seen her!'

'Yes. She has had some hard times in her young life, but she has enjoyed her birthday today.'

Then a shadow passed across her face.

'What is it?' asked Wendy, concerned.

'Oh, it's nothing...I just worry that when everything seems to be going well, something is bound to go wrong...it's just how I am!'

'I'm sure everything will be fine,' Wendy said, reassuringly.

Wendy looked at her own sons, tall, fair-haired and blue-eyed, like her, remembering when they used to chase each other around that same garden, all grey shorts and muddy knees, their arms stretched out tilted at an angle, playing aeroplanes. And now, at eighteen, Henry wanted to become a pilot for real. She consoled herself with the thought that at least she would have her younger son safely at home for a few more years.

She watched as Anthony turned the playing cards over faster and faster until with delight Gilda played the winning card and shouted 'SNAP! SNAP!', jumping up and down, shrieking with excitement, the whole game collapsing in laughter.

On the third of September both families gathered around the wireless to listen to the Prime Minister's address in which he declared, 'this country is at war with Germany'.

The women, in tears, hugged each other and the men shook hands, David saying, 'even though our countries are at war we will always be friends, whatever happens.'

Gilda watched them, uncomprehending. Anthony felt slightly embarrassed at this outbreak of emotion, but Henry was having none of it.

'That's it,' he announced. 'I'm not going to Oxford. I'm going to join the RAF and be a pilot!'

They all stared at him, open-mouthed, as he strode out of the room.

CHAPTER 3

Bath, 1939

Yom Kippur is the holiest day of the year in Judaism. Also known as the Day of Atonement, it is a time for repentance, when God will forgive and cleanse sins, and is celebrated with a period of fasting and intensive prayer.

That year at Mr Greenstein's hotel the small Jewish community in Bath observed the festival which fell just three weeks after the outbreak of war. Sonia allowed her mind to travel back to January when her husband had come home with news of the opportunity to leave, by train, that night. There was no time to say goodbye to her parents and her younger brother Franz and his wife. Karl had pleaded with her – implored her – to take this one chance, for the sake of their daughter.

After many tears Sonia had agreed to go, leaving a letter for her family begging them to forgive her for deserting them. Now, from the safety of her new home in Bath, Sonia feared that escaping to England had been an act of supreme selfishness, that she had betrayed those she had left behind. What gave her the right to be living here, in this beautiful city, when others were enduring the most terrible suffering?

She asked God to forgive her.

Karl also let his thoughts wander to the past. The treatment of Jews in Germany had become intolerable and, much as he'd hated the idea of deserting his country, he knew it was the only way to keep his family safe – that was why he'd put his family's name forward for the sponsorship scheme.

Communications were poor and in such febrile times he feared his case had been lost in the bureaucracy so when, at the shortest of notice, he was offered the opportunity to leave, he had to grab it. That night he and his family had boarded the train without any clear idea where they were headed, only knowing that the situation was desperate and that this may be their only chance to escape.

Now, safely in England, he too felt the guilt of the survivor and dread for those he had left behind. He had no siblings and could only imagine the devastation his parents must have felt when their only son abandoned them to their fate. He hoped they understood that he had taken that most difficult decision of his life for the benefit of his own child, and for the future. He asked God to forgive him.

Gilda remembered happy times at her grandparents' house when they used to tell stories and sing and dance while Uncle Franz played the violin. Then everything changed. Those horrible people, the Nazis, spat at them in the street and terrorised them, burning down Jews' homes and businesses.

She remembered her mother wakening her that night, bundling some clothes and her favourite doll into a suitcase and fleeing from the house.

On the train she was scared of the soldiers and had to stay very quiet. She had fallen asleep, they were on a ship, then the next thing she remembered was arriving in Bath and meeting the Roberts family. She liked Anthony, the tall, fair boy who was kind to her.

She had made a few friends at school but some of the children were nasty, calling her 'Kraut' and 'Jewess' and saying she was ugly and had a big nose. Some days she would run home in tears, then feel guilty because she had let her parents down. She asked God to forgive her.

CHAPTER 4

Bath, 1940

The early days of the war – the phoney war – were well-named. The City Council had been making preparations for months: air raid shelters had been built, sandbags were piled up in front of the Abbey, the Guildhall and other important buildings, fire drills held, gas masks issued and the blackout was enforced; but it all felt slightly unreal. And why would anyone want to attack Bath?

David continued his work at the local hospital and when Wendy enquired about resuming her nursing career she was snapped up straight away. Henry was welcomed by the RAF and sent to flying training school in Lincolnshire from where he wrote enthusiastic letters to his brother, urging him to join up when he was old enough.

Now officially 'the enemy' the Blumfeldts were taunted by some of the locals and told to go back where they'd come from. Thankfully the authorities seemed to appreciate their position as Jews and the worst they could do at this stage was make Karl give up his bicycle.

The families quickly adapted to change and the curtailment of freedoms which had previously been taken for granted. They listened to the wireless, learning with sorrow about the great evacuation from Dunkirk and the local servicemen who lost their lives there.

War was coming closer, and Bathonians grew accustomed to the drone of enemy aeroplanes flying overhead en route to Bristol and South Wales to bomb ports and factories.

There was even an occasional explosion over Bath when bombs intended for other targets went astray, and the city experienced its first casualties of war.

From mid-1940, as the Germans advanced across Europe, the threat from 'enemy aliens' was perceived to be serious and internment was enforced, even for Jewish refugees. The Blumfeldts were no exception. They came for them at 7 o'clock on a warm June evening.

'But this is preposterous!' cried David to the two policemen standing at his door. 'This is the sort of behaviour they came to England to get away from!'

'I'm sorry, sir' said the elder of the two officers, 'but these are my orders. They are to come with us tonight.'

Karl appeared and said, 'it's all right, David. We have been expecting this, haven't we?' Then he said to the policemen, 'May I ask you to give us a few minutes to pack our things, and we will come with you.' With that he went down to the basement, leaving David speechless and Wendy wringing her hands. Anthony came to see what was going on and the younger officer explained, 'we're just taking your Jewish friends away for a little while, for their own protection - people might think they are German spies. So the Government has set up camps where they'll be safe, amongst their own people, until things have settled down a bit.'

'But the Blumfeldts aren't spies!' cried Anthony, confused and angry. 'You can't make them go!'

'"I'm afraid they can,' said his father. 'There's nothing we can do.'

Karl returned with Sonia and Gilda, suitcases in hand, looking much as they had on their arrival in Bath eighteen months previously, albeit healthier and better-fed.

The younger officer, who had a daughter about the same age as Gilda, felt a moment of humanity. He wasn't a Nazi; he was just an English copper doing his job. He went over to the little girl, stooped forward, looked her in the eye and said, 'now, I don't want you to worry. The camps are quite nice – many are by the seaside and there will be games, and plenty of food, and a comfy bed. You will be quite safe and back here again in no time at all.'

Gilda stared at him, disbelieving.

Anthony had a sudden thought. 'Wait just a second please, I've got to go and fetch something.'

He dashed out of the room and returned a few moments later carrying a book. 'You must take this,' he said to Gilda. It was his copy of *The Wind in the Willows*. She quietly said, 'thank you,' and tucked the book under her arm.

Trying their best to maintain their dignity the Blumfeldts were escorted away by the policemen and David closed the door behind them.

'Do you think we'll ever see them again?' asked Anthony.

'Of course we will,' said Wendy. 'Of course we will…'

*

Henry had joined the RAF at the perfect time - the training programme had expanded and he was undertaking an intensive course which would enable him to gain his pilot's wings in just a year. His senior officers recognised immediately that Henry's enthusiasm was backed up by a natural aptitude for flying and had no doubt that he would make a successful pilot.

Wendy could scarcely believe that Henry, at just nineteen years old, had left home, never mind be in the forefront of such a critical part of the war. When he came home on a weekend pass he was completely changed from the schoolboy who had left – now, he oozed confidence and even had the beginnings of a moustache. Anthony was green with envy.

'I can't tell you, Anthony, how wonderful it feels to be up there, in the clouds…so liberating. There's loads to learn, and it's really interesting. I'm sure you'd love it – and there are lots of pretty WAAFs, too!'

Wendy had other worries. 'But you haven't been there long - surely they won't expect you to fight?'

'Mother, that's what I'm there for! We've got the most brilliant new planes, and the chaps I'm serving with really are top class. We'll beat those Germans, you'll see!'

Of course Henry didn't tell his parents all the details. He omitted to mention that some young pilots had crashed and been injured or killed during their training, and that the RAF was short of fully trained fighter pilots, so if things came to it he would be certain to fight. But he knew he would be safe because he was Flying Officer Henry Roberts, and he was invincible.

Henry's chance to prove himself came even more quickly than he'd expected. From July, hundreds of courageous young fighter pilots took to the skies to defend Great Britain from concerted attacks by the Luftwaffe.

On his first sortie Henry flew over the towns and villages of southern England that he loved, high on adrenaline, swooping and veering, ready to engage in aerial combat with the enemy to defend his country. Suddenly two Messerschmitts came out of nowhere and he was in a dog-fight, rapidly manoeuvring his Spitfire to gain advantage. He fired his guns and caught one on the wing, watching as the damaged aircraft spun downwards to earth. Then he fired at the other plane, and for a split second he saw the face of the terrified pilot before the fuel tank exploded and the plane blew to pieces.

Henry returned to Base, receiving praise from his colleagues, knowing that when it had come to it he had carried out his duty, and this time he had won. Kill or be killed: that was the lesson of war. And that was just the beginning; in the following weeks he shot down a dozen Nazi planes and substantially damaged many others, managing to return safely to Base after each sortie. He didn't think about the German pilots as people – they were the enemy, and it was his job to destroy their aircraft before they destroyed his.

Armed with this attitude he became every inch the Spitfire ace, finding combat exhilarating, revelling in the camaraderie, danger, and the chance to test his flying skills to the limit.

The worst thing by far was when his comrades didn't return or were injured. That was when he knew how deadly serious this battle was, and how crucial it was for the RAF to win it. 'Try telling that to my mother...' he'd think, as he wrote letters home assuring his family he was safe.

In September the Nazis began an intensive campaign to bomb London, deliberately targeting civilians as well as ports and industrial sites. Hundreds of people were being killed or injured and thousands made homeless. The London hospitals were in a desperate state and David arranged to spend a few days there each week to help out for as long as he was needed.

In November, when the Battle of Britain had been won, Henry was granted leave and arrived at Eagle House to a hero's welcome. Anthony couldn't wait to see him. By that stage, the daredevil pilot was exhausted, his boyish enthusiasm replaced by a cold, calculating display of nerve and skill. His family could see how battle had hardened him. Over a glass of whisky with his father Henry confessed how difficult he found it to cope with the loss of his comrades.

'It's the hardest thing,' said David. 'When I was serving in France I saw so much suffering, such a waste of life. You grow close to people in wartime. Everything is so intense, so urgent. You've coped well, Henry. I am proud of you.'

Henry didn't want to dampen his brother's enthusiasm about joining the RAF but felt a certain responsibility.

He lit a cigarette and told Anthony what he had learnt about the horrors of war.

'Look, old man,' he said, 'being a pilot is fantastic, but it's dangerous, too, and I'd hate the parents to have another one of us to worry about. I don't think you should rush to join up. It might all be over soon with a bit of luck.'

'But I want to do something!' cried Anthony, 'I'm fed up here. I can't do as much sport as I used to, Mum and Dad are working all the time, the Blumfeldts aren't here and school's so boring…'

'Well, whatever you decide to do, think carefully,' said Henry, taking a final draw on his cigarette then stubbing it out in an ashtray. 'That's all I'm saying.'

CHAPTER 5

Bath, 1941

During March and April some stray bombs fell on residential parts of Bath. Waiting in the queue for the butchers, Wendy heard a woman say twenty people had been killed – 'terrible,' she'd said, 'terrible. And now the Nazis know where we are, they'll be back, you mark my words!'

Once a week Anthony and his friends from school went to the Beau Nash cinema for some entertainment. Girls didn't feature in his life yet – he preferred the company of his classmates. They watched as the Pathé newsreel reported the latest news about the German-Italian alliance and the Eighth Army's action in Egypt and Africa. It seemed a world away. Then came an account of the RAF's latest exploits which made Anthony think jealously of his brother, leading a life of excitement while he had to stay at home keeping his parents company and studying for his exams.

For Wendy's birthday in June David took her and Anthony for lunch to the Pump Room, the Georgian meeting place for fashionable people, situated next to the Roman Baths. This historic building, beloved of Jane Austen's heroines, had been transformed for the duration into a new and important part of the nation's culture: a British Restaurant.

Wendy wore a new dress she had made for the occasion. With clothing being rationed, driven by necessity she had re-discovered her old Frister and Rossmann sewing machine up in the attic along with dress patterns and lengths of material she'd bought at a haberdasher's closing down sale years ago.

'You look beautiful, darling,' said David. 'And the band in your hat matches your dress!'

Wendy smiled. Her husband had always been good at noticing details like that.

'Doesn't your mother look lovely, Anthony?'

'I suppose so...'

'Forty five years old...and as stunning as the day we first met!' said David, gazing at his wife.

'Thanks for reminding me!' said Wendy.

David reached over, took Wendy's hand, lifted it to his lips and kissed it. Anthony cringed with embarrassment and was rescued by the waitress bringing them dessert.

'Never feel shy about telling a woman how beautiful she is,' David said to his son. 'You'll thank me for that advice one day!'

Anthony shrugged and tucked into his jam roly poly and custard.

Lincolnshire, 1941

At his RAF station in Lincolnshire, Henry was called in to see his Commanding Officer. He felt nervous in the same way as, on the odd occasion, he'd been summoned to the headmaster's study at school. His time flying Spitfires had left him exhausted and he hoped he hadn't done anything wrong.

However, his fears dissipated when he was offered a seat and a cigarette.

'We're impressed with your performance, Roberts. I'm pleased to tell you that you are being promoted to Flight Lieutenant.'

Henry nearly fell off his chair, he was so surprised.

'Now, we want to give you a change of scenery. You're being transferred to High Wycombe where you'll be flying bombers. We're stepping up the campaign in Germany and we need good pilots like you. Good luck.'

'Thank you, sir.'

Henry stood up, saluted, and marched out of the room.

Bath, 1941

One dark evening at the beginning of December Wendy answered the door to find the Blumfeldts standing there, suitcases in hand. After eighteen long months their internment had ended.

'Oh my goodness!' she cried, as her husband and Anthony came running to see what the commotion was all about. With hugs and kisses and tears of relief the Roberts welcomed them in, holding hands and standing back to look at each other.

'I cannot tell you how happy we are to be back!' said Karl, vigorously shaking David's hand. 'The Government decided in its wisdom that we are not a threat to national security. So here we are!'

Sonia said, 'I hope you don't mind – we have nowhere else to go…'

'Don't be silly!' said Wendy, 'this is your home! Your rooms are just as you left them. We've missed you so much!'

Then Wendy gave Gilda a hug. 'My, how you've grown! And your hair looks so pretty!'

Gilda's hair was braided and wound around her head in the German style.

'Thank you, Mrs Roberts. Old Frau Katz at the camp showed us how to do it, didn't she, Mama, she said I reminded her of her granddaughter. Oh, I am so happy to see you all!' Gilda's face had filled out, it was rounder, like her father's, and her cheeks were a healthy pink.

'Hello Gilda,' said Anthony, 'welcome home!'

'Anthony, I have missed you!' she cried, clinging to him.

'You are quite the young man, Anthony,' said Sonia, 'so tall! What are you doing now?'

'I'm still at school,' he said, 'but next year when I'm eighteen I'll be able to join the RAF, like Henry.'

'And how is your brother?'

'He's very well,' replied Anthony, 'he's even been promoted. He's flying b...'

'Yes, dear,' interrupted Wendy diplomatically, not wanting to go down that path at this stage. 'Now, come in, everyone. I'll make some tea and open that tin of shortbread I was saving for Christmas!'

The Blumfeldts were relieved to be back in the warmth and safety of Eagle House. They spared the Roberts the worst details about life in the internment camp.

For the first three months men had been separated from the women and children. When Karl had finally been reunited with his wife and daughter they were put in a room with Nazi sympathisers who spat in their food, calling them 'filthy Jews'. One of them attacked Karl with a knife but luckily a guard witnessed the incident and moved the Blumfeldts to another part of the camp housing Jewish families from Poland and life became more tolerable.

Teachers at the camp ran classes in a variety of subjects, and Gilda had attended an English reading group and started piano lessons.

'She loves the piano!' said Sonia, proud of her daughter. 'Karl's going to ask the music teacher at his school to continue with her lessons.'

'That's wonderful, Gilda,' said David, 'you can play the old upright in the drawing room whenever you wish.'

Gilda went to her room then returned with something for Anthony. 'Here is your book,' she said. 'I was so pleased to have it. I read it over and over again.'

'Good, I'm pleased it helped,' said Anthony. 'You can keep it, you know – it's yours now.'

Gilda beamed and gave him a kiss. 'Thank you,' she said.

She would never tell him how, on her way to class in the camp, she had been accosted by a tall, blue-eyed blonde girl, a few years older than herself. The girl had grabbed Gilda's arm, seized the book she was carrying and held it above her head, saying 'books are bad! You don't want this, you little Jewess. I'm going to burn it, like we do at home in Germany!'

'NO!' Gilda had shouted, jumping up to try and retrieve it, 'NO! Give it back!'

The blonde girl laughed at her, saying, 'it's a nice book, it will burn well!'

Gilda's anger was stronger than her fear. She kicked her tormentor hard on the shins, the girl screamed with pain and dropped the book which Gilda picked up then ran back to her room as fast as she could, clutching her most treasured possession – Anthony's copy of *The Wind in the Willows*.

*

One February afternoon on his way home from school Karl noticed a poster advocating people to grow their own food. This struck a chord with him; he gave the matter some thought and at the weekend when he happened to be standing next to David, looking out at the back garden, he decided to broach the subject.

'I love this time of year. Spring is coming and everything is coming alive again. Your garden is so lovely, and the lawn - so good for the children to play in. Do you remember the fun Gilda had on her birthday?'

'I certainly do,' said David.

'And yet,' Karl continued, 'in a garden as large as this, one could grow a lot of food…'

'I know…' said David, hesitantly. 'I've seen those posters too - *Dig for Victory!*'

'When I was in Germany I used to love growing vegetables and fruit - I always grew too much and had to give it away. They used to say I had green thumbs.'

'Fingers,' interjected David, 'in English we say 'green fingers'!'

35

He sighed. He could see exactly where Karl was headed, and knew he was right.

'I'll have to talk Wendy around,' he said. 'She loves the lawn – but I'm sure she'll understand. I'll get Anthony to give you a hand with the digging!'

'That would be marvellous,' said Karl.

Between them Karl and Anthony cut swathes through the lawn, making a series of beds for growing vegetables and fruit. A large part of the garden was given over to potatoes, then finally Karl planted some blackcurrant, redcurrant and gooseberry bushes.

Karl leant on his spade and surveyed the reformed garden with satisfaction.

'We've done a good job here, Anthony,' he said to his co-worker. 'We should see some green shoots appear in a few weeks, and the first crop of new potatoes should be ready for harvesting in May.'

Wendy approached them. 'Well done! You've both worked so hard!'

'Sorry about your lawn, Mum,' said Anthony.

She put his arm around him. 'It's for the best. And I can see all this exercise has given you some muscles, too!'

*

Henry was flying his first mission in a Lancaster bomber. As he manoeuvred the aircraft along the runway, gathered speed and took off, he marvelled at the engineering that had gone into this monster of a plane, heavy and throbbing with strength, so unlike his agile 'turn on a sixpence' Spitfire.

Henry was well-prepared for his new role and had confidence in his own abilities, his men and his machine.

Once the plane reached its designated height he reviewed the itinerary with his Observer.

'We're headed for Munich' said the Observer through his intercom, 'and we start dropping at a place called Ausberg.'

Henry nodded. Ausberg…the name rang a bell with him. Then he remembered. It was where the Blumfeldts came from.

CHAPTER 6

Bath, 1942

It was a sunny Saturday morning in April when Wendy said goodbye to her husband as he left Eagle House to walk to the railway station. They hardly drove their car now due to petrol rationing and had got used to walking or taking the bus for longer journeys. David had offered to work in London over the Easter weekend while staff took leave.

'Do take care, darling, it's so dangerous up there,' said Wendy.

'I'll be fine. Now you just take care of yourselves, don't worry about me.'

Wendy completed her own shift at the hospital and that evening, back home, she gratefully ate the meal Sonia had prepared for her. Just as she was settling down to listen to the wireless there was an urgent hammering on the door. Wendy answered it to find a young woman, frantic with worry.

'Is Dr Roberts in? We need help, urgently! It's my sister, Susan Fowler, she's gone into labour! She's in terrible pain, she's shouting the house down! Please, please can he come and help?'

'I'm sorry, my husband's away in London, but I can come if you like. I have delivered a few babies in my time!'

'Thank you, Mrs Roberts, that would be wonderful! She's just up the road, it's not far. Please come quickly!'

'I'll come straight away.' She called out to her son: 'Anthony – I've got to go and help Susan Fowler - she's gone into labour. Tell the Blumfeltds I've gone, will you? I'll be back later.'

Wendy quickly put on her coat, picked up her medical bag and followed the panicking woman out onto the street. It was a bright moonlit night and the blacked-out buildings were silhouetted against the sky. They hurried along to the house where Susan had a flat on the second storey, ran up the stairs and found her on the bedroom floor, clinging to the leg of the bed, screaming out in agony. Wendy helped her up and onto the bed, examined her and dispatched her sister, Ann, to fetch a basin of water and towels.

'The baby's on its way, there's no time to go to the hospital.'

Then the air raid siren started up – only slightly louder than Susan's cries. They ignored it at first – they'd got used to German planes flying overhead en route to Bristol and the hum of the engines had become a familiar sound. But it soon became apparent that this was the prelude to something entirely different.

'Should we go down to the shelter?' asked Ann.

'No chance!' said Wendy, 'it would distress her and the baby too much to move her. We'll just have to stay here and hope for the best.'

The rumbling of the planes grew louder and louder and suddenly the sky exploded with fire as sticks of incendiary bombs came tumbling down, followed by a massive explosion a few streets away which shook the walls of the house. The noise was terrifying and the three women clung together in shock while one bomb after another rained down on the city.

Orange flames danced, crackling and roaring as fires spread rapidly, then a bomb dropped nearby and the whole house quaked, shattering the windows and scattering broken glass everywhere.

Minutes passed, then an hour. The bombing was unrelenting, the explosions unending as the German planes approached in wave after wave, guided through the city by the bends of the River Avon, silver in the moonlight. A sudden ball of fire leapt skywards about half a mile away.

'It's the gasometer! It's exploded!' exclaimed Wendy.

Susan screamed out in pain and Wendy shouted 'push!' and 'breathe!', all the while agonising about Anthony and the Blumfeldts, and praying that her own house would be spared. Then at last the baby emerged.

'It's a girl!'

Wendy took the baby in her arms and, making her way carefully across the room through the broken glass, washed her, wrapped her in a towel and handed her to Susan who lay on the bed, exhausted. The three women wept with relief that the baby was safely delivered and listened as the roar of the aeroplane engines faded to a dull drone.

Just after midnight the all-clear sounded.

Wendy said, 'I must get home, I must see if Anthony and the Blumfeldts are all right. I'll come back later to check on the baby.'

Wendy left the house and could not believe the devastation around her. There were huge craters where houses used to be, lit up by fierce flames leaping into the night sky.

The front of one house had been completely blown off exposing its rooms like a dolls' house with its door wrenched open. The floors and furniture had disappeared into the wreckage beneath and a bath teetered precariously on a window ledge. Broken glass glistened everywhere. People were screaming, hurt, lost.

The emergency services and Civil Defence teams were in action, trying to put out fires in the burning buildings. Ambulance crews were treating the wounded and groups of people were desperately searching through the debris, calling for their loved ones.

Wendy made her way home, picking a path through the wreckage, her pace quickening as panic rose inside her. She turned the corner and didn't recognise the street she'd lived in for twenty years. Fires were ablaze in the blackness and cars parked in the street were covered in rubble. The acrid smoke which hung in the air made it difficult to breathe and she covered her mouth, her heart thumping and her eyes stinging as she staggered through the debris.

At last she reached her house and thanked God to find it still standing, albeit with superficial damage and broken windows. Even the stone eagles had survived, pock-marked, but defiantly in place. Wendy rushed inside to find Anthony and the Blumfeldts safe and uninjured.

'We were so worried about you, Mum!' cried Anthony. 'When we realised Bath was the target we took shelter in the cellar.'

Gilda was in tears and ran to Wendy for a hug.

'It was horrible!' she cried, 'I'm so pleased you're safe, Mrs Roberts!'

41

'And the baby?' asked Sonia.

'A girl! Safely delivered, right in the middle of the raid!'

Knowing everyone was out of danger Wendy went back into the night to assist the wardens who were rescuing people from the burning buildings. Anthony wanted to go with her but she insisted he stay at home with the Blumfeldts. After a few hours she returned home, filthy and exhausted, only to hear the air raid siren starting up again.

'I don't believe it! They're coming back!'

This time they all took refuge in the cellar together while above their heads German bombers, guided by the fires which still raged, came back to inflict a second wave of damage. As bombs and incendiaries ignited over the city Karl softly recited a prayer under his breath. Gilda sat between her mother and Wendy, gripping their hands, terrified that this time the bombs would get them. Anthony sat next to Karl, inwardly shaking but trying to put on a brave face, aware that in the absence of his father and brother it was his duty to protect his mother from danger but not knowing what to do.

They heard the thud, thud as explosives were dropped and the cackle of gunfire as the planes flew low, aiming at the emergency teams who were working to clear the devastation of the first attack.

Suddenly there was a massive explosion nearby which caused the walls of the house to shake and for a moment they all held their breath, looking up anxiously at the ceiling expecting it to fall in on top of them; but thankfully it stayed in place.

The raid continued unmercifully until dawn when the last of the planes left, the throb of its engines fading into the distance, and the all-clear sounded.

Slowly, the five of them left the cellar, their nerves shattered, fearful of what they might find above them. As they ascended the wooden staircase to the ground floor Gilda stumbled as one of the treads, weakened by the impact of the bombs, gave way underneath her. She screamed, and Anthony, who was following behind, caught her as she fell.

'Gilda!' cried her mother from the top of the staircase, 'are you all right?'

Gilda, in shock, couldn't speak, but Anthony called out, 'don't worry, she's OK, I've got her.' Holding the girl in his arms he climbed carefully up the damaged staircase, testing each tread as he went, until he emerged at the top and handed Gilda to her mother.

'How are you, *liebchen*?' she asked, anxiously, then to Anthony she said, 'thank you for rescuing her!'

'That's all right,' he replied, 'I think she's just shaken. No broken bones I hope.'

The next day, Easter Sunday, Wendy, Anthony and the Blumfeldts emerged from Eagle House having grabbed a couple of hours sleep. Gilda had escaped from her fall with some scratches and bruises, and although the whole episode had scared her, what she remembered most was Anthony holding her in his strong arms, carrying her up the stairs to safety.

Outside the air was thick with dust and fires continued to smoulder in the blackened buildings all around them.

43

Karl set about repairing the staircase and inspecting Eagle House for damage while Anthony went to help a party of men shifting debris from a crater where a row of houses had once stood.

Wendy assisted the Civil Defence teams, seeing to casualties and dealing with the walking wounded. Gilda followed her around helping where she could. Although only aged eleven she proved to be a useful assistant, unfazed by the sight of blood and supportive to patients, handing over bandages and plasters as Wendy saw to people's wounds. Wendy noticed Gilda's calm and reassuring manner and praised her saying, 'well done! You'll make a good nurse one day!'

Gilda blushed and said, 'thank you Mrs Roberts! I would like that very much.'

Bit by bit, news of the extent of the damage inflicted on the city emerged. Bath's famous Georgian landmarks - the Royal Crescent, the Circus, the Paragon, the Pump Room - none had been spared. The Assembly Rooms, which had only recently been renovated, had been gutted by fire. The station and the railway around it had been destroyed. Row upon row of terraced houses in Oldfield Park and Twerton had been hit, wiping out people's homes and whole communities.

Newly-homeless, bewildered people gathered in Victoria Park, unsure what to do or where to go. The council quickly set up emergency relief centres and people opened their homes to strangers who had lost everything, while some people left Bath altogether, fearful that the bombers would return.

Rumours were rife about the number of people killed and injured: three, four, five hundred dead?

Nobody knew for sure, but it was devastating for a small city.

Wendy desperately wanted to get a message to her husband to let him know they were safe, but the telephone wires and poles were down and it was impossible to communicate.

Then she spotted a doctor she knew.

'How are things at the hospital, Dr Richards?' she asked.

'We had a direct hit,' he said, 'the orthopaedic wing was completely destroyed. We managed to rescue some of the patients and move them to another ward but I'm afraid we lost Sister Whitehead in the blast, and several other staff were injured.'

'Oh, how terrible!'

'The windows fell in, ruining the blackout, so we had to switch off the lights and work by hurricane lamp. And we're admitting casualties all the time. It's pretty chaotic up there, I can tell you.'

'Should I come up and help?'

'No, Nurse Roberts. Quite frankly, the more people you can treat here the fewer will need to come to the hospital.'

'All right, I'll stay. Can I ask you – is there any way you could get a message to my husband, to let him know we're all safe?'

'I'll try. We do have a special phone connection to London which might still be working. I'll see what I can do.'

Gas and water mains had been hit and everyone was thankful when water carriers arrived from Bristol with supplies, including gallons of much-needed tea.

Sonia went to help distribute food and tea from the back of a lorry but one of the men she served noticed her accent and turned on her, calling her a 'murderous Kraut' and accusing her of being a spy who had guided the bombers to Bath. She rushed home in tears to find her husband sweeping up broken glass and china, and between sobs, she told him what had happened.

'We can't be safe anywhere!' she cried. 'We can't go home to Germany because we're Jewish, we can't stay here because we're German, whatever are we going to do? I felt safer in the internment camp!'

'Come here, *liebchen*,' he said gently to his wife. He put his arms around her and tried to comfort her. 'Shush, shush,' he whispered as he held her. 'Be thankful we are still alive! God has spared us this time. Have faith. People must understand that the Nazis who dropped these bombs are our enemy, too. The world must know what Hitler is doing to the Jews.'

Karl took a handkerchief from his pocket and gave it to his wife who wiped her eyes and blew her nose.

'We will keep praying,' she said.

'Things will get better,' he said.

Then, looking out the window into the back garden, pock-marked and covered with soot and ash, he kissed her on her forehead and quietly said, 'although I'm not so sure about my crop of new potatoes!'

David Roberts was relieved to receive a call confirming that his family had survived the attack and passed the good news to Henry at the Air Station.

Wendy worked all day, totally absorbed in her task until Karl went to find her, insisting she come home for a rest and something to eat. Sonia made her a sandwich and Anthony and Gilda joined her, all exhausted from their work and still unable to take in what had happened to their city. The suffering they saw that day on their very doorstep was beyond words, and they were just thankful to have survived.

Towards nine o'clock Sonia looked at Gilda who was asleep on her feet.

'Time for bed, daughter. You've done enough for one day. Say goodnight to everyone.'

Gilda went to Wendy and hugged her, saying, 'thank you for letting me help you today,' then to Anthony she said, 'and thank you for rescuing me from the cellar.'

He ruffled her hair and said, 'you're welcome!'

After Gilda had gone Anthony got up and said, 'I'm tired too – I think I'll go to bed. Goodnight all.'

Wendy dropped off to sleep for a while, then awoke with a start. 'I must go and see Susan Fowler and the new baby! I told them I'd be back...'

'Why don't you wait until the morning? You've done so much for everyone today and it's very late!' said Sonia.

'No, I will go – it won't take long. Tell Anthony I'll be back later.'

'All right, Wendy,' said Sonia, 'take care now!'

Wendy walked cautiously in the black-out, guided by the bright moonlight, seeking a path through the bomb-ravaged buildings until she reached Susan's flat.

Ann, Susan's sister, answered the door and showed her into the bedroom where Susan was sitting up, nursing the baby.

'Thank you so much for coming,' she said, 'we're all right, I've got her feeding now.'

Wendy was relieved to see mother and baby looking so well in the circumstances. She also noticed that someone had swept up the broken glass from the night before and boarded up the window.

'I wish I could tell Frank, my husband, about her, but he's away at sea, and…'

Susan was interrupted by the wail of the air raid siren. The bombers had returned.

They stayed in the bedroom, huddled together as they had the previous night, sheltering the tiny baby, trembling with fear as nearby explosions shook the house. This time the planes stayed low over the city for two hours sending down incendiaries, dive-bombing from only fifty feet and machine gunning anything that moved in the blazing streets below. Streams of tracer fire shot into the sky, seeking out the enemy, and anti-aircraft guns which had been brought in after the initial raids were deployed. The noise was deafening, even worse than before, the walls shuddered and the room filled with dust.

Wendy was thinking about how busy she would be the next day treating casualties from this latest raid when there was a massive explosion - a direct hit on the house. Everything smashed to pieces, the bed fell through the floor and masonry collapsed around them. Wendy fell down, down, down, helpless to save herself or the others as the walls of the house imploded and caved in on top of them.

*

'Help! – over here! – there's a baby crying!'

The warden climbed over the remains of the destroyed house and blew his whistle to call for the search party. Under a twisted piece of metal he found a woman with a broken arm and helped her to her feet. 'My sister...' she said.

Another woman was lying beside her, bleeding from a head wound and clinging to a baby.

'Get them to hospital!' shouted the warden, 'this baby can only be a few hours old!'

'Wait!' shouted his colleague. 'There's something more here – look...'

They saw an arm protruding from the rubble. Hurriedly they moved the bricks and lumps of concrete with their bare hands to reveal the body of a woman, her legs twisted horribly beneath her.

The warden checked her pulse, but the woman was clearly dead.

'Hang on,' said his colleague, 'I recognise her. It's the nurse who was helping us earlier – it's Dr Roberts' wife, Wendy.'

CHAPTER 7

Bath, 1942

David was bereft.

Wendy's funeral was held on 1st May, a few days after the raids, as part of a mass burial of the victims of the bombing. David stood at the service in a trance, his sons supporting him on either side – just one family among so many others. He listened to the words of the vicar and mouthed the words of the hymns but drew little solace from them. He had been called back from London in total shock, unable to believe that his beloved wife was dead. Henry was given leave to attend the funeral, equally unable to comprehend what had happened. Anthony was completely shattered and the Blumfeldts were devastated that the generous, compassionate woman who had offered them a home had been so violently killed.

On the evening of Wendy's funeral there was a knock at the door. Sonia answered it and showed a young woman into the lounge. David was asleep in his armchair, exhausted from the events of the day. Sonia gently woke him and said, 'there's a young lady here who wants to ask you something important.'

David looked up at the young woman and said, 'how may I help you?'

'My name is Susan Fowler' she said. 'Your wife delivered my baby girl, right in the middle of the raid, she was so brave, and I am so grateful. Then she came back to see me and she was with me and my sister when the house was hit and…' She started to cry.

'Sit down, my dear!' said David. 'Sonia, bring her some tea, will you?'

Susan sat down, wiped her eyes and continued. 'Well, what I want to ask is – I want to name my daughter 'Wendy', in honour of your wife. Would that be all right?'

Now it was David who had tears in his eyes. 'Of course, my dear, that would be wonderful.'

The night Wendy was killed was the last major raid on Bath. Most people knew in their hearts that they had to fight on: the famous wartime spirit which had sustained Londoners throughout the blitz was alive and well in Bath, too. Shops stuck signs on their boarded-up windows saying *'Business As Usual!'*, cinemas re-opened and local traders announced in the *Bath & Wilts Chronicle* that they were back in business.

Eagle House went into a week of mourning for Wendy. David acceded to the Jewish custom, allowing Sonia to cover the mirrors which had survived the bombing, and many visitors came, including Wendy's colleagues from the hospital who were terribly saddened at the loss of such a good nurse and a lovely woman.

When the period of mourning ended David threw himself into his work, the only way he knew how to cope.

51

Sonia assumed the duty of running the domestics, taking charge of both families' food and clothing coupons and doing all the shopping, cooking and cleaning. She even managed to source a chicken so that she could make some much-needed soup. As well as teaching, Karl took care of repairs to the house and set about trying to rescue the garden; and Anthony and Gilda went back to school. Life went on, day by day, but it was unreal, and grief pervaded Eagle House. Nothing would ever be the same again.

Mr Greenstein's hotel had survived the bombing and the German Jewish refugees gathered there to thank God they had been spared, drawing comfort from each other and more determined than ever to make Bath their permanent home.

Bath was honoured with a visit from King George VI and Queen Elizabeth, a much-needed boost to morale. Gilda wanted to see them and was delighted when Anthony offered to take her. Together they joined the crowds lining the ruined streets, standing near the Abbey which had emerged remarkably unscathed. The King and Queen walked slowly among them setting exactly the right tone, capturing that conflict between grieving and the need to carry on. They brought words of sympathy, looking sorrowfully at the damage that had been inflicted, but praising the people and congratulating the city on its response.

When they got home Gilda said to her mother, 'Mama, the Queen was so elegant, with her pretty hat and her pearls, and she spoke kindly to everyone. And the King listened carefully to what people said. It was so nice of them to come and see us!'

Anthony was also impressed by the royal visit. 'I just wish Mum could have seen them...' he said, and went to his room.

Slowly, the city began to re-build itself. Utilities were repaired and bombed buildings which teetered dangerously were demolished. 'Orphaned' pets were rounded up and sent to the Bath Cats and Dogs Home at Claverton. Plans were made to repair damaged historic buildings and to restore them to their former glory. The legacy left by the 'Bath Blitz', as it became known, would last for decades.

It was said that the raids were part of a deliberate German plan to attack places of historic and cultural interest and later they became known as the 'Baedeker' Raids, after the famous guide book. After Bath, the bombers' attention switched to Norwich, Exeter, Canterbury and York; but who knew when they might return?

Anthony put on a brave face but inside he was overcome with grief. He kept re-living that last night, thinking that if he'd stayed up longer he might have persuaded his mother not to go out; the thought kept going round and round in his head, driving him mad. He spent a lot of time on his own, walking around the bomb site where his mother had been killed, searching, looking, poking at wreckage with a stick hoping to retrieve something he had lost, trying to understand something which could never be understood.

One afternoon after school he was feeling particularly low. He had had a lousy day, failing a Maths test which he should have sailed through, and had copped a telling-off from his tutor.

He wandered the streets, ending up on the bomb site, and walked over the rubble towards a heap of fallen masonry where a chequered flag had been placed, marking the site of an unexploded bomb.

For an instant he considered climbing up to the flag and jumping up and down like a mad thing, wanting to blow himself to bits. But then he noticed something furry moving amongst the rubble, something black – not a rat, although the bomb sites were full of them... no, it was a little black cat.

'You stupid animal, you'll get yourself killed!' he shouted. The cat froze, its wide green eyes fixed on Anthony.

'Oh for heaven's sake! Come here!' The cat slowly made its way across a plank of wood and down the pile of rubble, finally leaping across a hole in the ground, then it ran up to Anthony and wound itself around his legs. He bent down to stroke the cat which started to purr.

'Hey, you had a narrow escape there, didn't you? Best to avoid those flags, I think!'

The cat was so thin Anthony could feel its bony skeleton under its fur.

'You could do with a good, meal, couldn't you? Looks like you haven't got a home to go to – the great round-up must have missed you. Come on, then!'

Anthony walked home and the cat followed, trotting along behind him.

Gilda was thrilled and named the cat Lucky. 'Thank you for rescuing her!' she said.

'I think it was the cat that rescued me...' said Anthony.

The Blumfeldts continued to eat down in the basement, with Sonia preparing a meal for David and Anthony and serving it to them in the dining room. One evening David said to her, 'why don't we all eat together? It seems silly for us two to be up here on our own.'

Sonia thought for a moment, then said, 'that would be nice, David – the five of us together. But how about Shabbat – would you like to join our celebration? You are more than welcome.'

The following Friday Sonia prepared a special dinner of rabbit stew with home-made bread and some potatoes Karl had managed to salvage from the garden. Sonia laid the table in the dining room and just before dark, when everyone was seated, she lit the Shabbat candles and recited a prayer, covering her eyes with the palms of her hands. David, aware of the significance of the meal, had fetched a bottle of wine from the cellar which Karl blessed and served to the adults. Other prayers and incantations in the strange Yiddish language followed, then finally Sonia served the meal and they could begin to eat. After a general murmuring of approval Sonia said to her daughter, 'so tell us what you've been doing at school this week, *liebchen.*'

From there the conversation flowed; the celebration of family and sharing of experience was as important as the food.

Later, when they were on their own, David lit his pipe and said to Anthony, 'do you know, I think we are quite privileged to be included in that strange Jewish ritual. I rather enjoyed it – and I think your mother would have approved.'

'Yes, she would,' said Anthony.

Henry, shattered by his mother's death, desperately wanted to stay at home to console his father and brother but had no choice in the matter. He grew another protective layer of armour and immersed himself in his work.

Two weeks later he was sent on his eleventh bombing mission. He steered the Lancaster along the runway, gathering speed, pulled back the controls and lifted the powerful machine into the air, heading once again for Germany.

The plane droned on steadily for what seemed like an age. All the crew were quiet tonight – they seemed to have run out of banter. Everyone was focussed on their task. At last they were nearing the vicinity of their target. As they approached, the full moon emerged from behind a cloud, lighting up the Rhine like a silver snake, guiding them to their destination. As the bomb aimer released the first bomb over the Ruhr valley Henry said, out loud, 'this one's for you, Mum.'

*

Anthony's Maths master, Mr Blake, invited Anthony to his rooms for tea to talk about the future.

'You have great potential, Roberts, and you should do well in your exams,' he said. 'I know you miss your mother, but you must concentrate on revising now – don't let the end go, just as you're getting to the critical point!'

'I know, sir…I'm sorry, it's just been so hard…'

Mr Blake poured some tea. 'You can put your University career on hold until the war is over – as long as you get good results your place at Oxford is secure.

You're coming up to eighteen and I know you're keen to join the RAF like your brother, but I must ask you: is that really what you want to do?'

Anthony sighed and scratched the back of his neck. 'I still want to join up. But I just feel so confused. And angry!'

Mr Blake sipped his tea. 'You know, I was about your age when I lost my father in the Great War. He was killed on the Somme. That loss is something you never really get over.'

'I'm sorry to hear that. It must have been very hard for you – and your mother.'

'It was - but we managed. And my mother's still alive – a very active seventy year old! And proud of what her children have achieved. You can't just stop, you see.'

Another deep sigh from Anthony. 'The thing is…' he began, slowly. 'The thing is…although I've always wanted to join the RAF, like Henry…I don't think I could bring myself to do it. To drop bombs, I mean.'

Mr Blake put down his teacup and listened.

'It's just that the way Mum died…I don't think I can do that. I don't think I can fly over Germany and drop bombs on somebody else's mother or father – even if they are the enemy. I know Henry manages to do it – but I can't.'

'That's quite understandable,' said Mr Blake.

'Don't get me wrong,' continued Anthony, 'I'm not a conscientious objector or anything like that. I just don't want to kill innocent people…'

'Look - I may have a suggestion for you. Leave it with me and we'll speak again soon.'

Anthony received a timely letter from his brother, brief and to the point:

'...*it's so difficult, especially for you, being at home without her. My only advice is to try and focus on something, something important. I've got my job, and you've got your exams. Try and do your best, won't you, old man? Make Mum proud of you. After all, you've got the brains of the family...*'

Anthony sighed. He really didn't have the heart to study – but perhaps he should try...

In August the families celebrated Gilda's twelfth birthday and watched as she charged round the revived vegetable patches in the garden with her new hockey stick, a gift from her parents. Sonia had saved up the sugar ration to bake her a cake and presented her with a pretty Summer frock she had made on Wendy's old sewing machine, using the stash of material up in the attic.

'There!' said Sonia to Karl, 'doesn't our daughter look lovely!'

'She does, my dear,' said her husband, 'she does.'

Anthony took his brother's advice on board and was rewarded with a pass in his Higher School Certificate with a distinction in Maths. Mr Blake congratulated him, knowing how difficult it had been for his prize pupil, then asked what Anthony thought was a rather strange question.

'You're good at sport, aren't you, Roberts?'

'Well, I won the House shield for cross-country last year...'

'And you were a Scout leader, weren't you?'

'Yes...'

'Fitness and leadership - those are the sorts of qualities they're looking for.'

'Who?'

'The Army!'

'What?!'

'Look, I've been speaking to my contact in the War Office and I think there's something that's perfect for you. They're introducing a new selection process for recruiting junior Army officers. You'd sail through it! Just think - you'd be in action, fighting other soldiers, then after the war you can take up your place at Oxford!'

Anthony was astonished.

'You don't have to follow the same path as your brother, you know – the Army might suit you better. Why don't you give it some thought?'

That weekend Henry happened to be home and Anthony broached the subject with him.

'My brother? A pongo?!' he cried, incredulously. 'Why on earth would you want to do that?'

'I just can't go dropping bombs on people,' said Anthony.

'But we're only doing to them what they're doing to us,' replied Henry. 'And we've got to keep on doing it until we win.'

Anthony shook his head. 'I don't think I can...I mean, flying would be great, but killing civilians...'

'Well, it's up to you. But don't think because you're on the ground you won't have contact with civvies. If you're really worried about that, you may as well join the Navy and blow up enemy ships!'

'No - I couldn't stand being cooped up in a tin box. And I'm sure I'd be seasick.'

David was equally surprised at his son's change of heart. He reminded him about his own experience as a Medical Officer in France.

'The Army will be tough,' he said, 'the discipline is harsh and you will be in danger. I'd miss you terribly. But I won't stand in your way, if that's what you really want to do.'

The more Anthony thought about it, the more he liked the idea. Being at home without his mother was unbearable and he desperately felt the need to get away, to do something different. He felt guilty at the prospect of leaving his father, but the Blumfeldts would look after him – thank goodness they were there. He filled in the application form and within the week received a reply from the War Office inviting him to report to Sandhurst in September for an interview.

At the next Shabbat dinner Anthony made his announcement.

'You all know that I want to do my bit. Well, I've applied to join the Army!'

There was a shocked silence, then David said, 'I know you've been considering your options, Anthony. I'm sure you will do well.'

'You will make a fine soldier!' said Karl.

'I wish you every success,' said Sonia.

Gilda was taken aback. 'I don't want you to go away!' she cried.

Anthony laughed and said, 'you'll manage without me!'

But Gilda didn't look so sure.

David got to his feet. 'A toast to my son!' he said, raising his glass.

'To Anthony!' they said.

Then Karl added, 'we wish you the best of luck - as we say, *'Mazel tov!'*

'Mazel tov!' said Gilda, quietly.

CHAPTER 8

Bath, 1942

Anthony breezed through the assessment interview for Army officer cadets. The year-long training programme began in October and as he left home, about to embark on the adventure of his life, he shook hands with his father who was still unable to believe that his younger son - this schoolboy! - was joining up to fight. Anthony felt a pang of remorse. His heart went out to his father; Wendy's death had left him somehow hollow, a lesser version of his former self.

'All the best to you,' said Karl.

'Take care of yourself,' said Sonia.

Gilda burst into tears. 'I'm going to miss you!' she cried, hugging him tightly.

Anthony kissed the top of her head and said, 'come on - I'll be back before you know it! Now, you be a good girl and look after everyone while I'm away, won't you?'

With that, Anthony took a deep breath, picked up his suitcase and with a last wave over his shoulder, left Eagle House.

Sandhurst, 1942

The first day at Sandhurst went by in a whirl of new uniforms, new boots, haircuts, dental checks and injections against numerous diseases.

Anthony's arm swelled up in reaction to one of the injections and that night, as he lay on his bunk in the dormitory feeling tired and unwell, it reminded him of when he'd had chickenpox as a kid.

He heard a woman's voice, speaking to him gently.

'Don't worry, darling, you'll feel better in the morning.'

'Thanks, Mum,' he replied, drowsily.

Realising what he'd just said, he sat up with a start and looked around, but no one was there.

The training programme was intense and merciless. They were to be whipped into shape by a crusty old Sergeant-Major who had seen service as a youngster on the Somme and explained how things were going to be.

'As prospective officers, while you are here, I will address you as 'sir'. You, in turn, will call me 'sir'. The only difference is that *you* will mean it!'

Anthony's first kit inspection was the cause of scornful laughter.

'Where's your razor?' barked the Sergeant-Major.

'I haven't got one, sir' Anthony replied.

'Why not?'

'I don't shave, sir.'

The cadets were issued with Lee-Enfield rifles, the British Army's standard weapon. Loaded with the 303 British cartridge, the rifle was the most important part of their kit and by the end of their training every man could strip it down, maintain and reassemble it, even in the dark.

They undertook daily route marches of up to twenty miles in the foul Winter weather carrying their equipment on their backs, their mess tins and tea mugs attached to their belts, singing bawdy songs to keep up their morale. The importance of observation was drummed into them.

'Always be aware of anything different, unusual - follow your instincts. If something doesn't seem right, then check everything again. Be suspicious. One day your life might depend upon it.'

They were issued with a pocket sketch book and with a bit of practice Anthony got quite good at drawing military scenes on Salisbury plain and sketching soldiers in the camp. They were taught First Aid and how to deal with casualties on the battlefield, dreading ever having to do it for real.

Christmas came – the first Anthony had spent away from home. He received a letter and gifts from his father and the Blumfeldts; it was strange to be celebrating the event with a Jewish family, his father told him, but all was well and Sonia was cooking a chicken. At Sandhurst they were served a goose with all the trimmings and in the evening there was a Christmas concert with carols followed by more upbeat music including some Glenn Miller tunes which reminded Anthony of home. Suddenly missing his family he went to his bunk and lay there, thinking about his mother and wishing he could be back at Eagle House with his father, eating a bowl of Sonia's chicken soup.

The Army's priority was to get the young officers ready to deploy to mainland Europe and the Far East, and in the new year, training intensified.

The cadets were toughened up, mentally and physically, their body-mass increased and Anthony soon had need of that razor. Another sign of adulthood came about simply from following orders:

'Fall out for a smoke!'

So he did.

Anthony learnt how to deal with the mickey-taking that goes as part of the territory of being in the military. Soldiers from the North teased him for his slightly posh accent and the way he pronounced 'Bath' with a long vowel rather than a short one, but he gave as good as he got. After a while he lost his inhibitions and learnt to shout out orders and swear like all the others when he needed to. It took him a little longer to stop wondering what his mother would think.

Bath, 1943

At the end of April a special service was held in Bath Abbey to commemorate the anniversary of the Bath Blitz. A year had passed since Wendy had been killed and the whole city stopped to remember the dead and injured. Henry and Anthony were both given leave to attend and sorrowfully accompanied their father to the ceremony, suffering their great loss all over again.

The brothers were incredibly pleased to see each other. Henry couldn't believe how mature Anthony had become and the pair of them struck a handsome picture as they strode along in their uniforms beside their father. At the service Anthony met his old Maths master, Mr Blake, and thanked him for pointing him in the direction of the Army.

'Although there have been moments when I wished you'd never suggested it!'

Sandhurst, 1943

At the mid-point of the year the cadets were required to decide in which Regiment they wanted to serve. Anthony chose the Corps of Royal Engineers – jacks of all trades going everywhere and turning their hands to pretty much everything. The panache of the Cavalry or living in a hole with the Infantry and getting amongst it with a bayonet were not for him.

A bit of light relief came with the annual Sandhurst Summer Ball which continued in a modified way in wartime conditions. In preparation the cadets were given dancing lessons – an important war-winning tactic – and Anthony was paired off with a rather dumpy but enthusiastic daughter of a Brigadier.

In the event the evening went reasonably well. The buffet and drinks were generous, Anthony managed not to step on any of his partners' toes and at the end of the evening the dumpy girl led him outside to some bushes where she allowed him to fumble with her breasts until she heard her father's voice and promptly ended their brief encounter, leaving Anthony feeling aroused, confused and deflated.

The cadets listened avidly to the wireless to follow the progress of the war, knowing it would soon be their turn to go and fight.

British forces had finally defeated the enemy in North Africa and proceeded to take Sicily, entering mainland Italy in September, at which point the Italians promptly switched sides and declared war on Germany. British forces were heavily engaged in Asia where terrible stories were emerging of the fighting conditions in the jungle and the treatment of Prisoners of War.

In December, David and Henry travelled to Sandhurst to see Anthony officially commissioned as a Second Lieutenant. For once Henry felt out-numbered in his Air Force blue, and although he still couldn't understand how his brother could prefer the Army to the RAF he respected his decision.

'A Subaltern – that's what they call you, isn't it?'

'That's right, until I become a Captain in a couple of years!'

'So chuffed for you, old man!'

Both brothers were able to get Christmas leave and enjoyed a very special few days with their father. The Blumfeldts were delighted to see them.

'You are so grown up already!' exclaimed Sonia.

'You look so well!' said Karl.

Gilda stared in awe at the strapping young men.

'Why don't you show Anthony your new room, *liebchen*?' Sonia said to her daughter.

Gilda grabbed his hand and led him up to the first floor of the house. Taking a heavy hint from Sonia, David had offered one of the guest rooms to Gilda, now aged thirteen, leaving her parents some privacy in the basement. Her father had given the room a lick of paint, put up some shelves for her growing collection of books and provided a desk where she could do her schoolwork. Sonia used Wendy's sewing machine to run up some new curtains and a matching bedspread, and Gilda was thrilled with the results.

'Now, tell me what you're doing at school,' said Anthony. 'I hear you're quite the athlete now – keeping fit, and playing lots of sports?'

She glowed with pride and told him all about it.

67

On Christmas Day Sonia announced, 'come, Gilda and I have prepared a special meal for us all,' leading them into the dining room. 'I hope you enjoy some home cooking. And the vegetables are from our own garden! After we've eaten, Gilda can play to us – you've been practising a new tune, haven't you, *liebchen*?'

It was soon time for Henry to return to his Unit. Anthony was off to Chatham, Kent, the home of the Corps of Royal Engineers, where he would undertake six months intensive training before joining his permanent station. As their father wished them goodbye he said, 'that was the happiest few days I have spent for a long time. I wonder what we'll all be doing next Christmas?'

CHAPTER 9

Chatham, 1944

Anthony had never been to Kent and suddenly became aware of what a West-country boy he was. The local accent sounded like a kind of strangled Cockney and the pace of life was faster than at home. The streets were alive with hustle and bustle, sailors swaying along in their bell-bottomed trousers carrying kit bags on their shoulders, often followed by giggling girls who would run after them shouting out 'touch your collar for luck, Jack!' The Dockyard was a hive of activity, crammed with warships and submarines being refitted and repaired by the Dockyard mateys in readiness for their return to sea.

The town had suffered terribly from bombing raids with houses and factories being destroyed as well as parts of the Dockyard itself. The nightly drone of German planes en route to London, thirty miles away, had become the norm and when the bombing of the Capital was particularly heavy an orange glow lit up the sky. People's resilience had to be admired; spending night after night in air raid shelters was exhausting, yet the following day folk would be up and about again, back to work.

Soldiers and sailors had been active in the area for centuries: three hundred years ago the Dutch fleet had dared to venture up the River Medway to Upnor Castle and attack Royal Navy ships before being forced to retreat. Nelson's flagship *HMS VICTORY* had been built at Chatham Dockyard. Previous generations of Royal Engineers had learnt their trade on this same stretch of water before going to Ladysmith and the Somme. Ghosts from history were all around them.

Anthony took on the role of platoon commander in charge of thirty 'Sappers', as privates in the Royal Engineers are known. They spent weeks on the Medway being taught how to assemble bridges and pontoons, and equally, the explosives techniques required to blow them up; and how to detect and defuse all types of mines. They also learnt to drive cars, jeeps, trucks and motorcycles, as mobility was all-important.

Anthony took to his new job with enthusiasm but there remained one area where his education was decidedly lacking. Occasionally the men would get a night off and Anthony was persuaded to go into town with one of the sergeants (a local man) and another young officer.

'Time you were introduced to the flesh pots of Chatham!' the sergeant said.

Anthony realised just how sheltered his upbringing had been and knew that for his credibility if nothing else he had to do something about it.

Their local guide knew all the pubs and where to find what he called 'willing women'. A lot of drink was taken and by the time they got to the unofficial brothel Anthony was the worse for wear.

The sergeant tipped his favourite girl the wink and she led the young man along to her room, like a lamb to the slaughter.

Later, Anthony said it had been 'the best Biology lesson I've ever had!'

Germany, 1944

Henry was flying his Lancaster on another bombing mission, this time to Berlin. By now he had lost track of the number of missions he had flown. Forty? Fifty? He knew it was a miracle he had lasted so long. He carefully checked his instruments to make sure everything was as it should be: there was no room for complacency.

They dropped fifteen thousand pounds of bombs that night leaving a trail of fire, death and destruction behind them. Henry remained cool, professional; there was no room inside his head to consider that there were real people down there; he was just carrying out his orders. He made a final sweep over the city and headed the plane for home.

Anti-aircraft guns were attacking from the ground but they were flying high enough to avoid them. They flew on, the noisy plane groaning and rattling, then suddenly, from beneath, a German fighter plane fired at them, hitting the port wing and fuselage. Henry looked out from the cockpit to see the wing on fire and his instrument panel was wrecked. The fuel tanks were alight and flames were engulfing the back of the plane. He grabbed his intercom.

'Evacuate! Evacuate! Use the forward escape hatch, it's the only one that's safe. Evacuate now!'

All six crew members managed to get through the hatch and use their parachutes. Henry was the last to leave, jumping out of the aircraft and plunging into the cold night air, watching as his beloved Lancaster plummeted into the earth below, sending a ball of flames skyward.

Bath, 1944

On 6th June, D-Day, the great operation to liberate North-West Europe from German occupation began. Some of the young officers would join the forces in France whose progress they had been following so keenly, but that was not to be Anthony's path. He and a dozen or so of his colleagues were to join the ranks of the Eighth Army as it drove German forces out of Italy. He was given a weekend pass, then he would be off.

Anthony took the train to Bath and walked through the damaged streets, past the blackened buildings, feeling like a stranger in his home city after six months away. His father and the Blumfeldts were overjoyed to see him, Gilda hugging him tightly and Sonia clucking around as if he were her own son, remarking on what a fine young man he had become. On Saturday he visited Wendy's grave with his father, neither of them yet used to the idea that she was gone.

'I came here in April with the Blumfeldts and we put some flowers down for your mother – it's two years now,' said David. 'Karl and Sonia have been a great support to me. And Susan Fowler brought her little girl Wendy to see me the other day, you remember, she was named after your mother.'

'I so wish my Wendy could have seen her. She is a delightful child, I must say. They live with Susan's sister in Bristol. Susan told me her husband's ship was sunk by a German torpedo and he never came home.'

Back at home David gave his son a gift to take to Italy. 'It's a phrasebook! You might find it useful if you need to communicate with the locals. You took Latin, didn't you? – you'll soon pick it up!'

On Sunday Gilda was on edge, watching wistfully while Anthony packed his kitbag. 'I'm worried that you won't come back!' she cried, 'I'm going to miss you so much!'

'Of course I'll come back! Now, you promise to be good, and keep practising that piano. It's your job to look after everyone here at home.'

Sonia answered a knock at the door and opened it to find a telegram messenger boy in his smart navy uniform.

'Telegram for Dr Roberts,' he said.

David heard his name and came to the door. He put on his reading glasses, took the telegram from the envelope, read it, then let it slip from his fingers as he put out his hand to steady himself. His face went deathly pale.

Sonia picked up the telegram, read it and caught her breath. 'It's Henry,' she said. 'He's Missing in Action.'

PART TWO

CHAPTER 10

Italy 1944

By July 1944 Italy had already seen some of the hardest and most ferocious fighting of the entire war. The Allies had finally taken Monte Cassino, with great loss of life, and were advancing beyond Rome, taking Florence and making rapid progress North. Anthony found himself posted to a Division working towards Rimini on the Adriatic coast, about to put into practice the skills he had learnt on the River Medway. He felt like an infinitesimal cog in a very tiny wheel, but against this backdrop of major world events each individual had their part to play, however small. And this was his.

Anthony was worried about his brother and had felt terrible, leaving his father that dreadful afternoon, but he had no choice. He passed the journey to Italy in a daze, boarding a ship, battling sea-sickness for a week until he was back on solid ground, then there was an interminable, hot, sweaty ride in a lorry until at last they reached a billet somewhere South West of Rimini.

Anthony met his new boss, Captain Baker, the Company Commander of a hundred men. He was in his mid-twenties, but years of battle had aged him. He welcomed some fresh blood. The Captain repeated the order he had been given himself, all that time ago:

'There are two things you must do: look after your men and know your job. You'll be in charge of a platoon of twenty-five. The Sergeant - Hawkins - is good. You can rely on his judgement. Watch out for Sapper Collins - nasty piece of work. But most of them are good chaps. You'll soon settle in.'

The soldiers looked askance at Anthony – young, fresh-faced, his map case and binoculars slung around his neck, looking for all the world as if he were on exercise on Salisbury plain. Most of these men had been away from home for two or three years, first in the North African desert then landing in Anzio and fighting their way North to their present location. They'd seen terrible things, fought the bloodiest battles, lost comrades, suffered injury. And these were the people they called the D-Day Dodgers. No amount of training could prepare a young officer for the look in these men's eyes.

Sergeant Hawkins came forward and said, 'right, sir, I'll show you around.'

'Thank you, sergeant,' Anthony replied, straightening himself up and trying at least to look as if he were ready to take command.

Soon after Anthony's arrival, by some miracle of the Army Post Office, the Company received a mail delivery. That feeling of connection was vital for morale and the men took their letters eagerly, giving the odd grunt, groan or chuckle as they read the news from home. Anthony was surprised and delighted to receive a letter from his father:

Dear Anthony,

This is to wish you a happy twentieth birthday. I expect this letter will take some time to get to you but I hope you were able to spend a reasonable day. We still have no news of Henry. I spoke to his Commanding Officer who told me Henry's plane hadn't returned from its mission so all the crew were reported as Missing In Action. He promised to let me know as soon as he hears anything further.

Your loving father…

With so much happening Anthony had only given his birthday a passing thought as he'd thrown up yet again over the side of the ship. But he appreciated his father thinking of him when Henry was the main concern.

It was blisteringly hot. It was Anthony's first time abroad and that Summer the Italian heat was exceptional. Like all the others his working uniform consisted of baggy khaki shorts, a brown leather belt and a khaki shirt, with sleeves rolled up during the day and down in the evening to prevent mosquito bites. Flies were a constant irritation and his clothes became sweat stained as soon as he put them on. But at least the supply lines were good and there was sufficient for them to eat and drink.

So, to work…

The Company began its advance towards Rimini. With some on foot and others travelling in trucks loaded with equipment they moved through what would in normal times have been gently rolling hills covered in vines and olive groves with picturesque rivers winding their way to the Adriatic Sea.

As it was, the landscape was scarred and burnt, the roads rugged and pot-holed, the sound of enemy fire never far away.

There were occasional raids from above when the men would take cover as bullets rained down on them from German planes. The first time it happened Anthony was terrified although he did his best not to show it. It reminded him of the bombing raids on Bath, but without a cellar to shelter in.

As they travelled he got to know the members of his platoon, a mix of regular Army men and volunteers including Sappers Davies and Jones from the coal mines of South Wales; Corporal Cummings who had been evacuated from Dunkirk then joined the Eighth Army in the desert; and Corporal Hastings, an older chap from the Post Office who had been in Rome after it was liberated. Sapper Collins was a quarryman from Wiltshire in his early twenties. Short, muscular and aggressive, you didn't want to be on the wrong end of his pickaxe. The Army had done an exceptional job in welding together this disparate bunch of people and training them as an effective fighting unit. Or so the theory went.

They were working alongside Divisions from all over the world - Americans, South Africans, Indians, French, Polish, Australians, New Zealanders - it was a marvel that these distinct forces were able to operate so well together, driven by a common cause.

There were also the partisans – native Italians who were fighting against Mussolini and Fascism in Italy's own civil war. Many of them hid out in the mountains in the North, poorly fed and supplied, but brave and committed fighters.

The Company stayed under canvas, bedded down in farm buildings or dug slit trenches, living in similar conditions to those their fathers had endured in France during the Great War. Cigarettes and tea kept them going. On their long march they passed through numerous villages, many razed to the ground by the German Army that had preceded them.

Occasionally a few survivors would run towards them, their hands held out, pleading for food. Buildings had been smashed to pieces by gunfire yet people still scratched a living in the ruins, farming the odd patch of land which had escaped damage and keeping a few animals.

Anthony was stunned by the poverty he witnessed but the worst sight by far was that of the numerous dead bodies they came across. The first time he saw the corpse of a German soldier lying face down by the side of the road he went over to it just as Sergeant Hawkins shouted out to him, 'No! Don't touch it!'

'But we can't just leave people like this, lying here!' cried Anthony.

'Stand back!' said the sergeant.

He kicked the body onto its back to reveal half-eaten, putrefying flesh, oozing with maggots and flies. A dozen rats scattered, their feast interrupted, and the stench was appalling. Anthony vomited violently. Square-bashing and route marches hadn't primed him for this.

'Come on,' Sergeant Hawkins said, 'they're everywhere. If we stopped to bury them all we'd never reach Rimini. It's war, all right? You'll get used to it.'

Going East meant crossing many rivers and Anthony's platoon was soon called upon to construct a temporary bridge. Sergeant Hawkins got everything organised; the men knew their roles and to Anthony's relief the whole operation went smoothly. 'It is easier when you're not being shot at!' commented Hawkins.

Every piece of German equipment left behind had to be treated as a potential booby-trap and Anthony led his men as they picked their way slowly and cautiously along the roads like beachcombers, clearing them of the lethal debris.

At last the months of preparation and practice paid off: Anthony knew what he was doing and led by example, each success bolstering his confidence and gradually increasing his standing in the eyes of his men.

As they approached a village called Villano, Captain Baker received intelligence indicating there had been enemy activity in an area adjacent to some nearby farmland. He ordered Anthony's platoon to look for anything suspicious, assess the dangers and make the area safe. The lives of their comrades lay in their hands.

Leading an advance party of ten men Anthony made contact with the farmer who owned the land in question. He seemed uneasy but came out to greet them, gave them some fresh eggs and a dozen bottles of wine from his vineyard, and invited them to sleep in a small stone barn that had previously been used as a cowshed.

They made good progress that day, working from side to side across a field next to the farmhouse under the burning sun, and found nothing untoward.

In the evening the men were able to rest up for a bit, eating their rations, cooking the eggs and drinking their way through the rough red wine.

Anthony took a moment to sit out in the cooler evening air to sketch the vineyard below which had escaped damage from the fighting. He relaxed as he drew rows of vines heavy with plump purple grapes, hearing crickets chirping in the fields and watching as fireflies twinkled in the distance as the sun disappeared behind a hill, a picture of tranquillity.

The barn was empty of cattle but teeming with rats. The soldiers made up beds on the straw and Sapper Davies amused himself by throwing his knife at the rats, seeing how many he could impale to the floor. The wine at least guaranteed some sleep.

Just after dawn Anthony awoke, disturbed by something crawling over his face. He sat up and watched the rat scuttling through the straw, its whiskers twitching. Anthony surveyed his comrades lying in contorted positions, mouths open, snoring, rodents running all over them. He got up, opened the door of the barn, went outside and lit a cigarette. He scanned the fields and vineyard he had sketched the day before, but now, in the early morning light, the place seemed different. No...no, it was more than that. Down among the rows of vines he noticed an unnatural movement and shadows which suggested a presence.

Something was wrong. He glanced up towards the farmhouse where the farmer was standing in the yard, but when he realised Anthony had seen him he turned and scurried inside.

Anthony remembered what he'd been told: Trust your instincts!

He put out his cigarette, grinding it into the earth with his foot, went back inside the barn and shook Sergeant Hawkins awake.

'Shhhhh…' he said, leaning over him. He whispered: 'there's something strange going on – I think we're in a trap. Wake the others, tell them to keep quiet and prepare for an attack!'

Anthony radioed his Captain to report his suspicions and ask for assistance.

The men, woken by the sergeant and now fully alert, primed their weapons and positioned themselves by the slit windows in the barn walls in readiness for the raid. And it came.

One moment there was eerie silence; the next the air was filled with the vicious rattle of machine gun fire and the dull crump of mortar bombs as they exploded. German soldiers emerged from the vines and ran up towards the barn, firing their guns. Anthony's troop shot back and a few fell but others continued to approach.

Anthony's mind went into overdrive, his heart was thumping, he was scared but excited at the chance to prove himself and put what he'd learned into action. He assessed that they were evenly matched in terms of numbers and that as the German soldiers had lost their main advantage – the element of surprise – his men were well-positioned to defend themselves.

Anthony took aim at one of the enemy soldiers. He hesitated for a split second, then pulled the trigger and the man fell to the ground. Sapper Collins, at his aggressive best, partly opened the barn door and hurled hand grenades at the advancing enemy.

Several men fell in the resulting explosions but one German soldier emerged from the smoke, reached the door and was about to open fire when Sapper Davies, well-practiced from the previous evening, propelled his knife at him and struck him in the neck. Some stray bullets ricocheted around the barn hitting Sapper Jones, giving him a flesh wound in his upper arm.

Anthony's troop fired a few more rounds then realised that mortar fire from their own side was exploding in front of them, finishing off the remaining enemy soldiers. Gunfire ceased; the brief battle was over.

Captain Baker appeared at the barn door with the Medical Officer who went over to attend to Jones.

'Right, let's check outside for any wounded and bury the dead.'

The Captain then spoke to Anthony.

'That little party must have stayed behind to welcome us. Well done, Lieutenant Roberts. Your first time in action!'

Later, as Anthony reflected on the morning's events, he remembered his brother telling him how exhilarating it was to take part in combat, gunning down enemy aircraft in his Spitfire. Kill or be killed, he'd said. Now Anthony had taken that step himself; by taking another man's life he felt as if he'd crossed some kind of threshold. No regrets. No guilt. And as he thought about his brave brother he felt sure in his heart that Henry was still out there, still strong, and that he would survive whatever ordeal he was going through.

CHAPTER 11

Italy, 1944

With one almighty thunderstorm Summer came abruptly to an end. The weather turned suddenly cooler and the Autumn rains quickly reduced the roads and tracks to mud. Progress was slow, a steady, monotonous edging forward across swollen rivers and waterlogged plains. Warm weather rig was replaced by serge battledress and the men's boots were permanently caked in mud, the main enemy.

The Germans relinquished Rimini and Anthony's troop pressed on towards the coast, clearing mines and building bridges along the way. After one particularly arduous week when they had successfully finished constructing a Bailey bridge over a strategically important river they were sitting in a barn brewing up tea, smoking and relaxing when Captain Baker arrived.

'You've all done a great job,' he said. 'That bridge is going to help keep us supplied through the Winter. Well done Roberts and your team. And, talking of supplies, we've had a delivery of beer...'

The men perked up instantly and helped themselves as the Captain carried crates of bottled beer into the barn. After a few drinks Sergeant Hawkins came and sat down on the floor next to Anthony and said, 'it's going well. You know, if you don't mind me saying...I had my doubts when you turned up. 'Blondie from Bath', that's what they call you, you know!'

Then he said, 'but after the business in the barn, when you copped those Jerries, and now, all those bridges we've built...it's going well, sir.'

'Thank you, Hawkins,' Anthony replied, surprised and pleased by his sergeant's praise.

But Sapper Collins, who heard the exchange, caught Anthony's eye, looked scornfully at him and turned away.

'What *is* the matter with that man?' asked Anthony.

'Oh – always been a rum one, him,' said Hawkins. 'They say he hasn't been the same since he saw his mate get his head blown off at Monte Cassino. Don't take any notice of him.'

December was bitterly cold. Old timers were predicting a Winter as terrible as the previous one, when blizzards and drifting snow had forced them to cease action all together and many men had suffered from frostbite and trench foot. Anthony wrote home to reassure everyone he was safe and well, letting his father know he had at least one son who was still alive.

At last, weary from the long trek and lack of sleep, they reached Ravenna, just North of Rimini, where they were to set up Winter quarters. Captain Baker called his Lieutenants together to brief them.

'The Colonel has made contact with the Mayor of Ravenna. Our Company is going to stay in a small town nearby called Affossa. We're requisitioning a school and a community hall there and some officers will be accommodated in private houses and farms. Offensive operations have ceased and can't resume until the Spring, so we'll be here about three months.

But this is not a holiday! There's a lot to be done in the area, repairing roads and bridges and checking for mines. But at least we'll be warm and dry.'

He then singled out Anthony.

'Lieutenant Roberts, you will be the Local Liaison Officer. I want you to make contact with the Affossa town representatives and see what needs to be done.'

As ordered, Anthony went to Affossa for a meeting with members of the local community, taking Sergeant Hawkins with him. They drove their jeep carefully along the winding road, avoiding potholes and fallen trees, and as they travelled the rain began to turn to snow.

The town had been the scene of bloody clashes between occupying Germans, Allied forces and Italian partisans, and was heavily damaged. However the *municipio*, the equivalent of the Town Hall, was still standing, having only recently been vacated by German soldiers who had used it as their temporary headquarters.

They entered the building and were immediately struck by the legacy of the previous occupants, most notably a photograph on the wall of one A. Hitler.

'Well that's going, for a start,' said Anthony, tearing it off and throwing it on the floor.

They were greeted by an official and ushered into a meeting room where about a dozen people were seated on one side of a long table. The man sitting in the centre got up, shook hands and gestured to them to sit down opposite him.

'Bit outnumbered, aren't we?' said Anthony to Hawkins, under his breath.

It was the first time Anthony had been in direct contact with the people who had initially been their enemy and were now their allies. It reminded him vaguely of the first time he'd met the Blumfeldts, only this time it was he who was the foreigner.

He had remembered to bring the Italian phrasebook his father had given him and thought he might try out a few words.

'*Allora,*' said the leader, a short man dressed in a too-tight suit with slicked-back black hair.

Anthony was encouraged. He knew that meant 'well, then.'

There followed a cascade of incomprehensible words at a hundred miles an hour, the man apparently speaking without drawing breath while gesticulating wildly. Eventually he stopped, folded his hands in front of him on the table, looked straight at Anthony and smiled.

The whole room fell silent.

Anthony felt his face reddening with embarrassment.

After a pause which seemed to last for hours, he heard the voice of an angel coming from the far end of the table:

'Signor Valentino says to you, we are very pleased to welcome English soldiers in our town. We hope your accommodation is comfortable. We have seen much fighting and hope you can help us with rebuilding our town.'

Anthony sighed with relief and looked along the table at the speaker, a pretty young woman of about his own age.

He looked at her and said, 'thank you. I'm afraid my Italian isn't very good. Please thank Signor Valentino for his welcome. The British Army will do all we can to help your community.'

The young woman translated and proceeded to act as interpreter for the rest of the meeting. Afterwards, Anthony approached her.

'You saved my life there!'

They shook hands.

'I am called Isabella Fortuno,' she said. 'Signor Valentino asked me to come because I speak a little English.'

'More than a little! That was marvellous!'

She looked up at him and smiled, and Anthony looked at her properly for the first time. He realised he hadn't actually seen a woman in months and as he took on board her long, dark, wavy hair, olive skin, dark brown eyes and slim figure he found himself becoming quite...

'Better be going, then, sir!' said Hawkins, beside him.

'Oh! Indeed, yes,' replied Anthony, still looking at Isabella. 'I hope to see you at our next meeting, Signorina Fortuno,' he managed to say.

'Yes, of course, Lieutenant Roberts,' she replied.

Isabella lay in her bed that night thinking about the English soldier. Tall and thin, with fair hair and blue eyes, his Aryan looks reminded her of the German troops who had occupied her town, first as allies, then as a cruel and vindictive enemy.

But she knew the British were on a mission of liberation, returning Italy to the Italian people. The young soldier was nice; friendly and sympathetic, he seemed genuinely interested in helping her community. Perhaps he might be useful?

Then her thoughts turned to Carlo, her brave fiancé, stocky and dark, his black eyes intense, her man of the earth. He was away in the North fighting with the partisans and wasn't expected home for months yet. She kissed his photograph as she did every night and prayed to the Holy Mother to keep him safe.

Germany, 1944

'Flight Lieutenant Henry Roberts.'

He repeated the mantra in answer to every question, just as he had been trained to do. Rank and Name, nothing more.

Eventually the German officer gave up. 'Take him back to his cell!' he ordered.

Flanked by two soldiers, Henry was hoisted to his feet and marched along a dark corridor. One of the soldiers flung him into a room and locked the door. Henry climbed onto the bunk and lay there, exhausted and in pain.

But alive.

CHAPTER 12

Bath, 1944

Sonia was busy doing the housework when the telephone rang. Expecting to hear a request for Dr Roberts, she was surprised when the caller asked to speak to her.

'Yes, this is Sonia Blumfeldt. How may I help you?'

'I am Miss Hickson, Gilda's form teacher. I'm sorry to tell you that your daughter has been involved in an incident.'

'Oh no! Is she all right?'

'Yes, she is. But we do need to speak to you and your husband about Gilda's behaviour.'

Sonia was dumbfounded. 'But this is ridiculous! Are you sure you've got the right person?'

'Definitely!' came the answer. 'Please come to School this afternoon to discuss the matter.'

After an anxious few hours Sonia and Karl arrived at the school and were taken to the Headmistress' office. Gilda stood in the corner, her head bowed.

'I am sorry to tell you that there have been a number of incidents on the hockey field,' the Headmistress said. 'Now, we tend to overlook the odd mishap – and girls will be girls - but earlier today your daughter attacked another girl from a rival team who had to be taken to hospital. Fortunately no bones were broken, but she was badly bruised and very shaken.'

'Gilda!' said Karl, 'is this correct?'

'Yes, Papa,' she said, quietly.

'What on earth got into you, child?'

Gilda hung her head and said nothing.

'What is it, *liebchen*?' asked Sonia. 'Is it something this girl did, or said to you?'

Tears formed in Gilda's eyes.

'She said horrible things to me…'

'Yes?'

'…she said my nose was big…that I was ugly…and then she said I should be in a camp with all the other Jews because that was the best place for us…'

The adults were horrified.

'…so I hit her on the legs with my hockey stick,' said Gilda.

There was a collective gasp.

'Well,' said the Headmistress, 'we know about this girl – she has a reputation as a bully but I had no idea she was anti-Semitic. This is dreadful. I will speak to her school and discuss what further action we should take.'

Turning to Gilda she continued, 'Now, it was wrong of you to attack her, however much she provoked you. Any more trouble and you will be expelled. But if anyone else says bad things to you about being Jewish, you come and report it to me straight away. Do you understand?'

'Yes, ma'am,' said Gilda.

On Saturday morning the Blumfeldts went to the Shabbat service and lunch at Mr Greenstein's hotel, as usual. Gilda felt self-conscious for some reason, imagining that people were looking at her strangely.

After the service, as they were walking into the dining room, a boy called Jacob sidled up to her. He was fifteen, a year older than her, and she remembered attending his *Bar Mitzvah*, although he had never paid any attention to her before.

'That was a good thing you did, Gilda,' he said.

'Sorry?'

He looked around surreptitiously.

'It's all right,' he said, 'everyone's heard about your prowess with a hockey stick!'

Gilda felt a flush of embarrassment.

'Don't be ashamed,' he continued, 'you did the right thing. It's about time we Jews started to fight back. When the war's over we'll get our chance, you'll see.'

Sonia appeared at their side. 'Is everything all right, *liebchen*?'

'Yes, Mama…'

Jacob smiled and went to talk to his friends.

Sonia whispered in her daughter's ear, 'don't pay any attention to what that boy says, he has some strange ideas…' Then, in her normal voice, she said, 'now, come and sit with your father and me and eat your stew.'

'Yes, Mama,' said Gilda, glancing towards Jacob who smiled at her again.

Italy, 1944

Anthony went along to his next meeting with the locals in good heart. Compared to the death and destruction he had witnessed during his journey it was a relief to meet townspeople who at least looked fed and reasonably well-dressed.

He was hoping to see Isabella the interpreter again and she was indeed there to greet him. When their discussions ended she said, 'tomorrow you meet me after mass and I show you my town. Yes?'

'Yes!' he replied.

The next day, Sunday, Anthony was off-duty and waited for Isabella outside the church while a light dusting of snow fell. At last she emerged, wearing a warm coat and a headscarf, accompanied by some other girls. She waved goodbye to her friends then greeted Anthony with a smile.

'Good morning! Today I show you around, but first we have a coffee. Come!'

They crossed over the road to a café and entered to a wall of cigarette smoke, steamed-up windows and a torrent of chatter. They sat at a table, lit cigarettes, then Isabella spoke to the waiter who brought two espressos. Anthony looked curiously at the tiny cups and the dense, dark liquid within them.

'You like coffee?' she asked him.

'Yes…but I've never seen it like this before…'

She looked at him strangely, downed her own drink in one and waited while he followed suit.

'Crikey!' he said as the bitter, strong taste invaded his mouth and he felt an instant hit from the caffeine. 'That's not like the powdered stuff we have at home!'

She didn't know what he meant, so continued, 'I want to show you the buildings in Affossa. It will help you…' she paused, searching for the right word. 'It will help you understand.'

They began with the church which had miraculously escaped significant war damage. As they entered, Isabella dipped her fingers in a bowl containing holy water, making the sign of the cross. Anthony gazed up at the impressive vaulted ceiling, the gold leaf, the massive candles on the altar and the pervading scent of incense – an evident display of the wealth of the Catholic Church. Isabella proudly showed Anthony around, pointing out the beauty of the stonework and carved wooden statues of saints painted in vivid colours. In one corner there was a Nativity scene on a grand scale, bigger than anything Anthony had ever seen in an English church, with life-like wooden models of the holy family and a menagerie of animals displayed in a sturdy-looking stable.

'For *Natale*,' she said. 'Christmas.'

Their footsteps on the stone floor echoed around the building as they walked past rows of chairs towards a side chapel where Isabella put a few lire into the collection box, took a thin white candle and lit it from the flame of another.

'Come,' she said, 'you light a candle too. There must be someone you would like to remember?'

Anthony wasn't particularly religious but it seemed a reasonable thing to do, so he also lit a candle, placed it alongside the others and said, 'for my mother.'

Next, Isabella showed Anthony the rest of the town. They walked briskly against the cold wind, his guide pointing out the many houses and public buildings which had been damaged and bore the scars of the hand-to-hand fighting which had taken place there.

The destruction reminded Anthony of Bath after the bombing raids and he recalled that dreadful feeling of loss and disbelief. But this was even worse: the Germans had actually been here, occupied the town, taken over its buildings, terrorised its people.

They passed a row of houses that had been reduced to rubble and Isabella said, 'this was not the war – there was an earthquake last year. We lost much property and many lives.'

Anthony shook his head – as if the war wasn't enough to contend with.

A group of children were playing among the ruins in the snow, some of them barefoot. 'Their parents cannot afford to buy them shoes,' explained Isabella, 'and some of them are orphans. The nuns look after them.'

A boy of about eight saw Isabella and ran over to her. They gabbled together for a few minutes then he ran back to join the others, leaving Isabella looking saddened.

'I knew this boy's parents,' she said, 'they were killed in the fighting here. He says his elder brother Paulo is very ill, he has a fever. They have no money for a doctor. The nuns are looking after him but it does not sound good. The priest is going to see him tomorrow.'

'Is there anything we can do?'

'No – I think the boy is beyond saving. Paulo di Paulo. That is how he is called, after his father - Paulo son of Paulo.'

They hurried on until they came to the main town square where Isabella stopped abruptly.

'What is it?' asked Anthony.

'This is where the Germans shot twenty of our people. They were partisans and the Germans called them traitors. I saw it.'

Anthony was shocked, imagining the horror. She looked personally wounded. What could he say?

'That's why we've got to keep fighting them,' he said, finally.

They made their way back to a street market where a dozen stall holders were standing around in shabby clothes, stamping their feet, trying to keep out the cold. Many foods were rationed but they had some Winter vegetables for sale along with cooking oil and smoked meats, and some cheap children's toys in anticipation of Christmas. As they walked, Isabella told Anthony about her life on her parents' farm up in the hills, just outside the town.

'I am nineteen and the oldest of six – I have four sisters and my little brother, the youngest, he is five years old. My parents say they had to wait a long time for a son! I suppose you would say we are a traditional Italian family. My father runs the farm and the vineyard, but Mama's word is the law! We have some soldiers staying with us. They are quite kind.'

'How did you learn English?'

'I enjoyed learning English at school. I would like to be a teacher, but I have to work on the farm.'

'Do you speak any other languages?'

She hesitated.

'Yes,' she replied, 'German.'

It suddenly occurred to him that Signor Valentino would have used her interpreting skills in his dealings with the occupying German forces.

He imagined her in that same room where he had first met her, sitting opposite a line of Nazi soldiers. The thought made him shudder.

The tour ended, but Anthony didn't want it to stop.

'May I buy you another of those coffees, Signorina?'

Germany, 1944

Henry lay on a bunk in his cell reflecting on the events of the last few months. He had crash-landed in a tree, his parachute entangled in its branches, and must have knocked himself out because the next thing he knew was coming to in a German doctor's surgery having stitches put in his forehead and his broken left arm put in plaster. Two soldiers had bundled him into a van and brought him to a camp where he'd been held in solitary confinement. He'd been interrogated but they hadn't got anything out of him.

A few weeks later he had been taken by ambulance, under guard, to hospital where a doctor removed the plaster cast from his arm. It was still painful to move but the doctor declared it mended and put his arm in a sling. Then he'd been brought to this cell where he'd been imprisoned, alone, ever since.

Suddenly Henry heard soldiers' voices and the door of the cell opened. They dragged him off his bunk and one of them said, 'on your feet, Roberts! We're taking you on a little journey…'

CHAPTER 13

Bath, 1944

Sonia was feeling weary. It was one of those days when, although she never stopped being grateful for their life in England, the war was grinding her down. Her husband and daughter caught the brunt of it.

'I went to the shops but there wasn't much there - stuff disappears as soon as it comes in. And everyone is looking so miserable, so suspicious of each other…In the end I found some tinned food at the market and some washing soda but it was a real schlep getting it all home. We've all had enough. When's it going to end, Papa?' She called her husband 'Papa' sometimes when she needed reassurance.

Karl looked at her over his newspaper and said, 'I know, *liebchen*, it is so hard. We can only be thankful for what we have, and pray. Who knows when it will end – we are in God's hands.'

'Well I hope He gets a move on!' said Sonia, irritably. She walked back to the kitchen, passing Gilda who was sitting at the table with a book. 'And is there something more useful you could be doing?'

'I'm reading, Mama!' said Gilda.

'Hmm…'*A History of the Jewish People*,' read Sonia, looking over Gilda's shoulder. 'Sounds serious!'

'Jacob lent it to me. He says you can't know where you're going unless you know where you came from…'

'That boy again! You be careful of him, he's a troublemaker! Now, if you want a boyfriend why don't you choose someone like that nice Daniel Dinkelberg - he's going to be a lawyer!'

'Mother, I don't want a boyfriend – or a husband for that matter! And I'm certainly not going to end up as *Mrs Dinkelberg*!'

With that she took her book and stormed off to her room.

Sonia stood, open-mouthed. 'What is the matter with her?' she asked.

'She's fourteen,' replied Karl, from behind his newspaper.

Italy, 1944

Captain Baker called his Company together to make an announcement.

'Following discussions between our Colonel and the Mayor it has been decided to hold various community activities over the Christmas period. First, there will be a special service in Affossa Church with music and carols. Padre, I will look to you to speak with the local priest to sort out the arrangements.'

The Padre nodded.

'Next, weather permitting, there will be a football match. It seems the Italians are quite good at football and the local team have challenged us to a match. Lieutenant Moore, I'm sure you can rustle up a team?'

There was a general murmur of interest from the Company.

'And finally, Allied Military Government officers have ordered us to distribute packages of food, sweets and clothing to war victim children in the region. We want to make a proper event of this so we're going to host a Christmas party. Orphans are the priority, but other children from the community are welcome too. Lieutenant Roberts, I want you to lead on this one. Let's make this a party those children will never forget!'

Anthony knew exactly where to begin.

He arranged to meet Isabella at the *municpio*, taking Corporal Hastings with him as he had five children and ought to know something about what was required. Following his tour of the town Anthony knew how important it was to gain the trust of the local people; Affossa had only just been vacated by one invading force and they mustn't feel that another had arrived to take its place. Putting on this Christmas party would be a good way to break the ice and give the children some much-needed fun.

Isabella was there to meet them and showed them into a room where a man and two women were sitting. After introductions Anthony asked, 'Signorina Fortuno, can you tell me how you celebrate Christmas here?'

'You mean when there is no war?' Isabella replied, wryly, then continued, 'the day before Christmas we eat a special meal and we go to the church. Christmas Day is time for the family together. Befana brings presents for the children on Epiphany, the 6th January.'

'Befana?'

'She is a little old woman, a witch, she carries presents in a sack and leaves them in stockings for the children.'

'Aah, like our Santa Claus. Well, this year the Allies are going to host a party for local children. We'll be distributing parcels of clothing, there will be presents, and plenty of food!'

'Food!' she exclaimed, her interest increasing.

'I suggest we hold the party the day after Christmas. Corporal Hastings here has some ideas for keeping the children amused. Perhaps some of the ladies could help out?'

Isabella turned to her colleagues to explain and there was a sudden eruption of enthusiasm with a torrent of words and gestures.

'Yes, they will help. What sort of food will there be?'

Using planning for the Christmas party as an excuse Anthony arranged to meet Isabella and took her for lunch at the café in Affossa. It was quieter than on the Sunday and easier to talk.

Isabella recommended a dish made from rice and mushrooms which didn't sound very appealing but turned out to be rich, creamy and totally delicious.

'We call it *risotto*,' Isabella explained, 'is very simple dish, a specialty of Northern Italy.'

'Never heard of it,' said Anthony, 'but it tastes remarkable!'

She shrugged.

'It is normal. But not many can afford to eat here, so I thank you for treating me today. Our food is rationed, each family is allowed only a small amount of flour to make the pasta, and a little meat. I expect in England you have plenty of food, no?'

'No, not at all! We are rationed too. There are very strict rules about what we're allowed. We grow vegetables in our garden which helps, and thankfully Mrs Blumfeldt is a good cook and does what she can.'

'Who is that?'

'The Blumfeldts - they're a German Jewish family, refugees who came to live with us before the war. Since my mother died they more or less run the place and look after my father. They have a daughter, Gilda, who must be – what – fourteen by now.'

Isabella was shocked.

'You have Germans living with you?'

'Yes. I suppose it sounds strange – but because they're Jewish we took them in. They'd be dead by now if they'd stayed in Germany.'

Isabella shook her head, uncomprehending.

'We had German officers staying in our farmhouse but we had no choice. I didn't like them. They used to shout at us and they drank all of Papa's best wine, and once when I was in the barn feeding the goats one of them tried to…'

She stopped, took a sharp intake of breath, and stared into her coffee cup.

'Anyway…' she continued, 'we were very pleased to see them go.'

'How awful for you! Well the Blumfeldts certainly aren't like that. You see, they hate the Nazis as much as we do and want to make England their home.'

104

'What happened to your mother?'

'She was killed in April '42, in a bombing raid on Bath.'

Isabella sat back in her chair and looked at him.

'The Germans kill your mother, but you are pleased to have a German family living with you? I don't understand you English!'

After lunch Anthony walked with Isabella through the town. As they passed the ruins where children were playing, the young boy who knew Isabella ran to her. He looked forlorn and Anthony could guess what he was saying.

After he left Isabella said, 'his brother, Paulo di Paulo, died last night. It is very sad. The funeral is tomorrow. So today one of the nuns goes to buy the shoes.'

'Shoes? What shoes?'

'They will dress Paulo properly in his best clothes and he must have shoes. Then he will go to heaven.'

'But you told me they couldn't afford to buy shoes!'

'No, not normally. But this is different.'

Anthony was baffled.

'So they have no money to buy shoes for the children when they are alive, but they find the money for them when they are dead?'

She shrugged. 'It is how we do things here.'

Anthony shook his head in disbelief.

'I don't understand you Italians!'

Germany, 1944

The Nazi officers holding Flight Lieutenant Henry Roberts had concluded that interrogating him was fruitless and wanted him off their hands. They put him on a train handcuffed to an armed guard and as they steamed through the flat, grey landscape of Eastern Europe Henry looked at the great outdoors for the first time in months, wondering where he was being taken.

At last his long, tedious journey came to an end. They dismounted the train and the guard marched Henry to *Stalag Luft 32*, a POW camp in what had been Western Poland, where he handed him over. Henry was taken to a hut where other RAF personnel were accommodated and met by a Wing Commander McFadden. They saluted and exchanged names.

Henry said, with relief, 'I've never been so pleased to see another RAF officer!'

'Good to meet you, Roberts,' said the Wing Commander, 'I'll give you a chance to settle in then perhaps we can have a chat in private.'

Henry knew this was code for a de-brief and a picking of his brains for any useful intelligence. The other prisoners approached Henry, wanting to know when he'd been captured and what had happened to him. Thin and exhausted, with dark circles under his eyes, a nasty scar on his forehead and his left arm in a dirty sling, he had clearly suffered at the hands of the enemy. Out of the gloom appeared a familiar face - Henry's Observer, Flying Officer Peter Harrison. He shook Henry's good hand enthusiastically, delighted to find that Henry had survived but devastated at the loss of their plane.

'Hancock, Phillips and Johnson have been taken prisoner,' said Harrison, 'they're being held in *Stalag Luft 40*. But Henderson and Jones didn't make it.'

Henry tried to take in all this new information but one thing was at the forefront of his mind.

He asked the Wing Commander:

'How can I get a message to my father?'

Bath 1944

Sonia heard the postman, picked up the pile of mail he had put through the letterbox and glanced through it as she walked back to the kitchen. One of the items made her stop and catch her breath – an envelope from Germany, addressed in what she was sure was Henry's handwriting.

'Dear God, he must be alive!' she said, and whispered a prayer of thanksgiving. Her hands shaking, she placed the envelope in the centre of the mantlepiece for David to open when he returned from the hospital.

CHAPTER 14

Italy, 1944

Christmas in Affossa turned out to be better than anyone could have expected. Supplies arrived from home and the troops had a terrific Christmas dinner- for once their mess tins weren't large enough to hold their ration and they had to queue twice to take on board portions of turkey, sausages with bacon, sprouts and roast potatoes followed by Christmas pudding with custard. Extra supplies of beer had been flown in, carols were sung, gifts from home were opened and even the snow arrived on cue. To top it all, along with a parcel containing warm socks, bars of chocolate and a new sketch pad and pencils, Anthony received a letter from his father:

My dearest Anthony,

I have the best news to tell you – Henry is alive! He is being held in a POW camp in Germany. His plane was shot down and he suffered some minor injuries but now he says he is fine and with other RAF personnel. I cannot tell you my relief when I read his letter! It is the best Christmas present we could wish for, isn't it? I am feeling much better now.

I'm sending you these small gifts and hope they find you well. I expect the Army will make sure you are well supplied at Christmas. I miss your mother so much. Sonia has been saving up our rations and is sure to cook us a good dinner on Christmas Day. They all send their love to you and Gilda sends you a kiss. Your loving father...'

Buoyed up by the marvellous news about his brother, Anthony awoke on Boxing Day in good spirits and ready to face the invasion of children coming to the party. All the arrangements were in place: the soldiers had done a splendid job, decorating the school hall with paper decorations, tinsel and balloons, and in a corner the Christmas tree sparkled magnificently.

First to arrive were the nuns with the orphans they were caring for. The children looked around the decorated hall in wonder, then spotted rows of tables, groaning with food, and charged towards them, the nuns trying to keep some kind of order whilst heaping up their own plates. Anthony recognised the boy that Isabella knew among the crowd and felt a wave of sympathy for him at the loss of his brother. More children arrived and Corporal Hastings organised them into teams for games, then there was a visit from Santa Claus, played by a corpulent sergeant in a red uniform with a very convincing white beard and a deep, mellow 'Ho-Ho-Ho!'

Anthony kept looking but hadn't yet seen one particular guest who was due to come. He took a break from the swarms of screaming children and went outside for a smoke. He met Corporal Cummings who was sitting on a bench with a cigarette, looking miserably at the ground, his solemn demeanour strangely at odds with his pink paper hat. Anthony went and sat beside him.

'What's up?'

Cummings gestured back to the hall where the children were running around.

'This is great,' he said, 'it's marvellous what we're doing – it's the best fun they've had in years.

But I wish I was at home with my own kids.'

He took a well-worn photograph from his pocket. 'Look, there's George – he's six now – and Evie, my little girl – she's four. Haven't seen them for two years, since I left.'

'You must miss them terribly.'

'Yes I do. But what's going to happen when I get back home? They've got their own lives now, and I feel like I'll just be in the way. Sometimes I think it might be better if I didn't go back at all...'

'Come on, Albert, you mustn't talk like that. Of course they want you back! They'll get used to you again – you'll see.'

'Mmm – I hope you're right. But I have my doubts.'

He looked unconvinced as he stood up and threw his cigarette butt into a pile of snow which had been shovelled up by the doorway.

'I guess there's only one thing for it,' he said.

Summoning his energy he took a deep breath and with an almighty roar he charged back into the hall, scooped up two of the smaller children, one in the cradle of each arm, and ran round and round in circles with them as they whooped with laughter.

Anthony was about to go back into the hall when Isabella arrived with three of her younger siblings.

'Signorina Fortuno! I'm pleased you've made it!'

'Sorry, Lieutenant Roberts, I had to finish some work at home before Mama would let us come. Now, go and play!' she said, shooing away the youngsters.

He hung up her coat then they walked together into the hall and hit a wall of noise as the mass of increasingly hysterical children hurtled around.

'It's going well!' he said, shouting to make himself heard over the din.

She laughed. 'Yes, it is good to see them having fun!'

'You look nice today,' he said, looking at her colourful, flower-patterned dress which showed her slender figure to perfection. She was wearing lipstick and her hair was pinned back from her face with a pretty silver hair slide.

'Thank you,' she said, flattered that he'd noticed.

At that very moment Anthony saw a green-faced child staggering towards them and he pulled Isabella aside just in time as the boy vomited on the floor.

'That was a narrow escape!'

'Too much cake I think!'

They moved out the way as an apologetic mother followed with a mop and bucket.

'The pleasure of children's parties!'

Isabella made her way to the tables where the food was laid out and helped herself to sandwiches which she ate hungrily, even if she wasn't sure what Spam was. They watched the children playing and Isabella, well-used to looking after little ones, joined in with the games while Anthony and his team gave out parcels of clothing and food.

It turned out that Sergeant Hawkins was a bit of an amateur magician and the children stared at him open-mouthed as he made coins, watches and all manner of things disappear before their very eyes and then reappear behind somebody's ear, under their hat or in his pocket.

Finally the party came to an end and it was time for the children to go home. Isabella watched as Anthony collected rubbish and put it in a sack.

'You look like Befana, carrying her sack on her back!' she said.

'I'm afraid it's not full of presents, though!'

She laughed. 'We've had a lovely time, Lieutenant Roberts. Please say thank you to all your people who have done this for us.'

'It's been a pleasure, Signorina Fortuno. We've enjoyed it too. It's good to see the children having fun after all they've been through.'

'I think now you call me Isabella.'

'Oh - thank you - Isabella. And you can call me Anthony.'

'An-th-ony' she repeated, slowly. 'That is like our Antonio, no?'

'Yes, I suppose so.'

'I will call you Antonio. Will we meet again soon?'

'Not for a few weeks, I'm afraid – we're off to do a few jobs. But I'll get in touch as soon as we're back.'

'That would be nice.'

They stood for a moment, looking at each other, then she called to her brother and sisters, 'come, children, it's time for us to go home. Say 'thank you' to the kind British soldiers who gave you such a good party!'

The three children in unison said a loud *'Grazie!'* and Anthony watched as they left, Isabella turning to give him one last wave. He waved back and sighed as he watched her disappear into the cold night.

As they made their way back home along the snow-covered path Isabella asked, 'so did you enjoy yourselves?'

'Of course!' the children shouted.

'You'll have lots to tell Mama and Papa!'

Guiseppe, the youngest, ran ahead, looping the loop with his toy aeroplane, the RAF insignia painted proudly on it wings. His sisters followed him, clutching their new dolls and bags of sweets.

Italian children would have good reason to remember their 1944 Christmas with the Allies.

Isabella had also enjoyed the party, albeit for different reasons. The British evidently had money and resources and she was pleased to see her community benefitting from them. For the first time since the Germans had left she had confidence that her town would be re-built, civic pride restored, and that life would, one day, return to something approaching normality.

Also, she liked the handsome young soldier she had named Antonio; she enjoyed his company and found him amusing with his strange English sense of humour. But more than that, he had revealed a whole new world to her with stories about this place called Bath, where English people were happy to open their homes to the enemy and where they seemed to know nothing about proper food. She would love to learn more about it.

Sometimes the thought of marrying Carlo, having babies and living a similar life to her parents scared her rigid. But in reality she knew she had no choice in the matter.

Carlo, ten years her senior, had loved her since she was a little girl and it was their parents' dream that the two families should be joined. It was her destiny to marry Carlo: so be it.

Germany, 1945

Henry gradually adjusted to life in the POW camp and began to feel more like his old self. Being back amongst his own kind had restored his morale; the dark circles under his eyes were fading, he had put on a few pounds and his moustache was back in place. He still suffered headaches from the gash to his head and his arm still hurt, but it could have been a lot worse.

He made friends with his fellow-captors, particularly Peter Harrison, his Observer. They had flown several missions together and held each other in mutual respect. It turned out that Peter was from a well-off family – his father had made a fortune in the burgeoning pharmaceutical industry – and they had their own estate in Berkshire. A couple of years younger than Henry, he, too, had joined up, full of enthusiasm, ambitious to be a pilot. He hadn't had the opportunity to gain his wings before they were shot down in the Lancaster but he fully intended to do so, and make a career for himself in the RAF, after the war.

'My parents want me to go into the City and become a Tory MP,' he said, 'but I can't think of anything more boring!'

Life at the camp was conducted under the terms of the Geneva Convention and was just about tolerable.

The food was barely adequate – a couple of slices of bread and watery potato soup was as good as it got – and without the Red Cross parcels life would have been dire. It was the camaraderie between the prisoners and communication with home that kept morale going, and in spite of all the horrors, better things emerged for those who were interested – there were classes in languages, history and science, a library, a theatre group and a band.

It put Henry in mind of the stories the Blumfeldts had told them about the internment camp in England and he was struck by how, in such adversity, people came together to share their experience and knowledge for the good of others.

Wing Commander McFadden made it clear that the duty of captured British servicemen, especially officers, was to escape. 'Roberts,' he said, 'I'd like you to join the Escape Committee. Our new tunnel should be finished in a few weeks. The last attempt was a bit of a cock-up, I'm afraid – the Goons rumbled us. I could do with your assistance...'

CHAPTER 15

Italy, 1945

In the new year Anthony's platoon was put to work around the Ravenna area repairing bridges and roads, enabling people and traffic to move again. The January weather was harsh and they had to carry out their tasks with bitter winds howling around them and frequent falls of snow. During their rest periods they would find shelter, sit and smoke, brew up tea and josh around to relieve the tension.

One evening the subject turned to women, as it often did, and Sapper Davies, no respecter of rank, said to Anthony,

'What about that pretty little Itie lass you've got your eye on then?'

'What about her?'

'Well – you know - have you managed to…?'

'No I certainly haven't! I've only met her a few times, and anyway…'

'You couldn't take your eyes off her at the party!' interjected Sapper Jones.

'Well, she did look nice that day.'

'Great tits!' said Sapper Collins, 'I wouldn't mind…'

Anthony felt embarrassed. He hadn't admitted his attraction to himself, never mind to this rabble.

'Look, shut up will you, and mind your own bloody business! I'm going outside for some fresh air.'

They laughed as he got up and left.

Outside, Anthony lit another cigarette. He was more irritated than annoyed by the banter and decided to ignore it. After a few minutes Sergeant Hawkins joined him.

'Don't worry about that lot, crude buggers,' he said, lighting up.

'Don't worry, I won't.'

After a pause the sergeant said, 'I've seen it all before, you know - you're away from home, the local girls are exciting and sometimes willing, too. All I'd say to you is – don't get involved. Have some fun – you're young and single, for God's sake! But then move on. It's the only way.'

Anthony nodded but said nothing.

At the beginning of February, the platoon returned to Base and dived on the pile of letters that was waiting for them. Anthony was thrilled to receive a note from his brother as well as an update from his father and the Blumfeldts. Then his thoughts turned to Isabella and he was wondering how to engineer a meeting with her when Captain Baker arrived with an invitation.

'A farmer who is accommodating some of our officers has invited us to their home for lunch as a 'thank you' for what we're doing for their town. It's a nice gesture so we should accept. Roberts, as Liaison Officer you ought to come, and bring a couple of your chaps with you. It's next Saturday at a farmhouse called *La Casa Bianca* - the farmer is a Signor Fortuno.'

The farmhouse was about a mile out of town, set among rolling hills and vines planted in rows, their misshapen branches still in their Winter dormancy. The surrounding fields were scarred with marks of battle but nature prevailed and patches of greenery were slowly emerging.

Anthony, impatient to see Isabella again, marched up the narrow track more quickly than was necessary, leaving Sergeant Hawkins and Corporal Hastings, his chosen companions, trailing behind. As he rounded a corner the two-storey, whitewashed farmhouse with its terracotta-tiled roof and assorted barns came into view.

'There it is!' cried Anthony, looking back to see Hawkins and Hastings a hundred yards behind him. '*La Casa Bianca* - the white house. Come on!'

When they reached the farmyard they were met by a flurry of clucking chickens, barking dogs and bleating goats. Half a dozen rabbits were kept in a cage outside, destined for the pot. Signor Fortuno and his wife burst out of the house to welcome them, he, a short, stout man with a shock of black hair and his wife of similar size and shape, her grey hair in a bun. They could both speak a little English and greeted the soldiers, shaking their hands vigorously, then ushered them inside.

As they entered Isabella emerged from the kitchen wearing a dark blue dress, her hair in a single long plait hanging down her back.

'Lieutenant Roberts!' she said, a smile lighting up her face. 'It is good to see you again. And your colleagues too…'

She looked even lovelier than Anthony remembered. She proceeded to present her four sisters and little brother, then said, 'please, take a seat, and we can talk later, but now I must go and help Mama.'

'Thank you,' he said, looking at her as she walked away, and sitting down next to a Canadian Army Captain.

The party gathered around a long table and Signor Fortuno poured them all a glass of red wine from his vineyard, including some for the older children, diluted with water. The volume of chatter in English and Italian rose as everyone relaxed together. Anthony kept glancing towards the kitchen where Isabella was working with her mother and sisters preparing the meal, hoping to catch a glimpse of her. At last lunch was served.

'You're in for a real treat!' said the Canadian, 'I've tasted food here like I've never tasted before!'

Signora Fortuno and Isabella came to the table carrying huge cooking pots, followed by a younger sister with a stack of plates. Signora Fortuno removed the lid from the first pot, sending a heavenly aroma of tomatoes and herbs into the room, then she raised the second to reveal a mountain of steaming spaghetti. She served generous portions of each and the guests passed the filled plates down the table.

A bowl of a finely grated cheese which Anthony gathered was called 'parmesan' was then passed around for each guest to sprinkle on the top. Anthony had never eaten spaghetti, so he copied the others as they wound the long strings of pasta around their forks and onto their spoons, slurping the delicious food into their mouths.

Anthony was astounded at the flavours that exploded on his tongue - the best food he had ever tasted. A sudden memory of chewy, grey, pig's liver and lumpy mashed potato served up for lunch at prep school flashed before him. He vowed never to eat like that again, now he'd had a taste of how food could be.

'This is fantastic!' he said, unable to contain his enthusiasm.

Signora Fortuno looked up at him from the other end of the table. She shrugged her shoulders and said, 'thank you. I am pleased you like it, but it is just spaghetti with tomatoes and herbs, and a little olive oil. Very simple!'

'Olive oil?' said Anthony, surprised. 'That's what Mum used to put in our ears to clear the wax! I had no idea you could eat it!'

For dessert they had oranges, fresh from the tree, then a cheese course and more red wine. While the women went back to the kitchen Signor Fortuno produced a bottle of his lethal, home-produced, *grappa* and passed it around the table. He stood to make a toast.

'To the Allies who have saved us from the enemy! We thank you!'

It fell to one of the resident British officers to respond.

'Thank you, Signor Fortuno, for your hospitality and for sharing such a delicious meal with us. We, your Allies, will soon be moving North finally to defeat the enemy. Then we will continue with the huge job of re-building our countries which have suffered so much.'

One of the farm workers, vocal after too much wine, got to his feet and recited a poem which was going the rounds:

Viva il Duce, viva il Re!
Francobolli non ce n'è
Alla fine della guerra
Paga tutto l'Inghilterra.

All the Italians laughed and cheered, slapping the backs of the soldiers. The British officer looked rather embarrassed and translated:

Long live the Chief, long live the King!
We don't have any stamps
At the end of the war
England will pay for everything

The Canadian officer diffused the tension, standing up and proposing a toast:

'To peace!' …and drinking resumed.

Signor Fortuno came and sat beside Anthony, whom he had noticed watching his daughter.

'You are the Lieutenant who organised the party for the children. It is much appreciated. Thank you.'

'It is our duty,' said Anthony. 'Thank you for welcoming us today. You have a lovely family. Your daughter has been very helpful translating at our meetings.'

'Aaah, Isabella. Yes, she is very clever, and beautiful, no? Her mother and I, we are proud of her. We are looking forward to the end of the war when her fiancé will return – he is away, fighting with the partisans.'

'Her fiancé?'

121

Anthony tried to stop his voice from cracking.

'*Si*, Carlo Spinetti. He is a good man. One day he will inherit his family's vineyard and we will join our businesses together. He will make Isabella a good husband and she will give him many children.'

He paused and looked at Anthony, meaningfully. 'It is how we do things here.'

'Of course,' said Anthony. 'I'm sure they will be very happy.'

He glanced up at Isabella and she smiled at him.

Anthony felt sick, and not because of the food.

Anthony excused himself and went outside for some air. He leant back against the wall of the house and lit a cigarette. Isabella came out to join him.

'So you enjoyed the spaghetti?' she asked.

'Yes, thank you, it was a lovely meal.'

He stood there, smoking, saying nothing.

'You are very quiet, Antonio. Is something the matter?'

He turned towards her, unable to hide the hurt he was feeling.

'I didn't know you had a fiancé. You're engaged to be married! When were you going to tell me?'

She shrugged. 'I didn't think it was important.'

'Not important?'

'Well…it's not as if...'

'As if what…?'

'Well…we are friends, but…'

Of course. What had he been thinking?

'Well, I like you,' he said, lamely. 'I wanted to get to know you better.'

'I like you too. We can still be friends. And I don't know when I'll ever see my fiancé again.'

Anthony dropped his cigarette stub on the ground and trod on it. He'd had enough of all this.

'We'll be going North next week, so maybe that's just as well,' he said, irritably.

'But you'll come back here?'

'Probably not. Well…I don't know. Who knows, with this stupid war?'

Anthony avoided looking at her, went back inside, sat down with the men and poured himself a large glass of wine. Isabella returned to the kitchen to join the women and he didn't speak to her again.

By the time he left the farmhouse with Hawkins and Hastings it was late afternoon and darkness was falling. They had made a big hole in the Fortuno's stock of wine and the three of them were drunk as skunks. As they staggered along the road, Hastings said:

'So, what about your Isabella, then? She's a cracker, isn't she!'

'She is not *my* Isabella,' replied Anthony, riled, 'and is never likely to be,' he said, drawing hard on the butt end of his cigarette. Feeling suddenly sober he angrily strode ahead, chucking away the cigarette stub, leaving it glowing in the dark at the side of the road.

Hawkins and Hastings looked at each other with raised eyebrows and kept quiet.

CHAPTER 16

Bath, 1945

At Mr Greenstein's the Rabbi was addressing the Shabbat service in sombre mood.

'My friends, I have very important news to tell you. The Allies are close to liberating our people from concentration camps in Germany and Poland and we are receiving the first reports about what has been happening in these unspeakably appalling places. Soviet forces have recently liberated a camp called Auschwitz and from what we hear it is a living vision of hell. More than a million prisoners were murdered there; those that survived are starving and disease-ridden; the dead are left unburied.'

The congregation gasped with horror.

The Rabbi paused, tears in his eyes, while his distressed congregation, many of whom had fallen to their knees, tried to absorb what he was telling them.

'In the coming months, more such camps will be liberated and similar atrocities will be found. Now, I must warn you all that these events are likely to be filmed and extracts from these films will be shown in newsreels at the cinema. I am not saying that it is wrong to show these pictures; on the contrary, it is right and proper that the whole world should see what has been going on in the camps, and the death and destruction the Nazis have wrought there.'

He paused again, then continued.

'We must remember that *all* the people you will see in these terrible pictures are our brothers and sisters. We must pray for every one of them. In time the truth will come out and we must ensure that the monsters who perpetuated these horrendous deeds are brought to justice; this will be our life's work. We must stand together and ensure that such atrocities never, ever, happen again.'

The Blumfeldts returned to Eagle House, white-faced with shock. David listened as Karl told him what the Rabbi had said.

'It is beyond our worst imaginings,' said Karl.

Sonia, thinking of the family she had left behind, started to cry, and so did Gilda.

David had no words, and thought of his wife.

Italy, 1945

The move North began and as they left Affossa behind them Anthony resolved to give up on women and concentrate on his job. It was a good decision because they were entering an extremely dangerous environment and everyone needed their wits about them. Booby traps were an ever-present danger and the men were alert to any suspicious-looking rock, branch, or vehicle. Anthony's troop took some jeeps up the line to check the area for mines left by the retreating German forces. The snow had subsided so the men were able to make their way carefully through the designated area, spotting mines, lifting their lids, extracting the detonators and kicking them into the next field. The work required total concentration, the men looking out for each other every step of the way.

A week into their progress they came across a point in the road where the enemy had blown up a dozen trees in order to block it, a classic scenario for a trap.

'Right, I'll go ahead,' said Anthony, 'Cummings and Jones, you follow behind me. Very slowly, now…'

There were possible trip wires among the branches of the lying trees and Anthony led his men through, inch by inch, to make a clear and safe path for the others. Then he saw a dead dog lying among the branches. He stopped and held up his hand to the men behind him.

'Watch out,' he said, 'there must be trip wires connected to mines, caught this poor animal here.'

Suddenly he saw a wire, painted green, attached to a mine, just a few inches from his legs.

'Ah, here we are…' he said, quietly, 'I've found the little bastard…'

He leant over and cut the wire, then waved Cummings and Jones forward and together they disarmed the mine. A few feet further on they found another one. The three men carefully repeated the process, then they were through.

'All clear!' shouted Anthony to the rest of the troop, 'it's safe to advance!'

Back in Affossa, Isabella was having regrets about how abruptly she and Antonio had parted company. She hadn't realised how interested he was in her and felt guilty that she hadn't been nicer to him. She went to the Base at Ravenna but the soldiers remained told her the Company had departed.

'How can I contact them?' she asked.

126

One of the soldiers looked her up and down and sniggered. He'd seen it all before.

'We don't give out that information for security reasons.'

She wasn't that naïve: she knew what he was thinking. She had to assert herself so she drew herself up to her full height of five foot four inches and said in her best English, 'I am the official interpreter of Affossa Council. I have important information regarding the town that will be of interest to the Company. Please give me their address.'

Another soldier joined the conversation and said, 'all right then – I don't suppose it will do any harm. You can send a message via the British Army Post Office. I'll write it down for you.'

Isabella took the piece of paper from the soldier, thanked him and turned on her heel.

When the next batch of mail arrived Anthony was thrilled to receive the latest news from his father and in addition there was a letter with an Italian stamp and unfamiliar handwriting. He opened it and read:

La Casa Bianca, Affossa

Dear Antonio,
I am sorry we parted in a bad way. I want to thank you for all you have done for me and my town. I wish to be your friend and hope that if you ever come back to Affossa you will get in touch with me.
     Yours, Isabella Fortuno

He snorted. As if he would ever get back to Affossa! He screwed up the letter and was going to throw it away, then changed his mind and put it in his pocket.

Bath, 1945

Jacob asked Gilda if she would like to go to the pictures with him one weekend. She didn't have much to do, so she accepted.

He took her to the Beau Nash where they watched the newsreel before the main film started. The report began with stirring music and showed the progress Allied forces were making in Europe, advancing towards Berlin. There were also pictures of soldiers in Italy, fearlessly pushing the Germans ever Northwards. Gilda wondered whether her brave hero, Anthony, was among them.

Next there was film of the King and Queen waving to crowds as they toured the country and Gilda remembered when Anthony had taken her to see them when they had visited Bath after the bombing, nearly three years ago.

Then, without warning, the music became sombre and they saw images appear on the screen of skeleton-like figures cowering on the ground, their helpless, hollow eyes staring at the camera, their bodies disease-ridden. There was a collective gasp of horror. Although the Rabbi had warned about such images, it still came as an almighty shock to see them.

The report was about the liberation of Auschwitz and the figures they could see were Jews.

They might even be people they and their parents had known: friends, neighbours, shopkeepers; but unrecognisable now, just hideous skin and bone, less than human. The report showed the courageous Russian soldiers who had found them and finished on the more optimistic note that the dead would be buried, survivors treated, and the monsters who had carried out these atrocities brought to justice.

Gilda and Jacob were so distressed they had to leave the cinema. Gilda was in tears and Jacob led her to a café where he ordered some tea.

'Don't cry, Gilda,' he said, 'this isn't the time for tears. We have to fight back! After the war we, the Jewish people, will have our own country. We will put a stop to the suffering, it has gone on long enough. It is up to our generation to do this work. Will you join us?'

For all the horror she felt, Gilda didn't know how to respond. The idea of creating a new country for Jews was beyond her grasp, and her parents had warned her not to get involved in politics as it was dangerous. And all she really wanted was to see Anthony again.

'I don't know, Jacob,' Gilda replied, 'I don't know…'

Germany, 1945

In keeping with tradition, the POWs drew lots to decide who would escape. Henry was amongst those who drew a long straw, meaning he could go. His friend Peter Harrison drew a short straw and had to remain. Although Henry was pleased he said to the Wing Commander, 'there's others who've been here a lot longer than me. Don't you think they should have priority?'

129

'Possibly - but it's how we've always done things,' he replied. 'Do you have anyone special waiting for you?'

'Well, my father, and my brother, although he's in Italy so God knows what he's up to…'

'No sweetheart, then?'

'No…I never had time for that. I mean, there was a barmaid at the Base, but everybody was in love with her…so, no one special, no.'

'Well, if you want to offer your place to somebody else, that's entirely up to you!'

Henry asked Peter but he refused on similar grounds, saying there were others in the hut who had been there a lot longer and had families to go back to. 'I've got my parents and two sisters at home but quite frankly they probably haven't even noticed I'm missing!' he said, cheerfully.

*

Tonight was the night. Everything was in place: the tunnel was robust, the timing took precise account of the Goons' nightly patrols, the new moon ensured darkness and a diversion was in place in the form of a concert by the resident band. At nine o'clock Wing Commander McFadden gave the signal.

'Good luck to you all!' he said, as the first man climbed down the hole in the hut under the floorboards, and into the tunnel. It would take fifteen minutes for each man to crawl along to the point where the tunnel emerged in a copse just beyond the perimeter fence. Another dozen men left, then another dozen. Henry had given up his place to a Flight Sergeant Dean, a married man from Bristol with four children who'd been in the camp for three years.

When he told Henry he hadn't even seen his youngest child Henry couldn't stand it, and insisted he take the chance to escape.

'Thanks again, sir,' said Dean, and shook Henry's hand as he disappeared down the hole.

The concert audience sung themselves hoarse, whistling and demanding encores – the best reception the band had ever had.

When the last man had gone, Henry and the Wing Commander replaced the floorboards and put everything in the hut back into its normal position. They had done all they could.

*

At roll-call the next morning it soon became apparent that a large number of men were missing. The Goons went into overdrive, herding the remaining POWs inside with reduced rations, setting the dogs loose and quickly organising patrols to track down the escapees. The prisoners waited anxiously inside their huts and it took only a few hours before half a dozen men were brought back to the camp in handcuffs and thrown into solitary. Later that day the camp Commandant triumphally announced that ten men had been shot dead whilst trying to evade the patrols and they had rounded up most of the others.

'Let this be a lesson to you,' he concluded, 'you will not escape from the German Army!'

Inside the hut, Wing Commander McFadden was philosophical.

'They always say that!' he said. 'Chances are that a good few of our men will get through. It's always worth a try.'

Henry wasn't so sure.

131

CHAPTER 17

Italy, 1945

The full might of the Eighth Army was making remarkable progress, driving German forces ever North, preparing for the final offensive. Anthony's troop moved forward mile by mile, re-building bridges and defusing mines, making the roads safe while Allied planes soared overhead. The work and its inherent danger became almost routine and old-stagers warned of the dangers of complacency and impatience.

Sapper Collins was easy to rise to anger and prone to showing off. Competent but over-ambitious, he was irritated, wanting to work more quickly. One afternoon as they were clearing a path through a road blockage he spotted a grenade wedged between the roots of a tree.

'Over 'ere, Lieutenant!' he called out.

Anthony ran over to see what Collins had found.

'That's a nasty one…' Anthony said, standing back and looking at the grenade. 'It's too risky to touch it - the slightest movement could set it off. We'll have to clear everyone out of the way and fire at it from a distance.'

'I can't be bothered with all that!' replied Collins with his usual bloody-mindedness. 'Leave 'er to me, I know what I'm doing.'

'No! Be careful you idiot!'

Before Anthony could stop him Collins tied a long string to the handle of the grenade.

He gave the string a quick pull.

The grenade exploded, hurtling Collins backwards, blowing off the lower half of his right arm. Anthony was thrown to the ground and covered with debris. He was unhurt but dizzy and took a moment to steady himself, then he got to his feet and rubbed the dust from his eyes to see blood spurting from the gaping hole in what was left of Collins' arm.

'Medic, over here, NOW!' shouted Anthony.

Anthony ran to the injured man who was writhing on the ground, screaming hysterically with pain and shock. He took off his belt and tied it tightly round the top of Collins' arm to stem the blood flow, then Collins passed out.

The Medical Officer arrived, gave Collins a shot of morphine and bandaged what remained of his arm.

'We must get him to hospital,' he said, 'he's going to need a blood transfusion, he's losing a hell of a lot…'

Captain Baker arrived and the M.O. gave his assessment.

'There's no field hospital near here. Best bet would be to get him to the hospital at Ravenna, that's the closest – but we must be quick!'

'Look, M.O.,' said Captain Baker, 'I can't spare you in case another idiot goes and injures himself. Roberts – could you drive him? Take one of the jeeps. Can you handle a patient on your own?'

'Yes, I think so.'

133

'M.O., do you trust Roberts to supply Collins with morphine?'

'Of course. Take plenty of bandages with you, keep him warm and get him there as fast as you can. I'll radio ahead to warn the hospital.'

Between them they carried Collins to a jeep and covered him with a blanket. Within minutes of the incident Anthony, spattered with blood, was driving back to Ravenna along the same route they had cleared, the patient unconscious beside him.

Ravenna was about forty miles away, a couple of hours drive in those conditions. It was difficult to avoid the potholes and bumps in the road caused by gunfire and explosions, and after an hour of jolting around Collins started to regain consciousness and become distressed. Anthony pulled over, gave him another shot of morphine and re-bandaged his arm. His face was deathly pale.

'Nearly there, old chap,' said Anthony, 'nearly there…'

It was getting dark. Blackout conditions were in force so they had to slow down and drive without headlights for the last part of the journey. When at last they reached the hospital at Ravenna the orderlies lifted Collins onto a stretcher and carried him away. Anthony stared after him, willing him to survive. He found a waiting room where he collapsed onto a chair and a nurse brought him a coffee. Just before midnight the Doctor emerged from the operating theatre and Anthony jumped up to speak to him.

'You're waiting for Frank Collins?'

'Sapper Collins, yes. I'm Lieutenant Roberts, his Commanding Officer. How is he?'

134

'Well, he's lost most of his right arm – couldn't save his elbow, I'm afraid. You got him here just in time – he's lost a lot of blood. The important thing now is to guard against infection so I want to keep him here for a few weeks to make sure the wound heals properly. No point in evacuating him home at this stage.'

'Thank you. Can I see him?'

'Not yet – he's still out from the anaesthetic. Why don't you fix up some accommodation and come back in the morning?'

When Anthony returned to the hospital he found Collins looking very weak, a massive dressing where his arm used to be.

'I'm so sorry,' said Anthony.

Collins opened his eyes and whispered, 'thanks for getting me 'ere.'

'You're welcome. Now you just rest, and I'll come back and see you soon.'

Anthony reported back to Captain Baker.

'Dreadful waste,' he said, 'but a salutary warning to the others about the dangers of complacency. Thank God you got him to the hospital in time.'

He paused, then continued, 'now, Roberts, something else has come up. I've had a request from one of the other Companies down in Ravenna. They're short of a Lieutenant – one of theirs was sent home on compassionate grounds – and they've been asking if they can borrow someone to do some mine clearance work. Seeing as you're there…how would you feel about joining them?'

'But what about my troop?'

135

'I'll put them under Lieutenant Moore. Look, it will mean you'll miss the action as we go for that final push…'

'Yes - I'd like to have been there. But if I can be useful here, I'll stay.'

'Very well, I'll put that in hand. Remain at the Base and await your orders.'

The following day Collins was sitting up in bed, looking a lot better, the colour restored to his face.

'Thanks for coming,' he said, his voice hoarse.

'That's all right,' said Anthony. 'In fact, I've been posted to a Company here so I'll pop in when I can. How are you feeling?'

'A bit stronger with all that new blood they give me. My arm do throb, like it's still there – they say that's normal. Don't feel sorry for me, for God's sake – it were me own stupid fault. Big-headed bastard.'

'You're not the first, and you won't be the last.'

The two were silent for a while.

Then Collins said, 'so you saved my life again.'

'What?'

'In that cowshed – we'd 'ave copped it if you 'adn't warned us about them Jerries. I thought you just got lucky - but now you done it again, got me 'ere, just in time.'

He paused.

'To be honest, I thought you'd be too soft out 'ere – 'Blondie from Bath'. But I guess I were wrong – sir.'

*

Anthony was seconded to a Company of Royal Engineers working alongside American forces in Ravenna. His new boss was a Captain Martin, a regular Army man in his thirties, who suffered from a shrapnel wound he'd got at Dunkirk.

'Welcome to the team, Roberts,' he said. 'I'm sorry you won't be chasing Germans up in the North – you'll find it a bit quieter here I'm afraid – but it's essential work. Should see us out, though…'

Anthony couldn't quite believe that fate had returned him to Ravenna, just a few miles from Affossa…

Collins remembered his boss's interest in the pretty Italian girl and, a sure sign that he was feeling better, decided to bait him.

'So 'ave you seen your girlfriend yet?' he asked.

'She is not my girlfriend! And no, I haven't.'

'Why not?'

'Well, we didn't part on the best of terms. And she's got a fiancé.'

Collins grunted. 'So?'

'Well I just don't think I should interfere…'

'Bollocks! If you really like 'er, get in touch for God's sake. Her fiancé isn't 'ere, is 'e? But you are. See 'er while you can. Tomorrow,' he said, pointing to himself with his good hand, 'this could be you!'

Maybe Collins had a point. Anthony re-read the letter Isabella had sent him and decided, at last, to write to her.

Dear Isabella,

For reasons I won't go into here, I am back in Ravenna serving with a different Company. I should be able to get some free time next Sunday. Would it be possible to meet?

  Yours, Anthony Roberts

Two days later he received a reply.

Dear Antonio,

I cannot believe you are back in Ravenna! I would be very happy to meet you. I will be at Church in Affossa on Sunday and can meet you after mass.

  Yours, Isabella Fortuno

That was more than he had expected. He folded the letter and put it in his shirt pocket.

*

Anthony was waiting outside Affossa church in the same place that he'd met Isabella on that cold Winter's day, just before Christmas. At least the weather was better this time, he thought, as he leant against a wall and lit a cigarette to steady his nerves. A minute later he saw Isabella emerge from the church, looking around for him, and his heart skipped a beat. He threw his cigarette away, half-smoked, and went to her. They shook hands then stood and looked at each other.

'Isabella' he said.

'Antonio' she said.

They laughed at their awkwardness and she said, 'shall we go for a coffee?'

138

They went into the café, sat down at a table, lit cigarettes and drank several of the now-familiar espressos. Anthony told Isabella about Collins' accident and driving him to hospital, then explained how he had been assigned to a new Company in Ravenna.

'This poor man, Collins,' she said, 'what will happen to him?'

'It depends how quickly his wound heals - they'll probably send him back to England in a few weeks. They reckon the war will be over soon so I expect they'll discharge him from the Army.'

'Thank goodness you got him to the hospital in time. You saved his life!'

'Not really, it's the doctors who did that – I just got him there.'

'Well, I think you were very brave.'

She paused and stared into her coffee cup.

'Antonio, I want to say to you, I am sorry about how we parted. I should have told you I was engaged, but...'

She sat back, shrugged her shoulders and held out her hands, palms upward, a typical Italian gesture that Anthony understood to mean, 'it wasn't my fault, don't blame me.'

'You see,' she continued, 'I've known Carlo all my life and our families have planned for so long that we should marry it is just something I...how to say...it is something I take for granted? I mean, I missed him at first when he went away, but so much has happened since then and I don't even know if he is still alive...'

Anthony took a deep breath.

'Isabella, please don't worry. I don't want to change anything between you and Carlo. I understand. For now, all I want is to be your friend and enjoy your company while I am still here in Italy. There is so much I would like to learn about your country and I would love you to show me.'

She leaned towards him and touched his hand.

'I would like that very much.'

Anthony met his new troop whose aim was to get through the next couple of months intact, by which time the war would be over and they could all go home. With his sergeant, Hargreaves, a Yorkshireman in his forties, they surveyed the zone where mines needed to be cleared and set to work. They drew up a plan under which they worked for six days then rested for one.

'If it's good enough for God, it's good enough for us,' said Anthony.

And he knew exactly how he wanted to spend his day off.

At his next visit Anthony was pleased to see that Collins was making a good recovery.

'So 'ave you seen your girlfriend yet?' he asked.

'She's not my girlfriend! But yes, I have.'

Collins gave a filthy laugh.

'Look, it's not like that…' protested Anthony.

'Hmmm,' said Collins, sceptically. 'My advice - fill your boots! What've you got you lose, eh?'

CHAPTER 18

Italy, 1945

Anthony soon found there were benefits to be had from working alongside American forces. At the canteen he saw a poster advertising a dance being held in the main hall the following Saturday night. It looked fun, and when he next saw Isabella he asked if she would like to go with him.

'It will be a bit American, but it should be OK,' he said.

'I'd love to go!' she said.

Anthony borrowed a jeep and picked up Isabella from the farm. She ran out of the house to meet him, looking lovely in the dress he remembered her wearing at the Christmas party and her hair pinned back with the silver hair slide. 'My mother says I must be back by midnight,' she said. 'I have to get up early to see to the animals.'

'She's worried you'll turn into a pumpkin!'

She laughed, although she didn't understand. 'What is a pumpkin?'

'I'll explain…' he said, as they drove off to the Base.

As soon as they entered the hall they felt as if they'd been transported across the Atlantic and magically dropped in some small town in Texas.

'It's like something from a film set!' cried Anthony above the noise, reminded of the movies he'd watched at the Beau Nash.

'It's wonderful!' cried Isabella, 'I've never seen anything like this before!'

A twelve-piece band was playing on the stage with a massive stars and stripes flag draped on the wall behind them. Red, white and blue balloons and streamers hung from the ceiling along with American and Italian flags and Union Jacks. Tables were laden with food and US and British service personnel were sitting with the locals, eating, drinking and laughing, the drawl of American accents lending a certain exoticism. But most impressive of all were the dancers – more than fifty couples, jiving and jitterbugging, the men flinging their partners up in the air, back down through their legs then twirling them around.

'I love this music!' said Anthony, already tapping his foot to the big band sound that he adored, and hoping to hear his favourite - Glenn Miller. He still hoped that his hero, whose plane had gone missing over the English Channel, might yet be found, but at least in the meantime they had his music.

'Let's get something to eat!' said Isabella.

They had never seen food like it – piles of bread rolls, slices of cold chicken and ham, potato crisps, frankfurters, gherkins and jars of thick yellow mustard. A friendly Yank explained to them how to put a hot dog together and told them to help themselves to drinks – bottles of beer, and a dark-coloured soft drink called Cola. Another table was piled high with cookies and doughnuts and bowls of candy. Isabella glanced around and quickly took some chocolate bars and put them in her handbag – 'for my brother and sisters!' she said.

142

They sat down, devouring their American buffet, and watched the couples dancing, not stopping for a moment, one tune leading straight into another.

'They didn't teach us this at Sandhurst!' said Anthony, suddenly recalling the dumpy girl at the Summer ball, then looking at Isabella, so slim and pretty.

'Let's dance!' he said.

They weren't up to the acrobatics being performed by the other dancers but Anthony and Isabella put on a good show, soon picking up the moves. Isabella noticed some girls she knew who were dancing with American soldiers and having a whale of a time. She was pleased she hadn't missed out.

'Thank you so much for bringing me here!' she said to Anthony, who couldn't hear her above the noise. He pulled her closer. She repeated what she'd said, and he replied, 'my pleasure. Thank you for coming, Signorina Fortuno…'

With that, he grasped her by the waist, lifted her high in the air and she shrieked with delight as he swung her round and around until they were dizzy.

Towards the end of the evening the music slowed down, the high-powered dance moves stopped and the couples grew more intimate. Anthony held Isabella close and when the band started to play 'Moonlight Serenade' he knew this was just the best moment of his entire life. His lips brushed the top of her head and as he held her tighter she looked up at him with her beautiful wide brown eyes. He was leaning down to kiss her when the tune ended, the lights came on with a blinding flash, and the party was over.

'I'd better get you back home!' he said, reluctantly letting her go.

They drove back to the farm in silence. Isabella knew her mother would be waiting up for her and as soon as they arrived she jumped out of the jeep.

'Thank you, Antonio, that was wonderful, but I must go.'

'Good night,' he said, as she disappeared indoors.

He turned the jeep around and headed back to Base, thinking about her. God, he wanted to be more than just her friend…

That night in bed Isabella didn't look at her photograph of Carlo.

The day after the dance Anthony met Isabella outside the church, their usual meeting place. She was with some of the girls who'd been at the Base the night before and he noticed them looking in his direction, teasing Isabella.

'What was all that about?' he asked her, as she ran up to him.

'They were just saying how well we danced! I think maybe they are jealous!'

He laughed. 'It was a wonderful evening.'

'Yes, it was, thank you,' she said, then continued, 'it is such a pleasant day, I think we will go to walk in the country, it is very beautiful.'

'That would be lovely,' he said, looking at her, then added, 'I hope your mother wasn't cross with you last night.'

'No, you got me home just in time. She doesn't mind us being friends.'

'That's good,' said Anthony, as he took her hand.

Isabella led him out of the town, up into the hills surrounding Affossa. As they left its bombed and ruined buildings behind it felt as if they were getting away from the war itself.

Isabella made her way along a narrow footpath and as Anthony followed he was transfixed by the delightful way her hips wiggled under her skirt and how her long hair, tied in a pony tail, swayed from side to side. Poetry in motion, he thought. She looked back over her shoulder at him and grinned.

'It is not far now, Antonio. I am sure you will enjoy the view!'

I am already, he thought.

At the top of the hill the path widened and they were able to walk alongside each other. She pointed out the local landmarks.

'Look, from here you can see right over Affossa, and Ravenna in the distance. And over there is the sea! See how it sparkles!'

'It looks marvellous,' said Anthony. 'Could we go there? Is there a beach?'

'There is a beach. We used to go every Summer. But with the war, the beach is covered with…how do you say - wire?'

'Barbed wire, yes. We have the same at home. What a shame, I would love to have gone to an Italian beach.'

'But you have lots of beaches in England!'

'Yes, but…' Anthony thought of pebbles, grey skies and freezing cold sea temperatures. '…it's not quite the same…'

She laughed, amused by the strange things he said, and went over to a spot in the grass where they sat down, watching the clouds scudding across the sky.

'So, Antonio, tell me about these English beaches...'

Anthony went to see Collins who was up and sitting in a chair next to his bed.

'So 'ow's your girlfriend?' he asked.

'She's not...' began Anthony, then smiled. 'She's very well, thank you. In fact, she's wonderful!'

Collins laughed. 'Good on yer!'

'But how are you?' asked Anthony.

'Not too bad,' said Collins, looking at the bandaged remains of his arm. 'They say it's healing up nicely and I'll 'ave a fine stump. Hey - light a fag for me, will you?'

Bath, 1945

'So do you think the war really is coming to an end, Papa?' asked Gilda.

'It looks like it, yes, *liebchen*,' Karl replied, putting down his newspaper. 'The Government expects the Germans to surrender soon, and our people will be free - at least, those that survive...'

'So Anthony will be back soon?' she asked, then added, 'and Henry?'

'God willing, yes. The campaign in Italy is almost over, and the prisoners of war will be liberated. We must have faith that God will return them to us.'

'We must pray for them,' she said.

146

Gilda kept her feelings to herself, but inside she was desperate to have Anthony safely back at Eagle House. She was eager for him to see her as she was now – she was nearly fifteen, almost a woman - not the little girl he had left behind. She wanted to talk to him about all the thoughts that were in her head, her dreams, her fears…he was the only person she wanted to confide in.

He was her hero. She remembered when he'd rescued her from the cellar after the bombing, how he'd carried her in his strong arms…the longer he had been away, the more important he had become in her mind. She started planning all sorts of scenarios about his return, and how he would see her in a new light…

CHAPTER 19

Italy, 1945

Having endured the stifling Summer of '44 and the icy Winter it came as a relief to everyone when Spring arrived. Trees full of blossom and colourful wild flowers emerged from the potholed, blasted countryside as if to declare that war, surely, must almost be over. Farmers were out working in the fields tending to their crops and vines, and in the towns people were sitting outside cafés enjoying the sunshine, away from the bombs and bullets.

It was one such beautiful Spring day when Anthony next saw Isabella. As they walked together up into the hills surrounding Affossa they chatted about their families and Anthony noticed that Isabella never mentioned Carlo, which suited him fine. Anthony had brought his sketchbook and pencils with him and when they reached the top of the hill he said, 'go and sit over there, will you, by that tree? I'd like to draw you.'

She did as he asked, and he spent the next hour scrutinising her, taking in every inch of her body. And as he studied the curves of her figure under her dress, her shapely bare legs and her olive skin, he longed to see her naked. He suddenly felt embarrassed by his train of thought, and needing a rapid change of subject within his head, he said,

'Oh – I've had an idea. Bit of a cock-up on the victualling front, so at Base we've got a surplus of porridge oats – tons of the stuff.'

Isabella looked at him blankly. She hadn't understood a word he'd said.

Anthony saw her quizzical expression and tried to explain. 'I thought you might like some oats to make porridge. It's delicious for breakfast. You mix the oats with water, and a bit of milk, cook it till it's nice and thick, and serve with a little sugar, if you have any – or honey. Some people prefer it with salt. We've got loads of it at the Base. I'll get them to send a sack up to the farm for you.'

Isabella looked doubtful but said, 'thank you – we will try your po-rich.'

Later, as they wandered hand-in-hand back down the hill into the town Isabella said, 'I love your drawing of me. You are very talented!'

He turned to her, gently pushed a strand of hair back from her face and said, 'and you are very beautiful.'

After studying her all afternoon he couldn't wait any longer. He took her in his arms and kissed her, and as their lips touched, each breathing in the scent of the other, she returned his kiss, melting into his body as he held her tightly.

Isabella was going about her daily duties at the farm, humming a tune to herself. She kept thinking about Antonio and smiled as she recalled the stories he had told her about his family and life in England. He could be so funny, and at other times very serious. She loved his voice, the way he laughed, the way he ran his hands though his lovely fair hair, the gentle way he touched her, his kiss…oh, that kiss! She couldn't wait to see him again.

Her mother noticed her daydreaming.

'Something on your mind, daughter?' she asked.

'No…I'm just feeling happy!'

Her mother snorted.

'Never mind 'happy'! Just make sure you get the goats milked before they burst!'

'Yes, Mama!'

*

'Next week is special, we celebrate *Pasqua*,' said Isabella – 'Easter. You must come to watch the parade with me!'

'I would love that!' replied Anthony.

'After the parade I will have to go home for our family meal. But *La Pasquetta* – on the Monday – we have a holiday. We could take food to eat outside. In Italian we call it a 'picnic'.'

'Yes! We have the same word.'

'Really?' she said, surprised that the English would even contemplate eating outside in their weather, never mind have a word for it.

On Easter Day Anthony met Isabella in Affossa to enjoy the celebrations. They stood in the main street among a huge, noisy crowd to watch the festive parade as it snaked its way through the town, led by a statue of the Virgin Mary held aloft on a palanquin, its four poles carried by young men dressed in traditional costumes. It vaguely reminded Anthony of the sedan chairs on display at the museum in Bath. The Virgin was followed by Catholic priests dressed in all their finery carrying a huge wooden cross, dispensing incense and blessing the assembled throng, with a choir chanting and singing hymns and incantations.

People of all ages lined the streets, children seated on their parents' shoulders so they could get a good view. The colourful procession and cheering crowd seemed to rise above the war-damaged buildings around them, lifting the spirits with a sense of optimism and new life – rather like the Easter message itself.

When the parade finished Anthony reluctantly had to let Isabella go, but they agreed to meet the following day at the farm for the picnic.

The Company Commander had 'gone native' and declared Easter Monday a holiday, so Anthony was free for the day. He went to the Motor Transport depot and found that all the jeeps were taken, but they offered him a motorcycle.

'All right, I'll take it,' he said.

He rode up to the farm, winding his way through the narrow lanes as fast as he could, his heart singing in anticipation of seeing Isabella again. When he arrived she came running out to meet him.

'Antonio! It is good to see you! Wait one moment and we will be with you!'

Isabella went back into the farmhouse and emerged with a wicker basket full of food and drinks…and one of her younger sisters.

'You remember Maria?' she said, when she emerged, 'Mama thought it would be nice if she could come to the picnic too!'

Anthony's face fell, momentarily, then he regained his composure.

'Of course! Although I only have the bike…'

'That's all right,' said Isabella, 'there's plenty of room for all of us!'

With that, Isabella climbed onto the motorbike behind Anthony. Maria, aged seventeen, was thankfully just as slim as her sister, if not quite so pretty. She climbed on at the back, carrying the picnic basket.

'Right,' said Anthony, bemused, but up for the challenge, 'let's go!' He revved up and they were off.

Isabella clasped her arms around his waist, holding on for dear life as he steered the bike around the sharp bends. She shouted directions in his ear and they motored on, into the countryside. Maria was half-hanging off the back of the bike, the wicker basket dangling over her arm. As they climbed up into the hills they saw some American soldiers working at the side of the road and Anthony slowed down. One of the men, stripped to the waist, sweating, stopped work, planted his shovel in the ground and watched as the party rode past.

'My achin' back, he's got two of them!' he said in a thick Texan drawl, hands on hips, looking at them. They heard what he said, the girls laughed and waved before clutching on to each other again as the bike moved on over the pot-holed road. Anthony smiled, thinking to himself, yes, I've got two of them – but there's only one that I want.

At the top of a hill the land levelled out and Isabella shouted in Anthony's ear, 'you can stop here!'

The three of them dismounted and Anthony pushed the bike off the road and onto the grass. The girls laid a blanket on the ground and unloaded the basket. Signora Fortuno had prepared a feast: newly-baked bread, goats' cheese, olives and some chewy ham, a speciality from Parma (which Anthony thought tasted like uncooked bacon), and a bottle of fresh lemonade.

The two girls chatted in Italian and laughed at Anthony's attempts to speak their language, encouraging him to copy their sing-song accent. He didn't mind – although it made him feel it was he who was the odd-one out in this group of three.

Maria got up and picked some small purple-blue flowers that were growing wild on a grassy bank near to where they were sitting. She made a posy from them and put them in the neck of the empty lemonade bottle.

'They're pretty,' said Anthony, 'what are they called?'

'They are pasqueflowers,' said Isabella – they come out at Easter time. They are lovely, no? We say the bright yellow centre is like the sun, surrounded by the deep blue sky of the petals.'

'Very poetic!'

'Why don't you draw them, Antonio?'

I'd rather draw you, he thought, but said, 'yes – good idea.'

He took his sketch book out of his pocket and quickly outlined the bell-shaped flowers with their feathery, grey-green leaves.

'That is beautiful,' said Isabella.

So are you, thought Anthony.

He was desperate to be alone with her and was trying to work out what to do when Maria stood up and announced that she was going for a walk. As she disappeared down the hill Isabella edged up to Anthony and said, 'I hope you don't mind Maria being here. I think Mama didn't want us to be on our own.'

'I'm sure she didn't!' said Anthony, 'but never mind, we are now!'

He put his arm around her and they kissed, lingeringly.

'That's better,' he said, 'I don't feel like the gooseberry any more.'

'Gooseberry?'

He laughed. 'I'll tell you later…'

When Maria returned they started to clear up, ready for their return trip on the bike. Anthony's eyes kept straying towards Isabella's blouse, so to keep his mind off its contents (which he had lovingly explored) he said, 'how did you get on with the porridge, by the way?'

Isabella pulled a face.

'We didn't like it. But our mother is feeding it to the chickens – they love it!'

As they packed up the picnic basket Isabella took one of the pasqueflowers from the lemonade bottle and put it between two clean sheets of paper in Anthony's sketch book.

'Put a weight on top and it will preserve it,' she instructed, 'then when you see the flower it will remind you what a lovely day we had!'

The three of them got back on the bike and Anthony steered them safely back to the farm. Signora Fortuno came out to greet them.

'Thank you, Lieutenant Roberts. You enjoyed the picnic?'

'Yes, very much!'

'And daughters, did you have a good day?'

'Yes, Mama,' they replied.

'And Maria, you were together all the time?'

'Of course, Mama!' she said.

154

Anthony could have sworn Maria looked back and winked at him as she followed her mother into the farmhouse.

The next morning Isabella was milking the goats in the barn but in her mind she was lying next to Antonio in the grass after the picnic. She had heard her friends say that Englishmen were cold and unfeeling, but they couldn't be more wrong.

Antonio was so handsome and when he'd taken his shirt off to reveal his smooth chest his body was more muscular than she'd imagined. She thought of how he'd held her in his strong arms, kissed her, gently caressed her…she had never felt such desire. Holy Mother, she wanted him…She had never felt this way about Carlo…

Isabella gasped at her wicked, sinful thoughts and crossed herself.

Anthony had been so taken up with Isabella he realised he hadn't been to see Collins for a while. He went to the hospital in Ravenna but couldn't find him and asked one of the nurses where he was.

'Frank Collins?' she said, consulting her notes. 'He left last week. He was making a good recovery and the chance came for him to get a ride back to the UK by plane, so he went.'

'That's great news!' said Anthony, 'I'm sorry I missed him. Do you know what will happen to him?'

'Probably get discharged from the Army as soon as the war's over. He'll be all right – he's a fit, determined young man. He won't let a missing arm keep him from a full life…'

CHAPTER 20

Italy 1945

Anthony and Isabella were walking hand-in-hand along by the river which ran through Affossa and which up until now Anthony had only seen through the eyes of a Royal Engineer. As they passed a temporary bridge he said, 'this is one of ours! Took us a week to build it - looks like it's bearing up well!'

Isabella was impressed. 'It is wonderful what you British soldiers have done for us.'

She was thoughtful for a while, then said, 'Antonio, do you think the war will be over soon? I heard some men in the town saying the Germans are close to surrender, and even *Il Duce* is running away.'

'Yes,' he replied, 'at our briefing the other day we were told we're pushing the Germans well into the North, it's just a matter of time. As for Mussolini, we heard he's heading for Switzerland with his mistress – but that might just be a rumour!'

'So what will happen after the war?'

'Who knows? I don't think anything will ever be the same again – there have been too many changes, so many lost…'

'But what about you?'

'Well, I'd like to go home to see my father - and my brother, hopefully…'

He paused, slipped his arm around her waist and said, half-jokingly, '…and after that, I'll come back here to be with you!'

Then they looked at each other and realised he wasn't joking at all.

In the middle of April Anthony's Company Commander called his troops together for a special briefing.

'I'm pleased to report that the German Army is retreating on all fronts. The Eighth Army has successfully crossed the River Po and is now advancing towards Venice and Trieste, our American Allies are driving towards Milan and into Austria, and the partisans have got Mussolini in their sights. Our long and bloody campaign is nearing its conclusion.'

The men cheered – events were moving fast and the end was in sight.

Then he changed tone and solemnly announced that American and British forces had liberated the concentration camps at Buchenwald and Bergen-Belsen. As he relayed the unspeakable horror of what they had found his audience fell silent, sickened by what they had heard, appalled on behalf of the victims and the comrades who had made these terrible discoveries and had to cope with the aftermath.

Anthony listened in a state of despair: man's inhumanity to man knew no bounds. He felt for those who had suffered so grievously; he felt for the Jewish people in general and the Blumfeldts in particular. Who knew what their fate might have been if they hadn't taken the chance to come to Bath, all those years ago?

157

Anthony had arranged to meet Isabella that evening; she had persuaded him to go to an opera. He hadn't been too keen and with the horrific news about Belsen he really wasn't in the mood for listening to a load of Italians singing, but he would agree to anything if it meant being with her.

He waited at their usual spot and when he saw her in the distance his spirits lifted instantly. As she ran towards him, smiling, his heart leapt, and he suddenly thought, what right did he have, with all these terrible, tragic events in the world, what right did he have to feel so happy?

When Isabella reached him he embraced her, holding her tight.

'I am *so* glad to see you,' he said.

The production of *Tosca* was taking place in an amphitheatre overlooking the river. Anthony's experience of live performance being limited to the odd play at Bath's Theatre Royal he was surprised how unstuffy the occasion was, with groups of people chatting, smoking, sharing food and drinking wine in the warmth of the evening. There was a buzz of anticipation and the theatre was filling up fast.

As they took their places on the stone steps Anthony asked, 'what's so special about the opera, then?'

'Everything!' Isabella exclaimed, surprised at his question. 'It's the beauty of the music, the passion – it's magical. We are taught famous arias at school, it's part of our heritage, our being.'

She took his hands in hers and said, 'Antonio, if you want to understand Italians – if you want to understand *me* - you have to learn about the opera.'

Isabella quickly explained the plot, a tragic tale of romance and politics set in Rome during the Napoleonic Wars with at its heart a beautiful woman, Tosca, who was loved by two very different men. Anthony noted the irony and wondered how this particular love story would play out.

'Don't worry if you can't understand the words, Antonio, just enjoy the music!'

The orchestra arrived to take their places and there was a ripple of applause around the theatre. The conductor entered and the performance began.

The power of Puccini's music soon had Anthony under its spell. He was surprised that the small orchestra could produce such a rich, deep, sound, and as the singers unleashed their vibrato and their voices echoed around the amphitheatre the atmosphere became intoxicating. The soaring violins and the rousing chords and cadences of the famous arias gave Anthony goose bumps, and when he looked at Isabella she smiled at him, tears streaming down her face, and grasped his arm.

As the final act commenced the sun disappeared over the horizon and darkness fell. Tosca's lover, in his prison cell, sung about the shining stars as if he were describing the actual scene above them. When the brass and strings came crashing down the theatre erupted, people stood and applauded, many in floods of tears, and Anthony was on his feet with the best of them.

The cheery saga of torture and death ended with both the lead male characters killed and Tosca hurling herself from the battlements. (Anthony hoped that the love triangle in which he found himself would have a less violent ending.) The audience gave a standing ovation with cries of '*Bellissimo!*' and the stage was strewn with flowers.

Eventually things quietened down and people began to leave. Isabella was still in a heightened emotional state, and Anthony took her hand.

'So, you see?' she asked him.

'Yes, I do,' he replied.

After the opera Anthony walked Isabella home. It was late and the farmhouse was in darkness; even her mother had gone to bed. Anthony leant down to kiss Isabella goodnight, but she stepped away from him and led him by the hand to the barn where the goats were sleeping peacefully. They lay down on the straw together and that night she taught him the only Italian words he really needed to know – *ti amo* – I love you.

Isabella was feeding the chickens, singing to them and scattering the last of the porridge oats. As they clucked and scuttled around her feet she could feel the warm sun on her back and a gentle breeze was blowing - a normal day, like thousands of other days she had spent at home on the farm. And yet today everything was different; she felt truly alive, happy, excited, in a way she never had before.

She reflected on the passionate night she had spent in the barn with Antonio.

160

They had slept in each other's arms until sunrise when he'd leapt up, hurriedly got dressed while kissing her at the same time, then rushed off to the Base to report for duty. Isabella had sneaked back into the farmhouse and managed to get up to the bedroom she shared with her sister Maria without waking anyone. She had lain in her bed in the knowledge that she had crossed a line and couldn't go back. She had no regrets: she wanted to be with this man more than anything and had never felt so happy in her life. She knew she had betrayed Carlo but pushed thoughts of him to the back of her mind. She knew she had committed a sin; but how could it be a sin when two people loved each other and it felt so right?

She should go to confession, but confessing without really meaning it seemed worse than not confessing at all. She had been pondering this as she fell into a deep sleep, only to be woken an hour later by her mother who told her it was time to get up and milk the goats.

She longed for Sunday when she would see Antonio again…

Anthony and his troop took a truck up to the zone where they were clearing mines to review the position.

'We've cleared about eighty percent of the target area,' reported Sergeant Hargreaves. 'Another couple of weeks and we'll be done.'

'Good work,' said Anthony, 'the men have done a great job. Let's make sure we finish it safely – don't want anyone to fall at the last hurdle.'

'Right. Then we'll be off, back to Blighty!'

'Yes…' said Anthony.

His thoughts went straight to Isabella. How could he leave her? Since that night in the barn he couldn't get her out of his mind. He hadn't known it was possible to feel such love, such desire. He smiled as he remembered how he had woken up, entwined around her, and had to make a mad dash back to Base before he was put on a charge. God, he longed for Sunday when he would see her again…

'We'll get on then, sir?' asked Hargreaves.

Anthony came back from his reverie.

'Er - yes, carry on!'

CHAPTER 21

Germany, 1945

The camp was buzzing with rumours. They'd heard that the Allies were tearing through Germany and surrender was imminent.

One morning Henry awoke to the distant sound of a plane – funny, it sounded just like one of his Lancasters. He sat up on his bunk as the thrumming of the engines grew louder. All the men were awake now, all with the same thought. As one, they charged outside just as a dozen Lancasters soared overhead, scattering leaflets. The men waved and cheered with joy at the sight, especially when one plane dived low enough for them to see the pilot giving the thumbs-up sign. As the planes flew away the Goons emerged and ordered the prisoners back into the huts.

Henry picked up one of the leaflets. It confirmed what they had thought - the Germans were in full retreat and the Allies were advancing on all fronts. The Soviets were liberating POW camps in the East, and their camp would be liberated very soon.

A few days later they were out in the exercise yard when they heard a deep rumbling sound in the distance. The sound grew louder, closer, until one of the men cried out,

'Tanks! British tanks! They're on their way!'

It really was true. All the men were outside now, the Goons standing back knowing there was nothing they could do. The tanks came closer, followed by a convoy of lorries and soldiers marching along behind - British soldiers.

The men whooped and cheered as the first tank smashed through the camp gate, standing back for their own safety as a second tank slammed through the barbed wire fence and demolished the watchtower. Then the soldiers arrived, throwing rations and cigarettes at the freed men who went wild with delight, mobbing their liberators, yelling, screaming, thanking them and asking for news about old friends and comrades.

Amongst this happy chaos the soldiers sought out prisoners who were so weak they were unable to get up, giving them food and medication.

Henry joined in the celebrations, realising how thin and emaciated they must look to their liberators.

'Never been so pleased to see a pongo!' he said, as one of them dished out bars of chocolate.

The Colonel in charge of the liberating force dealt with the Goons, taking them prisoner in their turn. His next priority was evacuating the sick. He then surveyed the remaining crowd of five hundred-odd men who had suffered so much and his heart went out to them. It would take a week for his convoy of trucks to take them all to the American airbase from which they would travel home. He hoped they could remain patient for a little longer.

Italy, 1945

Signor Fortuno rushed back from Affossa to tell his family the news.

'*Il Duce* is dead! *Il Duce* is dead!'

Mussolini, the great fascist dictator, loved by some and loathed by many, had been captured by Italian partisans and shot dead, near Lake Como.

He never made it to Switzerland, nor did his mistress, who was killed with him.

'They say they left him, hanging from a lamp post!'

*

On Sunday, Anthony met Isabella in Affossa outside the church. They couldn't wait to be alone and walked quickly up into the hills surrounding the town to their favourite spot. They sat down together on the grass, looking at the view towards Ravenna and the sea, and speaking for both of them Anthony said, 'let's not worry about what happens when the war ends. All I want is you.'

They kissed, deeply, passionately, and made love, oblivious to anything but each other, and nothing else mattered in the whole world.

*

Two days after Mussolini was shot, Hitler killed himself in his Berlin bunker. The full surrender of the German forces was imminent.

On the 2nd May hostilities in Italy were formally brought to an end. In Ravenna, the Company Commander announced the great news to the troops to shouts and cries of joy.

Anthony went straight to Affossa where the whole town was alive with excited crowds filling the streets, partying, drinking and dancing, thankful that at last the war had come to an end. He found Isabella there, celebrating with her friends. The couple joined in with the throng and ended up at the café where people were dancing on the tables, but although they celebrated among the crowd they only had eyes for each other.

One of Isabella's friends, Louisa, had a camera and took photographs of everyone enjoying the party. It was impossible to find a place to be alone that night so eventually Anthony had to let Isabella go home, then he returned to Base where the drinking continued.

A few days later Isabella met Louisa and they went to the café together. Louisa said, 'I have something for you,' giving Isabella an envelope. 'It's some photographs I took during the celebrations. It was a wonderful evening, wasn't it? I think we all had too much to drink! You may want to keep them…private…'

Isabella waited until she was alone in her room before she opened the envelope. She found a couple of photos of her with Antonio, smiling at the camera, cigarettes in hand, and another where he had his arm around her. The other photos taken later in the evening focussed on the crowd, but in a corner she could plainly see a couple locked in an increasingly passionate embrace, and realised it was her and Antonio. She was grateful for her friend's discretion and hid the photos away in a drawer.

*

Out of the blue, Anthony received a letter from his old Maths master, Mr Blake.

Dear Anthony,

You will be surprised to hear from me after all this time. I hope all is going well for you; your father was kind enough to pass me your address. I am writing to let you know that Oxford have been in touch and your place to study Maths is still open, should you wish to take it up when the war is over.

Now, I know that war can change many things, and, after the experiences you have had, it may be that studying for a degree may no longer appeal to you. Perhaps you want to stay on and make a career for yourself in the Army – I'm sure you would make a success of it. However, it is something you will wish to consider when looking at options for your future.

I am keeping well – I have been working with the Home Guard in Bath as well as teaching so have been keeping busy.

With best wishes,
Arthur Blake

Anthony read the letter as if it had come from another planet. It was kind of Mr Blake to write, but he hadn't thought about university for years and had no clue as to how he should respond. He really didn't want to think about the future. All he wanted was to be with his Isabella.

To add to his confusion, a few days later he received a letter from his father:

Dear Anthony,

I hope this finds you well. We are fine here; by all accounts the war is nearing its end and my greatest wish is to have both my sons home again. What a terrible ordeal it has been for us all.

I went with the Blumfeldts yesterday to put some flowers on your mother's grave. I can't believe she has been gone for three years. Some people here say we should try to forget, but I can't do that. I hope to hear from Henry soon, they say the POWs are being liberated so I'm hopeful for news.

Let me know how you are, Anthony, I haven't heard from you for a while.

Your loving father…

Anthony read his father's letter with increasing self-reproach. He had been so preoccupied with Isabella that he'd neglected his family, and Mr Blake's letter was a sharp reminder that he would have to make some decisions about his future, and soon. He sat down and wrote to his father straight away. He reassured him that all was well, the mine clearance task was almost complete and they had celebrated the end of hostilities in Italy. He also told him he'd lit a candle for his mother in the church (which he hadn't, actually, but intended to do the following Sunday.) He told him how much he'd enjoyed going to the opera. He gave his love to all and said he was sure Henry would be freed soon.

Then he paused.

He struggled to tell his father the whole truth: that he had fallen in love, that in spite of the horrors of war he was the happiest he had ever been. He couldn't say that once he had seen everyone at home he wanted to return to Italy to be with Isabella; he felt his father wasn't ready for that news. And somehow writing it down would spoil it, invite questions, questions he himself didn't want to think about right now. So for the moment he just wrote:

'...I have been very fortunate in my posting here. The work is interesting but not as dangerous as being on the front line...the local families are very hospitable and welcome us into their homes. They cook the most fantastic food here. And the girls are pretty too!'

He sighed. He hated telling these half-truths, but it was all he felt able to do at that time, so he sealed the envelope and posted the letter. A reply to Mr Blake would have to wait.

Isabella was outside sweeping the farmyard - hostilities may have ended, but life at the farm went on as usual. She had enjoyed the celebrations but she was worried about what she would do when Antonio went back to England. She wanted to be with him so much, longed for him, loved him...she crossed herself yet again for her sinful desires and deeds. Her thoughts were brought to an abrupt end when she caught sight of her mother walking along the road back to the farm, carrying a shopping basket over her arm. Isabella put down the broom and walked over to meet her.

169

'Did you buy anything nice, Mama?' she asked.

'Just a few bits and pieces…'

Signora Fortuno put the basket down and rested a moment – it was quite a climb up to the farm. Then she continued, 'I saw Carlo's mother in town this morning.'

Isabella caught her breath and a surge of guilt ran through her.

'Does she have any news?' she managed to ask.

'No - she hasn't heard anything since her younger son wrote to her, over a year ago. She's anxious to know what's happening. I do feel for her.'

'So she hasn't heard anything from Carlo?'

'Nothing. Now that hostilities have ended she is praying for them to come back, if they are still alive – the conditions in the North have been so dangerous. People say many didn't survive the Winter.'

'But Mama, Carlo will be all right, won't he? He is such a strong man.'

'It is not in our hands. All we can do is pray to the Holy Mother for his safe return…'

Then she fixed her daughter with a look and added, sceptically, '…if that is still what you want…'

Isabella was taken aback.

'Of course, Mama!'

Of course she wanted Carlo to come home safely. But how could she marry him, now, when she was so in love with somebody else?

170

CHAPTER 22

Germany, 1945

Henry, Peter and a dozen other men climbed into a truck, part of the convoy that would take them away from the camp and to freedom. As they left Henry said, 'I never want to see that place again as long as I live.' They arrived at the American airbase where they stayed for the night, then the next day they were boarded onto Dakota troop carriers and flown to Rheims in France where they were handed over to the RAF. They boarded the waiting Lancaster, passengers for once, and landed at an airfield near Weston-super-Mare where they were given a huge 'Welcome Home' tea party in an aeroplane hangar, waited on by the WAAF. It felt novel to hear English being spoken in feminine voices and to be treated with respect and consideration. Henry took a seat at a table laden with food and was hungrily eating a bully-beef sandwich when he recognised the face opposite him.

'Flight Sergeant Dean!' Henry exclaimed, getting up to shake his hand. 'How are you, old man? How far did you get?'

'Hello, sir! Good to see you again. Well, I ran for about a week, sleeping where I could, under bushes, in barns, but got re-captured near Frankfurt. They took me to another camp and we were liberated not long after. But it was worth a try, sir – I'm grateful you gave up your place for me.'

'It was the least I could do. You're local, aren't you?'

'Yes – tomorrow I'll be back with my wife and kids. Can't believe it!'

After hot baths, clean uniforms and new documentation the men stayed overnight in Bristol and were put on their various trains the next morning.

Henry caught the same train as Peter who was headed for his parents' home near Reading. As the train steamed out of Bristol Temple Meads Henry looked up at the colourful houses on Totterdown and the other familiar landmarks, still not quite believing he was really there. They whistled past Keynsham and Fry's chocolate factory (currently being used to make aeroplane engines, he heard someone say), then the train began to slow down as it approached Bath. Henry looked out the window as the famous Georgian terraces came into sight. The bombing raids may have left them looking like a set of bad teeth, but the inherent beauty of the city, nestling in a bowl at the foot of the hills, would never change.

The train squealed to a stop. Henry got up, picked up his kitbag and shook hands with Peter.

'Good luck, old chap. I'm sure our paths will cross again.'

'Thanks, Henry – yes, I'm sure they will. You must come down to the parents' place some time, they'd love to meet you.'

Henry nodded his thanks, disembarked, and waved as the train continued its journey to London. He began the walk back to Eagle House along roads which were familiar but different – blackened buildings, bombsites and holes where homes used to be.

In Victoria Park the cherry trees were in bloom, festooned with pink blossom against the blue sky. One day soon it would be a park fit for children to play in again, he thought, rather than a giant vegetable patch. He walked on, enjoying the warmth of this pleasant, sunny Spring day – an English Spring day. How good it felt to be home.

When Sonia opened the door she almost fainted. She hugged him, then cried out, 'it's Henry! He's home!'

Sonia brought Henry a cup of tea and some cake. He slurped his tea noisily, stuffed the cake into his mouth then looked up and wondered why they were all staring at him. He wiped his mouth on his sleeve and they all burst out laughing.

'Sorry! I suppose my manners aren't what they were!'

'Don't worry, son,' said David, 'we don't care! After what you've been through…'

'Yes…it wasn't the best year of my life. To tell you the truth, I rather want to forget all about it!'

'We are so pleased to have you back home, Henry,' said Karl.

'We've missed you,' said Gilda, 'it's wonderful to see you again.'

'It's wonderful to see you all too,' said Henry, 'and Gilda! You look so grown up!'

Gilda blushed and said, 'I am nearly fifteen…'

'Tonight we will cook Henry a special meal,' Sonia said to her daughter, then to Henry, 'you need feeding up!'

She looked at him with concern, taking in his thin figure, the scar on his hairline and gaunt face, exacerbated by the cropped hair the barber had given them all at the airbase.

'Nothing some of your chicken soup can't fix…' said Henry.

Later, once Henry had caught his breath, Gilda asked, 'do you think Anthony will be back soon?'

'Probably. I suppose it depends what Division he's in, and what they're doing. They can't send everybody home straight away.'

'I do hope he's all right.'

'I'm sure he is. Now, tell me what you've all been up to!'

Henry opted for an early night and some aspirin. It was the oddest feeling, being back in his childhood bedroom, the Sopwith Camel still on the shelf, pictures of aircraft still on the wall.

'I've left everything just as it was,' said his father.

'I keep expecting Mum to come in. It's so strange to be back here, but without her. I don't know how you've managed.'

'Yes, it's been very painful. I don't think you ever get used to it. But the important thing is, you're home now. Sleep well, son.'

'Good night, Dad.'

*

Italy, 1945

The next Sunday when the lovers met Anthony asked Isabella to go into the church with him so he could light the promised candle for his mother. They did so, then went to the café for a coffee. Afterwards they walked up into the hills, hand in hand, but both of them quiet.

'What is it, Antonio?' asked Isabella, 'are you thinking about your mother?'

He sighed and scratched the back of his neck.

'No,' he replied, then, 'well yes – in a way.'

He told Isabella about the letter he'd received from his father, how it had made him feel neglectful of his family, and worse, that he had been unable to tell his father about the love he had found.

'He sounded so keen to have me back home, I didn't have the heart to tell him I want to return to Italy – but I do, Isabella, I do! I can't bear to be without you!'

He pulled her towards him and kissed her, then continued, 'it's so hard to know what to do! I could stay in the Army, but God knows where my next posting might be. And I've heard from my old Maths master about taking up my place at university. But I don't want to do that anymore – it seems a world away. I'd rather come back here and work on the farm, I'd do anything if it means I can be with you.'

Then he had a thought.

'I suppose you could come to Bath…', then as soon as he said it he knew it would never work. Try as he might he could not picture his radiant Italian beauty in dull, grey England, trying to make the rations last the week.

175

'…or maybe not!'

She laughed as if he had read her mind.

They continued walking up the hill.

'Antonio,' said Isabella, 'it is a shame to lose your university place. You could have a good career. But I don't want to be without you!'

A cloud passed across her face and she said, quietly, '…and I am afraid of what will happen if Carlo returns…'

Carlo. She hadn't mentioned his name for ages, but he was still there, in the shadows.

They reached the top of the hill and walked over to their favourite, secluded place. Anthony stood and looked at the sea in the distance thinking about how the last few months had changed him. He had seen much in his long march across Italy - dead bodies by the roadside, disease, poverty, hardship. He had killed a man. He had saved men's lives. He had built bridges, defused mines. He had found the love of his life and was determined not to lose her. He had come a long way from being the schoolboy his father and schoolmaster remembered – 'Blondie from Bath'.

Anthony thought of Collins and his simple, direct approach to life. He wouldn't mess around. Find your fighting spirit!

Anthony grabbed Isabella's arm and pulled her towards him.

'Marry me!' he said. 'I'll go home, I'll tell my father how beautiful you are and that you're going to be my wife. Then I'll return and we can be married! And if Carlo comes back, and if your parents don't like it, well, it's too bad, we'll just have to go off somewhere and do it anyway…'

Isabella was shocked.

'Antonio! Of course I want to marry you! But it sounds...'

'Dangerous? Yes!'

He kissed her, hard on her mouth.

'Say yes! Say you will!'

'Antonio!'

He'd had enough of feeling guilty. To Hell with the future. He loved this woman and wanted her more than anything. He scooped her up in his arms then laid her on the ground, kissing her forcefully.

He couldn't stop himself; he pulled her clothes aside and entered her, possessing her, and then he felt her hands clasping his back, pulling him closer, responding to his body, his kisses...

Afterwards, as they lay on their backs, out of breath, she said, 'yes, Antonio. Yes, I will marry you!'

Bath, 1945

The 8th May was Victory in Europe Day. After nearly six years of fighting the war in Europe was at an end.

In Eagle House David broke out the whisky bottle and made a toast to peace with Henry, Sonia and Karl. Gilda and Jacob walked into the city to join in the festivities, passing houses decked with flags, people dancing and street parties in full flow. Crowds were flocking towards the Abbey churchyard where, at 3pm, Winston Churchill's speech on the wireless was relayed through loudspeakers to the masses who erupted with joy and relief.

As his sombre tones rang out the audience were reminded of the war with Japan which continued and of the tremendous losses which had been incurred in setting Europe free. But today was a day of celebration, and Bathonians took to it with gusto.

And Gilda was beside herself with joy, because she knew Anthony would be home soon.

Italy, 1945

On that very day, Anthony received a letter from his father with the best news – Henry had returned!

David described the relief at seeing his son again, that he was malnourished but would soon recover now he was eating proper food, and that all they wanted now was for Anthony to be home too.

In Affossa the celebrations surpassed even those of the previous week and everyone was out in the streets, dancing, drinking, laughing, singing. Anthony and Isabella celebrated along with everyone else. If they exuded an extra glow of happiness it was because of the secret promise they had made to each other: as soon as Anthony was back in Italy after seeing his family, Isabella would break off her engagement to Carlo and they would announce their plan to marry.

CHAPTER 23

Italy, 1945

For the first time since they had been posted to Italy the soldiers were showing some interest in the local shops.

'Well, I'd better take something back for the missus or she'll never forgive me!' said Sergeant Hargreaves.

Anthony splashed out and bought a carved wooden pipe and some tobacco for his father, a pen knife for Henry, a silk tie for Karl and silk scarves for Sonia and Gilda. He wasn't sure what to buy for Isabella so he went to the jewellers in Ravenna and tried to think what his mother would advise.

'Something she can look at and think of you.' He could hear her voice in his head.

He looked at engagement rings – that was what he longed to buy her, but it would have to wait until he returned. A bracelet? A necklace? May invite difficult questions. Then, in a glass display case he saw some delightful boxes made in marquetry, inlaid with mother-of pearl. He asked the jeweller if he could look at one of them. The man fetched the key, opened the glass case and took out a box, lovingly placing it in Anthony's hands. Anthony unlocked it, lifted the lid and only then realised that it was a musical box, playing none other than a tune he recognised from *Tosca*.

'See?' said the jeweller, 'it plays the beautiful tune, is lined with this lovely green silk and is large enough to keep jewellery, or a memento – a photograph perhaps?'

The old man seemed to read his mind.

'It's perfect! I'll take it,' said Anthony.

'Splendid!' said his mother.

*

Anthony's Company Commander called his men together to make a special announcement.

'I am pleased to tell you that our work here is complete and our Company will be among the first to be returning home. In fact - you will be leaving here by train tomorrow morning!'

The men cheered wildly, jumping up and slapping each other on the back – all save Anthony, who sat in stunned silence. Tomorrow…

The Commander called for hush to finish his announcement.

'I thank you all for what you have done, but our final thoughts must be with those who won't be coming back. This Italian campaign has been brutal and has cost British and Commonwealth forces fifty thousand lives.'

There was a gasp of horror at the enormity of it all.

'We give thanks to God for those of us that have survived.'

Anthony went back to his quarters, thinking fast. He packed all his belongings then borrowed a motorcycle and rode up to the farm, bringing Isabella's gift with him.

Signora Fortuno was in the yard collecting eggs.

'Lieutenant Roberts!' she said, greeting him, 'you have come to see my daughter?'

'Yes, I have,' he said.

'Are you leaving us soon?'

'I'm afraid so, yes,' he replied, 'tomorrow!'

Inwardly Signora Fortuno sighed with relief.

'You will be pleased to return to your family.'

'Of course,' he replied.

Isabella heard their voices and came out to see what was going on.

'Lieutenant Roberts is leaving us tomorrow!' her mother said, unable to hide a hint of pleasure in her voice. Isabella went pale and her hand went to her mouth.

'It's not true!' she cried.

'Take him inside, Isabella, and give him some coffee.'

They sat together at the kitchen table but it was impossible to speak privately with family members coming and going. Isabella whispered, 'I cannot believe you are going so soon…'

'I love you,' he said, softly, just as her little brother Guiseppe came charging in, playing with the toy aeroplane he'd been given at the Christmas party.

The Fortunos invited Anthony to share their lunch of bread and goats' cheese then went about their business, leaving them alone at last. They embraced and held each other, Isabella in tears and Anthony trying to console her, although he felt as wretched as she did at the thought of parting so soon.

181

He wiped the tears from her face and said, 'look, I've got a present for you.'

When Isabella opened the lid of the musical box and the tinkly tune from *Tosca* began to play it set her off again.

'It's beautiful!' she cried. 'I will never forget that night as long as I live!'

Anthony gave her a photograph of himself and said, 'would you like this? It's a bit formal – I'm in uniform – but it's all I've got.'

'You look very handsome!' she said, wiping her eyes.

He wrote on the back of the postcard-sized photograph, *To my beautiful Isabella, all my love, Anthony, May '45.'* Then he asked, 'what was that word you taught me, that means 'I will return'?'

'*Ritornerò*,' she said

He added the word on the back of the photo.

'*Ritornerò*,' he said, and kissed her.

'I will treasure it,' she said, placing the photo inside the box and locking it with its little silver key.

'Now,' she said, 'I have a present for you too! I will fetch it.'

She came back carrying a kind of attaché case made from dark green leather with brass fittings on the corners, a brass handle and a combination lock on the front.

'Oh, it's terrific!' said Anthony.

She was excited about it. 'Let me show you.'

She turned the combination lock and opened the lid.

The case was lined in finely cut black leather with pouches containing items of the barbers' trade – scissors, combs, a leather strop and razors.

'It belonged to my uncle who was a barber - he used to travel around the villages, shaving beards and cutting hair. He's dead now and no one else wants his case, so I thought you might like it. See, it is made from good Italian leather, and will last many years.'

Anthony examined the contents with fascination. The case was exquisite, although he wasn't convinced that he would ever use it.

'It's wonderful!' he said, kissing her, 'thank you so much.'

'I want to give you more things to put inside. Here...'

She unhooked the silver hair slide she often wore and gave it to him, shaking her hair loose.

'You can keep this to remember me. And I have some photos here, also.'

She gave him one of the photos Louisa had taken during the celebrations and another one of herself in a more formal pose.

'Papa took this one of me last year, on my eighteenth birthday,' she said. 'You can have it.'

She wrote on the back, '*To Antonio, with all my love, Isabella, May 1945.*'

'Thank you' he said, 'I will cherish it,' and he kissed her.

Isabella put the keepsakes carefully into one of the leather pouches inside the case.

Then Anthony took his sketch book out of his pocket. 'Would you like to have one of my drawings of you?'

'Yes please!'

She chose her favourite, the one of her sitting by a tree in the hills surrounding Affossa. He carefully tore the page from the book and gave it to her, then put his sketch book in his new leather case. Isabella showed him how the combination lock worked.

'Now, only you will be able to open it.'

The family invited Anthony to stay for their evening meal to mark his departure. Several glasses of wine later Anthony got up to go and Isabella walked him to the door. They were desperate to be alone one last time.

'Pretend to leave,' whispered Isabella, 'then come back in half an hour and I'll meet you in the barn.'

Anthony started up the motorcycle and rode a few hundred yards down the road where he switched off the engine and pushed it into a field. He waited there for a while, smoking, willing the time to go, then ran back up to the farm. Dusk was falling and the full moon was just coming out.

Isabella was in the barn as promised. She threw herself at him, crying '*Mi amore!*'

'I love you,' he responded, and they kissed, madly. They had no time to lose and within seconds they were naked in the straw together, crazy with desire, making love fervently, revelling in every touch, sound, smell and taste as they shared their bodies and their souls. In their ecstasy they lost all sense of time and place until at last they lay back on the straw, elated, exhausted.

Isabella sensed a movement outside and glanced towards the barn door which, in their haste, they had left ajar.

'What is it?' asked Anthony, as he lay beside her.

'I thought I heard something?'

'Probably the wind.'

Anthony got up and fastened the door, then returned to her.

'It's all right,' he said, 'there's no one around. Just us…'

They resumed their love making until they could give no more, then fell asleep, their bodies twisted around each other as one.

At sunrise Anthony knew he had to leave. They said their final goodbyes and kissed, devastated to part, but secure in the knowledge that when he returned they would marry and be together for the rest of their lives.

CHAPTER 24

Italy, 1945

The soldiers marched to the railway station carrying all manner of baggage in addition to their kitbags – souvenirs, lengths of material, bedding, gifts, food. Anthony proudly carried his essential new piece of kit – the green leather case. The men couldn't wait to get home, back to their loved ones. Anthony kept his emotions to himself – he wanted to see his father and brother, of course, but his mind was full of Isabella. He could still feel her, physically, as if she were there beside him. When they got to the station he sat and hurriedly scribbled a letter, telling her how much he loved her and couldn't wait to return.

He didn't have any stamps. *Francobolli non ce n'è.*

No matter, he would post it as soon as he had the opportunity. He put it away in his new case.

The train left Ravenna and travelled through the Italian countryside that they had marched across, a lifetime ago. Once over the French border they took another train North. The journey was long, slow and tedious. Anthony slept as much as he could, but the train was noisy and uncomfortable and he developed a painful headache he couldn't seem to shift. All the men were quiet, there was no banter now, they just wanted to get home.

Anthony looked out the carriage window at the devastation war had left in its wake. It seemed as if the wounds of the whole world were on display - houses, churches, villages were in ruins.

Processions of displaced people made their way slowly along broken roads, the lucky ones pulling a handcart containing all they possessed, the not so fortunate stumbling along with nothing at all to their name. What would happen to all these people? he wondered. Would they ever be able to make a home for themselves again? Would anything ever return to normality?

He closed his eyes so he could concentrate on his memory of Isabella.

They finally reached Calais and were billeted in an old hospital until a ship was ready to take them across the Channel. Adding seasickness to their woes in the unseasonably rough weather, Anthony couldn't care less about the white cliffs of Dover, he just wanted to get back to dry land. At last the soldiers disembarked and took the train to London. As they steamed through the suburbs Anthony looked out at rows of semi-detached houses, many bomb-damaged, and here and there a tree in Springtime green. England. It finally dawned on him that he was actually on his way home.

Anthony fell asleep, then awoke with a jolt as the train pulled into Charing Cross. There was a sudden rush as the men said goodbye and wished each other luck. No one knew or cared at that point about future reunions or ceremonies to commemorate comrades they'd lost; they just wanted to get home.

He and a few others who were West-country bound made their way to Paddington for the last leg of their journey. The train to Bristol was already crowded and they had to walk a long way down the corridor before they came to a compartment with some empty seats.

Anthony slid the door open, put his case on the luggage rack and flopped down onto a seat with his kit bag on the floor between his legs. He closed his eyes and tried not to think about his throbbing head. Isabella, he thought, I must try and concentrate on Isabella...

At last, with a hiss of steam and a blast from the whistle the train pulled out of Paddington and made its way past blackened homes, offices and factories until it left the city behind. It was late in the evening and outside it was getting dark. As the train gathered speed the motion made Anthony feel sick, just as bloody bad as crossing the Channel, he thought. A soldier sitting next to him, who he didn't know, offered him a cigarette, but Anthony refused and dashed to the toilet where he was violently ill. When he returned to the carriage, his face a pale shade of green, the soldier said, 'I thought you'd have got over travel sickness by now!'

Anthony tried to laugh it off, saying, 'yes, I know...I wish this bloody headache would go away though.'

The train stopped and started, passengers came and went. Anthony tried to sleep, but, God, his head hurt. He got up and walked into the corridor, pushed the window down to get some air but quickly closed it again when a rush of black smoke blew in.

He went back to his seat and lit a cigarette. It didn't help. He tried to concentrate on the rhythm of the train on the tracks, hoping it would lull him to sleep, but all he could feel was an excruciating pain which was getting more intense by the minute. The train pulled into Chippenham and he was alone in the compartment. Nearly there, he thought, if I can just make it to the next stop…

The train blew its piercing whistle as it entered Brunel's famous Box tunnel and everything went dark. And that was when the pounding inside his head became unbearable. Anthony clutched his head, trying to stop the searing pain which felt like a thousand daggers piercing his skull. He cried out but no one could hear him above the rattling of the train as it tore through the blackness. No longer in control, writhing in agony, he fell from the seat onto the carriage floor. And as the train emerged from the tunnel, just a few minutes away from Bath, he rolled over and sank into oblivion.

*

The train arrived late at Bristol Temple Meads, its final destination, due to an incident at Bath, which was annoying for the workers who had to clean the train for its return trip to London before they could go off shift. One of the staff, Hilda, worked her way from carriage to carriage with her refuse sack, picking up paper cups, old newspapers and discarded cigarette packets, muttering to herself about being late and wondering what she was going to have for her supper. In one of the compartments she found a dark green leather case on the luggage rack.

189

She took it down, tutting, saying to herself what a nice case, fancy leaving that behind. Once she'd finished her cleaning she took it to the Lost Property office, then went home. A nice boiled egg, she thought. With soldiers.

PART THREE

CHAPTER 25

Bath 1945

David and Henry rushed to the hospital as soon as they received the call.

'There must be some mistake!' David had said to the doctor on the phone, 'my son's in Italy!'

But when they saw the young man lying in a deep coma amongst a tangle of tubes and bleeping machinery, they knew there was no mistake. His hair was cropped short and his face tanned from the sun, but it was definitely Anthony.

'I'm sorry to tell you that Anthony has suffered a severe stroke – a blockage in the main artery to the brain,' said the doctor, gravely. 'It's an extremely serious condition and it is highly unlikely that he will regain consciousness. Most patients last a few days at most. I'm so very sorry.'

'Is there nothing you can do?' asked Henry.

'The damage has been done, but we can help his breathing and control any pain.'

David gasped and put his head in his hands. He was ashen.

'I have read of exceptional cases where patients have survived, but those that do are unable to communicate or resume any sort of a normal life,' said the doctor, ushering them away.

'I suggest you go home. We'll let you know straight away if there's any change in Anthony's condition.'

Completely devastated, David and Henry drove back to Eagle House to be met by Sonia who saw immediately that something dreadful had happened.

'Fetch Karl and Gilda, will you? I have the most awful news...' said David.

Henry, in a daze, poured some large brandies and sat down while his father told the Blumfeldts what had happened. Karl and Sonia gasped with horror; Gilda fainted. Karl gathered his daughter in his arms, laid her on the sofa, slapped her face to bring her round and gave her some brandy, then she sat up and started screaming hysterically:

'NO! NO! It can't be true! He can't be ill! He mustn't die! I've waited so long to see him, there must be some mistake...'

Her parents tried to comfort her but she fought them off, screaming, then got up and ran to her bedroom and slammed the door. Sonia went to her and the men looked at each other.

'Terrible news,' said Karl, 'terrible news. Poor Gilda, she's been so excited about Anthony coming home - as we all have...'

Sonia came back into the room.

'David, please give Gilda something to calm her down, she won't stop screaming!'

He fetched his medical bag and gave Gilda a sedative, wishing he could take one himself, anything to block out this dreadful pain.

That night, David, Henry and Karl sat together into the early hours. The hospital staff had given David Anthony's kitbag, the only remnant of his Army life, and the three men stared at it as it sat on the floor between them.

'We can only pray,' said Karl.

By some miracle Anthony survived the night and David and Henry returned to the intensive care ward to see him. David was not a strong believer, but he prayed with all his heart to God to help Anthony fight this battle. Henry did find some words of comfort for his father.

'Look, he's a young man, and a fighter. I've seen young pilots, terribly injured, burnt, disfigured – we were told they wouldn't make it, but several did. Young chaps like Anthony are surprisingly resilient. Don't give up hope, Dad.'

Then he held his brother's hand, saying, 'stay with us, old man. We've already lost Mum. We can't lose you too.'

Gilda was in turmoil. She had been praying to God to return Anthony safely to her, and what had He done? She had longed to have him back at Eagle House, but now she felt that all her foolish fantasies had come crashing down about her. She started to think that whatever had happened to Anthony had been her fault. She had been desperate to see him again and this was her punishment for her stupid, stupid imaginings.

Against the odds, Anthony held on to life and after a week he was transferred from intensive care to a private room.

The Blumfeldts were allowed to visit him and Gilda held back her tears as, led by her father, the three of them said prayers together in Yiddish. When they sat back a strange sense of peace pervaded the room.

'He is in a deep, deep sleep,' said Sonia, 'and I am sure, one day, he will wake up.'

After a while Karl and Sonia got up to leave.

Gilda said, 'can I stay with him, just for a minute?'

'Yes, child,' said Karl.

Gilda moved her chair nearer to Anthony. She stroked his cheek very gently with the backs of her fingers and touched his hair. As she looked at him, she could still see the old Anthony there and her heart melted with love.

'Don't worry, *liebchen*, I am here for you,' she said, softly, 'I will always be here for you…'

Italy, 1945

Isabella yearned for Antonio. She longed to hear from him but knew the post was bound to take ages to get from England to Italy. She consoled herself by opening the musical box he had given her and looking at his photograph, kissing it and remembering their last passionate night together, feeling the power of the bond they had created as if he were still there, by her side. About a week after he had left she woke up with a terrible headache and a profound sense of unease, but put it down to the intensity of her feelings.

Another two, three, four weeks went by and Isabella asked, out loud, 'why haven't you written to me, Antonio? You promised you would.'

So she found the address he had left her and wrote him a short note, cheering herself up with the thought that their letters would probably cross in the post, kissing the envelope as she put it in the mailbox.

Bath, 1945

Anthony's condition stabilised and, still in a deep coma, he was transferred to the stroke ward where his family and the Blumfeldts visited him every day.

Anthony's Company had been disbanded on its return to the UK and none of the soldiers he had served with during those last weeks at Ravenna were aware of his illness. An officer from Army Personnel came to see David to discuss the formal termination of Anthony's service. It was all terribly bureaucratic and impersonal.

When David and Henry finally unpacked Anthony's kitbag they were delighted to find the presents he'd bought for them all – the pipe, the penknife, the silk tie and scarves. But there was very little else of personal significance.

*

It was a Saturday morning and Gilda was at home, alone. Her parents had gone to the Shabbat service and lunch at the Hotel, but Gilda was feeling unwell – she suffered from period pains – so she stayed curled up on the sofa with a hot water bottle and Lucky the cat for company. David was visiting Anthony and Henry had gone out.

Around midday the postman came so she got herself up from the sofa, went into the hall to pick up the pile of letters, took them into the kitchen and put the kettle on to make herself some tea. She sat down and was skimming through the post when one particular envelope caught her eye. It had a foreign stamp and was addressed to Lieutenant A. Roberts; it came from Italy.

Gilda caught her breath. It wasn't an official-looking letter; it was personal. The buff-coloured envelope was flimsy, but the handwriting in black ink was regular and strong, the letters formed in the continental style.

It must be a letter from a friend he'd made – someone he'd known well enough to give his address to. A man? No, she thought, looking at the neat handwriting – a woman. The more Gilda stared at the envelope the more anxious she became. Who could this be? She felt nauseous.

The kettle boiled.

Gilda made her cup of tea, looked at the still-steaming kettle, and could not resist the idea. She knew it was wrong to read other people's mail but it would do no harm to look inside, she thought, then re-seal the envelope – no one need know. So she held the envelope over the steam, being careful not to scald herself, and eased it open.

Gilda sat down, her heart beating fast. She took the single sheet of paper from the envelope, unfolded it, her hands shaking, and read:

My Dearest Antonio,

I hope you had a safe journey back to England and that you are well. I hoped to hear from you by now. Please write to me! I miss you so much, amore mio, and I think about you every moment of the day. I am desperate without you and I will never forget our wonderful time together. Please come back to me soon!

Ti amo. I love you.
Your loving Isabella.

Gilda dropped the letter as if it had burnt into her skin. She felt sick and rushed over to the sink where she retched, violently. She took a drink of water but it could not quench the jealous rage she felt inside her. Who was this *'Isabella'* who was so desperate to see him again? And what right did this stranger have to call him *'My dearest Antonio'*?!

Gilda paced the room, her fists clenched, tears of anger stinging her eyes. 'No! No!' she cried, 'it is not possible!' All these months she had spent worrying about Anthony fighting the Nazis, but now she knew who her true enemy was. How could this *'Isabella'* claim him as her own? She can only have known him a few months, whereas she, Gilda, had known him – and, she now realised, loved him - all her life. Or, at least, her life since she had been in England, and that was all that counted. Heaven forbid, did he return this woman's love? It was too much to bear. She couldn't let anyone see this horrible letter. What good would it do? She thought of Anthony, lying unconscious in his hospital bed, unable to communicate, let alone read and reply to a letter. *'Isabella'* would just have to accept that she would never hear from him again.

199

Gilda looked at the clock – her parents would be home soon. She would have to act quickly. She took a box of matches from the kitchen drawer, put the letter and the envelope in a saucer and set light to them. The thin paper burnt quickly, leaving just a few ashes which she took outside and put in the dustbin. She came back into the kitchen and was gathering herself, drinking her tea, when she heard the front door open.

'Hello, we're back!' called her mother. 'How are you feeling, *liebchen*?'

CHAPTER 26

Italy, 1945

Isabella woke up feeling ill and had to rush outside to the toilet where she was sick. Her mother had just got up and was in the kitchen.

'What is it, daughter? Are you all right?'

'Yes, Mama – it must have been something I ate yesterday. I'm all right now.'

She went back upstairs to get dressed but still felt queasy. It would pass, she thought.

Six weeks after Antonio had left Italy Isabella had still heard nothing. Something must be wrong, badly wrong – she thought of the passionate times they had spent together and the promises they had made. She was sure he would get in touch somehow. She would write another letter to him - if only she didn't feel so sick. And, she realised, her period was late.

Signora Fortuna could no longer ignore her daughter's morning sickness. When they were finally alone in the house she confronted her.

'Tell me, honestly, Isabella, is it possible you could be pregnant?'

'Of course not, Mama!'

Her mother looked at her sceptically.

'Don't lie to me, Isabella. Is it possible?'

Isabella hesitated. She had hidden the truth from herself for long enough and the strain was driving her mad. Her lip trembled and she started to cry.

Signora Fortuno erupted and called her daughter all the names the rich Italian language had to describe the base morals and utter stupidity of this useless whore that she saw before her.

Isabella broke down, sobbing uncontrollably.

'You bring shame upon your family!' her mother cried, 'I knew the Englishman was trouble! They are always the same! You were a fool to fall for his charm, his foreign ways. I should never have let you see him!'

Between sobs, Isabella said, 'but we were such good friends…and then we fell in love…Mama, I do love him, and he loves me too. He's going to come back and we will be married!'

'Married! What rot! So why hasn't he written to you?'

'I don't know…' she said, dissolving into tears again. 'Mama, what am I going to do?'

Signora Fortuno composed herself.

'We will do the only thing we can. We must put our faith in the Holy Mother. You will go to confession. And we will pray. And don't say a word to anyone – especially your father…'

*

Isabella was peeling vegetables in the kitchen when she suddenly heard a scream and a clang of metal outside.

She looked out the window to see her mother, who had dropped a pail of goat's milk on the path and was standing in a puddle of the white liquid, her hands to her mouth.

Isabella ran out and her mother gestured towards a figure in the distance, a short, stocky, dark-haired man with his arm in a sling.

Both women crossed themselves. Signora Fortuno whispered a prayer of thanks to the Holy Mother. She was thinking fast.

'Isabella! Run to him! Run and tell your fiancé how much you've missed him!'

'Mama, I can't!' cried Isabella, 'I love Antonio!'

'Rubbish!' shouted her mother, 'you don't know what you are saying. Forget about him! Think about your future!'

Isabella was distraught. She didn't know what to do.

'For the sake of the Holy Mother and all the saints in heaven, GO!'

Isabella wavered for another few seconds, then turned and ran through the farmyard and onto the road where she met the man coming towards her.

'Carlo! Carlo! Is it really you? You're safe!' she cried.

'Bella!'

He embraced her with his good arm, holding her in a bear-like grip, his rough beard scratching her face. When he let her go she said, 'Carlo, I can't believe you are really here! Your arm, what happened?'

'It was a small wound to my shoulder. It will mend.'

Signora Fortuno joined them, kissed Carlo with joy, and the three of them walked back to the farmhouse where the rest of the family greeted him.

'Carlo! You've returned to us!' Signor Fortuno exclaimed, grasping Carlo's good shoulder, then standing back while the younger children hurled themselves at him in welcome.

Carlo wiped tears of emotion from his eyes and said, 'I cannot tell you, I am so happy to see you all…and especially Bella.' He took her hand. 'My beautiful Bella!' he cried. 'How I have missed you, *amore mio*! We must get married at once!'

The family had an impromptu feast to welcome their hero home. Everyone was firing questions so Signor Fortuno called for quiet and said, 'Carlo, we are so pleased to see you back safely. Please tell us a little of what you have been doing, then we will let you rest.'

'Thank you, Signor Fortuno. I have been fighting in the mountains these two years. It has been very hard – the Winters were cruel, we had little to eat, we had frostbite – I lost many comrades. My greatest sadness is that my young brother was killed by the Fascists. We were caught in an ambush, they shot him and I was left with this wound to my shoulder.'

The family murmured their condolences.

'But we must celebrate our victory! *Il Duce* is dead, the Fascists defeated and the war is over. All I want to do now is work at my farm and marry this beautiful girl who has been waiting for me.'

He looked lovingly at Isabella who felt her stomach churn with guilt.

Her mother kicked her under the table and Isabella replied, 'we have prayed every day for your safe return and give thanks. Welcome back, Carlo!'

After the meal the exhausted hero went upstairs to rest in one of the children's bedrooms. Signora Fortuno took her daughter to one side.

'The Holy Mother has answered our prayers! Tell him you will marry him!'

Isabella was in turmoil.

'But I can't! I love Antonio!'

'Don't be ridiculous! He's gone and he will never come back. Believe me, Isabella, I know it. I saw it in the last war – afterwards, when it is all over, when the soldiers go home, they meet their old friends and lovers and they forget! I'm not saying he didn't love you, but in a different place your mind changes, circumstances change. I have seen it. I know.'

'But Antonio isn't like that! He promised to come back and marry me!'

'Isabella – I am telling you – he won't come back. You must be realistic. You are pregnant. This man wants to marry you. Accept him!'

'But the baby?'

'Go to Carlo, Isabella – go to him this afternoon, while he is upstairs. Tell him you cannot wait.'

Isabella was shocked.

'But what if he doesn't want to…?'

'Of course he will! He's a man, isn't he? Go, now!'

*

Isabella lay in her bed that night, crying silently. She had acted her part well: she had pretended to be the virgin that she wasn't; she had sworn her love to Carlo; she had accepted his proposal of marriage. She made him the happiest man in the world, but when she left him she felt dirty, a cheat, and she had betrayed Antonio. Those few hours would determine the course of the rest of her life, and she had made her choice.

The following day Carlo continued his passage to his parents' home in Bassino, a village about fifteen kilometers from Affossa, where he would joyfully announce his forthcoming marriage.

The long-held wish of the families that the two would be joined was going to come true.

Isabella now dreaded the postman coming in case he should bring a letter from Antonio: what on earth would she do? But no letter came.

Signora Fortuna contacted the priest and the wedding arrangements were rapidly put in hand. Carlo took Isabella to Bassino to see his parents at their farmhouse – *La Casa sulla Collina* – 'The House on the Hill', a long, low building which had been extended over the years to accommodate new generations of the Spinetti family. After their marriage Carlo and Isabella would take the rooms at one end as their new home.

'You will be able to help my mother with the animals and in the vineyard,' Carlo said. 'And you can forget all about that job you were doing with the Council, no one needs interpreters now. Oh, Bella, we are going to be so happy!'

In other circumstances this visit would have been a wish come true, but that was before the war, before so many things had happened, before she had met Antonio. Now, she felt such a fraud.

Back home at *La Casa Bianca* Isabella's sister Maria asked, 'so are you looking forward to becoming Signora Spinetti?'

'Of course!' replied Isabella, unconvincingly.

'I see you look for the postman every day,' continued Maria, 'are you still waiting for a letter from England?'

Isabella couldn't keep up the façade and started to cry. 'He promised to write to me – he promised! He was going to come back and marry me! But I have heard nothing!'

'And now you have to marry Carlo.'

'I have no choice…'

Maria put a consoling arm around her sister and said, 'I know, Isabella. I know you have no choice…'

Isabella's heart skipped a beat.

'Don't worry, Isabella, you are my sister and I love you. I promise I won't say a word.'

Isabella and Carlo went to mass in Affossa and stayed behind to talk to the priest about their wedding plans. Isabella was thankful that a priest could not reveal the contents of a confession, and if he looked at her disapprovingly, Carlo didn't notice. When they left the church Carlo suggested going to the café. Isabella hesitated.

'I'd rather not…I don't feel too well…'

'All right, Bella, just have a glass of water, it will make you feel better.'

She reluctantly followed him into the café and immediately her memories of going there with Antonio came flooding back. When Carlo went to the bar to order drinks and said a general '*buon giorno*' a few people muttered the same in reply but avoided eye contact with him. The barman served him, glanced over at Isabella and smirked. Isabella couldn't stand it. She looked around at the other customers, imagining they were all laughing at her and got up, knocking her chair over in her haste, saying, 'I'm sorry, I must go!' as she ran out onto the street.

Carlo left the bar and went after her, conscious that people were staring, but putting Isabella's behaviour down to pre-wedding nerves.

Another week went by and as her wedding day approached Isabella began to accept that she may never hear from Antonio. In spite of what her mother said she couldn't believe that he would have gone home and forgotten all about her – surely? But what could she do? Things were moving so quickly and she had to stand by the decision she had made. She would never tell Carlo she had fallen in love with an English soldier. She didn't want to lose Carlo now and couldn't hurt him; he only had her best interests at heart and wanted nothing more than to make a home for her and raise children. If it hadn't been for the war she would have never known or wanted anything else.

She had cried enough tears over her lost lover. She would try to reconnect with her dark, hirsute husband-to-be and erase the memory of the lithe, fair-skinned Englishman she had once been so in love with.

The wedding took place in Affossa church on the first Saturday in August. As they received the bread and wine of the mass in front of their families and friends, Isabella and Carlo vowed to love each other for the rest of their lives. Signora Fortuno cried with joy and relief; Signor Fortuno welcomed his new son-in-law, looking forward to expanding his business.

Secretly, Isabella made a separate vow: she promised to love the child growing inside her, but took the piece of her heart that belonged to the English soldier who had cruelly abandoned her, and locked it away, forever.

Shortly after their wedding Isabella told Carlo she was expecting their child in the Spring. He was ecstatic.

Isabella's morning sickness had settled down and physically she was feeling well, but she had worries that she confided to her mother.

'What if the baby has fair hair?' she asked.

Her mother laughed. 'Don't worry about that – tell him your grandmother had fair hair – no one will know!'

'But what about the timing – won't he realise it's early?'

'Well, sometimes babies do come early! Look, Carlo is devoted to you. Even if he has suspicions, deep down, it will not change him – he will accept the child as his own. Don't worry, daughter, you have done the right thing.'

*

Carlo adored his wife, but from time to time he observed a distant look in her eyes and a certain sadness about her. His friends told him she'd been seen around with a British soldier while he was away and he suspected that she may have cheated on him. In his darkest moments he wondered if he really was the father of her baby – she had certainly been keen to lie with him the day he'd returned. But for all that, he loved her. He put her moods down to her pregnancy and consoled himself with the thought that if she had fallen for a foreigner he was long gone now - and they never came back.

*

In February, Isabella was at her mother's when a terrible pain shot across her belly. She doubled up in agony, cried out and fell to the floor.

'Mama, it's the baby – I think it's coming!'

'Holy Mother!' exclaimed Signora Fortuno, her mind racing. She called to her husband, 'the baby, it's coming early! You must fetch Carlo!'

She helped Isabella upstairs, comforting her while shouting at Maria to fetch hot water and towels. Carlo paced the floor all afternoon, chain smoking, until eventually, Isabella's screams subsided and a baby's cry was heard.

Signora Fortuno went downstairs to announce the news.

'Congratulations, Carlo. You have a son! He's come earlier than expected! He is small but healthy. And Isabella is doing very well. You can go up and see them now.'

Carlo charged up the stairs and entered the bedroom. His wife was sitting up in bed, exhausted, her hair wet with sweat. She held a bundle close to her.

'Thank heavens you are all right!' said Carlo. 'Now, let me see him…'

As Isabella carefully placed the child in his arms they exchanged a look which lasted only a moment, but which was to seal a deep understanding between them. Carlo's face fell. He knew, just looking at this tiny baby, its head covered with light-coloured down, he knew, instinctively, that the child was not his. The suspicions he had harboured since his return were correct. And yet, and yet…he loved this woman and couldn't bear to lose her. He would do what he must to keep her. He would go along with her charade and accept the child as his own, no matter what.

Isabella read his face and knew what he was thinking. He wasn't stupid – he was a good man and would be a good father.

She looked at him desperately, her eyes pleading with him to keep her secret and to forgive her.

Then Carlo said, quietly and carefully, 'there is only one thing I insist upon. He must be named after the brother I lost. He is to be called Antonio.'

Isabella stifled a gasp and managed to say:

'Yes…yes of course, Carlo, I know you loved your brother very much. Our son will be called…' She hesitated, then said, her voice cracking with emotion, 'our son will be called Antonio.'

Carlo took a deep breath, held the boy aloft and shouted out for all to hear, 'my son! My son! Let's celebrate!'

CHAPTER 27

England, 1946

In May it was a year since Anthony had suffered his stroke. He remained in a deep coma, totally unresponsive, but his consultant Dr Jones told David and the Blumfeldts never to give up hope. Gilda sat on the bed holding Anthony's hand, talking to him all the while, then she announced, 'Mrs Roberts once told me I'd make a good nurse and I've decided that's what I want to do. After my exams in the Summer I'm going to start Nursing School, then I can look after Anthony.'

'That would be wonderful, *liebchen*!' said Sonia, 'a good career for you, and I'm sure you will be very good at it.'

'Daughter, you are right to be giving some thought to your future,' said Karl, 'you will make a fine nurse.'

David felt quite emotional and was grateful that Gilda remembered his wife in such a fond and inspirational way. 'Thank you, Gilda,' he said, 'Wendy would be proud of you.'

The Winter of 1946 to 1947 was the worst in living memory. The steep hills of Bath were impassable, mountains of snow were heaped up alongside the roads, even potatoes were rationed and a shortage of fuel meant that it was cold simply everywhere.

In Eagle House everyone took to wearing Winter coats indoors and huddling around the one fire that was lit, Lucky the cat always managing to find the warmest spot.

It wasn't much better in the hospital where Anthony lay under a pile of blankets, oblivious to the freezing world around him. It came as a relief to the whole nation when the Spring came.

In April Henry took up a new post as a Squadron Leader at High Wycombe in Buckinghamshire. One morning he attended a meeting with some officers from the Air Ministry and spotted a familiar face around the table – his Observer and friend, Peter Harrison. When business was concluded, the two got up and shook hands.

'So pleased to see you, old chap!' said Henry, 'and I see you've been promoted!' he added, noting the extra stripe which showed Peter's new rank of Flight Lieutenant.

'And the same to you!' said Peter, 'I read about your DFC - congratulations! Well deserved!'

Henry had been awarded the Distinguished Flying Cross in recognition of his brave service during the Battle of Britain and his bombing missions over Germany. He was fairly low-key about it – it was his father who insisted on telling everyone – but he thanked Peter, all the same.

They had lunch together in the officers' mess, talking about their current jobs and avoiding any reference to the POW camp – a memory they both preferred to leave firmly in the past.

As Peter was leaving he said, 'you really must come down to the parents' place – you'd be very welcome. Let me know when you have a free weekend.'

'Actually, I will be free the weekend after next.'

'Super! That's settled then!'

Henry had invested a sizeable amount of his salary in a new car. Nothing gave him the same thrill as flying but motoring was the next best thing, especially in an open-topped car with sufficient horsepower for him to reach a decent speed on the quiet roads around the Station.

His latest purchase was a red MG TC two-seater sports car with an upright grille and spindly wire wheels of which he was inordinately proud. The basic petrol ration had been temporarily restored, so he relished the opportunity to drive down to Peter's parents' home in Berkshire.

Henry followed Peter's directions to a road just north of Reading where he located two stone pillars and a pair of iron gates with a sign marked 'Hathaway Manor'. He opened the gates and drove through, following the tree-lined driveway for about a mile until he saw the vast Tudor mansion set in acres of grounds. He whistled. Peter hadn't been exaggerating. It made Eagle House look like a peasant's hovel.

Henry was met by the butler who ushered him inside and carried his overnight bag up to his room. Peter came into the vast hallway to greet his guest.

'Welcome to Hathaway Manor! So good to see you here at last, old chap!'

Peter showed him into a sitting room and introduced Henry to his mother who remained seated so as not to disturb the small Yorkshire terrier perched on her knee. Elegantly dressed in a black Chanel suit, she was smoking a cigarette through a holder which she waved to one side as she gestured to Henry to sit down beside her.

'Delighted to meet you! I'm afraid my husband's away on business, you'll have to meet him another time.'

She rang a bell and a maid brought in a pot of tea and some cake.

'Now, Henry, tell me all about yourself.'

After tea Peter gave Henry a tour of the house, explaining how his father and uncles had started their pharmaceutical business after the Great War and expanded it, turning it into an international company and making millions. Peter's parents had bought the property on the back of their success. When they returned to the main sitting room a girl of about seventeen with long auburn hair was curled up in an armchair with a book.

'This is my little sister Celia,' said Peter. The girl looked up, languidly, said 'hello, welcome to the madhouse,' and returned to her reading.

They lit cigarettes and Peter was telling Henry about his father's collection of vintage cars when a tall, slim young woman with shoulder-length fair hair entered the room. She was wearing an off-white, short-sleeved jumper and beige slacks.

'I say, there's a rather nice MG outside,' she said.

'That will be Henry's,' said Peter, 'let me introduce you – Henry, this is my big sister, Matilda.'

'Tilly – everyone calls me Tilly,' she said, walking towards Henry. They shook hands and looked at each other.

The French expression *un coup de foudre* – a lightning strike - came to mind, although Peter was later to say it was more like a full-blown tropical storm.

The two stood, their hands glued together, their eyes locked.

Once the Earth had returned to its axis, Peter said, 'why don't you take Tilly for a spin?'

As he drove back to his Station on Sunday evening Henry felt elated, overjoyed, ecstatic...there weren't enough words in the dictionary. He had never been in love before – not really, properly in love – but now he was caught, hook, line and sinker. He knew he'd met his future wife.

And Tilly, who had never before taken much notice of her brother's friends, waved Henry goodbye, knowing that she had met her future husband.

Henry kept his feelings for Tilly private, but the next time he saw Anthony he couldn't keep quiet any longer, and after all, his brother was the one person he could rely upon to be discreet! It rather put him in mind of how a Roman Catholic must feel when they went to confession.

He sat down next to Anthony and said, 'I've got to tell you, I have just met the most wonderful girl! Honestly, old man, I can't tell you how lovely she is!

She really is the bee's knees…beautiful, and clever, too…but she's no blue stocking, she's great fun!
Basically – at the grand old age of twenty-seven - I'm in love!'

As Henry spoke, holding his brother's hand, it was as if the love that flowed from his heart transmitted itself to Anthony like an electrical charge. Suddenly, Henry felt Anthony squeeze his hand, and when he looked at him his eyes were open.

Henry was so shocked he jumped up, letting Anthony's hand go.

'Nurse!' he cried, 'NURSE!'

The nurse rushed in, then called the doctor who came straightaway and examined him.

Strange noises were coming from Anthony's throat and his left eyelid twitched erratically.

'Anthony! You are there, aren't you,' cried Henry, 'we always knew you'd wake up. Stay with us, old man!'

The doctor rang David who arrived with the Blumfeldts in tow and they all sat beside Anthony's bed, looking at him in wonder, thanking God that he had regained consciousness. Gilda couldn't contain herself and cried tears of joy.

Later, David asked Henry, 'what on earth did you say to him? It must have been pretty important to have that effect!'

Henry laughed and said, 'I haven't the faintest idea!'

This is extraordinary! I'm lying here, awake, and they tell me I've been in a coma for nearly two years. Two years! They say I had a major stroke when I was on the train, coming home from Italy, but I can't remember anything about it at all.

I can see and hear Dad, and Henry, and the Blumfeldts - but I can't move or speak. And I don't understand why Mum hasn't been to see me.

I just know that Henry was sitting next to me, holding my hand, telling me about his new love, and it reminded me of someone wonderful. I just wish I could remember who...

Italy, 1947

Isabella woke up with a start. It was as if something had been lying dormant inside her and had suddenly stirred.

She sat up in bed and looked around her, feeling confused, and thought she must have been dreaming.

Little Antonio started to cry so she went to his cot and picked him up before he disturbed Carlo who was lying on his back, snoring. She soothed her infant son, rocking him in her arms, and as she looked at him she could suddenly see her lover's face, and knew deep inside her that however much she tried to forget him, and however much he may have hurt her, she loved him still.

218

CHAPTER 28

England, 1947

At Hathaway Manor Henry was walking hand-in-hand with Tilly, telling her how Anthony had suddenly come back to life. 'It was incredible! After lying there for two years in a coma, I was talking to him when suddenly he opened his eyes and made this gurgling sound.'

'That's marvellous news! What a relief for you all! Do you know what triggered it, what brought him round?'

Henry hesitated.

'Well, actually…I was telling him all about you!'

'Me?!'

Henry turned to her, gently touched her face and looked into her sparkling blue eyes.

'I was telling him I'd fallen in love with the most beautiful, clever, wonderful girl…'

'What?!'

He took her in his arms and kissed her.

'Oh, Henry!' she cried, returning his kisses with passion.

The flame that had been lit when they first met had become a raging fire. Let it burn.

Later, the lovers resumed their walk, talking about their families, their schooldays and the war. Henry described his childhood fascination with aircraft ('just like Peter!' said Tilly), his flying career, and how he'd ended up with her brother in *Stalag Luft 32*.

'And you were awarded the DFC?'

'Well – yes.'

'You're unusual for a pilot – you're far too modest!'

Tilly continued, 'I enjoyed school, especially languages, and got my First at Cambridge – I was there during the first part of the war.'

'I was meant to go to Oxford to study Maths, but never got there – I was desperate to join up. The same went for Anthony…So, what did you do for the rest of the war, Tilly?'

'I spent most of the time in an office in Buckinghamshire, making tea for senior officers. I was never among the bombs and bullets, like you and your brother.'

'Well, the boring jobs can be just as important - those senior officers wouldn't have been able to function without all that tea!'

The next day Peter stood next to Tilly as they waved Henry goodbye.

'Looks like we'll be seeing a lot of him,' said Peter.

'Yes, we will,' said Tilly, giving her brother a kiss on the cheek.

*

David and Henry were called to the hospital for a meeting to discuss Anthony's future.

'Anthony's been conscious for two months now, and although he can't communicate, it is possible that he is aware of what's going on around him,' said Dr Jones. 'We must continue to engage with him in the hope that he might be able to understand.'

But then he added, 'I have to say there is little more we can do from a medical point of view.'

'So what happens now?' asked David.

'Well, one of my previous patients, a man in a similar condition to your son, moved back home to live with his parents. They had to adapt their house and employ round-the-clock care, but it worked out well for them, and the stimulus helped the patient. I think a similar arrangement might work for Anthony.'

David, Henry and Dr Jones discussed the matter in more detail and reached an important decision. David sat by his son's bed, held his hand and said, 'Anthony – you're coming home.'

This is good news. It will be wonderful to get out of hospital and go home. I get so frustrated, lying here – I want to shout out and tell them that inside this useless body I'm still here! About the only thing I can do is twitch my left eye, and I can squeeze somebody's hand if I really try. At least at home I'll have company and a different view to look at. And maybe being back among familiar things will help bring my memory back - my head is like a gruyère cheese, full of holes which I am desperate to fill...

In August, with much excitement, Anthony returned to Eagle House. David and Karl carefully manoeuvred him in his wheelchair up to the first floor where the builders, closely supervised by Sonia, had converted the old master bedroom at the front of the house into a living area for Anthony. They positioned his chair in the bay window overlooking the street and bought a new Bakelite radio and a wind-up gramophone to provide some entertainment.

There were plenty of chairs and a sofa for visitors to sit, bookshelves and a sideboard displaying Wendy's collection of Moorcroft pottery and family photographs. Henry's old bedroom was converted into a kitchenette and bathroom for Anthony's use, the pictures of aircraft and model planes packed in a cardboard box and put up in the loft.

Karl and Sonia insisted on becoming Anthony's carers, getting him up in the morning, washing, shaving and feeding him, giving him his medication and putting him to bed at night. The hospital sent a nurse to instruct them and Gilda, who had just completed her first year at Nursing School, joined in, eager to help. Extra assistance was required during the day so David engaged Mrs Potts, a widow with experience of caring for patients in Anthony's condition. Everything was in place to help Anthony lead his new life.

So here I am, back home at last.
Dad's explained to me about Mum — I remember now. She was killed in the Bath Blitz. It's so strange being here without her.
I'm desperately trying to piece together what happened to me. I can remember the nights the bombs fell, how scared I was...I should have protected Mum, and I didn't. I joined the Army but I think really I was running away. I remember just having to get on with things, and being in Italy...and then there was the girl, that beautiful girl...I catch glimpses of her, a flash of something silver, then she disappears, out of sight.

Henry brought Tilly, now his fiancée, to Eagle House to meet his father, brother and the Blumfeldts. Gilda felt nervous about it; she had developed an innate distrust of tall, blue-eyed girls with blonde hair.

However, as soon as she saw Tilly she knew she had no need for concern; Tilly's eyes were full of kindness and if anything, she reminded Gilda of Wendy.

A similar thought crossed David's mind when Tilly gave him a kiss on the cheek. He could see straight away why his son was smitten.

Amidst the cries of congratulations, Tilly sat down next to Anthony and took his hand in hers.

'Hello Anthony, I'm very pleased to meet you. I've heard so much about you! I bet you could tell me a few stories about your big brother! We joke around a lot together, but I want you to know, I really do love him.' She looked up at Henry and smiled.

Anthony's left eyelid twitched.

'So when will the wedding be?' asked Sonia.

'Next May,' said Henry, 'a year after we first met. It will give Tilly's mother time to get everything organised. You are all invited, of course. And, what's more,' he said, speaking to Anthony, '*you* are going to come!'

This is wonderful news about Henry and Tilly, it's given us all something to look forward to. I feel I've let everyone down, getting ill, and Henry's got to live for both of us now. But God knows how they're going to get me to Berkshire…

I'm getting used to the new routine. The Blumfeldts are marvellous, looking after me. They feed me brown gunge through a tube three times a day, give me physiotherapy and make sure I'm comfortable. Gilda's turning into a real treasure, so attentive, and she reads to me in the evenings. Even the cat comes and sits on my lap sometimes, which is rather nice.

Mrs Potts keeps me up to-date with all the gossip, although sometimes her incessant chatter drives me nuts. She talks twice as much to make up for what I can't say myself.

My main pastime is looking out the window, observing what's going on. Occasionally someone glances up and sees me sitting here, helpless, ga-ga. They look uncomfortable, embarrassed; then I can see the relief crossing their faces that it is me sitting here, not them; and then they straighten up, walk on and continue about their business. My old Maths master, Mr Blake, came to see me the other day. It was kind of him to come. I'll never take up my place at Oxford, though.

*

Henry and Tilly's special day went perfectly. The bride looked beautiful in an exquisite white silk dress, and the handsome groom was in uniform, proudly wearing his DFC. The traditional service was followed by the wedding breakfast in a marquee on the lawn at Hathaway Manor, and a society photographer took photos of the happy couple and their families to pass to Country Life magazine and local newspapers.

Henry had organised a specially adapted taxi to chauffeur Anthony, with Mrs Potts and Gilda accompanying him. David drove down with Karl and Sonia, his heart full of joy that his son was marrying the love of his life – and a millionaire's daughter, to boot. As Sonia said, 'the matchmaker herself couldn't have done a better job.'

Sonia had excelled herself, making dresses for herself and Gilda with nipped-in waists and full skirts, copying the 'New Look', and they both wore their shoulder length hair in a fashionable style.

Karl proudly linked arms with his lovely wife and daughter as they walked around, chatting to the other guests, enjoying the smart occasion and feeling equal to it.

'It's a marvellous day,' said Karl to David.

'It is,' he replied, 'if only Wendy were here to see it…'

When the dancing began Sonia pushed Anthony's wheelchair to one side. A couple of curious children came up and stared at him.

'Why can't you move, then?' said one.

'Can he feel anything?' said the other.

'I don't know – let's poke him and see what happens.'

Sonia spotted the children just in time.

'Leave him alone! He's a very brave man, you mustn't hurt him. Be off with you!'

Peter Harrison, Henry's Best Man, was thrilled that his friend and comrade was now his brother-in-law. He had his eye on one of Tilly's friends that he hadn't seen for years, and suspected it was only a matter of time before he'd be hearing wedding bells himself…

Gilda danced briefly with one of Henry's friends, then drew up a chair and sat down next to Anthony. Taking his hand she said, 'what a lovely day, *liebchen*! Henry and Tilly look so happy together, don't they?'

She felt his hand respond to hers. 'Anthony!' she exclaimed, delighted, 'you really are there, aren't you?'

I'm in the taxi with Mrs Potts and Gilda who is holding my hand tightly and won't let me go. It has been a wonderful, if exhausting, day. I am so pleased for Henry; he's on top of the world. But something is niggling at the back of my mind — wasn't I supposed to be going to another wedding? My own?

CHAPTER 29

Bath, 1948

Frank Collins was sitting in his house in Corsham, the *Bath & Wilts Chronicle* spread out in front of him on the dining room table. He turned the pages with his left hand while ash from the end of the cigarette perched between his lips fell onto the floor. The right sleeve of his shirt hung empty, useless, by his side. A headline and a photograph of a wedding caught his eye:

WAR HERO MARRIES

The wedding of Squadron Leader Henry Roberts, DFC, of Eagle House, Bath, and Miss Matilda Harrison took place at the Harrison's family home, Hathaway Manor in Berkshire. Sqn Ldr Roberts bravely flew many missions to Germany and suffered injury in the course of action. He is seen here with his brother, Lt Anthony Roberts of the Royal Engineers who served in Italy and tragically suffered a major stroke on his return to Bath. We wish the happy couple well…

Frank took the cigarette out of his mouth and put it in the ash tray.

'June!' he called to his wife.

She came in from the kitchen and he showed her the article, pointing to the figure in the wheelchair.

'This bloke 'ere – 'e was my Lieutenant - drove me to hospital when I got me arm blown off. Saved me life!'

He laughed to himself. "Blondie from Bath' we used to call 'im – we thought 'e were a right softie when 'e first joined us! But look at 'im now, poor bloke.'

'How sad!' replied June, 'you should go and see 'im – I'll look up the phone book, see if I can find a number.'

*

David was delighted to receive Frank's call and invited him to Eagle House the following Sunday. Sonia answered the door and led him upstairs where David welcomed him and shook Frank's proffered left hand.

'I'm so pleased to meet you! It is wonderful to speak to someone who served with my son. Now, tell me everything! Sonia, bring us some tea, will you?'

Frank pulled up a seat next to Anthony. Although he had seen the photograph in the newspaper it still came as a shock to see the good-looking young man he remembered, tall, energetic, full of vitality, sitting in this chair, unable to move.

'Hello, sir,' he said, 'it's Sapper Collins.'

Anthony's left eye twitched.

'Oh! I see what you mean! Christ!' exclaimed Frank, then apologised for his language.

'He can't speak, but we think he can hear us and knows what's going on,' said David.

Sonia came in with the tea, then left the room. Gilda remained; she wanted to know what the men were saying but didn't want to get involved in the conversation, so she sat at the back of the room and took out her sewing.

228

Frank told David all about their march through Italy and the incident in the barn when Anthony's quick thinking had saved the lives of his troop.

He talked about the Winter in Affossa, finally recounting how his arm had been blown off by a grenade and Anthony had driven him to the hospital in Ravenna.

'He saved my life, for the second time,' said Frank.

'And how are you managing now?' asked David.

'All right - thanks to me wife! I met June just after I got home — she were a widow with a young kiddie, and we got together. She's been wonderful.'

'And do you work?'

'Yes — I was a quarryman but can't do that anymore — filthy job anyway. I work for the Ministry in one o' them store depots underground in Corsham.'

'So, broadly, things have worked out for you?'

'Yes…' Frank smiled.

'…and talking of things working out - the Lieutenant took up a new post in Ravenna, so at least 'e got to see 'is girlfriend.'

Gilda caught her breath and listened.

'Well, well! I didn't know he had a girlfriend,' said David, surprised by this unexpected news, 'he never mentioned anyone in his letters.'

'He was a bit coy about it - but yes, 'e did. Isabella, she was called, a right cracker - 'e was crazy about 'er.'

Gilda felt her blood run cold. *'Isabella'* — the woman who had written that horrible letter - the letter she'd burnt…

229

She cried out in pain as she stabbed herself with her needle.

'Gilda, are you all right?' asked David, turning round and looking at her with concern.

'Yes - it was my own fault. I'll go and wash my finger under the tap.'

Gilda hurriedly left the room and the men resumed their conversation.

'Yes, 'e used to spend all his time with 'er – they were getting quite serious, I think. I used to tease 'im something chronic!'

'Well, I had no idea…'

Gilda slipped back into the room, unnoticed.

'I suppose she married 'er fiancé, if 'e ever came back,' said Frank.

'She was engaged?'

'Yes. I think Blondie…sorry, the Lieutenant, felt a bit awkward about it, to be honest, pinching someone else's girl. Mind you, I did encourage 'im! Different in wartime, though, isn't it?'

Suddenly Anthony made a strange noise, like a deep sigh. David quickly got up and went to him.

'That's odd,' he said, 'he hasn't made a sound like that before. Are you all right, Anthony?'

David looked intently at his son, whose left eye was twitching wildly.

'I think you might have triggered something there,' he said to Frank.

Gilda dashed over to Anthony who made the sighing noise again.

'What is it, *liebchen*?' she asked, smoothing his forehead, then turning to Frank she said, 'see, you've unsettled him with all this talk.'

Frank was worried. 'I'm sorry. Perhaps I shouldn't've come.'

'Not at all!' said David, 'it's been wonderful to meet you...'

'...but I think you should leave now,' said Gilda.

'Yes,' said Frank, concerned.

He offered his left hand to David who took it warmly. 'Please come back and see us again,' he said.

'I'll show you out,' said Gilda, leading him downstairs.

'I'm sorry if I upset 'im,' said Frank. 'Maybe I shouldn't come back.'

'Yes, that may be for the best,' said Gilda, as she shut the door behind him.

After Collins had left David proudly told Karl and Sonia what he had learnt about the brave things Anthony had done in Italy. 'He saved Collins' life! And it seems he had a lady-love, too - a girl called Isabella. She was already engaged, apparently. I wonder what happened to her?'

Gilda was sitting tensely, biting her lip.

'I expect her fiancé came back and she wanted to be with him,' said Karl.

'Yes...best to draw a line under it, I think,' said David. 'The main thing is that Anthony is home, safe, with us.'

Anthony's eye twitched, but Gilda chose to ignore it.

Sapper Collins! I never thought I'd be so pleased to see you! You've brought Isabella back to me! She's the one I've been grasping for, that figure just out of reach...I remember everything now. I loved her very, very much. I was going to return to Italy and marry her...

I wonder if her fiancé did come back? - Carlo, wasn't it? I feel a sudden pang of jealousy. I love her. She should be mine.

CHAPTER 30

Bath, 1948

After the Shabbat service and lunch Jacob, who was home from University for the Summer holidays, walked Gilda home through Victoria Park. He was studying politics and full of fervour for the Jewish cause; serious and intense, he had started wearing round, dark-rimmed spectacles which made him look older than his years. Not noticing the beauty of the trees in full leaf or the colourful flower beds, he spoke passionately about the creation of the new state of Israel which had been the subject of the Rabbi's sermon that morning.

'Imagine, Gilda!' Jacob cried, 'our own country, for our own people! It's what we've been fighting for all these years. It's our chance to show the world that we are not beaten – the Nazis tried to eradicate us, but they failed!'

'Yes, Jacob, it is very exciting,' said Gilda.

Jacob carried on talking but Gilda was more interested in the other news the Rabbi had told them - that Ausberg was being re-built, thanks to funding provided by the Allies. 'They blow us up, then they pay to re-build us!' he'd said. When she could get a word in edgeways Gilda asked, 'what do you think happened to those we left behind? Should we think the worst?'

233

'We'll never know for certain. Most people from Ausberg were taken to Auschwitz, and we all know what happened there…but Gilda, it's time to look to the future, not the past.'

They were almost back at Eagle House when he asked her, 'how are your nursing studies going, by the way?'

'Very well! I've passed my exams, and with our new National Health Service there are many opportunities,' she said, proudly. 'I'm going to specialise in neurology.'

He looked at her. 'Well done, Gilda, well done.'

When they reached the front gate Gilda glanced up and waved at Anthony who was in his usual position in the bay window. Jacob followed her eyes and stared with curiosity at Anthony for a few moments, then he turned back to Gilda and said, 'I must go now. I'll see you next week.' Jacob left and Gilda went indoors, running straight upstairs to Anthony's room.

I'm listening to the Glenn Miller orchestra on the Light programme – what happy memories it brings me! The music makes me want to tap my feet and dance, then they play 'Moonlight Serenade' and I start to feel my pulse racing. I can remember dancing with Isabella, holding her close…I can see her as plainly as if she were standing in this room. How I long to take her in my arms!

Gilda dashed in and turned off the wireless.

'I'm back, *liebchen*! You don't want to listen to the music now – I've got so much to tell you! The Rabbi was talking about Ausberg…'

234

Italy, 1948

The Autumn winds were blowing through Affossa when Isabella left the church after mass with her sister, Maria, two-year old Antonio toddling along between them holding their hands. They walked past the spot where Isabella used to meet someone, a long time ago, and past the café she never went to any more.

She spotted her husband's truck parked in a side street and they made their way over, climbing up onto the seat beside him. Isabella struggled; she was nine months pregnant and enormous. As she sat down she felt a searing pain across her belly and cried out.

'The baby!'

Carlo stepped on the accelerator, driving his truck as fast as it would go up to his in-laws' farmhouse. When they arrived Carlo helped his wife down from the truck while Maria carried Antonio indoors. Four hours later a baby's cry was heard from the bedroom.

'Carlo!' his mother-in-law called to him. 'You have a daughter! A beautiful daughter!'

Isabella looked down at her baby girl, Angelica, sucking at her breast. Isabella was content; Carlo was thrilled with his dark-haired daughter and told his wife over again how much he loved them both. Isabella knew she must put the past behind her; the birth of Angelica signalled the time to move on.

*

A year later, Isabella was in church, dressed in black, her face veiled.

Carlo's father, Luigi Spinetti, had died at the age of sixty-eight, worn out from years of hard work, and all the local community had turned out to pay their respects.

Back at *La Casa sulla Collina* after the service Carlo's mother, overcome with grief, declared that she had neither the will nor the energy to continue working and asked her son and his wife to take over the running of the farm and the vineyard.

Within days she moved her few possessions to the rooms at the end of the farmhouse so that Carlo, Isabella and their soon-to-be three children could move into the main part of the property. A new phase had begun.

Another change was underway at *La Casa Bianca* – Maria, Isabella's sister, was getting married to a factory worker she'd met at a dance in Ravenna. The heavily pregnant Isabella went to see her and the two sisters sat in the room they had shared for so long, surrounded by boxes that Maria was packing with clothes and other belongings.

'Mama wants me to clear the room so that Rosa can have it.'

Isabella laughed. Their younger sister had hankered after the room for years. Then, making sure no one was around, Maria got up and went to a drawer. 'I believe these are yours…' she said.

Isabella gasped as Maria produced a marquetry box inlaid with mother-of-pearl and an envelope containing some photographs. As she stared at the items she suddenly felt as if the last four years hadn't happened, that Antonio had left her only yesterday.

'Do you want them?' asked Maria.

What was the point?

Isabella took a deep breath. 'No, I don't...' she said, uncertainly.

She felt faint. Maria sat beside her and put her arm around her.

'Are you sure?' she said, gently.

Isabella wiped a tear from her eye.

'I could just throw them away,' said Maria.

'No! Please don't do that!'

For all of it, Isabella couldn't bear to see these relics of her past disappear. 'I'll take them,' she said.

When she got home Isabella went to the office at the back of the farmhouse. This was her new domain; she had happily taken on the role of managing the vineyard accounts and knew this was the one place Carlo would never step into. The wooden desk was ancient and had several drawers, some of which were hidden from view. She unlocked the most obscure, placed the box and the envelope containing the photos inside, and locked them away.

Her third child, Susanna, was born the following day.

England, 1950

In June, Tilly gave birth to Harriet, a blue-eyed cutie with curly blonde hair, and Henry was beside himself with joy. He could not believe how his life had altered in just a few years. Since his marriage he'd been promoted to Wing Commander, Tilly had used some of her father's cash to buy them a new family home near her parents, and now he was a father himself. He shared his thoughts with his brother.

237

'I'm so sorry you won't be able to have these things – a wife, a child. It seems so unfair. You know, sometimes I feel guilty that I can experience all this, and you can't. All I can do is try and share what I have with you, old man.'

Don't feel guilty on my behalf, Henry. In my mind I can see Isabella. I know that I have loved, and been loved.
Something has occurred to me though - I mean, I never took the precautions old Sergeant Hawkins used to warn all his soldiers to take. I just didn't think about it at the time, and in any case, being Catholic, Isabella probably wouldn't have wanted to anyway. But I do wonder…Christ…did I make her pregnant?

CHAPTER 31

Bath, 1951

In August Karl and Sonia held a party at Eagle House to celebrate Gilda's 21st birthday. It was a grand occasion; there were about forty guests, colleagues from the hospital, old schoolfriends, and several from the congregation at Mr Greenstein's hotel. Anthony was dressed in his best clothes and David stood back, rather enjoying this invasion of his house.

On the morning of the party Sonia and Karl presented their daughter with a gold Star of David pendant necklace. She went to the mirror, held it up against her and Karl stood behind her and fastened it.

'It's beautiful!' cried Gilda. 'I love it! Thank you, Mama, thank you Papa!' she cried, hugging them.

'We are so proud of you, *liebchen*!' they said, looking at their daughter who had blossomed into a fine, vivacious young woman.

For the party Sonia had made Gilda a red satin dress, its low décolletage displaying her best assets. Her black, curly hair tumbled around her shoulders, she was wearing red lipstick and her sparkling dark eyes were outlined with eyeliner. Gilda was pleased she felt well on this important occasion – the pains she suffered when it was her time of the month had been getting worse, but her mother told her that as a woman one had to put up with such things.

Sonia produced a banquet of kosher food and a birthday cake (saving up the still-present sugar ration) and by mid-afternoon the party was in full swing. Older guests who remembered Gilda as a little girl when she first arrived in Bath came up and kissed her, telling her how lovely she looked, and congratulating her on qualifying as a State Registered Nurse. She was considered a good match and various mothers thrust their sons in her direction, but they didn't interest her.

However, Gilda was pleased to see Jacob who had come down to Bath to visit his parents and join in the celebrations. They hadn't seen each other for a few months and there was a lot to catch up on. He had gained his degree in politics and found himself a job in London working for the *Jewish Chronicle* but what really excited him were all the new developments taking place in Israel.

'Do you know what they've done, Gilda? They've begun to plant a forest on the outskirts of Jerusalem called the Forest of the Martyrs. They're going to plant six million trees as a memorial to our people – all our relatives and friends who were murdered in the camps. We must never forget them. There is so much happening over there, Gilda! I'd love to be part of it!'

'You mean you want to go and live in Israel? What do your parents think?'

'Well, they know it's something I really want to do and I hope they'll support me. It's a wonderful opportunity!' he said, fervently.

At that point Henry and Tilly arrived with baby Harriet who immediately became the focus of attention.

David made a fuss of her saying, 'I still can't believe I'm a grandfather! What would Wendy think about *that*?'

Henry went over to Gilda and gave her a kiss. 'Happy birthday, Gilda! You look marvellous!' Then, turning to his brother, he said, 'doesn't she, Anthony?'

The afternoon took a musical turn with the birthday girl performing a couple of her favourite piano pieces, then one of the Jewish men took out his violin and played a plaintive, traditional song which made Sonia cry. Gilda recognised it as one her Uncle Franz used to play when they were in Ausberg. When the violinist finished a hush descended over the gathering. Then, without any further words, and mindful of the occasion, he struck up a joyful tune and everyone began to dance.

'I think it's a Jewish thing,' whispered Henry to Tilly — 'they're sad and maudlin one minute, and cheerful and laughing the next!'

Later, after a lot of wine had been consumed, the guests began to leave. Jacob had drunk his fair share and unsteadily beckoned Gilda out into the garden where they walked together in the fading light.

'Gilda,' he said, 'I have known you a long time and I'm pleased you are happy. You look beautiful today.'

She felt herself blushing. 'Thank you, Jacob. You have been a good friend to me.'

'I was serious earlier when I said about going to Israel.'

He turned to her.

'I want you to come with me!'

'WHAT?'

He took her hands in his. 'Come with me, Gilda! There are so many opportunities there for people like us – young people who believe in the future of Israel. You with your nursing, me with my politics and journalism...we could achieve so much together!'

She was stunned. 'But I couldn't, Jacob! England is my home now!'

'Be brave! Take a risk!' He paused. 'We could even get married if you want...'

Gilda gasped and withdrew her hands.

'No! No, Jacob, I don't want to marry you. It all sounds very exciting but I'm not the right person to do this with you. You don't need me!'

Jacob was so frustrated he paced around, practically tearing his hair out.

'But this is such a big chance! To be there, at the birth of a new country – what our people have been fighting for, for centuries!'

'I know, but I want to stay here. I can't leave my parents and I don't want to leave Anthony...'

'Aaah, Anthony...' he said, 'I should have known. It always comes down to him, doesn't it? It's unnatural, Gilda. You can't stay here forever, looking after that cripple!'

Gilda was shocked.

'How *dare* you call him that! He can't help being ill! He has done brave things, saved people's lives...' (some of Collins' words came back to her). 'And he was so kind to me when I was growing up, the least I can do is take care of him. I want nothing more.'

Jacob knew he was defeated.

'Very well - I'll go on my own. But I hate to see you wasting your life.'

He turned his back and stormed away, leaving Gilda standing in the garden, bewildered and unsure what had happened.

Well, that was quite a party. Gilda looked lovely today and I'm sure she enjoyed herself. One strange thing, though – after everyone had gone she sat with me for a while holding my hand, looking pensive. When her parents came to put me to bed she kissed me on the forehead as always and whispered, 'he's right, you know – it always comes down to you...'

*

David didn't want to get involved in personal matters but couldn't help but notice how Gilda was increasingly suffering every month, having to take to her bed and being in considerable pain. He felt he had to say something to Sonia.

'Has Gilda seen a doctor?'

'No - we keep hoping it will get better as she gets older.'

'But instead it's getting worse? Look, Sonia, it's none of my business, but I think Gilda really needs to see someone. Women don't have to suffer anymore - and with our new National Health Service you don't need to pay either! It's not just about false teeth and spectacles, you know! Look, why don't you make an appointment to take her to the GP?'

Gilda was worried but had reached the stage where she would do anything to have a normal life.

The doctor referred her to a consultant gynaecologist who examined her and called her back the following week for the test results.

'Miss Blumfeldt, I'm sorry to tell you that you are suffering from a serious condition called endometriosis. If we leave things alone your symptoms will worsen and you will suffer increasing pain. I recommend you have a hysterectomy. Do you understand what that is, Miss Blumfeldt?'

'Of course I do – I am a nurse!'

'Yes, of course, I'm sorry. But you understand what this means for you, personally? You won't be able to have children.'

Gilda nodded. She understood.

'Go home and discuss it with your parents, and let me know when you reach a decision.'

It took a while for the impact to sink in. Sonia was distressed at the prospect of never having grandchildren because Gilda was the end of the family line. But Karl said his daughter's health outweighed everything else, and if that was the best way to treat her condition, so be it. David agreed from a medical point of view, although it was sad for this to happen to such a young woman.

Gilda had never been sure whether she wanted children, but this was the harshest way for the decision to be made. It seemed she had little choice in the matter.

She was put on the waiting list and operated on two months later.

Her parents went to the hospital to see her.

'How are you, *liebchen*?'

'I feel weak, but I'm going to be all right.'

Gilda took several weeks off work to recuperate. She appreciated the extra time she had to spend with Anthony and would sit with him for hours, finding it comforting, being in his company.

'What an odd pair we are,' she said to him, 'in our twenties, but single and never to have any children…'

Poor Gilda. She's had a rough time of it. I squeeze her hand and she smiles at me as we sit, together.

CHAPTER 32

Italy, 1960

Isabella made regular trips to Milan to see Carlo's younger brother, Alberto, who had moved to the city to manage the marketing side of the expanding Spinetti-Fortuno wine business. She enjoyed her brother-in-law's company – he was more sophisticated than Carlo, closer to her own age, and acted as her guide, telling her about the latest fashions and happenings.

Since the end of the war, largely thanks to American money, Italian factories had thrived and entrepreneurs were helping cars, fashion, food and drink become the cornerstone of the country's recovery. Isabella longed to be part of these changes and to make her own contribution to Italy's growth and stature in the world.

On her next visit she took Antonio with her leaving Angelica, Susanna and her twin daughters, aged five, in the care of her mother. She felt it was time for her fourteen-year-old son to see the city and be introduced to the wider aspects of the wine trade. He was a bright, intelligent boy, interested in the family business and growing up fast. His eyes were hazel in colour and in his features he resembled Isabella, although his fair hair made him feel self-conscious and the object of teasing from his schoolmates.

They stayed in Alberto's apartment overnight and the next day he took them to the wine merchants who sold their produce and the fashionable cafés and restaurants that bought it. Antonio was fascinated. He loved the buzz and excitement of the big city - he had visited his Aunt Maria in Ravenna a few times, but Milan was something else.

In the afternoon they went to a pavement café and sat in the sunshine, wearing their sunglasses, watching the world go by. Alberto ordered a cola for Antonio and beers for himself and Isabella. Antonio watched, transfixed by the crowds of people, young men with smart suits and slicked-back hair, girls in mini-skirts and stiletto heels, Vespa scooters buzzing their way through the heavy traffic. Alberto looked at his nephew and laughed.

'It is exciting, being in the big city, no?'

'I have never seen anything like this before!'

Alberto sat back in his chair and lit a cigarette, his expensive watch glinting in the sunlight.

'See the people passing – watch them. You get ideas from them – what they buy, how they dress, how they laugh together. And when they come into the café, watch what they order – what is popular to drink. This is how I get ideas for our business.'

He paused.

'And...' he added with a wink, 'it's a good way to meet the prettiest girls!'

On their way back to Alberto's apartment Isabella looked in the shop windows displaying exquisite handbags and shoes, mostly manufactured in France.

'These are lovely, but it makes me so annoyed!' exclaimed Isabella. 'We Italians can produce designer goods just as well as the French, but we don't promote them enough. It's the same with our wine…'

They passed a shop selling fashions by a new, young Italian designer called Valentino.

'This is more like it!' said Isabella, 'I have read about him. His clothes are so beautiful, so glamorous…' she said, drooling over them.

Antonio said, 'one day, Mama, I will buy you a beautiful dress like this!'

She laughed.

'Did you hear that, Alberto? You can be my witness!'

Bath, 1961

In Bath, the post-war re-building programme was progressing apace. Large areas of inadequate housing had been cleared on the outskirts of the city, replaced by huge modern council estates which were not to everyone's taste, but people needed somewhere to live.

The city centre was crammed with cranes and construction equipment and chosen buildings were having a face-lift, covered in scaffolding and tarpaulins with water applied at high pressure to remove layers of soot and grime that had built up since the blitz.

David was interested in all the changes afoot and one evening he went along to the Guildhall to attend a public meeting with the enticing title: *Bath: a Vision for the Future!*

248

He watched as a young architect proudly unveiled a scale-model of the next phase of work revealing an extraordinary collection of ugly, cubist buildings and multi-storey blocks of flats in the city centre, wide new roads, bridges, schools and car parks. Huge swathes of Georgian and Victorian terraces were to be demolished to make way for this revolutionary new landscape which would increase business opportunities and bring prosperity to the city.

Someone in the audience mentioned preserving the city's historic past but they were quickly shouted down by those who said it was time to drag Bath into the twentieth century.

'Our city has seen many changes in its history and now is the time to make the next step,' said the architect. 'We must be brave and bold in the choices we make. What we decide today we will be living with for the next fifty, a hundred years. My belief is that a modern look is exactly what Bath needs.'

David was horrified by the proposals but held his tongue until a member of the public said the Germans had done them a favour when they had bombed the city, as it gave the chance to sweep away the slums and build anew.

David couldn't believe what he had heard. He stood up to protest on behalf of all those who had lost loved ones, called the new proposals a travesty, and insisted that the least the Council could do was to erect a memorial to those who had died in the Bath Blitz. Then he walked out.

Back at home David told the Blumfeldts what he had learnt.

'I mean, to destroy all those historic buildings without a thought. And what really made me angry was the way they want to forget about the blitz, as if those who were killed and injured don't matter! They're not even planning a memorial!'

The Blumfeldts were sympathetic, but it was only later when he was alone that David reflected that however much he had lost in the war, the Blumfeldts had lost much, much more.

*

Sonia was at the hairdressers, having her hair fashioned into the new 'beehive' style and chatting to a friend she knew from Mr Greenstein's. When she got home and her husband had got over the shock of seeing her new look, she mentioned something her friend had told her. Karl listened, patiently, and seeing the excitement on his wife's face said, 'well, if it would make you happy, *liebchen,* it sounds a good idea. Why don't you see what David thinks?'

So, that evening, Sonia broached the subject.

'Mr Greenstein's brother runs a hotel in Bournemouth,' she said, 'and he also owns apartments which he rents by the week, overlooking the sea. It's a popular place for Jewish people for holidays, apparently, and my friend who's just been there said it was lovely.'

David looked at her over the top of his newspaper and waited for her to get to the point.

'Well, I was thinking, perhaps we could go there for a holiday – all of us. Karl and Gilda, yourself, and Anthony.'

'We could hire the taxi to take Anthony, like we did when we went to Henry's wedding. In fact, Henry and Tilly could come too, with the children! Wouldn't that be wonderful!' She clapped her hands together, smiling at the thought. 'And we don't even have to worry about the cat any more...' added Sonia, with a touch of sadness at Lucky's demise.

David put his newspaper down.

'Maybe that's not such a bad idea,' he said. 'It would do us all good to get away for a break, get some sea air. We haven't had a holiday by the sea since the boys were small...' He thought for a moment of happy times when they stayed with Wendy's parents on the Isle of Wight, before the war – an age ago.

'All right, Sonia, let's have a look at some dates and see how it fits with everybody. Maybe we'll go for two weeks!'

And so it happened that in August the Roberts and Blumfeldts found themselves sitting together on a beach in Bournemouth, surrounded by the usual paraphernalia of an English seaside holiday – deckchairs, buckets and spades, picnic baskets, ice creams and beach balls. Anthony's chair was positioned in the centre of the group, ensuring he had a good view of the sea. Luckily the weather was good, sunny and warm with a pleasant breeze.

The children - Harriet, eleven years old, and her little brother Freddie, six, were playing happily together, running in and out of the cold sea, shrieking when they were caught by the waves. Henry and Tilly were thrilled to have a son, and Harriet loved having her new playmate to teach about life as she knew it.

251

Tilly was walking along the beach with Gilda, arm in arm, chatting, enjoying her company and the sea air. David and Karl were sitting reading their newspapers, and Sonia and Mrs Potts had brought their knitting. Henry had been buried in the sand by his children.

They ate their picnic lunch, with added sand, then Gilda went for a swim. She waved from the sea towards the group, smiling and laughing, and they waved back at her.

Sonia said to David, 'it is good to see her looking so happy. She has known some hard times, but she is very happy now.'

'Yes' said David, 'she's become a fine young woman. It's her birthday soon, isn't it? How old will she be?'

'Thirty-one.'

David paused.

'I wonder why she hasn't married? I know it's a shame she can't have children, but I'd have thought someone would have snapped her up by now…'

'Oh, I think we know the answer to that one!' said Sonia.

'What do you mean?'

'Well, David…I know we've never spoken of it, but I thought it would have been obvious…?'

'Sorry, I'm not following you. Unless you mean - she prefers other women? I always thought she was rather…'sporty'…?'

Sonia was shocked.

'Of course not! I'm surprised at you, David! How could you think of my daughter in that way! No, no, I didn't mean that at all!'

252

Sonia caught her breath and continued.

'On the contrary - Gilda has made good friends with some young men over the years – in fact there was one that I particularly liked, a good Jewish boy, too. But there's only ever been one man who has interested her…'

Gilda came bounding up the beach towards them, her ample breasts swaying, barely constrained by her swimming costume. She grabbed a towel and dried herself off. Exhilarated by the seawater and the waves, she smiled broadly as she shook out her wet hair.

'Oh, that was such fun!' she cried.

Then she stood behind Anthony's chair, put her hands on his shoulders and said, 'and are you enjoying yourself, *liebchen*? Could you see me waving to you, when I was in the water?'

She laughed and kissed the top of his head, then sat down on the ground beside his chair and hooked her arm around his leg.

Sonia gave David a knowing look.

We're back home now, after an exhausting but enjoyable holiday by the sea. I find it hard to cope with new routines, it saps my energy, but it was worth it.
And then there is Gilda...
Ever since that revelation on the beach…it's got me wondering, how do I feel about her? Grateful for all she does for me, of course, but - love?

CHAPTER 33

Isabella was feeling weary. She had been working hard in the vineyard, the girls had been playing up and at the grand age of thirty-six she was pregnant again. She prayed fervently for a son: Carlo was a wonderful father to Antonio, but the unspoken truth that lay between them had put a constant strain on their marriage which she hoped might be lessened if she could give her husband a son of his very own.

All she wanted to do was rest, so she went into her office, lay down on the couch and within minutes she was sound asleep.

In the living room Antonio, who didn't realise his mother was sleeping in the room next door, put a record on the gramophone.

Isabella is dreaming. She can hear the strains of an opera which she recognises - an aria from Tosca. She is transported to the amphitheatre in Affossa on a warm May evening with Antonio, her handsome English soldier. She is trying to explain to him why opera is so important and is feeling emotional. At the end of the performance she turns to him, loving him, desiring him. She leads him to the barn behind her parents' farmhouse where they take off their clothes and lie down together beside the sleeping goats. She can feel the straw, scratchy against her back, and the smooth skin of her lover, delighting in their nakedness as she guides him into her...

'*Antonio*!' she cried out.

Her son heard her, realised she was in her office and went to see if she was all right.

'What is it, Mama?' he said, kneeling down beside her, 'is it the baby?'

'*Antonio*,' she repeated, with a strange look in her eyes, her hand reaching out.

The boy took her hand. 'I'm here, Mama, don't worry. I think you were dreaming…'

Suddenly Isabella was wide awake.

'Antonio!' she exclaimed, seeing her son.

She could hear the music on the gramophone.

'Why are you playing that?' she said, angrily, sitting up.

'We're studying *Tosca* at school, the music teacher lent us the record to listen to. Why, Mama, don't you like it?'

'No, I don't!' she said, pushing herself up from the couch. She went into the lounge, snatched the record from the gramophone and threw it across the room where it smashed to pieces.

The boy was terribly upset. He had never seen his mother so angry.

'Mama, see what you've done – it's not mine, it belongs to the school! I'll get into trouble!' he cried, his eyes brimming with hot tears of incomprehension.

'Never play that again!' she shouted, and left the room.

Later, contrite, she apologised to her son.

'I'm sorry I was so angry earlier – forgive me. I have been so tired.'

'Here,' she said, giving him some money, 'go and buy a new record for your school, and treat yourself to something too.'

Antonio remained puzzled, but took the money gratefully.

In the Spring Isabella gave birth to a son, a healthy, strong boy with dark eyes and black hair. At last she had given Carlo what he craved and they named the boy Luigi, after Carlo's father. The girls adored him and the oldest, Angelica, at fourteen, proved to be a great help, assisting her mother with the baby and looking after her younger sisters.

Antonio was pleased for his family but at the same time felt removed from it; he wasn't interested in babies and the way his father clucked over this dark, new arrival made him feel left out and slightly jealous.

Antonio had hit adolescence with a vengeance and grown several inches in a year, his limbs becoming long and gangly. Although he ate like a horse he looked so skinny you could see his ribs; it was as if he had been stretched and thinned-out. At the age of sixteen he was nearly six feet tall, towering over his siblings and his parents, his features became more angular and his hair remained stubbornly fair.

He was painfully aware of the changes taking place in his body and how different he looked from all the other members of his family, feeling like a stranger in his own home. He spent as little time there as possible, preferring to be with his friends, and realised that some girls found his unusual looks attractive.

One in particular called Joanna took a shine to him and during the Summer holidays he started seeing her at her parents' farm just outside Bassino. The two rode horses together, taking picnics into the countryside, and she tried to kiss him, but Antonio froze and didn't know how to respond to her. They let it pass and remained friends.

When Joanna's brother Ricco returned home from university in Ravenna the three of them went riding together. Ricco talked about life in the city and Antonio found himself warming to this older, more worldly boy with his charming smile.

One afternoon they returned to the farm, exhilarated by their canter through the fields. They settled the horses and gave them a rub down, then Joanna went indoors leaving the boys alone together.

'That was fun,' said Ricco. 'You ride well. It's been good meeting you.'

Then he turned to Antonio, looked at him and touched his face.

'You are handsome,' he said. 'I love your fair hair. It is so different from most people round here. Where did you get that from, I wonder?'

Antonio, feeling embarrassed, said, 'my mother tells me it is from my great-grandmother.'

Ricco sniggered.

'That's what she told you, eh?'

'Yes' said Antonio, awkwardly.

Ricco ruffled his hair.

'And you believe your Mama because you love her!'

'Of course!'

Ricco put his hands on Antonio's shoulders.

'It doesn't matter where it's from,' he said, 'I find you very attractive.'

And he kissed him, full on the lips.

Antonio was shocked. He pushed Ricco away and swore at him, but he just laughed.

'Go, then, run away home! But next time you come to see Joanna, make sure you see me too!'

Antonio ran all the way back to *La Casa sulla Collina*, wiping his mouth with the back of his hand but unable to remove the lingering taste of Ricco's kiss.

Antonio didn't go up to the farm again that Summer, he was too confused by what Ricco had said and done. Antonio couldn't get the boy out of his mind; his kiss had both aroused and repelled him, and Ricco's comments about his hair brought to the surface doubts he had harboured for years. Why would his mother lie to him? The more Antonio thought about it, he'd been aware all his life of people looking at him in a strange way, as if he didn't belong. Even Aunt Maria treated him as if he were different from his siblings. He began to question everything he had ever known. Was it possible that Carlo wasn't his real father? And if he wasn't, who was?

CHAPTER 34

England, 1962

Group Captain Henry Roberts was watching from his office window as a squadron of 'V'- bombers took off from the Air Station.

'Let's see how they get on then, sir,' said his second-in-command.

'Indeed,' said Henry. 'I'll join you in the briefing room in half an hour.'

'Yes, sir.'

As Henry watched the jets go, part of him wanted to be out there with them, getting a piece of the action, but age and rank dictated otherwise and as Station Commander his role was to direct rather than to do. It felt good to be back at the sharp-end of his business – flying planes. He wasn't personally in the cockpit, but tactical air warfare was familiar territory and his experience was being put to good use.

He sat down and lit his pipe. The situation was serious. Tensions between the Soviet Union and the United States were mounting and the threat of nuclear war was palpable. The RAF was in the frontline of Britain's defences and 'V' bombers had become the guardian of the country's nuclear deterrent.

On this occasion, it was an exercise: the jets had taken off in response to a practice alert and were headed towards Eastern Europe, flying low over potential targets. But next time it could be for real.

Henry looked at the framed photographs on his desk – a black and white portrait of his beautiful wife and an informal picture of her playing with Harriet and Freddie on the beach at Bournemouth last year. He couldn't bear the thought of another war. That's why what he was doing was so important - the RAF had a vital role to play in keeping the peace and he was proud to be part of it.

Back at home, Tilly was bored. Their home was organised just as she wanted it, she employed a housekeeper to deal with the routine jobs and Freddie was away at school. Even her younger sister Celia had upped sticks and moved to Australia – she'd gone there to study marine biology, fallen in love with a rugged-looking deep-sea diver and stayed there. And Tilly hardly saw her brother Peter now he was married with children.

She missed Henry, away at the Station in Lincolnshire all week, and sometimes at the weekends too. She knew how important his work was and in truth she was rather envious of him. He never spoke to her about the Top Secret tasks for which he was responsible but, from her own experiences during the War, she could guess what was involved. How she missed the excitement of those days! Much as she loved her home and family, sometimes she wished she was back in the Hut at Bletchley Park with Beatrice and the rest of the gang…

Tilly completed the *Times* crossword as she always did, speedily, every morning, and the long day stretched ahead. She picked up a copy of the village magazine and was browsing through it when among the adverts for handymen and gardeners an article caught her eye. A woman she knew – the mother of one of Harriet's friends – was organising a charity event to raise money for disabled ex-servicemen. This was a cause close to their hearts, so Tilly rang her and asked if she could help.

'That would be marvellous, darling!' said the woman, 'we're having a committee meeting this afternoon, do come over!'

Henry came home for the weekend to find the study full of giant teddy bears, cheap and tacky gifts, gaily painted signs, hessian sacks full of coconuts and other paraphernalia of an English fete.

'What the…?!'

'Well there was nowhere else to put it all,' said Tilly, 'and it's all in a good cause. You don't mind, do you, darling? I've been so bored with you being away. It's either this or I find myself a lover…'

*

It was a year for public disgrace, and every day seemed to bring a new tale of trouble in high places. Reading her *Daily Mail* Mrs Potts was engrossed by the shocking reports of sex scandals, corruption, spy rings and sleaze, forcing her to read long extracts to Anthony, savouring all the lurid details.

'Who'd have thought it?' she said to Anthony, 'all those posh people behaving so badly. I heard a rumour, you know, that some of them meet up at a house near Corsham...can you imagine all the goings-on!'

I listen with interest and not a little jealousy! I'm afraid sex parties and shenanigans have passed me by - the only excitement I ever get is watching our new television!

Life is pretty routine nowadays. I miss Henry — he's so busy with work that he doesn't have much time to come down and see us. I'd love to have a proper conversation with him about his job - I'm proud of him and his achievements. His family are so important to him. I can see how he draws his strength from his children, and Tilly is marvellous — there is definitely something special about her. God, I wonder what sort of a father I might have made, if things had been different...

CHAPTER 35

Italy, 1962

One cold and rainy weekend in October Isabella had a migraine and stayed in bed. She lay there with her eyes closed then suddenly remembered something. She struggled out of bed and called to her son.

'Antonio – I'm sorry, *caro*, I am not well. But I need your help. The auditor is coming today.'

Antonio went upstairs to her.

'What is it, Mama?'

'Here are my office keys. Please will you go there and get the account books? I keep them in the top drawer of my desk. You can give them to the auditor when he arrives.'

'Yes, of course, Mama,' said Antonio, 'You must rest. I hope you feel better soon.'

'Thank you,' she said, weakly, and lay back on her bed.

Antonio went down to the office to the ancient desk and tried several keys before he found the correct one. He took out the books, locked the drawer, then, out of curiosity, tried some of the other keys to see what else was in there – his mother guarded her desk fiercely and he'd never had the chance to look inside before.

In one drawer he was surprised to find a significant amount of lire squirrelled away; the vineyard workers were due to be paid, but this was more than was needed for that. Perhaps his mother had a secret nest egg?

In another he found some old photos of his mother as a baby with her parents at *La Casa Bianca*. Then, hidden away at the back of the desk, he opened a drawer containing a marquetry box, inlaid with mother-of-pearl, and an envelope.

He took out the box, unlocked it with its little silver key, lifted the lid and was surprised to hear the tune from *Tosca* that had so enraged his mother when he had played the record on the gramophone. Inside, he found a sepia photograph of a fair-haired young man, a soldier in British Army uniform. Antonio gasped. It was like looking in a mirror. In his shock he dropped the box and the photo fluttered to the floor. He picked it up, his hands shaking, turned it over and read:

'To my beautiful Isabella, all my love, Anthony, May '45. Ritornerò.'

His heart was thumping and his mind was racing.

May '45. He could do the arithmetic. This man, this foreign stranger, his look-a-like, must be his father. And he was called Anthony - isn't that English for Antonio?

Antonio put the photo in his trouser pocket then took the envelope from the drawer, looked inside and found more photos of his beautiful, young mother with the same soldier at some kind of celebration, obviously in love, clutched in a passionate embrace…

Antonio couldn't cope with all this. He tore up the photographs, threw the pieces into the air and fled from the office. He ran out of the farmhouse into the rain and kept going, he didn't know where, tears streaming down his face.

What should he do? Should he challenge his mother? Did Carlo know about this? How could he look his parents in the eye again?

When he had no breath left he stopped running and found he was near Joanna's parents' farm. He stood there, not knowing what to do, when he saw Ricco walking towards him.

'Antonio! It is good to see you! But what is the matter, my friend?'

Antonio couldn't speak but was grateful for the attention. Together they walked into the farmhouse where Ricco fetched him a drink.

'Now, Antonio,' he said, sitting beside him, 'take your time. If you want to talk, I will listen.'

Any awkwardness Antonio felt about seeing Ricco again evaporated in the face of this new discovery. He showed him the photograph he'd found in the wooden box.

Ricco whistled.

'He certainly does look a lot like you...' he said, then, looking at the date, added, 'your Mama must have been pregnant with you when she married your Papa. It must have been very difficult for her...'

'So it's all my fault!' exclaimed Antonio, distraught.

'Of course not! And she loves you. But I wonder what happened to the soldier?'

'He deserted her!' said Antonio, growing angry, 'he said he would return, but he didn't. I hate him!'

'But you don't know what happened - there might be all sorts of reasons why he didn't come back. I don't suppose even your Mama knows.' He paused. 'So what are you going to do?'

'I don't know…' said Antonio. 'I can't stay on the farm. I won't be able to look at my father – Carlo. Or my mother.'

'But where else would you go?'

'I don't know…oh, this is so hard!'

Ricco put a comforting arm around him and Antonio let himself be held. There was something about this older boy with his muscular arms and soothing voice that he found reassuring.

Ricco's mother came in from the farmyard and said, 'Antonio! How nice to see you! Are you all right?'

'Antonio had an argument at home,' said Ricco, 'but I think he is feeling better now – aren't you?'

'Stay and eat with us!' said his mother. 'I've made my special lasagne!'

'Come on,' said Ricco – 'my Mama's lasagne is the best!'

'All right,' said Antonio, 'that's very kind of you.'

After the meal and several glasses of wine, Ricco walked Antonio back home. Darkness was falling.

'You need to make a plan,' said Ricco. 'You could come and stay with me in Ravenna for a few days if you want...'

'Thank you – I'll think about it…'

As they approached *La Casa sulla Collina* Antonio, unsteady on his feet due to the wine, grasped Ricco's shoulder and said, 'thank you, Ricco, you have really helped me today.'

'That's all right. I'm very happy to help the best-looking boy in town.'

Ricco drew Antonio towards him and kissed him on the mouth, lingeringly. This time, Antonio returned his kiss. This was going to be easier than Ricco had thought. He looked around for somewhere to go.

He spotted a barn with its door ajar and guided Antonio towards it, kissing him all the while. He led him inside and within minutes they were having sex in ways that Antonio hadn't even known were possible.

*

Isabella, still feeling rough, had got up to make the evening meal for the family. Later, she went out into the farmyard to get some air and check on the animals before locking up for the night. As she walked past the barn she heard strange noises, heavy breathing and a whimpering sound, like an animal in trouble. She opened the barn door and shined her torch inside.

She couldn't believe what she saw.

There was Antonio, her son, naked in the straw with his lover, arms and legs, fair hair and dark hair tangled together, their bodies moving in a way which was familiar, but different...

For a split second she had a flashback to that last night in the barn with her own lover, before he had gone away, forever.

Then a thunderbolt struck as she came back to the present. Her beloved son was with a man.

She screamed with shock, dropped the torch, and screamed again.

As Carlo came running out of the house Ricco shot out of the barn carrying a bundle of clothes and sprinted away into the night, his white buttocks visible in the moonlight.

Isabella was still screaming.

Carlo went into the barn and dragged Antonio to his feet.

'Put some clothes on, you disgusting pervert!' he cried.

Angelica came out to see what was happening; all the commotion had wakened the children.

'Go back inside!' Isabella shouted at her, 'now! And keep the children upstairs! Tell them...tell them Mama was hurt by one of the goats, but she'll be all right. Tell them to go back to sleep...'

Angelica, horrified at the look on her parents' faces, ran back indoors.

'What is this?' cried Carlo, angry, incredulous, repulsed. 'What do you think you are doing? You are worse than an animal! You bring shame on your family!'

He turned away from Antonio in revulsion.

Isabella was weeping, saying, 'it's a sin, you will go to Hell for this!'

'I cannot believe that any son of mine could commit so horrible an act!' shouted Carlo. 'You disgust me! Get out of my house!'

Antonio looked at him and screamed back, 'don't worry, I'm going. And anyway, I'm not your son!'

Isabella fell to the ground and Carlo knelt beside her, holding her.

'How dare you say that! See what you have done to your mother!'

'I don't care! It's the truth! You're not my father, Carlo. Didn't you know? Didn't my whore of a mother tell you?'

Antonio's words struck Isabella to the core.

'GET OUT!' she screamed at him, 'get out of my sight, NOW! I never want to see you again, you filthy, worthless…'

Carlo got up and swung his fist at Antonio but he dodged the blow and turned and ran.

Isabella stayed on the ground, crying hysterically. Carlo got down beside her and the two clung together in a helpless state as Antonio disappeared into the blackness.

*

After Antonio had fled Isabella and Carlo struggled to their feet and went back inside the farmhouse, saying nothing. Carlo went upstairs to bed; he couldn't bear to look at his wife. Isabella took refuge in her office. She could see what had happened: the desk drawers were open and the musical box was on the floor surrounded by torn-up photographs.

Isabella gasped and cursed herself for having kept these wretched souvenirs of her past. It was so long ago she'd forgotten they were there. She couldn't bear the shambles around her, the mess she had made of her life. Her face wet with tears she checked to see if the money was still in the drawer - the lire she had saved to give her children when they were older. She saw with relief that it was.

Her son may be a sodomite – Holy Mother, it pained her even to think the word - but he wasn't a thief.

Still crying, Isabella picked up the scattered pieces of photographs and the wooden box, took them into the kitchen where the stove was always lit, and put them on the fire.

She watched as the photos singed, curled up and turned to ash. The wooden box caught fire, sparking and crackling, the silver key and the mother-of-pearl melting away in the heat, the musical mechanism disintegrating until nothing was left.

CHAPTER 36

Italy, 1962

Antonio ran and ran through the night until he was exhausted and collapsed under a tree where he stayed, sleeping on and off until sunrise. He awoke and started walking, soaked to the skin, until he reached the main road to Ravenna. He thought about going there to find Ricco, although judging by the way he had bolted out of the barn the night before, Antonio wasn't sure he'd be welcome. All he wanted was to be as far away from home as possible. He stuck out his thumb as he had seen hitchhikers do and eventually a lorry pulled up at the side of the road. The driver opened the passenger door.

'Where are you headed?' he asked, looking at the bedraggled figure.

Antonio turned the question around.

'Where are *you* headed?' he asked.

'Milan.'

Antonio nodded, and climbed up beside the driver.

They arrived in Milan late in the afternoon. The lorry driver had taken pity on the young lad who had no money or possessions with him; Antonio told him he'd left in a hurry after a row with his parents and needed to get away for a few days. The driver bought him a meal which Antonio ate ravenously and gratefully, then dropped him in the city centre.

'You know someone here?' he asked.

'Yes, my uncle.'

'Best of luck, kid,' said the driver, and went on his way.

It was only during the journey that Antonio had thought about Uncle Alberto. Of all his relatives, he might be willing to help him. He remembered roughly where Alberto lived from when he and his mother had stayed there two years ago. It seemed like an age away.

Antonio walked the streets and it was late evening when he found Alberto's apartment. He pressed the bell and after the shock of seeing his nephew standing there, dishevelled and clearly in a bad way, Alberto ushered him inside. He knew better than to ask questions so he ran Antonio a bath, found him some clean clothes and shared his meal with him. It was only then that Alberto sat back, lit a cigarette, looked at his nephew and said, '*Allora*? – well, then?'

'I had a big row with Mama and Papa and they threw me out. But Carlo is not my father, this man is.' Antonio took the photograph from his pocket and showed him.

Alberto examined the picture and the message written on the back. He raised an eyebrow.

'So, a British soldier…' he said, nodding, as if something made sense.

'There!' cried Antonio, picking up on his uncle's reaction, 'I'm beginning to think that everybody knew except me!'

Antonio told his uncle how he'd run from the farmhouse and sought comfort with a friend. 'And then…Mama found us together in the barn…'

He stopped talking and reddened.

'Aaah, I see. So you have the problem with your Papa and the problem with the girl. Have you got her into trouble, Antonio?'

Antonio looked at the floor, embarrassed.

'It's not so easy…' He hesitated. He may as well be honest, he had nothing to lose.

'Uncle, it wasn't a girl…'

Alberto nearly choked on his cigarette. Even he was shocked.

'God in heaven! Well, no wonder your parents were so upset!'

Alberto considered himself a man of the world who mixed with a sophisticated group of people, but his own nephew…He thought for a moment, then said, 'Antonio, I am sorry this has happened. You are still very young. Sometimes at your age it isn't always easy to know if you prefer the boys or the girls - but going with boys is more dangerous…'

He was thinking fast. In their country homosexuality was an issue of religion and morality, rather than a criminal matter. It wasn't illegal as such, but he was concerned that the family name and business could be tainted. He had to get his nephew away from here.

Alberto lit another cigarette and said, 'look, Antonio, if you really think that is what you want – if that is how God made you – then you must go somewhere where it is safe. Now, I have an idea. I have a friend in Amsterdam who runs a restaurant - he owes me a favour. I will write to him saying you need work experience and somewhere to stay.'

'I have been to Amsterdam, Antonio, and I know that these - what can I say – 'relations with men' - are more acceptable than here in Italy. But it can be a dangerous world - you must be discreet and you must be careful. I will do this for you because you are my nephew and I love you. But don't mess it up!'

In truth Antonio wasn't even sure where Amsterdam was, but if it meant being far away from his parents, having a job and somewhere to stay he was all for it. For the first time he could begin to see a way out of his troubles.

'Uncle, that would be wonderful!' he exclaimed, 'Thank you! Please tell your friend I'll work really hard. And don't tell Mama or Papa where I am - not that they care, anyway…'

'I will give you your train fare. But after that, you are on your own. Understand?'

*

Isabella spent the night on the couch in her office and cried herself to sleep. She awoke at dawn, got up and took herself up to their bedroom where she found Carlo, also awake, sitting on the side of the bed, his head in his hands. She sat down beside him.

'I never want to see him again,' said Carlo, quietly. 'I have loved and raised him as my own, but the things he said…the things he did…I can't, Bella. I can't…'

They sat together for a moment, then Isabella, her throat dry from all the tears she had shed, whispered, 'but what are we going to say to the children? And to our parents?'

Carlo rubbed his face with his gnarled hands.

'I don't know, Bella. But we certainly can't tell them the truth!'

They sat in silence. Outside the morning was slowly coming to life, the cock crowed and the goats were bleating, needing to be milked.

Carlo had been turning ideas over in his mind all night. There was one that just might work.

'Look – we could tell them he's gone to join the Army. He'd be due to do his military service in a couple of years anyway, so what if we say he was so keen, he couldn't wait, and a friend of his persuaded him…'

'…we objected and had a big argument…' continued Isabella,

'…and he walked out!' Carlo concluded.

They looked at each other.

'It might work,' said Isabella, nodding her head slowly. 'But where shall we say he's gone?'

'Italian East Africa!' said Carlo.

'Perfect!' exclaimed Isabella, surprised at her husband's inventiveness.

'I can tell you, Bella, when I was with the partisans during the war I met some soldiers who had served out there. It's certainly a long way away.'

'Carlo, you are a genius!' said Isabella. Then she paused. They had many other things to discuss.

'*Caro*…we will have to talk. I don't know if you can ever forgive me…'

Carlo turned to her, his face furrowed and leathery from years working outside under the hot sun. Even his beautiful Bella looked her age this morning.

The slender, young girl he had loved so much had gone. Six children and hard work had thickened her waist, drawn fine lines on her face, and now, after the row with Antonio, her eyes were full of sorrow.

Moreover, the implicit understanding they had had for so long had been shattered.

'Bella,' he said to her, gently, 'I can't forgive you – not yet. Things have changed between us. We need time to mend ourselves. And we have five more children to raise. We'll tell them our story, as we've agreed – who knows, we may even end up believing it ourselves! But the other things...I need time, Bella – I need time...'

He kissed her on her forehead.

'Just one thing,' he concluded. 'For the moment I'd prefer to sleep alone, in the spare room.'

Isabella felt humbled. She had never heard her husband speaking so seriously or so wisely.

'Yes, *caro*, I understand,' she said.

At breakfast Carlo announced to the family that Antonio had gone and they didn't know when he would be coming back. The older children weren't convinced by the reasons he gave and the younger ones cried, upset that their beloved big brother had left them without saying goodbye. To stop further speculation Carlo said, 'your mother is very upset by all of this. Please don't make it worse for her by asking questions.'

With that the children were dispatched to school, Carlo went into the vineyard and Isabella went to church in Bassino where she spent the whole morning on her knees in prayer.

She blamed herself for what had happened: she had deceived everyone about Antonio's true father and this was her punishment. She prayed to the Holy Mother and begged forgiveness for her sins, but she couldn't bring herself to forgive Antonio for his.

Isabella didn't know where her son had gone, didn't care what happened to him and never wanted to see him again.

Amsterdam, 1962

Antonio was washing dishes in the restaurant, tedious work but at least he had somewhere to sleep and plenty to eat. Max, the restaurant owner, was happy to let the nephew of his friend Alberto have a room as long as he worked hard and did what he was told. He had no interest in why the kid had left home and asked no questions.

Antonio couldn't stop thinking about the British soldier whose photo he had kept. He still found it hard to accept the truth; he would always think of Carlo, the man who had raised and loved him, as his 'real' father. Antonio questioned his own identity: he was half-English, for God's sake! And what about his feelings for Ricco? When it all came too much to bear Antonio took solace in a nearby brown café, smoking strange cigarettes which helped dull the pain.

After weeks of being stuck in the kitchen Antonio never wanted to wash another dish again, so when one of the bar staff got sick he saw his opportunity and offered to help. Max agreed and showed him the basics. Unaware of the irony he also taught Antonio some rudimentary English, being a more useful language than Dutch.

The bar was always busy; Amsterdam was a cosmopolitan city, thriving in the post-war boom, and all nationalities and types were catered for. The young, blonde Italian soon became a favourite with the customers and one evening a well-built, distinguished man started chatting to him and invited him to a party.

'Come when you finish your shift,' he said, giving him a card with his address. 'My name is Leo. You'll have fun…'

After work Antonio found the house in a fashionable part of the city. Music was blaring, all the lights were on and through the window he could see semi-naked people dancing. A drunk young woman answered the door and pulled him inside.

'Leo invited me?' said Antonio.

'Come in!' cried the woman. 'Leo! One of your boys is here…nice, isn't he?'

'Welcome, Antonio! Come and meet my friends!' Leo put his arm around Antonio's shoulders and ushered him into a room at the back of the house where a dozen or so middle-aged men were drinking and smoking cannabis. They flocked around Antonio and looked him up and down.

'Very nice…'

'I haven't had an Italian for a long time…'

'And so tall, so fair…!'

'How old are you, sweetheart?'

'Sixteen.'

'Aaahhh…sixteen…' leered one of the men.

Antonio was unnerved. 'I think I'd better go…' he said, turning to leave.

'Certainly not!' cried Leo, grasping his arm, firmly. 'Here, have a drink.'

278

To steady his nerves Antonio gulped down the strong alcohol while Leo said, 'now, young man, how would you like to earn yourself a lot of money?'

Italy, 1962

Isabella was in Milan for a business meeting with Alberto. He was apprehensive about seeing her, wondering what she might say about Antonio. When they met at their usual café he was shocked by her appearance - in just a few months she had aged and her eyes had a dullness to them. The bitter estrangement from her son was hitting her badly. He didn't make any comment, just reduced the level of his usual bonhomie and gently gestured to her to sit down while he ordered a bottle of wine. When they were settled Isabella said,

'Alberto, I have some news. Antonio has joined the Army! He's gone to Africa!'

Alberto spluttered and spilt wine over his trousers. Wiping himself down with his napkin, he managed to say, 'really?'

'Yes!' proclaimed Isabella. 'A friend persuaded him to go. Carlo and I were against it and we had a big row, and he left!'

'Well, that is a surprise…!' said Alberto, thinking, nobody will believe it, but it's probably the best they could cook up. 'So what happens now?'

'Well, the children are terribly upset. I don't think his father and I will ever be able to forgive him. So, we are putting him out of our minds. I am teaching Angelica about the business – she is a fast learner.'

'That's good,' said Alberto, who liked his oldest niece and suspected that Isabella had neglected her in favour of Antonio.

'I'm sure she will be an asset to you. You must bring her with you next time you come.'

Antonio never did go back to the bar. Max heard on the grapevine that Leo had taken him under his wing and took no further interest.

At first, life was good. Antonio was Leo's favourite and he liked having the handsome young Italian on his arm when he went to fancy restaurants and clubs, as well as in his bed. He bought him smart suits from fashionable London designers, gold chains to wear around his neck and an expensive watch. He also gave him pills which gave Antonio the highest highs but to which he quickly became addicted.

After a few months another young man caught Leo's eye so he moved Antonio out of his house and installed him in a small flat on the outskirts of the city. It was a simple arrangement: Leo sent men to him for sex and paid him in cash which Antonio stashed under his mattress. Antonio had no choice: he was addicted to the pills Leo fed him and was completely under his control.

*

When Antonio turned eighteen Leo chucked him out. 'Sorry, *mio amore Italiano*,' he said, holding Antonio's face between his hands, 'you've been wonderful, but my customers prefer younger boys. I'm giving you a day's notice then I want you gone.'

Antonio was in despair. He had nowhere to go and when he looked under his mattress all his money had vanished.

CHAPTER 37

London, 1964

Henry was fed up. He sat at his London desk looking out the window onto Whitehall, then back at the pile of papers in front of him that he had to deal with, many with red flags labelled 'IMMEDIATE!' Some days he yearned to be a Flying Officer again, soaring through the skies in his beloved Spitfire, but in this career the further up the ranks you travelled the further away it took you from why you joined in the first place.

The phone rang.

'Air Commodore Roberts, the appointers want to see you. An opportunity's come up which might appeal to you...'

Henry returned home on Friday evening as usual, found his wife in the kitchen and said,

'Tilly, darling – how do you fancy going to Paris?'

'That would be lovely – what, for the weekend?'

'No,' Henry replied, 'for three years!'

He produced a bunch of flowers from behind his back, picked her up, twirled her around and kissed her.

'You're looking at the next Air Attaché to Her Majesty's Embassy in Paris!'

I'm thrilled about Henry and his new job. It's a great opportunity for him and his family. Dad and I will miss them, though – it does lighten things up a bit when the children come to see us. Dad is slowing down now, and Karl and Sonia aren't getting any younger. It's Gilda that keeps us all going.

Paris, 1964

Henry came home from his first meeting with the Ambassador and his senior staff looking rather subdued.

'How did it go, darling?' asked Tilly, bringing him a whisky. He looked like he needed it.

He sat down on the Louis Quinze sofa and sighed.

'Quite honestly, Tilly, I found the whole thing difficult to follow - it was as if they were speaking in some kind of code. I'm almost wondering if I'm up to this…'

'Don't say that, darling - whatever do you mean?'

'Well…they don't really discuss events, or facts – they seem to pick up signals which I'm just not tuned into – a raised eyebrow, a scratch of the nose…and they were all fawning over some tweedy woman, a bigwig from the Foreign Office…'

'Aah - welcome to the world of the diplomat!' said Tilly.

'Yes - of course, that's what it is!' said Henry in realisation. 'Look, I'm a simple pilot – I can fly a plane, but this is beyond me. Have you got any advice?'

The actual move to Paris had gone well - they were allocated an extensive, beautifully furnished apartment close to the Embassy and the children were found places at the International School. Henry had learnt it was best to let Tilly get on with things and she was in her element, organising their new world. All Henry needed was a little time to adjust to this most unusual job, grow confident in speaking French and learn what the hell he was supposed to be doing.

Two weeks after their arrival they attended their first reception at the Embassy. The president of an obscure African country was visiting and the Air Attaché and his wife were required to put in an appearance. At home they prepared themselves for the evening, Henry in his best dress uniform with his DFC and Tilly with her hair up, wearing a midnight blue, satin gown and a stunning diamond necklace her mother had lent her for just this sort of occasion.

'What a handsome pair we make!' she said as they stood in front of the long, gilt-edged mirror in the vast hallway of their Paris apartment.

'You look beautiful, darling!' said Henry, and kissed her.

They arrived at the Embassy and entered the historic, ornate room hung with chandeliers where the reception was being held. It was noisy with people chattering, waiters serving drinks and canapés from silver trays and a string quartet playing in the background. Tilly, instantly at home, sensed her husband's unease and squeezed his arm.

'Don't worry, you'll be fine!' she whispered to him, encouragingly.

They approached a few familiar faces then worked their way around the crowd. Henry spotted the woman he'd seen at his meeting the previous week and pointed her out to his wife.

'At least she's looking less tweedy tonight!' he said. Tilly looked over at the woman who was wearing an elegant black dress and exclaimed, 'good God!'

She walked over to her, leaving Henry trailing in her wake, and when the woman saw Tilly there were cries of delight, kissing of cheeks and a hug.

'Beatrice!'

'Tilly! What on earth are you doing here?'

'I'm with my husband…' Tilly looked around for him and Henry arrived, looking slightly bemused.

'The new Air Attaché…' she said, shaking Henry's hand, 'I had no idea you were Tilly's husband!'

'Beatrice and I were in the same year at Cambridge,' said Tilly, by way of explanation, 'then we worked together during the War…'

'Oh, I see,' said Henry. 'You used to make the tea as well, did you?'

The women looked at him, then at each other, and laughed.

'Well they did used to drink an awful lot, didn't they?' said Beatrice. 'Now, come and tell me all about yourselves…'

Henry learnt that night that being 'Tilly's husband' opened doors that he hadn't even known were there. He was also intrigued that his wife was so friendly with, and had worked alongside, a formidable senior diplomat. As they got ready for bed Henry looked at Tilly sitting at the dressing table taking off her necklace.

She caught his reflection in the mirror as he stared at her.

'What are you looking at?'

He stretched out on the bed.

'I'm looking at my beautiful wife to whom I have been married for sixteen years…and I still find her full of surprises.'

Tilly raised her eyebrows.

'So talented, so clever…so good at making tea…!'

She smiled. 'If you must know,' she said, getting into bed, 'I may have done the odd bit of typing as well…'

He laughed, took her in his arms and kissed her.

'Tilly Roberts, you are phenomenal!'

*

September 1965 saw the twenty-fifth anniversary of the Battle of Britain. As Air Attaché Henry was responsible for organising the celebrations and the fact that he was a war hero with a DFC who had actually taken part in the Battle was beyond the Ambassador's wildest dreams.

'This will be the best one yet!' he declared to Henry. 'No pressure!'

David and Tilly's brother Peter flew over for the special event which involved a garden party in the Embassy grounds for dignitaries and veterans from all the countries involved, speeches and a fly-past of vintage aircraft. Henry gave a stirring speech, vividly recalling his part in the Battle and emphasising the themes of reconciliation and remembrance of those of all nationalities who had been killed or injured.

Later, when he and Tilly were alone, Henry declared, 'I'm pleased that's over!'

'But darling, your speech was marvellous! You said all the right things.'

'Thank you. But - I'm not sure I meant all of them. Tilly, I know I shouldn't say it, but I still struggle, dealing with the Germans…'

'Even though we're all friends now?'

'Exactly. But I can't forget. And I'm not sure whether I'll ever be able to forgive…'

Amsterdam, 1965

A man and a woman from a charity for the homeless and two volunteer helpers were conducting their usual patrol along the canals and bridges on the outskirts of Amsterdam where homeless people, drunks and drug addicts congregated under the dark archways, seeking shelter during the cold nights. The four walked along, lighting their way by torchlight, giving out food and checking to see if anyone needed help. One of their regulars beckoned to them out of the shadows.

'This chap here,' he said, pointing to a figure cowering in a corner, 'he's not right – keeps shivering and shouting out in some foreign language. He's dead thin. I don't think he'll last the night. Can you help him?'

*

Antonio woke up in hospital. He had very little memory of the past year and nothing to his name. Even the photograph of the soldier he'd carried with him ever since he'd run away from home was lost, washed down the drain with his self-respect.

CHAPTER 38

Bath, 1966

Gilda was at work on the Stroke Ward when Dr Jones, the consultant, said, 'Nurse Blumfeldt, can I have a word with you in my office?' She dropped what she was doing and followed him down the corridor, walking quickly to keep up with him, curious to know what he wanted. He closed the door and beckoned her to take a seat.

Gilda didn't know it, but Dr Jones had rather a soft spot for her. He admired how this attractive, vivacious woman who did so much to raise the morale of her patients on the ward had devoted her life at home to caring for Anthony.

'I've just come back from a conference and there's been an important development that I want to talk to you about,' said Dr Jones. 'Some American neurologists have identified a condition which they're calling 'locked-in syndrome'. It usually arises as the result of a major stroke and leaves patients unable to move or speak, but what they've discovered - and this is the important thing – is that the person is still conscious. Still mentally alert, able to see, hear, think. It's just that they can't tell you.'

Gilda listened intently.

'Now, with regard to your Anthony,' he continued, 'we've suspected for some time that he knows what's going on. But these new developments will help us to prove it...'

Gilda held her breath while Dr Jones picked up a piece of paper and started to write out the alphabet in large letters.

'People with locked-in syndrome can usually move an eyelid,' he said.

'Yes, Anthony can.'

'Now, this is so simple I can't believe we haven't done it before.'

Taking his pencil, he pointed to each letter in turn. 'When the person blinks, that is the letter they want to spell out. It's been done in America – it takes ages at first, but once you get the hang of it it's easy. They're even making special cards which have the most common letters first, and words like 'yes' and 'no'. Do you see, Gilda? With the aid of this system, you can help Anthony find his voice!'

Gilda was stunned.

'But it's so obvious! I've always believed that Anthony was still there, that he could hear us, but with this he can talk back! Doctor, this is amazing!'

'I knew you'd be interested. Now, Anthony's annual check-up is due soon, isn't it. What I suggest is that you bring him in tomorrow. I'll examine him, explain to him what I've just told you and we'll try him out with the spelling card. And we'll see how our other patients here in the Stroke Ward get on as well – it won't suit everyone, but it's definitely worth a try!'

Gilda was overwhelmed. 'That's marvellous! Thank you so much!'

They both got up and Gilda looked so thrilled Dr Jones couldn't help but open his arms and give her a hug. 'I do hope it works for you!' he said.

'Thank you!' she replied.

Then returning to business he let her go saying, 'you'd better get back to the ward now, Nurse Blumfeldt.'

'Yes, Dr Jones,' she said, smiling fit to burst.

The following day David drove Anthony to hospital for this very important appointment. Gilda led them to Dr Jones who conducted Anthony's physical examination then positioned him in front of the spelling card and explained what he was going to do.

'Now, I want you to think of a short word – a name, perhaps. I am going to point out each letter in turn and when I come to the letter you want, you must blink, once. Do you understand, Anthony?'

Anthony blinked, once.

'All right…here we go.'

Starting with 'A', Dr Jones moved his pencil along the line of letters and when he reached 'G', Antony blinked, once.

The doctor wrote it down.

The second time they got as far as 'I', followed by 'L', 'D' and 'A'.

'GILDA'!

They were all silent for a moment, catching their breath, then Dr Jones sat back and exhaled.

'My God, it works!' he exclaimed.

Back at Eagle House, David, overjoyed, phoned Henry to tell him the news.

Sonia was beside herself. 'Anthony, *liebchen*!' she cried, 'there must be so much you want to tell us!'

Karl said, 'this is marvellous! We must thank God for these miracles.'

Gilda tried the board and Anthony spelt a few simple words but then his concentration lapsed.

'He's tired,' said Gilda, 'I think we should leave any more till the morning.' Then she took his hands in hers and said, 'but there's no hurry, dearest. We have the rest of our lives!'

This is truly amazing. I never thought there could be so much power in the blink of an eye. I owe Dr Jones so much. My life has taken on a whole new meaning. At last I'll be able to tell people how I feel, what I think, and to thank them for what they do for me. It will take hours, days...but I've got nothing else to do, have I?

Henry's come over from Paris especially to see me. It's wonderful to have him here again and for the first time in over twenty years I've actually been able to 'talk' to him. It's a painstaking process, but better than not being able to say anything at all. I'm pleased he's happy – he and the family are having a ball in Paris. I wish I could go there...I wish I could do lots of things...

Italy 1967

Isabella and Angelica were at their favourite café in Milan for a business meeting with Alberto. They sat in the warm sunshine drinking espressos, watching people go by, with Angelica, at nineteen, thrilled to be in the city that was fast becoming the fashion capital of Italy. Alberto was impressed by his young niece – she was intelligent as well as pretty, with lovely long wavy hair and good legs like her mother. Dressed in a smart jacket and a short skirt she looked every inch the young professional.

Alberto asked after the family.

290

Antonio wasn't mentioned – in the five years since he had left home they had heard nothing from him and he could be dead, for all they knew. At first the younger children used to wonder what adventures their big brother was having in Africa but Angelica would shush them, saying, 'don't mention Antonio, you know it upsets Mama…' And after a while they forgot to ask.

Alberto lit a cigarette and launched into his new marketing idea.

'I think we should expand our sales into England,' he said. 'Wine-drinking is becoming more popular over there now and I think we would do well. We can't let the French take all their business.'

Isabella was suddenly irritated.

'No, not England,' she said.

'Why not?'

'I don't like it – it's too cold and grey in that country for them to appreciate our wine.'

Alberto shrugged his shoulders, holding out his hands, palms upwards, saying 'but Isabella! The weather over there isn't bad all the time…perhaps drinking our wine will cheer them up!'

'No,' said Isabella, firmly. 'No, I don't think it's a good idea.'

In the back of his mind Alberto remembered the photograph of the British soldier, but surely Isabella wouldn't let the past influence a business opportunity?

'All right, we'll leave it for now,' he said, knowing there was no point in arguing.

He called the waiter for some more coffees and they sat in silence for a moment, then Alberto noticed Angelica staring at two men who were sitting at a table nearby.

She suppressed a giggle. Alberto was having trouble with these women today.

'What's the matter with you?' he asked his niece.

She whispered, 'they're holding hands!'

Isabella, shocked, looked at the men and muttered 'disgusting!' while Alberto and Angelica tried not to laugh. The two men heard her and looked over at them. Alberto turned and said, 'I apologise, it's none of our business.'

'It's all right, we're used to it!' said one of the men who then, for good measure, kissed his partner full on the lips.

Isabella mouthed a prayer and crossed herself.

'It's all right, Isabella, it's how God made them!' said Alberto, 'it's even legal now in many countries.'

'But it's a sin!' exclaimed Isabella.

Alberto looked deep into her eyes.

'And you, of course, have never sinned!'

His look was so intense and knowing she nearly choked on her coffee. She had the strangest feeling that he knew more about her than he let on, and that all her secrets were laid bare.

Paris, 1967

The Embassy was due to host a summit meeting of world leaders and Henry had his work cut out making sure that everything went without a hitch. He had learnt over the years that there was no substitution for eye-balling things himself and had scheduled a meeting with the head chef in the kitchens, down in the basement of the Embassy building.

He proceeded to check over the menus and delivery of fresh food and wines making it clear to all the staff that he expected them to do their best to make the important event a success.

Afterwards, as Henry walked back along the narrow corridor towards the staircase, he saw a young man coming towards him pushing a trolley loaded with crates of champagne. He was tall and thin, good looking, with short fair hair, and as he grew closer Henry felt his blood run cold. He was the image of his brother when he was about the same age.

As they slowed to pass each other the man smiled charmingly, said, '*Bonjour Monsieur*,' and Henry replied in the same way. My God, he even had Anthony's smile! Henry turned to watch as the man made his way towards the wine cellar, a shiver running through him as if someone had walked over his grave.

When Henry got back to his office Sylvia, his secretary, looked at him with concern.

'Are you all right, sir? You look as if you've seen a ghost!'

'Oh – it's nothing – just a funny thing. There was a young delivery man down below, reminded me of my brother, that's all. Tall fair-haired chap – unusual for a Frenchman.'

'Aaah,' said Sylvia, 'I know who you mean, he's rather a dish! He works at the wine merchants and brings the champagne deliveries. All the girls look forward to seeing him! He's not French, actually – he's Italian. His name's Antonio.'

CHAPTER 39

Bath, 1968

After Anthony's annual check-up Dr Jones chatted to David about his son's progress.

'It really is quite incredible to see how well Anthony is doing,' he said. 'I know it sounds ridiculous, but apart from the fact he can't move he's actually in very good health – heart, weight, blood pressure are all perfect for a man of forty-one. There's no reason why he shouldn't live to a ripe old age! As long as he has someone close to look after him…'

'That's good to hear!' said David, 'and now we can communicate things are so much better. It's a laborious process, but it works.'

'We've been using the spelling board with other patients and having a good success rate.' Dr Jones spoke briefly to one of the nurses, then continued, 'in fact, I was reading the other day that in America a 'locked-in' patient married his carer! He was able to take his vows using the board – remarkable!'

Back at Eagle House David told Anthony and the Blumfeldts what Dr Jones had said.

'Married! Isn't that incredible!' said David, 'must have been marvellous for the chap's morale.'

'And good for the morale of his carer, too…' added Sonia.

In July, after a long period of drought, a phenomenal downpour overwhelmed Bath's fledgling flood defences and the city suffered a massive inundation as the River Avon burst its banks.

Torrents of water swept through Bath and surrounding villages, cascading down the hills, submerging shops in the city centre and flooding many homes. The cricket ground resembled a lake and main roads were impassable. Water sources were contaminated and for many weeks drinking water had to be boiled. Eagle House escaped the deluge although David's car, which was in the garage at the bottom of the hill for servicing, was submerged and had to be written-off. Many people had it a lot worse and at Mr Greenstein's the Rabbi said prayers for those afflicted by the worst damage to hit Bath since the Blitz.

The flooding didn't stop the double celebration planned at Eagle House in August: Karl was sixty-five, retiring from teaching and it was David's seventy-fifth birthday. Henry, Tilly and the children, now back from Paris, joined them. After a lunch of salt beef and pickles, Karl's favourite, he stood to make an announcement.

'Thank you for all your good wishes. I am looking forward to spending more time at home and there is plenty of work to do in the garden. But my main desire is to devote more time to studying our faith. I have recently been visiting a synagogue in Bristol and have arranged with the Rabbi to spend two days a week there, with other Jewish scholars, to study the Torah and discuss the learned books.'

'Goodness!' exclaimed Sonia, who had been unaware of her husband's plans, 'but that is good, Karl! You deserve to spend your time as you wish.'

'I think it is wonderful, Papa,' said Gilda.

'Well done,' said David, 'I hope it helps you to find peace.'

Later, David had a quiet word with Henry.

'I've been thinking about the future too,' he said. 'I won't be here forever. When I die, Eagle House will pass to you and Anthony. It's up to you what you do with it – but I need to know that Anthony will be looked after, and also that the Blumfeldts will be secure - it's their home as well as our own.'

'Dad, I've got a lovely house and a wife with pots of money. I don't need to keep any financial interest in Eagle House - Anthony and the Blumfeldts can stay here forever as far as I'm concerned.'

'Thank you, Henry. I knew you'd understand. I'll go to see my solicitor and see what he suggests.'

I appreciate Dad's concerns about the future, although I'm sure he'll be around for a long time yet. But since I've been able to communicate with the world something has become very clear to me. I've heard the discussions, and I can take Sonia's hints. I may sit here, helpless, in this wheelchair, but there is something obvious I can do which will put everyone's mind at rest.

I loved Isabella, a long time ago, but that is all in the past and I'll never see her again. Now, in a different sort of way, I have come to love Gilda. She is totally devoted to me. What more could a man in my position want? I think it's time I did the decent thing...

Gilda came in from her shift, tired, but her heart always lifted when she saw Anthony. She ate her meal with her parents then went to sit beside him with her book, the new Radio 2 station playing some light music in the background, enjoying an ordinary evening like many others they had spent together.

Anthony twitched his eye.

'Do you want something, *liebchen*?' she asked, picking up the spelling board.

It took just a few seconds to spell out the two important words:

'M-A-R-R-Y M-E'

'*Marry me*? Whatever do you mean, Anthony? Are you proposing?'

'YES'

Gilda was stunned.

'Anthony…oh, I don't believe it!'

She got up and her book fell to the floor, then she was kneeling in front of him, taking his hands in hers and kissing them. Her heart overflowed with joy – the moment she had dreamed of but never believed would happen.

'Yes, Anthony, I will marry you. I will!'

Sonia came in, wondering what was going on.

'Mama…'

Gilda got up and ran to her mother, hugging her, unable to contain her tears of happiness.

'Mama, Anthony's asked me to marry him!'

*

The plans for this most unconventional of weddings quickly took shape.

David and Karl had a meeting with the city Registrar to discuss the arrangements for conducting the ceremony at Eagle House; Dr Jones attested that Anthony was capable of communicating his vows, with Henry given legal powers to sign documents on his behalf; and Karl and Sonia saw the Rabbi regarding the religious ceremony and asked him to instruct Anthony on marrying into the Jewish faith.

The big day came at last. Anthony was dressed in his best suit and wearing a skullcap. Gilda, in a white organza creation made by her mother which accentuated her curvaceous figure, radiated happiness. The wedding guests crammed into Eagle House to witness the ceremonies, culminating with all the guests shouting '*Mazel tov!*'

Word about the unusual wedding had spread and a small crowd gathered outside to watch the man in the wheelchair marry the woman who had cared for him for so long. At the end of the ceremony Gilda turned Anthony's chair around to face the window and waved to the people outside, feeling like the Royal family on the balcony at Buckingham Palace.

David spoke of his joy at seeing his son marry the woman who had loved him for many years and wished the couple as much happiness as he had known with his own wife, Wendy. Karl gave a moving speech relating how the Roberts family had welcomed them in those dark days after their escape from Germany.

'We arrived with nothing, and now we have everything!' he said, looking gratefully around him.

'We have a good life in this lovely city, and we are so proud and happy for our beautiful daughter. Our only sadness is that our relatives cannot be here to see her…'

He then read out a telegram of congratulations from Jacob and his family in Tel Aviv which Gilda found very touching. She was pleased Jacob had made a success of his life in Israel and looked forward to receiving his letters. He was working for the Government, had married a law student and they had two children.

Mrs Potts, who had retired, was thrilled to be at the wedding she had never dreamt would happen. She found it miraculous to be able to communicate with Anthony after years of not even being sure whether he was 'in there' and hoped her chatting to him over the years had kept up his morale.

David took Karl to one side and said, 'when I went to see my solicitor the other day I found out something that will interest you. Many years ago, you asked me whether Eagle House had a connection to Germany. Well, now I know the answer! According to the deeds of the house it was built, as I thought, in the 1880s, and the architect was a man called Goldblum, who was German – and a Jew!'

'Really! That's remarkable!' exclaimed Karl.

'Yes! It's as if fate brought you here! And Karl, I want you to know, I've arranged that this will always be your home, for all of you.'

High on the emotion of the day the two looked at each other, shook hands then hugged in an unmanly way, Karl saying, 'thank you, David, thank you so much!'

Sonia, relishing her role as mother of the bride and wearing a pink bouclé suit and matching hat, noticed them and went over to find out what was going on.

'Sonia, David has the most wonderful news…'

David had tracked down Frank Collins, who introduced his wife June to Gilda and Anthony, 'the man who saved my life, twice'. As they moved away Frank whispered to June, 'well, Gilda's more friendly than the last time I came to visit!'

'That's because she's got 'er claws into 'im now!' June whispered back.

Mr Greenstein presented Gilda with a special gift – a *mezuzah*, a small decorative case containing a piece of parchment inscribed with Hebrew verses. Mindful of what David had just told him, Karl knew exactly what was required. He fetched his tool kit and with Sonia and Gilda beside him, nailed the *mezuzah* to the wall by the front door.

'Now this is a proper Jewish house!' Gilda proclaimed, hugging her parents.

The feasting began with kosher food, wine and champagne, and one of the guests produced schnapps, direct from Germany. There was music and dancing and the volume of enjoyment became louder and louder. Henry and Tilly stood and watched the celebrations with a mix of fascination and bewilderment, entranced by the vibrant Jewish community that had taken root in Eagle House. As the guests sang a selection of traditional songs in Yiddish and German Henry whispered to Tilly, 'I love the Blumfeldts, but I still can't get used to all this German stuff. It feels like a takeover!'

'Shhh, you mustn't say things like that!' she replied, digging him with her elbow, but she knew what he meant. Harriet and Freddie overheard and sniggered, and their mother glared at them to keep quiet.

Frank and June Collins came over and Harriet listened attentively while Frank re-told his story about serving in Italy with Anthony.

'And did you ever meet her – Isabella?' she asked, curiously.

'Yes – well, I never really spoke to 'er, but I saw 'er a few times. A real Italian beauty!'

Harriet sighed. The story of her uncle and his doomed love affair never ceased to fascinate her.

June said, 'we shouldn't be thinking about that today, though, should we? We should be congratulating Anthony and Gilda on finding happiness together.'

'You're right, love,' said Frank, and changing the subject he said to Freddie, aged thirteen and looking bored, 'and what're you going to do when you're older – join the RAF, like your Dad?'

'No!' said Freddie, firmly, 'I'm going to be an astronaut!'

'He's fascinated by the Apollo programme,' said Harriet, 'he has pictures of rockets all over his bedroom wall, don't you?'

While Freddie told Frank all he knew about space science, June asked Harriet about her own plans.

'I've got a place at Cambridge to study languages,' she said, 'I'll be starting in September. It's the same course that Mummy followed. But afterwards I'm going to teach – it's what I've always wanted to do.'

'Good for you!' said June. 'I suppose one astronaut in the family's enough!'

301

Tilly went to see whether Sonia needed any help in the kitchen and found her there, crying.

'Sonia!' said Tilly, giving her a hug.

'I'm sorry, Tilly,' she said, wiping her eyes, 'it's been an emotional day. I just wish...I just wish my family could have seen Gilda today, so happy...'

She started to cry again.

'My parents! My brother! I can't bear to think about it...but I can't stop myself!'

'You suffered a huge loss,' said Tilly. 'Do you want to talk about it?'

Gradually the guests began to leave. Sonia hugged Tilly tightly and said 'thank you, *liebchen*'.

As they drove back home in the Rover Henry said, 'what was all that about, with Sonia?'

'Well - she opened up to me a bit about their life before they came to England.'

'Really? They don't normally like taking about it, do they – understandably.'

'Indeed. She told me that coming here was the best thing, and the worst thing, they had ever done. She still feels guilty about those they left behind.'

'That's war, though, isn't it?' said Henry. 'Dreadful things happen, people die. The Nazis were monsters. But the Blumfeldts have a good life here, thanks to my parents, and now they have a secure future too. Maybe it's time they let the past go.'

'I suppose so...but it's so hard, isn't it? You've admitted that yourself – you still have difficulty with the Germans, don't you? One needs patience and time to forgive, they say. But how awful, to have loved ones, and not know for sure whether they are alive or dead...'

302

On the wedding night Gilda and her mother got Anthony ready as usual, washing and changing him, giving him his medication and manoeuvring him into bed. Then instead of going to her own room Gilda said, 'from now on I'll sleep here, with my husband.'

'Of course,' said Sonia. She gave her daughter a hug.

'I am so happy for you, *liebchen*.'

'Thank you, Mama.'

Sonia left the room.

Gilda looked at Anthony who was already asleep. She took off her clothes and slipped into bed beside him. Naked and aroused, she pleasured herself, and as she reached her climax she stifled a cry and thrust herself against his warm but unresponsive body.

It was enough.

PART FOUR

CHAPTER 40

Bath, 1974

Since we got married Gilda's gone into overdrive - she's loving being mistress of Eagle House. She's completely overhauled the place, had a new kitchen and bathrooms fitted, all the rooms redecorated, new carpets, curtains, gilt-edged mirrors, the lot. Her parents still live in the flat downstairs, updated with all mod cons. She's swept the past away and made a new start for us all. Dad seems quite happy about it; he's in his eighties, quite frail now, and happy to leave everything in Gilda's hands. All he does is foot the bill. But in fairness, Gilda is marvellous – she manages the domestics, works at the hospital part-time and looks after me. She's put on a bit of weight and looks older now - her hair is going grey, and so is mine for that matter. She's a wonderful wife. I'm not sure whether I'm much of a husband, though…

I spend my time as usual, sitting looking out the window. Even on a rainy October day like today there's always something to see. The road is busier than it used to be – more people, more traffic, changing fashions, more foreigners and an endless stream of salesmen coming to the door.

Actually, here comes one now – although she's better looking than the usual greasy-haired, bri-nylon shirt brigade. This one's a rather striking tall, thin, redhead, wearing a bright orange coat and carrying a case. What's she selling?

The bell rings, I can hear voices, then Gilda shuts the door, abruptly, and runs up to her old room. The young woman walks back along the path and closes the gate behind her. Standing on the pavement outside the house she looks up and sees me for the first time. She stares at me, curiously, as if trying to work out a puzzle, then goes on her way. And she is no longer carrying the case.

Lizzie James returned home disappointed, deflated. An Art teacher, she collected vintage clothes and accessories and when she spotted the dark green leather case at Bath antiques market it immediately intrigued her. The seller told her he'd bought it from a dealer in Bristol who said it was pre-war and had originally come from a British Rail lost property sale back in the 1950s. But no one had been able to open it without damaging the combination lock. It was heavy – there was definitely something inside it – but what?

'Probably somebody's pre-war sandwiches!' her husband Mark commented, unhelpfully.

Lizzie negotiated the sale down to twenty pounds. She took it home and cleaned the leather, lubricated the four-figure combination lock and tried some obvious numbers, but without success.

'You do realise that the odds of finding the right combination are millions to one?' said Mark, 'you'd have more chance winning the football pools!'

'I know, but I'm going to keep trying. I just have a feeling there's something important inside…'

Lizzie worked her way methodically through various combinations but couldn't crack the code.

One Saturday afternoon while her husband was out with his pals watching Bath rugby she played around with some random numbers - her birthday, Mark's birthday - then she tried their wedding anniversary, the 31st July: 3107.

Click! The lock opened.

Shocked and excited Lizzie carefully opened the case and was surprised to find various implements for grooming and cutting hair – a kit for a mobile barber! She explored the individual pockets of fine black leather and found a silver hair slide - a keepsake, perhaps? - and a small black and white photograph of a young couple, gazing at each other, clearly in love, at some kind of celebration. There was a larger sepia photo, a formal portrait of the same girl, and a sealed envelope addressed to a town in Italy. Lizzie sensed that she had discovered some extraordinary treasures. But whose were they?

The answer was to be found in the last item she retrieved from the bottom of the case - a small sketch book with an inscription on the inside page:

'Anthony Roberts, Eagle House, Bath.'

Bath!

The case had come home.

Lizzie was determined to reunite case with owner, so having tracked down the address it was with a mixture of anticipation and trepidation that she had gone to Eagle House that day. Hence her disappointment at the short shrift she'd been given by the unfriendly woman who answered the door – Anthony's wife.

'She didn't show much interest in the case at all, the old bat,' said Lizzie.

'Well what did you expect?' said Mark, 'a total stranger turning up like that. But I wonder what the story is about Anthony Roberts?'

Gilda put the case on her bed, stood back and looked at it as if it were an unexploded bomb. If it really did belong to Anthony it must be at least thirty years old - where had it been all this time? And how had this woman managed to open it and trace its owner? Gilda had a horrible feeling in the pit of her stomach. She dreaded what secrets it might contain – things from Italy, the woman had said – things that might be better left undiscovered. Gilda didn't want her comfortable life disrupted by relics from Anthony's past. The case may have found its way back to him like some sort of miracle but she couldn't bear to look at it so she picked it up by its brass handle, keeping it at arm's length, and hid it under her bed.

It was Lizzie's birthday on 9th December so Mark took her out to a new Chinese restaurant in the city centre. Just after nine o'clock, as they were enjoying their banana fritters, they heard a loud blast and the room shook. The owner of the restaurant said it was probably a gas explosion and told his clients not to worry. A few minutes later they heard sirens and saw flashing blue lights, and Mark, who was a retained fireman, couldn't sit still any longer.

'Stay here!' he said to Lizzie, 'I'm going to find out what's going on.'

310

He joined a crowd of people gathering near The Corridor, an arcade of shops, but couldn't get close as the police had cordoned it off. Everyone wondered what had shattered the peace of the night, then the word went around – it was an IRA bomb. Mark dashed back to the restaurant to tell Lizzie and the next day the news was confirmed. Thankfully no injuries were reported, although several shops in the arcade suffered damage. A similar terrorist attack occurred in Bristol two days later.

When David and the Blumfeldts heard about the bombing their minds went straight back to the war and the memory of the devastation that had been wrought by the Luftwaffe. The question 'why Bath?' hung in the air again, but during the Troubles the IRA spared no one.

In the new year, after the shock of the bomb blast and a busy time preparing for Christmas, Lizzie's thoughts turned again to Anthony Roberts. She was disappointed not to have heard anything from his family and was still curious. She took to walking past Eagle House, looking up at the man in his wheelchair, but, not wanting a confrontation with the unhelpful woman, she didn't ring the doorbell.

I can see a tall redhead in a bright orange coat walking up and down outside, looking at me. She's the one who brought a case here a couple of months ago and left without it. This has been bugging me and at last I've worked it out. I lost the case and somehow she found it.

The case she brought here is mine.

311

CHAPTER 41

Bath, 1975

Anthony knew he couldn't trust Gilda on the matter of his case so he waited until Henry's next visit to make his move. He twitched his eye, indicating that he wanted the spelling board. Henry wasn't as quick at interpreting as Gilda, so he called for her to come.

'What is it, *liebchen*? What do you want to say?'

She held up the board as Anthony spelt out his message.

'I W-A-N-T M-Y C-A-S-E'

'What case? What do you mean?'

'G-I-R-L B-R-O-U-G-H-T M-Y C-A-S-E'

Gilda hesitated. She understood exactly what he meant, but how on earth did Anthony know about it? She flushed with guilt.

Henry noted something amiss and said, 'what's all that about, Gilda?'

She couldn't avoid it. 'Oh – I think I remember,' she said, trying to sound casual. 'A woman came here a while ago with a case she thought might belong to Anthony, but I didn't want to bother him with it, so I put it away...'

Inside, Anthony was seething. His brother understood and spoke for him.

'I think you'd better go and get it, then.'

Gilda returned and rather sheepishly gave the case to Henry along with the combination written on the back of the woman's business card.

'Three – one – zero – seven. Of course – the 31st July! Anthony's birthday!'

David joined them and watched as Henry worked the combination. The lock clicked and he opened the lid.

'Well, well!' he said, 'it looks like a case for a travelling barber! What on earth was Anthony doing with this?'

He found the sketch book.

'Look, Dad! His name and address are on the inside cover – that must be how the woman traced him.'

'That's marvellous!' said David, 'I always wondered what had happened to his sketch book!'

Henry flicked through it, admiring the scenes of battle-strewn landscapes, vineyards and drawings of a pretty girl with long, wavy hair.

A sepia photo fell to the floor, a formal portrait of the same girl.

David picked it up, turned it over and read, '*To Antonio, with all my love, Isabella, May 1945.*'

'So this, then, is Isabella - the girl Collins told us about. She called him 'Antonio'!'

Henry found the small black and white photograph of Anthony and Isabella together and knelt down next to his brother, holding the photo so he could see it properly. 'You loved her very much, didn't you. She is beautiful.'

Henry felt Anthony squeeze his hand in confirmation.

'How wonderful that these things have been found!'

This was all too much for Gilda. She had stood to one side, looking on while the men poured over these hidden treasures, but couldn't take any more. 'Isabella' – would that wretched woman never go away? Stifling a cry of anger and jealousy, she ran from the room.

David and Henry watched her go.

'She's taking it badly,' said Henry. 'The girl who found the case must have told her what was in it and Gilda couldn't face it. Good job you realised what was going on, old man,' he said to his brother.

They found a silver hair slide, the one Isabella was wearing in the photographs, and finally an envelope addressed in Anthony's handwriting to Signorina Isabella Fortuno.

'That's strange - he wrote her a letter but never posted it,' said Henry. 'What should we do with it?'

'Mmm…best leave it unopened, I think,' said David. 'What Anthony wanted to tell her was private between themselves, and it should stay that way. And she won't want a strange letter from England turning up after all these years.'

'Let's ask Anthony what he thinks.'

Henry took the spelling board. Slowly, he helped as Anthony spelled out,

'I L-O-V-E-D H-E-R'

Henry had tears in his eyes.

'Yes, old man, I can see that. And I'm sure she loved you too. You wanted to go back to Italy and marry her, didn't you?'

'YES'

Then followed the words,

'L-E-T   H-E-R   G-O'

'Let her go,' repeated Henry. 'We've got to let her go. That's the right thing to do, isn't it, Dad?'

'Yes, it is,' replied David. 'It's a long time ago. Things change. Isabella will have made her own way in life. And Anthony is happily married to Gilda now, isn't he – he'd be lost without her.'

Anthony had one more message to convey:

'T-H-A-N-K   T-H-E   G-I-R-L'

'Yes, of course,' said Henry, picking up the business card of the woman who had brought them the case. '*Elizabeth James, The Old Priory School,*' he read. 'How strange - that's where Harriet teaches! I wonder if she knows her?'

In the flat downstairs Gilda was in tears, her parents, uncomprehending, comforting her as best they could until Gilda was able to tell them what had happened.

'I always loved him!' she cried, 'but he was in love with that Italian girl!'

'There, there, *liebchen*,' said Sonia, 'strange things happen in wartime, but then it's over and people move on. Come, Gilda, you are Anthony's wife! He loves you! What could be better than that? She only knew him for a short time, and you have him forever!'

Gilda knew her mother was right. But did Anthony still think of this Italian woman? Did he miss her? Did he still yearn for her, after all these years? It had been bad enough when Frank Collins had told them about Isabella, all that time ago, but seeing photographs of her and the evidence of her love affair with Anthony was too much to bear.

315

Then Sonia said, 'it must have been hard for her, never hearing from him. How awful, not to know what happened to the man she loved…'

For a reason Sonia couldn't fathom, this thought set her daughter off again as she dissolved into tears of resentment and guilt.

When Sonia and Karl came to put me to bed Karl said, 'please be patient with Gilda. It's hard for her to know that you once loved someone else. But she is your wife now. In time she will accept the past and you will both be happy again.'

He's right, of course. I love Gilda and marrying her was the right thing to do. But it is a different sort of love…

Just to see Isabella's photograph again makes me so happy. I loved her so much, and I still do. She was clever, and ambitious – I hope she's made a success of her life. Now I have to let her go, but I will never, ever forget her.

Usually so doting, so patient, Gilda's jealousy was burning inside and over the next few days she was quite irascible with Anthony, tetchy as she washed and changed him, wrestling with his clothes, muttering under her breath as she carried out routine caring tasks. She was sleeping in her old room for the first time since they'd been married.

David noticed and said to Anthony, 'don't worry, she'll get over it. Give her time – and keep telling her you love her.'

Henry got in touch with Lizzie James and invited her and her husband to Eagle House to meet Anthony and the rest of the family.

Gilda dreaded the day but her father gave her a shot of whisky and told her to bear up.

Lizzie, who arrived in a shocking pink mini-dress which clashed with her red hair, was pleased finally to meet this enigmatic figure, Anthony Roberts, knowing her instinct about the importance of returning the case to its owner had been right. Using the spelling board Gilda, through gritted teeth, conveyed Anthony's message of gratitude, saying how much it meant to him to see his belongings again.

Tilly introduced herself to Lizzie saying, 'well done on your detective work! You're like me – you love solving puzzles!'

Harriet was amazed that it was one of her colleagues who had found the case. She only knew Lizzie in passing, mostly noticing her individual style in clothes. They were about the same age and Harriet was pleased to have the chance to find out more about her. Harriet was enjoying living in Bath - after qualifying as a teacher she'd taken a job in the city she'd got to know and love as a child, and her parents had bought her a small flat in a Georgian house on Lansdown Hill.

Having heard the story from Frank Collins Harriet was thrilled to see an actual photograph of Isabella and the mementos of her love affair with Anthony. 'I can't believe you found all these treasures!' she said to Lizzie, 'it means so much. It brings the past to life!'

Lizzie, who was equally pleased and surprised to meet Harriet, agreed, saying, 'there was just something special about the case – when I saw it at the market it was as if it spoke to me…'

Gilda went to prepare tea and when she returned David was showing Karl Anthony's sketch book.

'He was always good at drawing, I'm pleased he kept it up,' he said.

As Karl leafed through the book he found a pressed flower, stuck between two pages. He carefully lifted it out and inspected it.

'Sonia!' he said, holding it in the palm of his hand to show his wife, 'look! *Eine Pasqueblume!*'

'Karl!' she exclaimed, 'oh my goodness!'

Sonia kissed her husband full on the lips and Gilda looked at her parents with surprise. Sonia noticed, blushed, and said, 'this brings back so many happy memories! These flowers grow in Germany – we used to see them in the meadows near our home where we used to go walking…'

'…when we were courting!' said Karl.

'Yes!' said Sonia. 'I think in English they are called pasqueflowers – the Easter flower. They grow all over Europe, but not so much in England. I haven't seen one since we left. Anthony must have kept it to remind him of his time in Italy.'

She stood by Anthony's chair and took his hand in hers.

'My dear boy, I am so pleased to know that you have had happy moments in your life. No one can take your memories away.'

She beckoned Gilda to her, took her hand and, standing between them, said, 'and now, you are lucky enough to have found love again, with my beautiful daughter. Please,' she said, looking at Gilda, 'please try!

318

With God's help you can both be happy again! You and Anthony have so much, together, and what is past is past.'

Gilda's resistance was weakening. She loved her mother, she loved Anthony, she was so lucky...

'Yes, Mama,' she said, hugging her, tears in her eyes.

Then Gilda cupped Anthony's face in her hands and kissed him on the lips.

'I'm sorry, *liebchen*,' she said. 'Forgive me. I love you.'

CHAPTER 42

England, 1975

Henry and Tilly were enjoying a leisurely breakfast at home. Tilly had completed the *Times* crossword, as usual, and was working her way through the morning post.

'Oh!' she exclaimed, opening a letter, 'it's from Beatrice – she's taken up a new post at the Embassy in Bonn.'

'Really? And what have the Germans done to deserve that?'

'Don't be horrible, darling. I'm sure she's doing something wonderful.'

Tilly read the letter, engrossed, then said to Henry, 'she's enjoying herself. What a fascinating time to be there. Anyway, the interesting bit as far as we're concerned is that she has access to the archive holding records from the concentration camps. They always say that the Nazis kept good records, don't they, and it seems to be true.'

'What a cheerful thought on a Saturday morning! And that is interesting for us because…?'

'Why, the Blumfeldts, of course! Haven't you heard Sonia and Karl talk about the relatives they left behind in Germany?'

'Yes, but…'

'Well, now we might be able to find out what happened to them! Beatrice remembered me telling her their story and she's offered to help – if they would like her to.'

'Goodness! That would be remarkable, after all this time.'

Tilly picked up the letter and turned to the last page.

'She concludes:

I can think of nothing worse than not knowing whether the people one loves are alive or dead. Do ask your friends if they would like to try and trace their missing relatives – if they want me to help I am happy to do so.'

'Next time we go to Bath I'll talk to the Blumfeldts and see what they think.'

When Tilly told Sonia about Beatrice's proposal, Sonia was uncertain.

'It's very kind of your friend to offer to help us, but is it good to dig up the past, or better to leave it?'

Gilda wasn't keen on the idea, saying, 'I think we should let things rest.'

Then Karl said, 'your mother and I are not getting any younger. Perhaps before we die we should finally know the truth about what happened to our families, for better or worse. I'll have a word with the Rabbi. And we will pray. Then we will decide.'

A few weeks later, Karl telephoned Tilly.

'God has given us guidance,' he said. 'Please tell your friend we gratefully accept her offer. We will provide her with as much information as we can.'

*

321

As Harriet got ready for another week at school she reflected on her love-life which was not particularly great. She was bored by most of the men she met and was looking for excitement, not security, in a relationship. She put herself in the position of Isabella, a young Italian girl, falling in love with a foreign soldier during wartime, choosing him over her absent fiancé.

Now, that must have felt exciting. But how she must have missed her lover when he went away, never to return…

Although the family had agreed to leave well alone Harriet couldn't stop thinking about the case and its contents. Wouldn't it be wonderful to deliver Anthony's letter to Isabella and explain at last why he hadn't gone back to her?

Harriet got in her car and put the radio on. The Carpenters had a recent hit which they kept playing all the time – *'Please Mr Postman…deliver the letter, the sooner the better…'* they sang, as if to her.

The issue simmered at the back of her mind and Harriet concluded that a trip to Italy during the Easter holidays was just what she needed. She'd visited Rome when studying for her degree and could speak basic Italian but had never been to the North of the country and didn't really want to go on her own. The next time she saw Lizzie she asked her whether she had any plans for the Easter break - since the discovery of the case the two had become friends, going shopping together in the new precinct and having lunch at Fishy Evans.

'Not really,' Lizzie replied, 'Mark's on duty so I'm just going to be hanging around at home.'

'Well - I've got this idea…'

Harriet told her Grandad about her plans to go to Italy as a part of her personal journey, to see the places her Uncle Anthony had seen and to practise speaking the language. If they happened to find themselves in the vicinity where Isabella lived, well…

David, who could never refuse her anything, knew he was being played but raised no objection.

Anthony must have been equally susceptible because when Harriet asked his permission to borrow the photo of Isabella and the letter addressed to her he signalled his agreement, with one proviso:

'O-N-L-Y T-O H-E-R'

'You only want me to give the letter to Isabella, not to anyone else?' asked Harriet.

'YES.'

When she heard about Harriet's plan Gilda was livid. She cornered her when they were alone in the kitchen and gave her a diatribe.

'I thought we'd all agreed to leave well alone. You shouldn't go digging up other people's pasts, you don't know what you might find.'

'But you want to find out about your family, don't you? And I want to learn more about what Uncle Anthony did in Italy. You can't stop me!'

Gilda took a deep breath and stood back. She recognised the same determination in Harriet's eyes that Tilly had when she was set on something and nothing would stand in her way.

She weakened. 'All right, Harriet, but be careful – I know it's all ancient history to you, but the past is important. Treat it with respect.'

CHAPTER 43

Italy, 1975

When the Easter holidays came Harriet and Lizzie caught a plane to Milan. They spent a couple of days there, loving the buzz of the sophisticated city, the art and the extraordinary fashions, then they picked up a hire car and set off on the road to Ravenna.

As soon as they left the city they were captivated by the stunningly beautiful scenery set against the azure sky. The steep hillsides were covered in row upon row of vines, stitched together like a patchwork quilt, punctuated by cypress trees, patches of wild flowers, white cottages perched up high and rivers below snaking towards the coast. As they drove along the winding roads Harriet felt herself falling in love with the place, as if this was where she were meant to be.

They stopped in a village for lunch at a café-bar where they ate the creamiest, most delicious mushroom risotto they had ever tasted. Harriet listened-in to the locals speaking, trying to attune her ear to follow what they said, while rejecting the advances of the waiter who wanted to know what the beautiful ladies were doing later. They finished their meal with strong espressos then resumed their drive.

Further on in the distance they noticed rows of tiny white dots on a hill, making a similar pattern to the rows of vines they had been admiring all day.

But as they grew closer they could see that these were nothing to do with vines; they were gravestones.

They had come across one of the many war cemeteries that were scattered across the region, a memorial to the Allied forces who had been killed liberating Italy from the Nazis. Harriet and Lizzie stopped the car and walked over to a stone memorial with hundreds of names carved upon it. It served as a sharp reminder of why Anthony had been in Italy in the first place – his journey had been no holiday.

An elderly woman was there, putting flowers on one of the graves. She looked up, saw the two English women and spoke to them with a strong American accent.

'Good morning to you. Beautiful day, isn't it?'

She went on to tell them, 'this is my son's grave. He was here during the war, based at Ravenna. He used to write and tell us about the good times but we knew that was only part of the story. He was killed in the fighting here in '44. I come over every few years to pay my respects.'

'So sorry for your loss,' said Lizzie. 'How old was your son?'

'Just twenty-one. My only child.'

They stood in silence for a moment.

'We're on our way to Ravenna. We had no idea this was here,' said Lizzie, looking around and gesturing with her arm.

'People forget,' said the woman. 'And this cemetery is tiny compared to the ones further South – especially at Cassino. Thousands of men were lost there – thousands…'

'My uncle fought here with the British Army,' said Harriet, 'we're tracing some of the places he went to. He's not well enough to travel so we're here for him.'

'What are those flowers called?' asked Lizzie, looking at the delicate blue flowers with a bright yellow centre the woman had placed on her son's grave.

'They're pasqueflowers. Back home in Dakota we call them the prairie crocus. They grow wild all around here at Easter time. Pretty, ain't they?'

'Yes, they're beautiful.'

'Do you remember?' said Harriet, 'there was a pressed flower like that in Uncle Anthony's sketch book – the Blumfeldts recognised it. It's lovely to see them for real.'

Harriet and Lizzie walked slowly around the graves of the doomed youth, each with their own tragic tale. 'At least Uncle Anthony came home,' said Harriet.

As they walked back to the car the American woman said, 'it was lovely to meet you. I hope you find what you're looking for.'

They reached Ravenna, which was larger and more industrial than they had expected, and booked into the hotel where they had arranged rooms for the next couple of nights.

In the morning they set off for Affossa, Harriet in her denim bell-bottom jeans and T-shirt and Lizzie in shorts and a cheesecloth shirt tied around her midriff, and spent a few hours looking around the market and buying gifts to take home.

They tried to see the town through Anthony's eyes - the destruction, poverty and streets full of foreign soldiers. But being in tourist mode themselves and with modern apartments and office blocks all around them it was difficult to picture. Then, in the main town square, they came across a plaque dedicated to twenty partisans who had been shot there in cold blood by the Germans in 1943.

'How terrible,' said Harriet, 'it shows you what we were fighting for.'

Some buildings remained in ruins and picking up the locals' chatter Harriet said, 'they had an earthquake here a couple of years ago – there was a lot of damage and they haven't got the funds to re-build. Sounds horrible, and quite a few people died, apparently.'

They looked inside the impressive church then had lunch at a nearby café, speculating as to whether Anthony and Isabella may have gone there. Harriet asked the barman if he knew *La Casa Bianca*, the address on Anthony's letter, and he gave her directions.

In the afternoon they found the narrow road that led up to the farmhouse. As they reached the top Harriet cried, 'there it is! *La Casa Bianca* – the white house. Isn't it charming!' They drove to the front gate, got out the car and looked around.

'Shall we?' asked Lizzie, her hand hovering by a brass bell on a wooden stand.

Harriet hesitated for a moment, feeling suddenly nervous at the prospect of actually meeting Isabella. Maybe Gilda had been right to caution her. But they had come all this way…

Harriet took a deep breath.

'Yes!' she said.

Lizzie rang the bell and a dog began to bark. A short, dark man in his mid-thirties, dressed in his working clothes, came out of the house and walked towards them.

'*Buon giorno Signorinas*. How can I help you?'

Harriet attempted her best Italian.

'*Buon giorno*, Signor. We are sorry to disturb you. We're on holiday from England. We're looking for someone called Isabella Fortuno. Is this her home? Do you know her?'

'Isabella? She's my sister. But she has not lived here for years – she moved away when she got married, a long time ago. What do you want with her?'

'Well, we have an old photo of her that belongs to my uncle. He was a soldier here during the war. He wrote a letter to her, which he never posted, and that is how we found this address. We wondered if we could contact her?'

The farmer felt uneasy. He distrusted these foreign women who seemed to know something about his sister. 'Where is this photo?'

'Here,' said Harriet, producing the sepia photograph from her bag and handing it to him.

He caught his breath.

'*Madre mia…*'

He crossed himself. The years disappeared as he looked at the pretty young girl smiling at the camera. Visibly moved his attitude softened and he said, 'yes – yes that is her. That is my beautiful sister – Isabella.' Collecting himself, he looked at the back of the photo.

'So who is this 'Antonio' that she gave this to?'

'My uncle – Anthony. We think she liked to call him 'Antonio'.'

'Antonio is the name of her son,' he said.

'She has a son?'

'She has two sons and four daughters. Antonio is the oldest. He was named after his father's brother who died fighting with the partisans. I have never heard of this other Antonio, an Englishman.'

'Do you remember foreign soldiers being here during the war?' asked Lizzie.

'Yes, I do, but I was very young. First we had the Germans, then Americans and the British. Some of them stayed here at the farm.'

He paused, thinking back to his childhood.

'In Christmas '44 the British soldiers organised a party for the children of the town.' He grinned at the recollection. 'Isabella took me and my sisters. I had never seen so much food!'

A woman approached from the farmhouse.

'Guiseppe! Are you all right? Who are you talking to?'

He turned and shouted to his wife.

'These English ladies were asking me about my sister Isabella. Their uncle knew her during the war.'

The woman snorted.

'We had too many foreign soldiers here in the war,' she said, dismissively. 'We don't talk about those days now. Come, husband, it's time to feed the animals.'

'Yes, my love, I'll come now.'

His wife turned back to the house.

'I must go,' he said.

'Thank you for your help,' said Harriet, then added, 'could you tell us where your sister lives now?'

'Yes - *La Casa sulla Collina* in Bassino. It's about fifteen kilometres away on the road to Ravenna – Isabella's lived there since she married her husband, Carlo Spinetti. Now I must go.'

'Thank you so much!'

'Good day to you.'

The farmer walked back towards his house. Half-way along the path he turned, looked at the women and waved. Something gnawed at his memory but it was too vague, he couldn't place it.

'Guiseppe!' his wife called.

'Yes! I'm coming, *caro*.'

Harriet put the photo back in her bag.

'Mention of the war does stir up so many memories for people, doesn't it - and obviously his wife isn't very keen on talking about it!'

'Yes, you have to tread very carefully,' said Lizzie. 'So Isabella did marry Carlo and have lots of children, as we'd suspected. But isn't it strange that her son is called Antonio?'

'Yes, after his uncle. Pure coincidence I expect. And now we have an address for Signora Isabella Spinetti. Let's go to Bassino!'

They got out the map, found the spot, and set off.

*

Lying in bed that night Guiseppe Fortuno found it hard to sleep. Speaking to the English women had triggered many memories of that time - Isabella, so young and beautiful, and his parents, kind and loving, working hard to give their family a good life.

And yet, beneath those happy memories there was something troubling him that he couldn't quite recall…

When he finally fell asleep, he had a disturbing dream.

He was a small boy, five or six years old. He'd been playing out in the field and hadn't realised how late it was. He was hurrying home when, passing the barn, he heard strange noises. The door was slightly ajar and he looked inside. In the moonlight he could see a khaki uniform and a woman's clothing, discarded, on the ground. The noises were coming from a pile of straw in the corner. He saw somebody's arm – a leg – a head of fair hair – a bottom? – moving around, and a panting sound, like the sound the horse made after a canter through the field. The young Guiseppe stood and stared, then there came a stifled cry from the man, a sigh from the woman. The woman turned her head towards the barn door and he saw her face, for a split second, before he ran away as fast as his legs would carry him, back to the farmhouse.

Guiseppe awoke with a start and sat up in bed, his heart thumping.

His wife stirred beside him. 'What's the matter, *caro*?' she mumbled, half asleep.

Guiseppe recovered his breath and came back to the present.

'I'm all right. Just a bad dream. Go back to sleep.'

But he knew it wasn't just a dream. He remembered everything, now – the feelings of curiosity and guilt, the implicit knowledge that he must keep what he'd witnessed a secret and the overriding need to protect the woman he'd seen with a foreign soldier in the barn that evening - his sister, Isabella.

CHAPTER 44

Italy, 1975

La Casa sulla Collina turned out to be quite an enterprise. Acres of terraced vines covered the steep hills around the house, there was a collection of barns and stables for farm animals, then to one side stood some ugly concrete buildings, a factory and a warehouse, out of place amongst the greenery. This was wine-making on an industrial scale. Harriet and Lizzie drove up to the house and followed signs to a parking area where they found a fifty-seater coach with '*Gute Reisen!*' emblazoned across the side, discharging its cargo of German tourists. Harriet and Lizzie parked the car and followed the throng.

A stocky, dark teenage boy saw them trailing behind and beckoned to them, saying in Italian, 'come, come! The tour begins in five minutes!'

The two looked at each other and thought, why not?

They tagged along with the tourists, trying to follow the curious mix of Italian and German being spoken as the guide, a smartly dressed woman in her early-twenties, explained how the grapes were harvested, crushed and fermented in vast stainless steel vats, and how red and white varieties were made. They visited the bottling and labelling plant and were then ushered into yet another room where the tasting was to take place.

A second woman appeared alongside the guide, causing some merriment as the two were identical. 'Yes, we're twins!' said the guide, as she and her sister poured a selection of wines into rows of glasses.

They put on quite an act, swirling the wine around, savouring the bouquet and talking up the qualities of 'the best wine in Italy' while the visitors enthusiastically followed suit. Harriet and Lizzie joined in the tasting, almost forgetting the reason for their visit. Finally the party was ushered through to the shop where a spending spree ensued, everyone buying cases of wine which the driver piled up and wheeled back to his coach with a trolley. Eventually the party left and the coach drove away leaving Harriet and Lizzie in the shop, each holding their purchases. Another, slightly older Italian woman appeared, checked the till receipts and discussed with the twins how much money they'd made. They sounded pleased – tourist trips were obviously a good earner.

The older woman noticed Harriet and Lizzie, heard them speaking and said in English, 'so you are not with the party?'

'No,' said Harriet.

'Aaah, so you enjoyed a free visit today?'

The two felt embarrassed and offered to pay.

'It's all right,' laughed the woman, 'I'm pleased you enjoyed it, and now you can tell all your English friends to come and visit the Spinetti-Fortuno vineyard!'

The mention of the name brought Lizzie to the point of their visit.

'Actually, it's Signora Spinetti we hoped to see.'

'My mother? She's not here – she's away in Milan, on business. Why do you want to see her?'

Harriet, who had inherited her mother's knack of getting people to open up to her, knew she had to handle this very carefully and said, 'could we sit down, please? We have something to show you…'

The woman, who introduced herself as Angelica Spinetti, ushered them over to a seating area, looked at them curiously and waited for them to speak. Harriet explained who they were and the reason for their visit, showing her the unposted letter and the photograph of Isabella which had only recently come to light.

Angelica was visibly moved – and suspicious. 'So your uncle knew my mother? She has never mentioned him. She never speaks about the war.'

Angelica took the photograph and looked at the message written on the back.

'She called him 'Antonio' – that's my brother's name! But I know nothing about this other Antonio.'

Harriet and Lizzie could hear the shock in her voice.

'So, Mama, you had a wartime romance…' said Angelica, talking to the photo of her mother, so young, so beautiful. 'You must have met the English soldier while my Papa was away, fighting…'

'My uncle intended to return to Italy but couldn't because he was taken ill,' said Harriet. 'He had a major stroke. He was unconscious for two years!'

'How dreadful!' said Angelica, then added, 'but my parents married just after the war ended, so it's just as well your uncle didn't come back!'

They sat for a moment while the news sunk in then Lizzie asked, 'is your father still alive?'

'Yes - but his health is not good. He stays in the house most of the time. My sister Susanna looks after him. I won't tell him about this – I don't want to worry him.'

Harriet looked at Angelica, touched her arm gently and said, 'I'm sorry, this has all come as rather a shock. Thank you for listening to us.'

Then she added, 'my uncle wanted us to pass on a message to your mother – to say he hopes she has a happy life.'

Angelica looked at Harriet, this English woman of about her own age, with her kind blue eyes and disarming smile. Something about her made Angelica feel willing to talk.

'I'm sorry about your uncle's illness and I will pass on his message. You can tell him my mother is a much-loved lady and a good wife. It is thanks to her vision and hard work that our wine business is the success it is today. If you want to give me the letter I can pass it to her.'

'Er – no, thank you,' said Harriet, 'I promised my uncle I would only give it to her personally.'

'Very well.'

Lizzie had been looking around the room and asked, 'what's that display over there?'

'That is our museum! There are a few old tools, some of our original wine bottles and family photographs. Would you like to see?'

'Please!' said Lizzie.

'My father's family have made wine for generations but it was only after he married my mother that the business really took off,' Angelica explained.

'When the Spinetti's and the Fortuno's joined together they expanded the enterprise and now we export our wine all over the world!'

She pointed to a display board with a blown-up black and white photo. 'This is our family,' she said, proudly. 'See, my father and mother – Carlo and Isabella. And here am I - aged about twelve, with my sisters, before my little brother was born.'

'And this is…?' asked Harriet, transfixed by the incongruously tall, thin, fair-haired boy at the end of the row, smiling into the camera.

Angelica hesitated.

'That is Antonio - my elder brother,' she said.

Harriet looked at Angelica, willing her to say more.

She added, quietly, 'I haven't seen him for thirteen years.'

'Really?'

'It was very sad. He had a big row with my parents and left home, suddenly. I haven't seen him since – none of us have. I miss him so much. Mama and Papa never speak of him.'

'How awful! Do you know where he is?'

'No. Mama and Papa told us he'd gone to Africa with the Army, but…'

She sounded doubtful.

They let the matter hang for a moment, then Harriet said, 'well, thank you for your time, Angelica. I'm sorry this has been difficult. Perhaps we shouldn't have come.'

'Some say it is better to leave the past alone…' Angelica replied.

She deliberated for a moment, then added, '…but sometimes one needs answers, to know the truth. I'll tell my mother about your visit when she gets back. Thank you for coming.'

Harriet handed Angelica her business card, saying, 'these are my details if you ever want to contact me.'

Harriet and Lizzie thanked her again, picked up their wine, left the shop and walked to the car where they sat, stunned.

'It's got to be, hasn't it,' said Harriet. 'I mean, Grandad's got photos of Anthony when he was young all over the house – you'll have seen them – and that boy is his image…'

'Yes - and the timing's right, isn't it…' said Lizzie.

'I wonder how Isabella and her husband dealt with it all those years, bringing him up – like a cuckoo in the nest. Maybe that's why Antonio left home in such a hurry – perhaps he found out the truth and couldn't handle it?'

'And he's been away ever since!'

'Angelica wasn't convinced about Africa, was she - perhaps they just said that to keep the children quiet. I wonder where he really is? Oh, Lizzie, wouldn't it be wonderful if we could find him!'

*

Angelica watched as the English women drove away and tried to absorb all this new information. So her Mama had betrayed her Papa while he was away! No wonder she'd kept quiet about what she did during the war.

338

Angelica looked again at the family photograph. As a child it had never occurred to her, but as she stared at the elder brother she loved and missed so much the realisation struck her like a blow to the head. Knowing what she knew now, it was as clear as day.

Her mother may not like talking about the war but Angelica couldn't, wouldn't, let her stay silent any longer.

CHAPTER 45

Bath, 1975

Harriet and Lizzie made their way back to Milan to catch their return flight then drove straight to Eagle House where the family were eager to know what they'd discovered. First, Harriet returned the undelivered letter and Isabella's photograph to Anthony and told them about the Spinetti-Fortuno vineyard. Then she announced, 'there's no easy way to tell you this. We saw a photograph of Isabella's oldest child - and he is the image of Anthony when he was young. We are sure he must be Anthony's son! He's called Antonio – after his uncle, apparently.'

Gilda nearly fainted, then recovered herself.

'But how can you be sure? It was only a photograph!'

Harriet grabbed one of the photos of Anthony on the sideboard and pointed at it. 'Honestly,' she said, 'this could be his twin!'

'So where is this son?' asked David.

'We don't know,' said Harriet, 'he had a big row with his parents thirteen years ago and left home, and they haven't seen him since.'

'So let's leave well alone then!' said Gilda. 'I warned you about digging up the past, it can't bring any good.'

'Let's see what Anthony says, shall we?' said David, picking up the spelling board.

But Antony was twitching so much David couldn't make any sense of it.

'Look,' he said, 'this is obviously too much for him – and for me! We need some time to reflect.'

Karl spoke up. 'You are right, David. It's a fascinating story – but it all happened a long time ago. The good thing, from what Harriet has told us, is that Isabella is leading a happy and successful life. And if her oldest child – well, not a child – he'd be, what, about thirty? – if he is Anthony's that would be wonderful, but...'

Gilda stifled a sob and her father took her hand. 'Wait, Gilda – let me finish. It would be wonderful, but, if this man has been missing for thirteen years and no one knows where he is, isn't it all rather academic? And if his own family neither know nor care, why should we? He might be in all sorts of trouble – or even dead...'

'But Angelica misses him,' said Harriet, 'she'd love to have him back!'

A discussion ensued with everyone talking at once.

Henry was listening intently. He suddenly remembered the young, fair-haired man he'd seen at the Embassy, delivering champagne...it must have been a coincidence, surely? He dismissed his foolish thought.

Eventually David had to call a halt.

'Harriet and Lizzie – your trip has raised more questions than it has answered. I suggest we wait until Anthony has had time to consider all this. But my own view is that we should let the matter rest.'

341

Christ, so I did make her pregnant! I have a son! Incredible! Although....poor Isabella, you must have suffered so much, bringing a foreign bastard into your Catholic world. I can imagine the problems: having a child that looks like me in your community must have raised some eyebrows.

The questions he must have asked himself as an adolescent! And when he found out, which somehow he must have done – God, how awful! I expect that's why he left home. He probably thinks I deserted his mother and hates me.

And I'm worried about Gilda - she's suffered enough with all these stories about my time in Italy. She'll find it really difficult to accept that I have a son. She's right – stirring up the past does bring its troubles. But if no one knows where Antonio is there's nothing more to be done. As Dad said - we should let the matter rest.

Italy, 1975

As soon as Isabella returned home and they were alone, Angelica told her mother about the visit from the two English women from Bath.

'The one called Harriet Roberts had a letter addressed to you, Mama, and a photo you'd given her uncle, a British soldier called Anthony, during the war.'

Isabella turned pale. She felt faint and sat down, suddenly remembering the first time she'd met Lieutenant Anthony Roberts at the *municipio* in Affossa.

Angelica fetched her a drink of water.

'I'm sorry, Mama, I know this is a terrible shock.'

'So what did they tell you?' Isabella asked, hesitatingly.

342

As Angelica told her what she had learnt, Isabella's mind drifted back thirty years. She'd always known in her heart that something dreadful must have happened to prevent Antonio from returning to her. It appalled her to learn that he had spent his life in a wheelchair, barely able to move or communicate…it was all too much to take in. Her heart went out to him, wanting to sympathise, to comfort. Although she had tried to forget him it had been impossible - he was still there inside her, the man she had loved so much…still loved…

She couldn't tell her daughter how she felt, it would cause too much hurt. What good would it do? Some things were better left unsaid.

Angelica knelt by her mother's side and put her arm around her.

'There was a message from Anthony – hoping that you had a happy life - so I told them about our family and the success you have made of the vineyard.'

Isabella nodded, stifling a sob, her eyes filled with tears.

'It was the war,' she managed to say at last. 'We were very young - we had no idea about anything! But now I understand why he didn't come back.'

'You loved him, didn't you?'

'Yes…yes, I did. But it was a long time ago, Angelica.'

Angelica knew what she had to say next.

'Mama, I know…I know about my brother, Antonio. I know it is the Englishman who is his real father, not Papa…'

Isabella caught her breath - hearing the truth spoken by her daughter shook her to the core.

343

'Angelica, you mustn't say anything! Your Papa has been hurt enough. And the younger children don't need to know.'

'But Mama, we are all grown up now! We can accept it. And I suppose that is why you argued, why Antonio left home. Mama, can't you forgive him?'

Isabella suddenly turned angry.

'Angelica!' she cried, 'you think you know everything, but you don't! Antonio has sinned, Angelica – I cannot forgive him! Never mention him again!'

With that she got up and fled from the room, overwhelmed by grief and anger, sorrow and regret.

Angelica watched her go, feeling even more perplexed and confused than ever. What else was her mother hiding from her? Why had her brother left home in such disgrace?

There was only one person who could tell the truth – Antonio. She had to find him. But how?

London, 1975

Henry didn't say anything to Tilly – the whole idea seemed ridiculous, yet it kept nagging at the back of his mind…

But Tilly was about to go away for a few days and she need never know. When he got to his desk in Whitehall he put through a call to the Embassy in Paris. He was surprised to hear his former secretary answering his old number.

'Sylvia! You're still there! It's Henry Roberts speaking.'

'Air Commodore! How nice to hear you! Yes, I'm still here – part of the furniture, me! What can I do for you?'

344

'Well, this may seem rather an odd question, but I wondered if you were still in contact with the wine merchants we used to deal with?'

'Yes – we still use the same one.'

'Excellent! Would you mind doing me a favour? Ask them if they have an Antonio Spinetti working for them? Or if not, whether they have any idea where he might be? And I'd appreciate your discretion…'

'Of course, sir…'

CHAPTER 46

Bonn, 1975

It took several weeks to gather all the required information together. The Blumfeldts forwarded details of names and significant dates, Mr Greenstein provided information about Ausberg and Beatrice organised matters at her end. At last everything was in place for the search to begin. Karl and Sonia told Gilda they did not feel strong enough to travel to Germany and asked her to go in their place. Having overcome her initial reluctance, Gilda now saw it as her duty to find out as much as she could about what had happened to her family, and that is how she came to be with Tilly on a plane bound for Bonn.

It was the first time Gilda had been abroad since she had arrived in Bath at the age of eight, so it was with a mix of nervous anticipation, curiosity and excitement that she embarked on her journey. She was pleased to have Tilly as her companion; her self-assurance rubbed off on Gilda, giving her confidence a much-needed boost as she set off on her very own voyage of discovery. And Tilly was expert at navigating the horrors of Heathrow.

For her part, Tilly was pleased the Blumfeldts had decided to go ahead. It was exciting to be embarking on a new venture and she was looking forward to having a break away from home, spending time with Gilda and seeing Beatrice again.

Harriet had had her Italian adventure and Freddie had moved to America to pursue his career in space science. Now it was her to turn to do something different. Even Henry had been pre-occupied lately - she couldn't work out why. Perhaps a few days apart might do them good.

Beatrice met them at the airport and drove them into the city where she lived in an apartment in the diplomatic quarter. They whisked along beside the Rhine on wide, straight, tree-lined roads, passing austere office blocks which housed the seat of the West German Government, then arrived at the hotel where Beatrice had reserved rooms. She left her guests to settle in and returned later to take them out to dinner.

Gilda was mesmerised by the bustling city, taking in the street names and shop signs written in German gothic style. Hearing the guttural inflections of the language, words that had once been instinctive came back to her. Some of the older people at Mr Greenstein's still spoke German but over the years Gilda had tried to distance herself from her origins - it was her faith, not her nationality, that defined her. Since her marriage she had proudly become a British citizen and to be back here, a foreigner in her native land, was an extraordinary sensation.

The next morning Beatrice took Tilly and Gilda to the library where the archives were kept. She escorted them down to the brightly-lit, air-conditioned basement where rows and rows of shelves containing boxes of files extended as far as the eye could see. Beatrice ushered her guests into an office and made the introductions.

'This is my chief researcher, Herr Müller. He's an expert at finding needles in haystacks, aren't you, Heinrich?' she said. 'I'll leave you in his capable hands.'

Herr Müller smiled and opened the vast ledger in front of him.

'Good morning, ladies. Let's begin our journey.'

*

Evacuations from Ausberg had begun in 1941 with most Jews being taken to the Lodz ghetto in Poland, then to Auschwitz-Birkenau. After a couple of hours, working methodically page by page, row by row, name by name, Herr Müller announced, 'Aahh: Blumfeldt…I've found something. Here, look…'

Tilly and Gilda peered at the neat handwriting and identified the names of Josef Blumfeldt and his wife Ingrid who had been admitted to Auschwitz in January 1942. The dates and places of birth tallied. They had been killed just one month later.

'Papa's parents!' exclaimed Gilda, sickened at the reality that these rows of names represented. 'It must be them.'

She stared at the page, looking at other names and recognising a few from Ausberg – neighbours, friends…

Herr Müller let the information sink in, then asked, 'that is all from your father's family?'

'Yes,' said Gilda.

He looked kindly at them and said, 'why don't we take a break now? Go outside and get some fresh air. We can resume our work this afternoon.'

*

Their next search was for Sonia's parents, Benjamin Schneider and his wife Hannelore. By late afternoon, having picked his way meticulously through the records, Herr Müller found that they, too, had been taken to Lodz shortly after the Blumfeldts, then to Auschwitz in late 1942 where they were killed in the gas chambers in January 1943. Again, the shock of the terrible reality struck home. Tilly took Gilda's hand, beginning to wish they hadn't come.

Herr Müller said, 'this is enough for today. Now at least you know what happened to your grandparents, Gilda. Tomorrow we will try and find your mother's brother and his wife.'

'Uncle Franz…'

'Yes. Now, go for a walk, clear your minds, and have something to eat. It is a very brave thing you are doing, ladies. I will look forward to seeing you again in the morning.'

That night Gilda had a terrible nightmare. She was at the cinema with Jacob when pictures of Jews in Belsen appeared, skeletal, disease-ridden, hollow-eyed, but this time she recognised them – she could make out her father and her mother, and their parents, then there was a young girl, so thin and frail, haunted, and she realised the girl was herself.

The next day, anticipating the worst, Tilly and Gilda returned to the library and Herr Müller resumed the search. The now familiar pattern emerged: Franz and his wife Anne Frieda had been taken to Lodz in 1942, then transferred to Auschwitz in March 1943. But this time something was different.

'Now, this is interesting…' said Herr Müller, carefully checking the entry on the page. 'This shows that Franz gave his occupation as 'musician'. Is that correct?'

'Well, he played the violin,' said Gilda, 'but he was a carpenter by trade.'

'He may have known that the Nazis sometimes spared musicians for entertainment purposes. I can't find a date of death. His presence of mind may have saved his life!'

'Really?' said Gilda and Tilly together. 'And what about his wife?'

The researcher moved down several pages before he halted at another entry.

'Not so good,' he said. 'Anne Frieda Schneider died in September 1943.'

'How terrible!' said Tilly. 'She didn't escape the gas chambers.'

Herr Müller paused and looked again at the entry. 'Actually, she did,' he said. 'She died in childbirth! Look, see the entry here – one Jew gone, another one born…'

'Dear God!' cried Gilda, 'she was pregnant when she went to the camp! But how sad that she died…What about the baby? Did it live?'

'Yes - a boy, named Benjamin Isaac Schneider.'

'Benjamin - after his grandfather!'

'So what happened to him?' asked Tilly.

'Let's find out, shall we?' said Herr Müller.

Not wanting to raise their hopes, Herr Müller told Gilda and Tilly that although thousands of babies were born in Auschwitz, very few survived.

The majority were drowned at birth, some were given away for adoption and others were used in foul experimentations or succumbed to disease.

'Would Uncle Franz have known that he had a son?' Gilda asked.

'It's doubtful, although word may have got to him somehow. Another woman would take care of a baby as her own – it was the only way the little ones survived.'

Gilda and Tilly waited anxiously while Herr Müller traced the records to January 1945 when the camp was liberated by the Soviets. Finally he said, 'here we are. Franz Schneider and Benjamin Isaac Schneider were sent to a camp for Displaced Persons in Bavaria.'

'So father and son were united!' cried Gilda, joyfully.

'Indeed!' said Herr Müller, 'quite remarkable!'

'And what were these camps?' asked Tilly.

'Resettlement camps – they were established by the Allies to provide survivors with a temporary home until they were fit enough to begin new lives in Europe, America or Israel. I should be able to get hold of the records – then we'll be able to see what happened to Franz and Benjamin.'

Herr Müller sat back in his chair and took off his spectacles.

'You have had a harrowing time, ladies, but from it all we have found some hope. Why don't you take a break tomorrow, let me do some more research, then come back and see me the day after?'

'That would be wonderful. Thank you so much!' cried Gilda.

Before they left, Tilly had a question.

'Herr Müller, may I ask you – do you know anything about what happened to the old Prisoner of War camps? My husband and my brother were – and still are – in the Royal Air Force. They were both captured and held in *Stalag Luft 32.*'

'In fact most POW camps were razed to the ground after the war. Some have had factories or housing built on them, others have just disappeared back into the woods. I'll see what I can find out.'

'Thank you. I'd appreciate that.'

That night at the hotel Tilly and Gilda drank their way through a couple of bottles of wine, going over what they had learnt and talking through the possibilities. They lay on Tilly's bed together, quite tipsy, and Gilda said, 'Tilly, I had a terrible nightmare last night. I'm scared to sleep on my own. Can I stay here with you?'

'Of course you can,' said Tilly, putting her comforting arms around her.

Gilda and Tilly returned to the library where Herr Müller produced the records of the Bavarian resettlement camp.

'They were both admitted in January 1945,' he began. Looking through the records he traced their movements from one camp to another over the next two years until he came to an entry in March 1947.

'That was when they finally left Germany,' he said. 'Do you see this entry here? Franz Schneider, aged thirty-seven, and his son Benjamin, aged three. They embarked on southbound train, headed for Palestine – to what would become, Israel.'

Herr Müller closed the ledger, stood up and said, 'and that, ladies, is where our trail ends.'

'So do you think they ever reached Israel?' asked Tilly.

'It is possible - you would need to check with the Israeli authorities, but I'm afraid I don't have any contacts there.'

'No...' said Gilda, 'but I do!'

That evening Beatrice joined Tilly and Gilda at the hotel for their final meal together.

'What an extraordinary few days you've had,' said Beatrice. 'I am so sorry about your grandparents, Gilda, but at least now you know the truth. And how wonderful, to find that your uncle and his son survived! You'll be contacting your friend in Israel?'

'Jacob – yes. When we get home I'll write to him with all the details Herr Müller gave us and see what he can find out.'

'Do let me know what happens, won't you?'

'Of course! We couldn't have done it without you! We're so grateful to you, Beatrice!'

'I'm pleased to have been of help. The 'not knowing' must have been dreadful for your family all these years.'

'Yes...' said Gilda, then her voice trailed off and she started to cry.

'I'm sorry, Gilda,' said Beatrice, 'it's been an emotional time. You must be exhausted. You must rest now.'

Before they left Bonn, Tilly and Gilda went back to see Herr Müller to give him a bottle of whisky.

'It is not necessary,' he said, 'but thank you.'

Then, turning to Tilly he said, 'I found out about *Stalag Luft 32*. As I expected - it was bulldozed after the war and now it is overgrown, taken back by the forest.'

'Like it never existed…' said Tilly. 'But we must never forget.'

Then she added, 'if you don't mind me asking, Herr Müller, did you lose loved ones during the war?'

A shadow passed across his face.

'Yes,' he replied. 'Both my parents worked in a factory in the Ruhr valley. They were killed in a raid by the Royal Air Force.'

Tilly nodded, and said, 'I am sorry for your loss.'

'It was war,' he said. 'We must remember those who died, and move on.'

CHAPTER 47

Bath, 1975

Tilly and Gilda travelled back to Bath where Sonia and Karl were overwhelmed by their news. They sat with David and Anthony, transfixed, wanting to know every detail of the search, mourning their losses but celebrating the survivors with Sonia repeating over and over again, 'thank God! Thank God! Franz is alive! He has a son! A son! I don't believe it!', sinking to her knees in prayer. On Shabbat the Blumfeldts went to Mr Greenstein's where prayers of thanksgiving were said.

A few weeks later Gilda received a phone call.

'Gilda – it's Jacob. I've managed to track down your relatives – it hasn't been easy – but now I have an address for them, here, in Tel Aviv. The son, Benjamin, is a lawyer – my wife knows of him! What do you want me to do?'

Two weeks after Jacob's call a letter arrived from Israel. The Blumfeldts were beside themselves with joy – Sonia clasped the letter in her brother's handwriting to her breast, reading and re-reading it to herself and anyone else who would listen.

There was a separate page in a more youthful hand from Benjamin saying how extraordinary it had been to receive a call from Jacob, whose wife he had come across on the legal circuit.

They were overjoyed to learn that Sonia, Karl and Gilda had successfully made their home in Bath and wondered if it would be all right to come over to visit them in the Autumn? His father was not in the best of health, but they would love to see them all…

This was all too much for Sonia who collapsed into her husband's arms and was only revived by a strong shot of brandy.

Henry and Tilly came to Eagle House, delighted to hear that Franz and Benjamin were planning to visit. Gilda and Tilly had grown close during their trip to Bonn and as they walked around the garden together Tilly sensed that, for all the wonderful news, something was wrong.

'You've been so brave, Gilda, doing this for your family,' she said, gently.

Gilda stifled a sob. Tilly gave her a handkerchief, put her arm around her and asked 'what is it, Gilda? Is there something you want to tell me?'

Gilda wiped her eyes, then blurted out, 'we're glad because Uncle Franz has a son…but what about Anthony? He has a son too! And he never knew, all this time, and we don't know where he is, and it's all my fault!'

Tilly was taken aback. 'I don't understand, Gilda. Of course it's not your fault!'

'But it is! She wrote a letter to Anthony…' Gilda sobbed.

'What do you mean? Who wrote to him?'

Gilda had kept her secret since she was fourteen years old, but she couldn't stay quiet any longer.

'Isabella!' The word came out like a piece of food caught in her gullet. 'She wrote to Anthony, just a few weeks after he got back from Italy…'

'What?!'

'I opened the letter…I know I shouldn't have done, but I did…'

'And you read it?'

Gilda nodded and said, 'she told him she loved him, she couldn't wait till he returned to her. But Tilly, he was so ill! He was in a coma! We all thought he was going to die! What was the point in telling him?'

'What happened to the letter, Gilda?'

'I…I burnt it! I was so jealous, so angry, I wanted Anthony for myself. And I was so young…I just wanted her gone. So I burnt it, and never told a soul until now!'

Tilly took in this revelation then asked, 'did she say she was pregnant?'

'No…' said Gilda, 'no, there was nothing about that. It was too soon – she probably didn't even know...and now I keep thinking about that young girl, so in love, wondering why he didn't return to her. I should have told someone…we could have written and explained that Anthony was ill…'

Tilly held her, trying to console her.

'Well, she knows now, doesn't she? Her daughter Angelica will have told her about Harriet's visit.'

'Yes, but she could have known years ago! And Tilly, I've been thinking about how Uncle Franz and Benjamin found each other, how important it was…

Anthony needs to see his son, and I mustn't stand in his way. If only we could find him! I feel so guilty about it all. I have prayed to God to forgive me, but I don't think He has...'

Tilly faced Gilda, put her hands on her shoulders and looked directly at her.

'Yes, you must pray to your God, Gilda,' she said. 'But if you want Him to forgive you there is something you must do first. You must apologise to the two people that really matter - Anthony, and somehow, one day, to Isabella. But I'm not sure how we're going to find Antonio...'

That night in bed, Tilly told Henry about Gilda's confession.

'Wow!' exclaimed Henry, 'the jealous little bitch! How on earth did you get her to confess all that? You didn't pull her toenails out, did you?'

'Well, I do have my methods...! But I had the feeling something was on her mind, ever since Bonn...'

Tonight, Gilda knelt in front of me, took my hands, and told me the secret she'd kept since she was fourteen years old...she told me about Isabella's letter.

What can I say? I had no idea back then that Gilda had such strong feelings for me – she was just a kid as far as I was concerned. And who knows what would have happened if someone had written to Isabella to tell her I was ill?

Gilda was distraught tonight but I think she's suffered enough. I twitched my eye, she fetched the spelling board, and I spelt out:

'I F-O-R-G-I-V-E Y-O-U'

London, 1975

'Good morning, Air Commodore, it's Sylvia. I've managed to track down Antonio Spinetti. He still works at the wine merchants - he's their Marketing Director. They have an office just off the Champs-Elysées.'

'Really?'

Henry was overwhelmed, amazed that his hunch had proved correct.

'Er...do you want me to do anything? Set up a meeting?'

Henry thought for a moment.

'That's an excellent idea. Ask him to come to the Embassy – make up some excuse, like planning for a special event perhaps? And I'll come over and join you. Look, to let you into a secret, Sylvia - he's my long-lost nephew!'

CHAPTER 48

Italy, 1975

Carlo, knowing he had little time left, was thinking back over his life – his happy childhood, terminated by the terrible war; his fight against the Fascists and the tragic loss of his brother; and his love for Isabella. He was so proud of his family and what they had achieved together. He only wished his and Isabella's parents had lived long enough to see their success. But behind it all something troubled him, and it went back to that fateful evening when Antonio had left. And now, as death approached, he felt compelled to say something, do something, before meeting God.

Carlo asked his daughter Susanna to bring the priest to him. He came, they said prayers together, then the priest asked, 'do you want to make a confession?' Carlo nodded, and the priest sat closer to him.

In a rasping voice, Carlo began, 'I have sinned. I have been wronged by people I love and I have not been able to forgive them. But I am dying, Father, and before I meet my Maker I need to say how sorry I am. What can I do?'

The priest replied, 'it is not too late. If you feel your heart has opened towards these people, if you still love them in spite of what they did, then, you are ready to forgive. Tell them, while you can. Then God will forgive you.'

Carlo carefully considered the priest's words and decided the time had come to speak to his wife. Isabella realised her husband was nearing the end and knelt at his bedside as he told her he forgave her and Antonio.

Isabella, full of remorse, said, 'but Carlo, I do not deserve your forgiveness. I deceived you. You brought up Antonio as your own, you worked night and day to support our family and I never even thanked you.'

'It was my choice. I loved you.'

'When Antonio left that night I lost you too.'

'I'm sorry, said Carlo, 'that was the hardest time.'

'Yes, *caro*. And that was when I realised how strong and wise you are. But now it's too late for you to love me again.'

Carlo shook his head.

'No, Bella – I still love you. I forgive you – and I forgive Antonio. And so must you.'

That night, Carlo died in his sleep.

*

Isabella was bereft. She attended Carlo's funeral overcome by grief and afterwards, back at their house her children gathered around her, cocooning her with their love. Her younger son Luigi, soothing her, said, 'don't worry, Mama, I will look after you. I am the man of the house now.' She nodded and squeezed his hand. He was so like his father.

But something was gnawing at her heart. She couldn't stop thinking about Carlo's last words to her – that she must forgive Antonio. If Carlo could, so could she. And that evening, alone by her bed, she knelt and prayed and wept and finally, she forgave.

Paris, 1975

Henry felt strange, being back at the Embassy.

'Sylvia!' He greeted his old secretary and co-conspirator with a kiss.

She was almost excited as he was at the prospect of this mysterious meeting.

'I've put you in the interview room and left a pot of coffee for you both. Signor Spinetti should be here in a few minutes.'

As soon as Antonio entered the room Henry knew he was the same person he'd seen at the Embassy eight years ago. He'd matured from delivery boy to business executive, tall, thin, with shoulder-length fair hair, hazel eyes and a smart suit. They shook hands.

He introduced himself. 'Antonio Spinetti. How may I help you?'

*

Antonio was stunned. Henry showed him photos of Anthony and Isabella and he stared at them, saying, 'this…this is the same photo I had, but I lost it…And this picture of my mother…I don't believe it!'

He listened carefully as Henry told him about Anthony's illness and how he communicated using a spelling board.

'I had no idea. But you say that your daughter – Harriet? – she has been to Italy and met my sister Angelica?'

'Yes. And Angelica would love to see you again – she misses you.'

Antonio shook his head. 'I don't know…it has been too long. And I don't know whether my parents will ever forgive me…'

'I can't say. But time does heal – and unless you approach them, you'll never know.'

Henry offered Antonio a cigarette and they both sat back and inhaled deeply.

Then Henry said, 'look, Antonio, I want to invite you to Bath, to meet Anthony – and the rest of your English family. It would give us much pleasure.'

'Really?'

Antonio thought for a moment. 'This has come as a shock to me – but yes, I would like to come to England and meet you all. I have never been there. But…'

'But…?'

Antonio sighed and scratched the back of his neck. 'Perhaps, first, I should go home. I owe them that. I need to see my parents again before I meet Anthony.'

'Yes. Yes, of course…that's a good idea. I hope it goes well.'

At home in their flat in the Marais - a fashionable and bohemian part of Paris, once the city's Jewish quarter - Antonio told his partner Alain about his extraordinary meeting with Henry and how he had invited him to England.

'But I have decided that first, I must go home to Bassino.'

'Do you want me to come with you?' Alain asked.

'No – not this time, anyway. But thank you. It's something I need to do on my own.'

Bath, 1975

Henry came back from Paris with the most astonishing news – somehow, he tracked down and met Antonio – my son. I can't believe it. What a phenomenal brother I have. He told me that Antonio's a handsome young man who has made a successful career for himself in the wine trade. And one day soon I hope to meet him.

I think that Gilda will be able to handle it – she seems to be reconciled to the situation now and won't stand in the way. And she's curious to see what he looks like...

Tilly said, 'good God, Henry, how did you manage that?'

Henry replied, 'I had this hunch...it seemed such a long shot, I didn't want to tell you. But it worked!'

Then he took her in his arms, looked at her and said, 'so you see, Mrs Roberts, you're not the only one around here with the right contacts and a knack for solving puzzles...'

CHAPTER 49

Italy, 1975

Antonio left Paris early, stopping overnight in Lyon then continuing his journey the next day. He drove on to Milan in his Alfa-Romeo, thinking about the time he had hitch-hiked there seeking refuge with Uncle Alberto, and reached Bassino in the late afternoon.

La Casa sulla Collina looked different – ugly new buildings had sprung up, a factory, a warehouse, concrete roads and a car park. He suddenly felt nervous, realising how much had changed. Would they even remember who he was?

A teenage boy approached him.

'*Buon giorno, signor*, can I help you?'

Antonio looked at the boy who reminded him of someone, then it dawned on him that he was a younger version of Carlo. This must be Luigi, his little brother – who clearly had no idea who this visitor was. Then a young woman appeared at the door of the house. She looked at the fair-haired man wearing designer jeans and a white shirt, standing by his sports car, lighting a cigarette and she felt the earth move under her feet. She ran to him, crying out 'Antonio!' and flung her arms around his neck.

Luigi stood back, totally bemused by the scene.

The woman reminded Antonio of his Mama and it took him a second to register that it was his little sister, Angelica. He hugged her in turn, saying, 'Angelica! You are so grown-up!'

'I can't believe it's really you!' she cried, just as her mother appeared in the doorway.

Isabella looked at the young couple. She caught her breath and her knees buckled beneath her. As she fell to the ground she said a prayer to the Holy Mother and crossed herself. What was this apparition? She could see the ghosts of herself and her lover Antonio there, right in front of her. She looked up at the sky. 'Is this your doing, Carlo?' she asked, 'have you sent these spirits down from heaven?' Then the ghosts turned and saw her, and as they walked towards her she saw they were flesh and blood – her own flesh and blood…

'Mama,' said Antonio, taking her hands and helping her to her feet. She had changed – she seemed smaller, her face was lined and her dark hair, tied back from her face in a bun, was flecked with silver. She was wearing black. They looked at each other, then he took her in his arms and held her, tightly.

'Go inside,' said Angelica, gently, 'you need some time alone.'

They did as she said, then Angelica went over to Luigi and announced, 'it's Antonio – our big brother. He's come home!'

Luigi looked distinctly unimpressed. 'So I see…' he said.

Isabella and Antonio sat as one, their arms around each other, crying, touching, measuring the changes in their faces. Explanations were pointless; all that mattered was that they were together again.

'And Papa,' said Antonio, 'where is Papa?'

Isabella's face fell.

'He is dead, *caro*. He had been ill, for a long time. He died two months ago.'

Antonio was stunned; in his mind his strong, sturdy Papa was invincible.

'But before he died, he forgave you,' said Isabella, 'and I forgive you too.'

Tears formed in Antonio's eyes. 'Papa…I am so sorry. I wanted to see him again. I do not deserve your forgiveness. I'm so sorry for hurting him, and you. You must miss him, Mama.'

'I do…but I have been aching to see you, my son.'

Then she asked, 'what made you decide to come back?'

*

'So now I know, Mama – I know about you and the English soldier, how you loved him – and I understand why he didn't return to you. And…I must tell you that his brother, Henry, the one who got in touch with me – he's invited me to Bath, to meet Anthony and the rest of his family.'

Isabella caught her breath. This foreign place her lover Antonio used to tell her about so many years ago, these people he had spoken of…she had never thought in a million years that her son would go there and actually meet them…

When they heard that Antonio was back his other sisters flocked around him, excited to see their big brother again even if their memories of him were vague.

Isabella looked at her daughters – the twins were both married now, with babies of their own, and Susanna had nursed her Papa for many years. She thought of the lies and half-truths she had told them in the past, to protect them – and herself. Now they were old enough to hear the truth about her love affair and so, at last, she told them.

They were shocked, but knew that strange things happened in wartime, and understood. Thirteen-year old Luigi feigned little interest but inwardly he was upset to learn that his Mama had betrayed his beloved Papa – and that Antonio was the result.

But Angelica still had something on her mind. After her mother had gone to bed she sat up late, talking to her brother, drinking the best Spinetti-Fortuno red wine.

Angelica said, 'when you had that big row with Mama and Papa that awful night…it was about your English father, wasn't it? But I am sure there is something else that Mama hasn't told me…'

'Aaah,' said Antonio. He faced her and took her hand. 'Angelica, your big brother has been very bad. He has said and done some terrible things. He has sinned. And he will carry on sinning…Angelica, that was the night I discovered that I prefer men.'

*

Isabella rang Alberto to tell him Antonio had come back home.

'So, the prodigal son has returned,' he said.

*

368

The grape harvest was in full swing and Isabella welcomed Antonio's offer to stay and help. She showed him around the vineyard and the factory complex, proudly explaining the changes they had made to increase productivity and improve the efficiency of the business.

Isabella had tried to force the truth about her son's sexuality to the back of her mind but now she couldn't ignore it any longer. Wasn't one meant to be more tolerant about such things these days? – that's what Alberto had told her. So as they walked together through the rows of vines she said, '*caro*, tell me about your friend – Alain?'

Antonio had been expecting this, sooner or later. He hesitated for a moment then said, slowly, 'Alain rescued me, Mama – I was in a lot of trouble. Without him and his friends I would be dead. I was very ill and in hospital for a long time…'

Isabella gasped, wracked with guilt that she hadn't been there when her son needed her.

'…and he helped me get better. He visited me, we became friends and when I recovered I went to live with him on his canal barge in Amsterdam.'

'Amsterdam?'

'Yes. And he found me a job at the wine merchants where he worked. Then after a year or so the company opened a new branch in Paris – Alain's home city – and we moved there. We have a flat in the Marais.'

They paused while Isabella absorbed this information.

Antonio faced his mother and took her hands.

'It's how God made me, Mama…'

His words echoed with her for some reason.

'I know, *caro*,' she said, looking into his hazel eyes. 'I will try and understand. But are you happy?'

'Yes, very happy. Although we are beginning to tire of life in the city. For a while we've been talking about moving out and buying our own vineyard. In fact we've got our eye on some land near Trieste.'

'So you would be back in Italy? Antonio, that would be wonderful!'

'Yes! And do you know,' he gestured around him, 'being back here makes me realise how much I've missed my own country and working outdoors, tending the vines.'

'But will your - friend - mind leaving France?'

'No, he's ready to move on. And also we're thinking about producing sparkling wine. It's impossible to buy land in the Champagne region but in Italy it is still available.'

'That sounds a good idea,' said Isabella, 'it's a developing market.'

'Yes, so I believe.'

Then Antonio said, 'you must meet Alain, Mama. He's really nice, and kind…'

'Yes, Antonio. I would like that.'

*

As they worked together on the harvest Antonio chatted to his sisters, pleased to get to know them again. Just one thing bothered him.

'Mama,' he asked, 'why do they keep asking me about Africa?'

'Aaah…' she said, embarrassed.

He guessed what had happened.

'It's all right – I just said it was very hot. And I told them a story about how I fought off a man-eating lion!'

His brother Luigi wasn't so easy to pacify.

'Luigi is working hard at school,' Isabella told Antonio. Turning to her younger son she said, 'you're going to study hard for your exams and you want to go to College, don't you, *caro*?'

'Maybe…but now Papa is dead I would rather work here with the vines like he used to.'

'No, Luigi, it is better to get qualifications.'

'I'm not so sure,' he said, adding sarcastically, 'but now *Antonio* is here you won't need me anyway!'

Isabella and Antonio stood and watched as he stormed off.

After their dinner that evening Antonio took Luigi to one side and offered him a cigarette, which he took.

'Luigi, I know you are finding things hard without Papa,' said Antonio, as they lit up.

'*My* Papa. Yes, I really miss him.'

'I want you to know, I'm not planning to stay here – I needed to come back to see Mama but I'm not going to interfere – you are the man of the house now and Mama needs you.'

Luigi looked up at him.

'So you're not going to move back here?'

'No, I'm not. I have other plans.'

Luigi visibly relaxed.

'Good! I mean, Antonio, you are my brother – well, half-brother – and I am pleased for Mama's sake that you have come back to see us. But I want to be the man here. Papa taught me everything he knew. And I don't want to waste my time at school.'

Antonio exhaled, a plume of smoke surrounding him. 'I wish I'd gone to College,' he said. 'I was meant to. My life would have been so different.'

Luigi looked at him, curiously. 'But you're doing all right now, aren't you?'

'Yes - but it's taken many years. I was in a bad place for a long time, Luigi…'

The two stood and finished their cigarettes.

'Just try and make Mama proud,' said Antonio.

When Antonio came to leave he embraced his mother and said, 'I will let you know about Trieste - when we're settled in you must come up and see us.'

'I would love to, *caro*,' she said. 'In fact, I would like to help you with your business. I never told you, but for years I saved money for my children. And I have kept some for you, Antonio. I always knew you would come back one day. It's time it was put to good use!'

'Mama, I couldn't…'

CHAPTER 50

Bath, 1975

With a roar from its diesel engine the inter-city 125 express entered Bath Spa station and slowly squealed to a stop. Passengers disembarked, those waiting climbed aboard and with another deafening bellow from the rear engine the train departed towards Bristol.

Karl and Sonia stood, anxiously looking around the crowded platform, then they saw them - an elderly, frail gentleman with white hair, leaning on the arm of a younger man, both carrying leather suitcases. The older man was wearing a dark suit, collar and tie with a raincoat folded over his arm, the younger man more casual in a light waterproof jacket and jeans.

As Karl and Sonia walked towards them the old man put down his suitcase, moved away from the support of his son and opened his arms to embrace the sister he had not seen for nearly forty years.

For a moment, time stood still. Then, after much shaking of hands, hugs and tears, Karl said, 'welcome to England. Let's get you home.'

Back at Eagle House, David, Anthony and Gilda were waiting for their special guests in a heightened state of expectation.

Gilda was shocked to see her uncle looking so frail and old beyond his years but when he kissed her and said, 'my little Gilda! How grown up you are, and how beautiful!' she recognised his voice, and looking into his dark brown eyes she could see it really was him –Uncle Franz.

Her cousin, Benjamin, had the same dark, curly hair her uncle had when he was young. He felt in awe at discovering this extended family that, just a few months ago, he had known very little about.

They all went upstairs to the living room to meet Anthony who had prepared some words of welcome which Gilda read out to them. The rest of the day passed in a blur of talk and reminiscence, and it being a Friday, an outstanding Shabbat dinner was served.

After the celebrations Franz, exhausted from his journey and the emotions of the day, withdrew to his room. Sonia went to make sure he was comfortable and sat on the bed next to him – her little brother.

'I cannot believe you are here,' she said.

'I cannot believe it either.'

She took his hand, then noticed a mark on his arm under the sleeve of his pyjama jacket.

She gasped. She knew what it was.

He looked at her and pulled up his sleeve to expose the row of numbers the Nazis had tattooed on his arm.

'I heard the screams, Sonia,' he said, gravely. 'I can still hear them. We must never forget.'

At the weekend Henry and Tilly came to Eagle House to join the reunion. Tilly felt very emotional, meeting the real people behind the names in Herr Müller's ledger. There were so many questions, only some of which had answers.

'So do you remember anything about the camp?' Gilda asked Benjamin.

'Nothing at all,' he replied. 'My first memories are of living in a big house with lots of other families. It was cold and dark inside, and Papa used to work, making things from wood. And we would go to the synagogue and pray.'

'We lived in Tel Aviv,' said Franz, 'I took casual work, I played violin on the streets for money while Benjamin was at school. It was hard, and my health was poor. My first stroke of luck was when the woman who owned the house where we stayed gave me some woodworking tools that had belonged to her husband. I learnt how to use them again and worked as a jobbing carpenter until we had enough money to rent a little workshop with rooms above. We lived there for many years, didn't we, son?'

'Yes, Papa, just you and me. They were good years.'

'We took Israeli citizenship – a wise decision. Eventually we made enough to buy our own flat, and Benjamin did so well at school...'

'I wanted to be a lawyer and worked to put myself through college. My first job was in a solicitor's office where I met my wife – she's a secretary. And now our son, Franz, is eight years old and our daughter, Ruth, is five. Papa lives with us, so we can look after him.'

Sonia clapped her hands with pleasure. 'And I thought our family had come to the end of its line! Benjamin, this makes me so happy! One day you must bring them all here to meet us.'

Tilly asked, 'Franz, when you were in the camp, how did you find out that you had a son?'

Franz paused, collecting his thoughts, then said, 'men were separated from the women but certain workers would pass messages for us. I had no idea Anne Frieda was pregnant, then one day we heard that a woman from Ausberg had died in childbirth. And someone else found out her name…'

Franz took a breath and continued. 'When the camp was liberated I sought out the child and found the woman who'd been looking after him. We travelled to the resettlement camp together and for a while we were a family, but then she died…she was so weak…we all were...'

'It's a miracle that you found each other!' said Tilly.

'Yes, it was,' said Franz, 'I thank God every day. I just wish our parents could have known…'

Franz paused, staring into the past, then turned to Tilly and Gilda and said, 'but it is thanks to you and your friends that Benjamin and I can be here now, with you all, in Bath. We would never have known how to find our family without your help. This must be a truly blessed house.'

David listened, reflecting that when he and Wendy had offered the Blumfeldts a home they'd had no idea how far-reaching their decision would be.

He watched Gilda, now his daughter-in-law, and her mother, who could barely take her eyes off her long-lost brother, and marvelled at what a strange world it was. How he wished Wendy could have been there to share the moment with him.

David asked Franz about the current situation in Israel.

'For us, war is never far away,' said Franz. 'The Six-Day war in '67 was very frightening - we used to watch the jets flying overhead and hear the gunfire, but thankfully we escaped harm. And every day there are terrorist threats. One has to be vigilant all the time. We face many political problems in our country and there is no easy answer...'

'But Tel Aviv is a thriving city now, Papa,' interjected Benjamin. 'They've demolished many old buildings, we have new housing and green spaces, and a real mix of people from all over the world. It is a very exciting place to live, especially for young people.'

Gilda listened and it suddenly struck her that if she'd gone to Israel with Jacob this might have been her life. Then she looked at her husband, his family and her own parents, safe in the security and peace of Eagle House, knowing that for all the excitement Israel offered this was where she was meant to be. She had made the right decision.

Franz and Benjamin were the stars at Mr Greenstein's, given the VIP treatment as they spoke of their lives in Tel Aviv. Jacob's mother had almost equal billing, thrilled that it was her son who had finally traced the family to their home.

Other members of the congregation flocked around Franz asking for information about their own lost relatives and he was able to remember a few names which provided some comfort. At the service the Rabbi spoke of how vital it was to preserve these memories for future generations so that what had happened would never be forgotten. Gilda prayed along with everyone else, thanking God for those who survived the camps and for His help in finding Franz and Benjamin.

Her faith was as strong as ever, but privately she added a separate prayer to thank Tilly, Beatrice and Jacob, without whose help even God would have struggled…

One thing had been niggling at Sonia's mind. 'Franz, after Karl and Gilda and I left Ausberg, did you try and contact us? We wrote letters to you and to Mama and Papa…'

'Sonia, we never received them - the Nazis burnt everything. None of us heard any news from England, it was all destroyed. Even if we'd known where you were, they would have burnt our letters.'

'Of course,' said Sonia, sorrowfully. 'But we felt so awful, abandoning you all.'

'You mustn't say that, Sonia! You did exactly the right thing. We prayed for you, always. Then there was Lodz and the camp and it was all so terrible…one lost track of time. By the time we were free everything was so different and I was so weak…'

'But we're together now,' said Benjamin, 'that is the main thing.'

The week went by too quickly. Sonia and Karl proudly showed their guests around Bath, their adopted city and home. Franz and Benjamin admired the architecture, historic and new, but Sonia and Karl also told them about their own internment and the horrors of those terrible nights when the bombs fell and Wendy was killed. No one had escaped from the devastation of war.

On the visitors' last night Sonia invited some friends to Eagle House and after their meal they put on some musical entertainment. One woman sung some traditional Jewish songs and Gilda played the piano, then one of the men produced a violin. He carried it over to Franz and said, 'please play to us.'

Without a word Franz slowly got to his feet, placed the violin under his chin and played a mournful folk song he had learnt as a boy. In his mind he saw another audience: men in the black uniforms of the SS, relaxing in their chairs, smoking cigarettes, watching him while he played for his very life.

When he finished he sat down, looking at no one. There was a moment's silence, then everyone applauded, tears in their eyes.

Franz handed the violin back to its owner then took Sonia's hand in his and they sat, not letting each other go, for the rest of the evening.

*

Karl, Sonia and Gilda waved goodbye as the train taking Franz and Benjamin to London for their flight home disappeared into the distance.

'We have had a long life,' said Karl, 'and that was one of the most remarkable weeks we have ever spent.'

'I can die happy now,' said Sonia.

'But not yet, Mama!' said Gilda.

Then she added, 'I wonder if we'll see them again?'

'Of course we will, *liebchen*! Of course we will.'

CHAPTER 51

England, 1976

After a brilliant thirty-six year career the time had come for Henry to retire. As he celebrated with drinks at the RAF club in London he remarked ironically, 'at least now I'll have more time to fly!'

For the last few years he had been a member of his local flying club, flying light aircraft over the Home Counties at the weekends. It had kept his hand in and he never ceased to be thrilled by the sense of freedom and movement he felt as soon as he left the ground. It gave him the will to go back to his desk in Whitehall on Monday mornings – but now, his working days were over.

Aside from flying, the plan was that Henry and Tilly would help Tilly's parents who were having a wing of Hathaway Manor converted into a rehabilitation centre for injured ex-servicemen and women. But before they became submerged in doing-good for others, Tilly knew there was something her husband longed to do for his own satisfaction.

One bright weekend in early Spring, accompanied by Harriet and Freddie who had come home for the occasion, Henry and Tilly went to the aerodrome where, waiting on the runway, was a Spitfire.

The vintage planes were becoming rare but Tilly had worked her usual magic and arranged for one to be made available for her husband to take for a spin.

Henry felt ridiculously excited at having the chance to fly his favourite aircraft once more. After some initial checks with the ground crew he turned to give the thumbs-up sign to his family who waved to him from the edge of the airfield, then he clambered into the cockpit. He'd forgotten what a tight fit it was – even more so now, with the extra few pounds he was carrying – but once he got himself strapped in it felt comfortable and he was instantly at home. He switched on the engine which spluttered into life, checked his instruments and was given the all-clear to take off. As the plane trundled down the runway and rose slowly into the air the distinctive sound of its Merlin engine sent shivers down his spine. There was nothing else like it.

As the plane rose into the sky time slipped away and in his head he was twenty again, flying high over the English countryside he loved and had been prepared to die for. All the comrades he'd lost, all the battles he'd ever fought, every dog-fight he'd ever had came back fresh into his mind and suddenly, deep from within his memory emerged the face of a German pilot, frozen in sheer terror in the split second before Henry fired at him, blowing his plane to pieces.

Air traffic control spoke through the headphones and Henry came back to the present. Now, testing his skills he soared high into the sky, revelling in the responsiveness of this magnificent machine which felt like part of his own body.

With a nudge of the joystick he was turning on his side, dropping through the wispy clouds, free from the earth, gripped by the sheer joy of being back in his beloved Spitfire.

As the flight neared its end Henry's thoughts returned to the young man he had been, and to the German pilot. He thought how strange it was that two intelligent men of about the same age and similar background, with a love of flying, had somehow ended up trying to kill each other. At the time they were enemies, doing what they had to do. But now? A new generation had taken over; things were different. Patience and time, Tilly had said to him. He would never forget, but was he finally ready to forgive?

Air traffic control called him in. Henry flew low over the airfield in a final Victory roll then came into land and brought the plane to a stop. He sat for a moment to recover his breath, then opened the cockpit as the aircrew and his family ran over to him.

He climbed out of the plane and Tilly greeted him with a hug.

'Was it as good as you remember?' she asked.

'Yes…' said Henry, his head still in the clouds.

She looked at him. He seemed different – exhilarated, yet dazed and thoughtful. All at once.

He pulled himself together and looked at his family.

'Yes!' he declared, 'it was magnificent! Absolutely magnificent! Thank you so much!'

CHAPTER 52

Bath, 1976

The airliner touched down at Bristol airport on time. Henry and Tilly waited anxiously in the arrivals hall as passengers emerged until at last, among the businessmen and holidaying families, they spotted Antonio and a smartly dressed woman in her fifties, pulling suitcases behind them. Henry took a deep breath and Tilly gave his arm a squeeze.

'Here we go!' he said.

He waved and the pair made their way over to them.

'Antonio!' said Henry, shaking his hand, 'so good to see you again! This is Tilly, my wife.'

'Welcome to England!' said Tilly, as Antonio gave her a kiss on the cheek.

'It is wonderful to be here. May I present my mother, Isabella Spinetti.'

'Delighted to meet you,' said Henry, shaking her hand, and Tilly followed.

'I am pleased to meet you both,' said Isabella.

Then she turned to her son and spoke a torrent of words in Italian. Henry was concerned for a moment but Antonio said, 'my mother says it is a long time since she has spoken any English. It will take her a while to be fluent again. But she is overjoyed to be here and to meet you.'

Isabella smiled at them, her eyes moist. Tilly saw a formidable woman with excellent deportment in a dove-grey Armani trouser suit, her dark hair streaked with silver and pulled into a neat chignon, wearing some seriously expensive jewellery. Henry noticed her wide, dark eyes, and beneath the lines on her face he could see the beauty, the sparkle of the young girl who had captured his brother's heart so many years ago.

It had been Antonio's suggestion. When he had finally contacted Henry to make arrangements to come to Bath he'd asked if he could bring his mother with him. Since Antonio had moved to Trieste he and Isabella had spent time getting to know one another again and Antonio had convinced his mother that she really ought to take this chance to come to Bath with him. Henry thought it was an excellent idea and persuaded Anthony and Gilda, who were as ready as they would ever be, to agree.

The four of them proceeded to the exit, Henry fetched the Rover, put the suitcases in the boot and they drove to Bath. Isabella looked out curiously at the English countryside.

'The sun is shining!' she said, surprised, 'I thought it rained all the time in England!'

'Of course not!' said Henry, 'whoever told you that?'

When they arrived at Eagle House Isabella looked up at the first floor window and saw a man with short fair hair, sitting in a wheelchair. She knew it was Antonio – her Antonio. She faltered in her step and leaned on her son's arm.

David greeted them at the door, overcome at meeting the grandson he hadn't known existed until a year ago, and his mother Isabella, an elegant beauty. He showed them upstairs where Gilda was waiting, her anxiety levels high at the prospect of finally meeting her old rival. But somehow the reality of the situation gave both women courage, and when they shook hands they recognised in each other someone who had suffered in their lives, overcome many difficulties, and who just happened to love the same man.

Gilda caught her breath when she saw Antonio. He was so like his father, and when he took her hand and kissed her on the cheek she felt an extraordinary sensation, as if that was how Anthony might have been – should have been...

Gilda composed herself and said, 'welcome to Eagle House, Isabella. Come and see Anthony.' She guided her over to the window and sat her down on a chair next to him, then said, 'we'll leave you both alone for a while.'

*

Isabella took Anthony's hands in hers and looked at him.

'*Amore mio*,' she said, as her tears flowed.

She kissed his hands and gently touched his face. She felt him squeeze her hand, strongly. She was surprised – she hadn't expected him to be able to respond at all. She stood up, looked deeply into his eyes, cupped his face in her hands and kissed him on the lips. He made a strange sound in his throat, Isabella willing him to communicate.

'Yes, Antonio, it is me, Isabella. You couldn't come back to me, *caro*, so I have come to you. It is thanks to both our families that we have found each other.'

She looked at him, the man she had liked, then loved, then hated, the man she had tried to forget so many times, but who, deep in her heart, she had never stopped loving. And even though he was so very ill she could still see her own Antonio there, and her heart melted.

Their son Antonio entered the room and joined them, the three embracing, Isabella saying, 'our son...our son...'

I am overwhelmed. She is as beautiful as I remember. I'm longing to hold her, to take her in my arms, I hear her voice and the years disappear. You are the love of my life, Isabella.

And I have met Antonio, the son I didn't know I had.

Antonio was transfixed by this man that he resembled so closely. He stared at the figure in the chair, his fair hair turning white, his long limbs, his strong features, and thought, this is where I'm from. And he couldn't help but wonder, if Anthony hadn't been taken ill – if he had returned to Italy and married Isabella – what sort of life they would have had, and how different his own life would have been. How strange things were.

So he sat, holding Anthony's hands, looking into his eyes, saying over and over again, 'my English father.'

Sonia and Karl were next to be introduced to the visitors, fascinated to see Anthony's Italian connection made real. They understood only too well the thrill of meeting those who were once thought lost and had now been found.

Later that evening Gilda and Isabella talked together, telling each other about their families and, inevitably, about the war.

'Your relatives suffered so much,' said Isabella. 'How lovely that you were reunited with them, here in Bath.'

'Yes, it was wonderful,' said Gilda. 'And – Isabella – I can understand how difficult it was for you, all those years, not knowing what had happened to Anthony…'

She paused.

'Isabella, there is something I must tell you.'

Gilda confessed how she had burnt her letter.

Isabella was shocked, but at the same time something made sense.

'I always wondered why no one wrote to me. I just assumed the letter was lost. And then so many other things happened…'

'It was wrong of me. It's plagued me for so many years. I am so sorry. Can you ever forgive me?'

'You were very young – and so was I. Who knows what difference it would have made? Yes, Gilda, I forgive you.'

*

The following day Harriet arrived with Lizzie, both delighted to meet the man they had identified as Anthony's son in the photograph in Bassino. He was strikingly handsome and yet they both sensed that, for all his charm, he wasn't the usual type of skirt-chasing Italian they had come across during their trip. His mother, who was just as beautiful and stylish as they had imagined, obviously doted on him: whatever had happened that night when Antonio had left home in disgrace had been forgiven, if not forgotten.

Harriet could see a strong family resemblance between Antonio and her brother Freddie, who was back in America, and wished he could have been there to meet their Italian cousin.

Lizzie recounted how she had found the green leather case and tracked down its owner, befriending Harriet in the process, and how it had led them to *La Casa Bianca* and the Fortuno family. Then Henry produced the case and Isabella gave a sharp intake of breath. Her memory of the day she gave it to Anthony was clear in her mind.

Sitting next to Anthony, her hands shaking, Isabella put on her reading glasses and opened the letter he had written to her in May 1945 only moments after he had left her following their last passionate night together.

She read the short note in silence, having trouble keeping her composure, her cheeks damp with tears. Then she put the note back in its envelope and quietly said to Anthony, 'thank you, *caro*. I no longer have the presents you gave me, but now I have this. I will treasure it forever.'

Gilda showed Isabella how to use the spelling board so that she and Anthony could communicate. It was difficult, but over the next few days they were able to remember Affossa and the wonderful times they had spent together, enjoying the pleasure of being in each other's company once more. Isabella told Anthony about her life with Carlo and their children, and the success of their business. She glossed over the bad times, sparing him the details of the night Antonio had left home, concentrating instead on their son's plans and hopes for the future. She described Antonio's new home which he shared with Alain, saying how much she had enjoyed her visit, especially the day they'd taken her on a shopping trip to Milan where Antonio bought her an exquisite designer dress by Valentino...

It is blissful to be with you again, Isabella. Although we both found happiness with other people, I never stopped loving you. Our son is a fine young man - you and Carlo raised him well. There must have been times when it was hard for you both, and you still haven't told me why Antonio was in exile for so long. I suspect it was partly because of me, and partly because he's homosexual - it's obvious to me, anyway, and it doesn't bother me at all, but I expect you consider it to be a sin. You'll get used to it in time, Isabella...we all get used to things, in time...

David wanted to show Isabella the garden and she walked with him, slowly, her arm linked in his. He pointed out the plants and vegetable plots Karl had nurtured over the years, then led her to a paved area bordered by rose bushes where they sat down on a garden bench.

390

'I often come and sit here,' he said. 'It's where I do my thinking.'

'And what do you think about?' Isabella asked.

David lit his pipe – an old habit, thought unhealthy now, but one he still enjoyed. 'Oh…my family – my sons and how proud I am of them both. People I knew at the hospital. But mostly I think about my wife.'

Isabella nodded. 'She must have been a very special lady. Antonio – Anthony – used to speak about her a lot. I know he really missed her and loved her very much.'

'Really? That's good to know.'

Then David said, 'I wasn't here, you see…the night the bombs fell – the night Wendy was killed. I was working at the hospital in London.'

'You were doing important work.'

David sighed. 'Yes…but if I'd only been here, things might have been different. I've never told anyone this, Isabella, but I still can't forgive myself for not being here to protect her.'

'That's what Anthony used to say,' she said.

'What?'

'Anthony used to say that he should have stopped her going out that night.'

'Really?'

Isabella took his hands in hers.

'Yes. And I will say to you the same thing I said to him: it wasn't your fault. You mustn't blame yourself. David, all our lives are full of 'maybes' and 'if only's'…I know that more than anyone! You were doing your job and Wendy was doing hers. Her loss was tragic, but there is nothing you could have done to prevent it.'

391

David paused, then said, 'thank you, Isabella. That gives me great comfort.'

'It was war,' she said, 'but some good came from it. Anthony and I were so in love…and I have Antonio. And now you have us as well!'

David smiled at her. 'Thank you my dear. That means a lot.'

*

Henry said to Antonio, 'so, tell us about your vineyard.'

'With pleasure!' said Antonio, his eyes bright with enthusiasm. 'It's early days yet, but the soil is good and we grow Chardonnay and Glera grapes. Alain - my business partner – is working on a plan to produce sparkling wine and export it. We might even bring it to England! It's a whole new venture. It's a bit risky, but Mama has confidence and has invested some money to help us get started.'

He looked at his mother and smiled. 'Mama was always ambitious…'

Anthony made a strange noise and Antonio laughed, as if at some private joke between them.

'It sounds fabulous,' said Harriet.

'It is. It is so beautiful there. We're looking forward to our first Summer. Can you imagine, Alain and I will be sitting outside in the warm evening air, looking at the sun going down behind the hill, the fireflies glowing in the distance, a glass of wine in our hands…' He smiled at the thought then added, 'you should come and visit us, Harriet!'

'I would love to!' she said, already mentally booking her flight, while at the same time the penny finally dropped that her cousin was gay.

'So, where is this vineyard, exactly?' she asked.

'In the far North East of Italy. We live near a little village called Prosecco.'

*

The visitors enjoyed playing the tourist, showing an interest in Bath's heritage and architecture. The Springtime weather remained fine, and as Isabella admired the cherry blossom and flower displays she said, 'I did not expect England to be so beautiful!' But she remained unconvinced about the food.

One evening, after a lot of wine had been taken, Tilly found herself alone with Antonio in the kitchen.

'You speak very good English,' she said. 'You don't even have an Italian accent. Where did you learn?'

He hesitated.

'I was in Amsterdam for a while,' he said.

'Really? Interesting place…' said Tilly.

'Mmm – it depends…' said Antonio.

That night in bed Henry said to his wife, 'you were talking to Antonio for a long time - what was that all about?'

Tilly was quiet for a moment.

'He was telling me about his time in Amsterdam.' She paused. 'He was in a very bad place, Henry, for a couple of years. He hit rock bottom. I don't think we should tell the others.'

'Really?' said Henry. 'All right, whatever you say.'

Then he added, 'I don't know how you do it, Tilly. You could get a confession out of the Pope!'

The week passed so quickly. The visitors promised to return the following year and as they said their farewells Antonio kissed Anthony on the forehead, saying, 'goodbye, my English father. I am so pleased we have met at last.'

He turned to Gilda and said, 'thank you for looking after him.'

Gilda looked at Antonio, matter-of-factly, and replied, 'I love him. I have always loved him.'

When Isabella said her final goodbye she kissed Anthony and he spelt out one last time the only words he ever needed to say: '*Ti amo*'.

Henry and Tilly took Isabella and Antonio to the airport and waved goodbye to the visitors as they made their way through passport control and disappeared into the departure lounge.

Henry said, 'well, that was a success, thank heaven!'

'Incredible,' said Tilly, 'so much emotion. They really were in love, weren't they…'

She looked momentarily distant, concerned.

'What's bothering you, darling?'

'I'm just thinking - what if something like that had happened to us? How would we have coped?'

'I suppose it shows that if the bond is strong enough it won't break, no matter how much fate tries to weaken it. Love is a powerful thing.'

'And we are so lucky to have found it.'

And they embraced, there and then, in the airport lounge, oblivious to the rest of the world that passed them by.

Gilda had Anthony to herself again.

'Oh, *liebchen*, what an extraordinary time we've had! You've seen your Isabella at last, and your son. You know this hasn't been easy for me, but, with God's help, I will cope…'

I've prepared a message for Gilda which takes me a long time to spell out, but basically says:

'Thank you Gilda. You are a good wife. I cannot deny that I still love Isabella but I love you too. Without your care I would have died long ago. You are a brave and dutiful woman. It is you who looks after me, it is you I live with every day and it is you I sleep with at night. I don't know what I would do without you.'

CHAPTER 53

Italy, 1977

Isabella had driven over to *La Casa Bianca* to see her brother Guiseppe. She hadn't seen him for a while and had been intrigued by something he'd said on the phone. She was welcomed by him and his wife, then after a coffee he said, 'I've been clearing out your old room, the one you used to share with Maria. I found this stuck in the back of a drawer. I liked it so much I framed it – it is you, isn't it?' He handed her a pencil drawing, torn from a sketch book, of a young woman sitting by a tree.

Isabella gazed at the image of her younger self, seen through Anthony's eyes, and her heart skipped a beat. She remembered everything about that beautiful Spring day - the warm breeze, the joy of living in the moment, the pleasure of being in the company of the handsome English soldier. And she remembered their first kiss, the thrill of growing close to him, on the brink of falling in love.

Guiseppe brought her back to the present. 'Would you like to keep the picture?'

'Yes,' she said, 'thank you. I would like it very much.'

Suddenly the glass and china on the dresser started to rattle, some wine bottles fell from a shelf, smashing on the floor, a deep rumbling noise came from under their feet and the ground began to shake.

'What the...?'

Bath, 1977

That very same day, Gilda was in the kitchen preparing Anthony's liquid lunch when she suddenly heard a cry, the strangest noise, like a wounded animal. She rushed back into the room to find him having a fit and as she reached him he gasped, stared straight at her and grasped her arm.

'Anthony!' she screamed.

With a final convulsion, he crumpled into a heap, dead.

Italy, 1977

The day after the earthquake the rescue party worked their way through the collapsed farmhouse, stepping carefully around broken blocks of concrete and protruding metal, searching for signs of life. One of the men called for help – he could see some clothing and a foot sticking out from under a pile of rubble. The party hastily removed the debris to reveal the body of a woman curled up on her side, her arms folded tightly across her body, holding something close to her.

As they lifted her up, one of her lifeless arms dropped to one side revealing the precious object she had clung to in her last moments – a framed picture, its glass smashed, of a young woman sitting by a tree.

Time recedes, and when I meet Isabella in our usual place outside the church she is young again, and so am I. She runs up to me, smiling, we kiss, then I take her hand and together we walk up into the hills surrounding Affossa. At the top we find our favourite spot, next to a grassy bank covered in pasqueflowers, and we sit contentedly, as one, looking at the view of Ravenna in the distance and beyond to the sparkling sea.

Epilogue

The Roberts family, along with many others, were gathered together in Victoria Park for a special occasion.

Henry and Tilly, a distinguished couple in their eighties, were standing with Harriet, who had flown back to England with her Italian husband and two children. Freddie wasn't able to be there due to work commitments in America. Gilda was with Franz, her cousin Benjamin's son, and a young student, Zac, who was staying with her at Eagle House. Since David's death the house had been gifted to a Jewish educational society and was open to young Jewish people who came to England to study.

Antonio had come to Bath with his partner Alain to pay his respects to the grandmother he had never known. And Wendy Mason, née Fowler, who had celebrated her birthday the previous day, was there to remember the brave nurse who had delivered her and after whom she had been named.

And so it was that, sixty-one years after the bombing raid on Bath, a ceremony was finally held to unveil and dedicate a memorial to the 417 residents and visitors in Bath who died as a result of the air raids.

The families stood in silence as the names of the victims were read out, including that of Wendy Roberts.

At last they could rest in peace.

When Bombs Fell On Bath

Original artwork by Maggie Rayner

About the Author

Originally from Kent, Maggie moved to Bath at the
age of eleven and lived and worked in the city for
many years.
She is now retired and lives in Wiltshire.

Also available from Amazon:

'Moonflight and Other Tales from Wiltshire and the
West'

Printed in Great Britain
by Amazon